lphur Wells

mbo-Limbo

Matlacha

Sandy Hook

DOC FORD
COUNTRY

CORAL

D0054215

Bull Sharks

PINE
ISLAND

St. James City

und

Woodring's Point

Sanibel
Flats

Tarpon Bay

No Más

Dinkin's Bay
Marina

Doc Ford's
Lab

Causeway Blvd.

Sanibel
Marina

bel – Captiva Rd.

Periwinkle Way

Bait Box

Sanibel
Lighthouse

Nave's

Tarpon Bay Rd.

Timbers

Casa Ybel Rd.

Bailey's
General

W. Gulf Dr.

Gray Gables

FORT MYERS RSW
INTERNATIONAL
AIRPORT (25 miles) →

ORIDA

© 2007 Randy Wayne White
Rendering by Meighan Cavanaugh

BONE
DEEP

ALSO BY RANDY WAYNE WHITE

BONE DEEP

Randy Wayne White

PUTNAM

G. P. Putnam's Sons
Publishers Since 1838
Published by the Penguin Group
Penguin Group (USA) LLC
375 Hudson Street
New York, New York 10014

USA • Canada • UK • Ireland • Australia
New Zealand • India • South Africa • China

penguin.com
A Penguin Random House Company

Library of Congress Cataloging-in-Publication Data

White, Randy Wayne.
Bone Deep / Randy Wayne White.
p.   cm—(A Doc Ford novel ; 18)
ISBN 978-0-399-15813-1
1. Ford, Doc (Fictitious character)—Fiction.   2. Marine biologists—Fiction.   3. Crow Indians—Fiction.
4. Florida—Fiction.   5. Suspense fiction.   I. Title.
PS3573.H47473B66   2014   2013049644
813'.54—dc23

Printed in the United States of America
1   3   5   7   9   10   8   6   4   2

BOOK DESIGN BY GRETCHEN ACHILLES

This book is for my pal and traveling partner, Dr. Brian Hummel,

and his brilliant family: Kristin, Sydney, Jordan, Andrea, John,

Chris, Allison, Kipling, Theodore, Amary, Stephen, Kris, Asher,

Maggie, Jon McConnel, Harlan, Peggy, and dear Joyce

Sanibel and Captiva Islands are real places, faithfully described, but used fictitiously in this novel. The same is true of certain businesses, marinas, bars, and other places frequented by Doc Ford, Tomlinson, and pals.

In all other respects, however, this novel is a work of fiction. Names (unless used by permission), characters, places, and incidents are either the product of the author's imagination or are used fictitiously. Any resemblance to actual persons, living or dead, or to actual events or locales is unintentional and coincidental.

Contact Mr. White at www.docford.com

AUTHOR'S NOTE

I learned long ago, whether writing fiction or nonfiction, an author loses credibility if he's caught in a factual error. I take research seriously, and am lucky to benefit from the kindness of experts in varied fields. Before recognizing those who provided assistance, though, I would like to remind the reader that all errors, exaggerations, and/or misinterpretations of fact, if any, are entirely my fault.

I have wanted to use Florida's Bone Valley as a setting for many years, but it was a conversation with two Florida Fish & Wildlife (FWC) officers that finally provided material for a plotline. Much thanks goes to Maj. Curtis Brown, who walked me step-by-step through various artifact theft scenarios. Col. Jim Brown (Ret.) was also helpful, plus he correctly pointed out that Doc Ford owns a tactical boat built in Florida exclusively by Brunswick, not by a French manufacturer as I had wrongly assumed.

Phosphate mining in Bone Valley is controversial, which is why the Mosaic Company—one of the world's leading producers—deserves high marks for having the professionalism and confidence to allow me to tour their mining operation and reclamation projects in Central Florida. Especially helpful were John Courtney and Diana Youmans. Through their eyes and experience, I learned much about Bone Valley and the history that lies beneath.

In this book, Doc Ford references "snag fishing" for tarpon in Boca Grande Pass on Florida's Gulf Coast. Thanks to Kenneth W. Wright—Florida Environmentalist of the Decade, in the minds of many anglers—this "jigging" technique has finally been exposed as a fraud. Mr. Wright, and a group of knowledgeable, courageous FWC commissioners, voted unanimously to ban the technique, and Florida is a better place because of them. In this and other areas, biologists Dr. Jonathan Shenker, Diane and Dr. Phil Motta, and Justin Grubbich also deserve thanks, as does Maria Laura Habegger for her work on bull sharks. While writing this book, I learned that Dr. John Miller, of Mote Marine and University of North Carolina, died in July 2013. He was a fine man; his advice regarding Doc Ford will be missed.

Much thanks goes to friends and advisers Dr. Justin White, Dr. Marybeth B. Saunders, Dr. Peggy C. Kalkounos, Ron Iossi, Jerry Rehfuss, and Dr. P. D. Miller. Sports psychologist Don Carman, once again, contributed unerring insights into human behavior, aberrant and otherwise, and his advice regarding Marion Ford's fitness routine is much appreciated.

Bill Lee, and his orbiting star, Diana, as always, have guided the author, safely—for the most part—into the strange but fun and enlightened world of our mutual friend, the Rev. Sighurdhr M. Tomlinson. Equal thanks go to Gary and Donna Terwilliger, Wendy Webb, my wife and trusted friend, Stephen Grendon, my devoted SOB, the angelic Mrs. Iris Tanner, and my partners and pals, Mark Marinello, Marty, and Brenda Harrity.

By virtue of their affection for Florida and all good causes, special thanks go to Mollie B. Nelson, Ryan J. Farley, Matt and Maggie Farley Bradfield, Will Andrew Derco, Capt. John C. Comstock Jr., Ann Miller Ekas, Sue Depré, Lisa Bowling, Linda Comstock Teel, Tom Braciszewski, Kirsten Dickerson, Shane Traugott, Joey Ann Kempson, lovely Marla J. Martin, and to my wonderful fourth-grade teacher, Mrs. France Crow, of Pioneer, Ohio, who recently celebrated her one hundredth birthday.

Much of this novel was written at corner tables before and after hours at Doc Ford's Rum Bar and Grille on Sanibel Island and San Carlos Island, where staff were tolerant beyond the call of duty. Thanks go to Liz Harris, Chef Kris Zook, Juan Gomez, Kim McGonnell, Ma-Donna Butz, Jeff Kelley, Jose Sanchez, Allyson Parzero, Amanda Rodriguez, Ashley Rodeheffer, Christine Sabater, Amazing Cindy Porter, Desiree Olson, Kara Sarros, Big Khusan Ismatullaev, Marvelous Milita Kennedy, Olga Qlgita Jarrard, Detroit Rachel Songalewski, Rebecca Harris, Sarah Carnithan, Tall Sean Lamont, Hi Shawn Scott, T. J. Grace, Yakh'yo Yakubov, Darlene Mazzulo, Gabrielle Moschitta, Maria Jimenez, Mario Martinez, Charles Hill, Tall Cheyne Diaz, Chris Jenkins, Dale Hempseed, Dylan Wussler, Tyler Wussler, Richard Decosta, Big Boston Brian Cunningham, Jim Rainville, and Nathaniel Buffam.

At the Rum Bar on San Carlos Island, Fort Myers Beach: Dan Howes, Kandice Salvador, John Goetz, Corey Allen, Charity Owen, Heriberto Ramos, John Rhoads, Jamie Allen, Nora Billheimer, Seth Bishop, Kassee Buonano, Dan Busby, Astrid Cobble, Allison Dell, Sue DeMartini, Brian DeMartinis, Jessica Foster, Samantha George, Ashley Griner, Nicole Hinchcliffe, Eric Hines, Mark Hines, Janell Jambon, Netta Kramb, Jesse Kane, Anthony Kelhower, Meredith Martin, Katy McBride, Megan McNeill, Grace Novak, Kerra Pike, Cris Rentas, Kevin Reynolds, Dustin Rickards, Sandy Rodriquez,

AUTHOR'S NOTE

Deon Schoeman, Michael Scopel, Jon Spellman, Heidi Stacy, Josh Vega, Lee Washington, Erin Montgomery, Ali, Pereira, Kylie Pyrll, LaToya Trotta, Kevin Tully, Molly Brewer, Katie Kovacs, Natalie Ramos, Taylor Recny, Jordan Van Leuven, Emily Heth, Anthony Howes, Justin Voskuhl, David Werner, Nick Howes, Bronson Joney, Andreas Ramon, Reyes Ramon, and Marcus Summ.

At Doc Ford's on Captiva Island: Mighty Jean Crenshaw, Raynauld Bentley, Clark Kent Hill, Chef Greg Nelson, Chef James King, Alexis Marcinkowski, Amy Charron, Cheryl Erickson, Chris "Go Bulldogs" Orr, Erica Debacker, Heather Walk, Holly Emmons, Isabel Garcia, Julie Grzeszak, Karen Bove, Larissa Holmes, Matt Ginn, Sarah Ginn, Shelbi Muske, Nick Hopkins, Thayne Fugal, Jon Calupca, Alexa Mozes, Hope McNulty, Ashley Foster, Chad Chupurdia, Daniel Flint, Dominic Cervio, Stephen Day, and Mojito Greg Barker.

Finally, I would like to thank my sons, Lee and Rogan White, for helping me finish this, the twenty-first novel in the Doc Ford series. Quite a ride, huh?

—RANDY WAYNE WHITE

Casa de Piña

Sanibel Island, Florida

Florida archaeologists . . . found a mastodon tusk, scarred by circular cut marks from a knife. The tusk was 14,500 years old. The age was surprising, even shocking, for it suddenly made the Aucilla [Florida] sinkhole one of the earliest places in the Americas to betray the presence of human beings.

Smithsonian Magazine, FEBRUARY 2013

BONE DEEP

ONE

A BIG CHUNK OF CENTRAL FLORIDA IS KNOWN AS BONE VALLEY TO GEOLOGISTS and antiquities thieves, as I was reminded by a stranger wearing braids and wrangler denim who appeared on my porch one stormy June morning.

The man claimed to be on the trail of artifacts stolen from Crow tribal land in Montana.

"Stone carvings about yay high," he said, holding his fingers apart. "They didn't come from Bone Valley, but Florida is where a lot of tribal stuff ends up."

My stilthouse on Sanibel Island, the Gulf Coast, is four hours from Orlando, and two thousand miles from Big Sky Country. "You sure you have the right Marion Ford?"

"You're Doc?"

"Yeah, but not the kind you need."

"A marine biologist who doesn't read his horoscope, that's what I heard. You could be just the guy."

I was standing outside my lab, water slapping at pilings below my feet, thunderheads sliding our way. "What does astrology have to do with stolen artifacts?"

The man, who had introduced himself as Duncan Fallsdown, said, "Tonight, at what's supposed to be a sweat lodge, it would be nice to have a buffer. You know, someone who talks about something other than Mother Earth and spirit quests—all the standard stuff I've heard a million times. A hawk circles overhead, a guy like you figures the bird's hungry, looking for a mouse. A snake, maybe. No big deal. Am I right?"

I said, "A sweat lodge in June? If that's an invitation, no thanks."

"Not the best timing, but I'm committed," Fallsdown replied, his eyes moving to the bay where a sailboat was anchored. The boat's boom was strung with laundry that flapped in the breeze: a tie-dyed shirt, several sarongs, and what appeared to be women's lingerie. Suddenly, the nonsensical was redefined as commonplace.

"Tomlinson's behind this," I said. "How long have you known him?" I was referring to a lecherous, cannabis-growing anarchist turned Zen master who lives aboard the sailboat, an old Morgan, *No Más* in faded script on the stern.

"Long enough to leave last night, when he chugged a tray of Jell-O shooters and invited some women to go skinny-dipping," the man replied. "That was around one. I flew in late yesterday afternoon."

Yep—definitely bras and panties clipped to the Morgan's halyard, all doomed to be soaked by the rain rumbling toward us. "You *do* know him," I said. "How many?"

"Women? At least one that was married, so I didn't bother counting. They're here because of the sweat lodge." Fallsdown considered the squall, then looked beyond me through the screen door. "Man . . . you've got a bunch of aquariums in there. As a kid, I always wanted one. What kind of fish?"

It was a request to escape the rain, so I opened the door, asking, "What time did Tomlinson start drinking this morning?"

Fallsdown's shoulders filled the doorway, his Indian braids black on blue cowboy denim, and I got a whiff of what might have been smoke—mesquite, maybe, not tobacco or marijuana.

"Answer that one," he replied, "I'd have to know what time he stopped last night, wouldn't I?"

DUNCAN FALLSDOWN, who told me to call him Dunk with a *k*, accepted a bottle of Gatorade after refusing a beer, saying, "I'm hop-tose intolerant," which might have meant ten a.m. was too early—or the gentle rebuff of an alcoholic. A man in his mid-forties acquires seismic markers at the corners of the eyes—harsh winters, smoky barrooms, is what I saw.

I dumped my coffee and made fresh while wind blew the first fat drops of rain against the roof. Twice, while water boiled, I went to the door and whistled, then made small talk until Fallsdown followed me outside, across the breezeway, into the old ice house I have converted into a lab. I showed him around, explained what I do for a living—collect and sell marine specimens, plus environmental consulting—then went to the door again, "When you crossed the boardwalk, did you happen to see a dog swimming around near my house?"

"That was a *dog*?" Fallsdown replied.

Surprise with a tinge of wariness—the typical reaction of a newcomer who thinks he has seen what is probably an alligator but could be a giant otter. A few minutes later, I returned, and my yellow-eyed retriever was drying in the breezeway, a fresh bone to occupy him, while Fallsdown and I talked above the hiss of rain.

"These stone carvings, someone I know wants them back. Dollarwise, they're fairly valuable, but that's not the reason. The person's in a hurry. Tomorrow, there's a flea market near Venice I want to hit. Then a gun show in Lakeland."

"You don't know where the artifacts are?"

"I've got some contacts, and Tomlinson's working on some others—that's why I'm here. MapQuest says the trip's three hours."

Over an hour to Venice, then two hours to Lakeland, I guessed. "But double that if Tomlinson's driving."

Fallsdown, focusing on fish tanks along the wall, kept his back to me. "You know the guy better than I do. He's not as flaky as he pretends, sometimes. He's got good instincts, too, and people trust him. Better than having just me show up, a cowboy-Indian dressed like Billy Jack, asking questions about artifacts that might sell for fifty, sixty grand. See what I'm saying?"

I was surprised by the numbers. "At a flea market?"

"It's the sort of place dealers use now. Used to be, the quality stuff was sold at auctions or antiquities shows. Coins, arrowheads, fossils—Florida had some of the biggest shows in the country. Vegas was big. New Mexico used to be, but the Indian relics trade has mostly gone underground. States are cracking down, Florida included, but it's still one of the world's best places for *finding* fossils and relics. The money's here, so the dealers keep coming."

I was sitting at my computer and broke a personal rule by turning on the Wi-Fi before I'd finished the morning grunt work required of an aquarist who owns two boats. "These artifacts, do you have a link where I can find photos?

"I've got a folder in my rental car when the rain slows down. The carvings don't look like much—black soapstone—steatite, it's called. Some say the pieces look like owl faces."

"Just the face?"

"Judge for yourself, but they're plain-looking stones. Not nearly as pretty as agate coral. They find a lot of that near Tampa, but other areas, too. Phosphate quarries are best."

There were plenty of quarries. Phosphate mining has been a major Florida industry since the early 1900s, which Fallsdown already knew.

"A million years ago," he said, "inland Florida was high ground with rivers, and animals that collected there in the river basins and watering holes died there. That's why they call the area Bone Valley. Awesome fossils mixed in with stone tools from the Paleo era—sort of one-stop shopping. Spend an afternoon digging the right spot, you could buy a car with what you find. Hell, a ranch, if you really got lucky." Fallsdown looked around, his expression congenial; he had the easygoing confidence of a plumber or an electrician, but that didn't quite mesh with his knowledge of Florida geology.

"Are you a private investigator?"

"Not hardly."

"Studied the field sciences in college?" On the computer screen I had opened photos of agate corals, all polished pink, silver, or cinnamon by the pressure of eons, each piece uniquely hollowed like a geode or miniature cave.

Fallsdown replied, "Nope. But I did three years in the joint, two as library trustee—Deer Lodge state prison. Lots of reading time."

I said, "Oh," while he focused on a hundred-gallon tank where I had isolated three fingerling snook—a triad of silver blades suspended above a mangrove diorama.

"But you are a . . . a *member* of the Crow tribe."

"I'm an Indian—a Skin, if that's what you mean. You don't have to be careful around me. I make decent money putting on shows for tourists, and the politically correct bullshit really gets old. That's how Tomlinson and I met. Sedona, Arizona. Sedona attracts every UFO kook and crystal worshipper around, but we hit it off. That was back in my drinking days, so I forgot what a pain in the ass he can be." Fallsdown put his face closer to the aquarium glass. "What are those spiny things?"

He meant the sea urchins. Then he asked about tunicates and barnacles—their rhythmic, feathered appendages were actually modified legs—and the anomaly of pregnant male sea horses, before he got back to the subject. "Look up 'Mastodon tusks' and see what they sell for. Most are from phosphate quarries, or rivers south of Orlando. Maybe 'Clovis tools,' too, or 'Charmstones,' but don't get your hopes up. Dealers have stopped selling over the Internet."

The man sipped at his Gatorade while I banged away with two fingers at the keyboard. Then Fallsdown decided to trust me with more information.

"It's my aunt who wants the carvings back. She did some crazy stuff after she ran off and left her husband and kids. Organized protests, the whole nine yards, even got her picture in newspapers when AIM had a standoff with the feds. Which sort of puts me in an awkward spot."

I stopped what I was doing and chose my words carefully. "Awkward because of what your aunt did? Or because she . . . *knows* Tomlinson?" My strange pal is a womanizer, and had mentioned his involvement with the American Indian Movement many times.

The man from Montana thought about that for a few seconds. "Maybe that hippie snake did sleep with her—it would explain a lot. But, no, what I mean is, she—Rachel—Rachel switched from being a radical to traditional a few years back. Now she has pancreatic cancer. She says she can't die in peace until the carvings are returned to the tribe. That's why I can't waste time with Tomlinson's touchy-feely bullshit."

"You have to find the artifacts before your aunt dies," I said. Rather than add *But she'll die anyway*, I swiveled around in my chair, done with the computer.

"Find anything?"

"Enough," I said. "A few years back, a complete mastodon tusk was stolen from a private collection. No photos, but it had primitive carving on it, a sort of lacework thatching. The thing was insured for half a million. Also a flint spearpoint—'orange plains chert,' they call it—supposedly worth ten thousand. You're right, nothing currently for sale on the Internet. I had no idea that kind of money was involved."

"Fossilized ivory," Fallsdown said. "Is that the tusk they found in the Suwannee River? I heard it was a yard long and weighed fifty pounds. Paleo man—the early Skins—used ivory for weapons, but also as totems. That makes it a lot more valuable."

"Because it was worked," I said, but was guessing.

"Not only that, ivory used by the Paleo Indians holds up better. I don't know why, but I'd take the time to find out if I lived here. Some believe there's an Ice Age graveyard where mastodons went to die. Mammoths, too, probably, but I'm not sure. Wouldn't that be something to find?"

I said, "In Florida?" The legend about elephant graveyards originated in Africa, not Florida, and it had been debunked long ago.

Fallsdown gestured to indicate he kept an open mind.

I said what I had been thinking: "Are you sure you're not here to sell something? Or do some collecting on your own?"

Fallsdown remained unruffled. "I might. Depends on how it goes tonight. I'm supposed to do that sweat lodge for the wife and daughters of a family in the phosphate business. They might know the names of serious collectors, because collectors drive the phosphate companies nuts, begging permission to hunt, trespassing. These women, or whoever runs the business, might have access to a list."

I said, "And you just happened to remember your good ol' hippie buddy from the Sedona days." My tone was cool enough to be an accusation.

Fallsdown took it calmly, even smiled. "Don't worry. I know all about that pond owned by a friend of yours, and the arrowheads, pottery, and other stuff you found in a cave. Tomlinson even offered to take me diving there, but no thanks, man. Find the two pieces I'm after, I'm outta here."

For Tomlinson—who had nearly died in that pond—to risk another dive said a lot about the respect he had for a man I had just insulted. I said, "Sorry. It's a bad habit of mine, thinking when I should be listening. It's just that you know a lot about the relics trade for someone who's not an investigator or a tribal cop."

Fallsdown was pleased, not offended. "See? You're a man who uses his head. That's what I was hoping. Why not tag along with Tomlinson and me, at least tonight? Might be good for you."

I asked, "How?"

"Well . . . I'll just come out and say it. I heard you got dumped by your girlfriend, and it might get your mind off things. The women are damn good-looking—twin sisters and a blonde—their stepmother, I guess. Used to be a big-time fashion model according to Tomlinson. We're taking a water taxi to a private island they own north of here."

As he spoke, my dog banged the door open with his nose . . . trotted toward Fallsdown, gave his hand a sniff . . . did the same to me . . . then spun a few circles in the corner before collapsing on the floor.

"He's not what you'd call an affectionate animal, is he?" Fallsdown remarked, but sounded impressed. "What's his name?"

Instead of answering, I replied, "Tomlinson has a big mouth. I wasn't dumped—in fact, I had dinner with the woman he was talking about last night."

"Oh. Then you are still dating."

"Umm . . . not exactly," I said, "but it was a mutual decision. We're still good friends."

"Mutual, huh?" He smiled, amused by the lie. "Then invite her along. You'll understand why I need a buffer when you hear the whole story."

"If I want to sweat, I'll wait 'til this rain stops and go stand in the parking lot," I told him.

Fallsdown's faith in me had been validated. *"Perfect,"* he said. "You can help me calm down Tomlinson after he finds out what I really have planned."

TWO

AN HOUR BEFORE SUNSET, THE FISHING GUIDES CROSSED THE FLATS, THREE boats in formation, so I put away the photos Dunk Fallsdown had loaned me—stone carvings that did, indeed, resemble owls—and walked to the marina to enjoy the show.

Business hours at Dinkin's Bay Marina are seven a.m. to six p.m., but Mack, the owner, doesn't lock the parking lot gate until later, especially in summer. Tourists were gathering on the dock to watch the guides clean fish, and tourists have money.

Mack, a big man with a cigar, was standing at the office door, surveying what his eyes perceived as profit. He waved and panto-mimed pulling the lever of a cash register as I passed. Jeth Nicholes, one of the guides, had gone inside to use the toilet, and I walked with him to the cleaning table—a slab of wood with a wash-down hose—where captains Felix and Neville were sharpening their knives.

"There was a school of spinner sharks off the lighthouse," Jeth said, stuttering some but not worried about it. "I brought one back for steaks, if you want to check its stomach."

I did, but said I would wait for the crowd to thin. A semicircle had formed around the cleaning table, people snapping photos, clients posing with fish, while gulls bickered with terns, and a flotilla of pelicans waited below, their heads swaying as if fillet knives were conductors' batons. Captains Felix and Neville, buckets at their feet, had had a good day catching sea trout, mackerel, pompano—a big cobia, too, that might weigh sixty pounds.

Jeth said, "I saw Hannah's boat near the river. Her clients were fly-fishing. Two guys—but they weren't what you'd call good-looking."

He was referring to Hannah Smith, an elite fly-fishing guide, and the woman, who according to rumor, had dumped me. Which is why Jeth had stuttered a little more when he described her clients.

"We had dinner last night," I reassured him. Then asked if he would remind Felix to save the cobia carcass so I could have a look inside its belly.

Jeff is built like a farm boy linebacker, but he's sensitive, so he showed his relief. "Sure," he said. "Good." Then he maneuvered his way through the crowd and got to work.

When there was no one around to offend, I opened the bellies of the spinner shark and the cobia. The shark had been feeding on thread herring. The cobia was loaded with crabs and two sea horses. I washed my hands, and said hello to Rhonda and Joann, who live aboard an old Chris-Craft yacht, *Tiger Lilly*. The stop required another reference to my date with Hannah to defuse the gossip. Same when Eleanor intercepted me at the Red Pelican Gift Shop and offered a consoling piece of fudge.

Mack, at least, had other interests when he took me aside and asked, "You meet Tomlinson's Indian pal from Montana? Nice fella. Not like most of the oddballs who show up asking for His Guruness."

After what Fallsdown had told me, I couldn't help chuckling. "He stopped by the lab."

"Yeah? What's so funny?"

I didn't have permission to share details, but I could say, "Tomlinson's driving the poor guy nuts."

"Nothing unusual about that," Mack said, waiting for the punch line.

"Duncan will be back in the morning. Get him to tell you."

"*Dunk*, you mean? He did tell me something. Tomlinson thinks Dunk is a big shot with his tribe back in Montana, the head medicine man or something. So Tomlinson volunteered him to put on a show for some rich folks, the ones who own Albright Key. The two of them left to catch a water taxi half an hour ago."

"The Albright family, yeah," I said. "Twin daughters, both out of college, and Mrs. Albright, the wife."

"Are those the three blondes from last night?" Mack smiled when I nodded. "Okay, now it sort of makes sense. But sitting in some tent—a sweat lodge—in June?"

"That's the funny part," I said, and told him that Tomlinson was in for a disappointment. Duncan was conducting a shaman drum ceremony, not a sweat lodge.

Mack got the joke. "Hah! Wish I could see the look on the horny bastard's face when he finds out. No sweat lodge means the women won't have to take their clothes off, right? Mosquitoes will be bad enough as is."

I said, "That's why I'll be wearing pants and a long-sleeved shirt."

Mack sobered. "You're going?"

"Wouldn't miss it," I said. "Jeth will let my dog out, once you lock the gate. I'd take him, but people who own islands are fussy about dogs."

Mack, relighting his cigar, said, "You don't give a damn about any shaman drum ceremony. And that island's forty minutes by water, even in your boat. What's the real reason?"

"I've never been on Albright Key," I answered, which was true, but not the whole story.

Fallsdown had asked me for a harmless favor—or so it seemed at the time.

IN THE CRIMSON DUSK OF A JUNE SUNSET, I left the mouth of Dinkin's Bay and flew my boat northeast, pretending the quickest route was backcountry past the village of Sulfur Wells. The detour was a silly excuse to wave at Hannah, the long-legged fishing guide, if she happened to be on the dock, or topside on her small blue live-aboard cruiser.

She wasn't—but a sleek runabout I recognized was tied there, which suggested Hannah was below, entertaining a guest. A male guest. I knew the runabout and I knew the guy. He was a wealthy Brazilian who kept his yacht at Dinkin's Bay when he wasn't traveling the world, one or more fake passports in hand.

Hannah trusted that bastard?

Worse, while I rubbernecked, my port engine snagged a crab trap and nearly threw me out of the boat, so it was dark, and Fallsdown was already drumming, when I got to Albright Key. The island was forty acres of foliage intersected by a shell ridge where, by day, a Mediterranean mansion spread itself on columns, bone white, above the bay, but now showed only windows and a lighted portico of marble. There was a boathouse off the channel where *No Trespassing* signs included threats of prosecution.

I tied up anyway. Through the trees, I could see a golden bouncing light that was a ceremonial fire. The Albright family, plus Tom-linson, would be gathered there, so why interrupt? My clothes were soaked after going overboard to cut that damn crab trap free, so I pawed through the emergency bag I keep aboard and soon stepped onto the dock wearing a chambray shirt and jeans.

Only then did I notice a man coming toward me from the shad-ows. A very tall man who spoke articulately but sounded weary when he said, "Unless you're invited to this circus, get back in your boat. I've got the local deputy on speed dial." He had to raise his voice to be heard over the thumpa-thumping of the drum.

I introduced myself, and looked toward the fire. "That noise has to get on your nerves after a while," I said.

"Then why are you here?" The man's tone insinuated *All the way from Sanibel . . . at night?*

"I've passed this island a hundred times and wasn't going to miss an invitation to come ashore. I was hoping to meet the owner and have a look around."

He made a sighing sound. "My daughters own the place, appar-ently. And my wife. Otherwise, I wouldn't have to listen to that mad-dening bullshit. Any idea how long it'll go on?"

From the elevated dock, I could see the fire and the silhouettes of four people, their backs to me. Tomlinson's hair, tied Samaria style, was as distinctive as a woodpecker's crest. Fallsdown faced his audi-ence, a drum between his knees, but was dressed normally, not like a stage medicine man. "Not a clue," I answered. "In my cooler, I've got beer on ice. Maybe it'll take your mind off the noise."

The man switched on dock lights to get a better look at me. "Never seen a rig like that," he commented, meaning my twenty-six-foot rigid-hulled inflatable—a boat ringed with a heavy foam-filled collar. It had a T-top, twin Mercs, and an electronics tower. I'd bought it through contacts at the specials ops base at MacDill in Tampa—a confiscated drug runner's vessel, supposedly, and that's the story I stuck with when I told the man about it. But I was honest when I added, "It's made by Brunswick in Edgewater, Florida. That's where Boston Whaler has its tactical division."

"I didn't know Whaler made tactical boats," he said. "It's not a Zodiac?"

I had made the same assumption, which felt odd to admit, then explained that Brunswick, depending on the buyer, followed black ops protocols when it came to labeling. The manufacturer's name wasn't on the registration. Impact was the model. Or B-Impact Tactical—BIT, for short.

"Military types love acronyms," the man said, following along, then asked for permission to step aboard.

He liked gadgets, and we talked about the springy decking and seats for a while—*shock mitigation*, is the term, nice to have in rough seas. He claimed he was interested in buying a RHIB design—a rigid-hulled inflatable—but I got the impression he was bored, just wanted to talk. After I'd demonstrated the electronics—impressed him with the night vision system; FLIR thermal imaging, too—he said, "If you want to come inside and see the house, I've got liquor and beer. It'll be quieter," and then finally told me his name.

I followed Leland Albright, heir to his grandfather's fortune, up the ridge into the mansion.

THREE

"I WAS READING THIS BOOK THAT SAYS IT TAKES THREE GENERATIONS TO PISS away a family fortune," Albright said, pouring another vodka rocks while I sipped my beer. "One to make it, one to mismanage it, and then a spoiled third generation to squander what's left."

He straightened and tested the air for the faint thumping of the drum. "I think I'm an exception. But my daughters and wife seem determined to prove the book right."

He had seen me noting the walls blistered by a leaking roof, the corroded faucets in the kitchen, and obviously felt the need to explain why a vacation home they seldom used wasn't in the best of shape.

"I thought a caretaker lived here," I said. "The times I've gone by, there's usually a boat tied up."

"Drunks and druggies," Albright explained, then returned to the subject of his family. "They have no concept of what it takes to make money. Find business contemptible, I guess, the twins especially. They'd rather save the world by giving it all away."

"Your daughters?"

"By my second marriage. Esther and Tricia. Thirty-one years old, with degrees in environmental studies, and they're worried sick about carbon footprints, global warming—but they still love flying to Palm Beach to shop. Otherwise, to hell with the family business. That's how they finally bonded with my new wife. Now it's me against them, and they're starting to wear me down."

I said, "I'm the wrong one to ask for advice about women, but isn't it odd for daughters to side with a new wife?"

Albright started to answer, then reconsidered, aware that his second vodka, or maybe his fourth or fifth, was causing him to open up to a stranger. We were sitting in a room of tile and coral rock, which had probably been mined in the Keys way back, an elegant space with maharajah accents—Persian rugs, carved elephants— but the furniture was 1960s bamboo, glass tables, and floral prints more commonly found at yard sales. The chairs were positioned to offer a panoramic view, on this moonless night, of the village lights of distant Boca Grande, miles of black water between. To the left, beneath trees, we could see the ceremonial fire where two angelic- haired blondes were thumping away on a log while Tomlinson shuffled to the rhythm. Albright put his drink on the table and de- cided to find out more about me. "You said you run a marine supply business? A boat like yours isn't cheap."

I replied, "A small business," and got a few sentences into de- scribing my lab, and what I do, when I was stopped by the stricken look on his face. "Is something wrong?"

"You're a *biologist*?"

"Yeah . . . ?"

"I thought you meant marine supply as in selling yachting hardware."

"More like selling sea horses to schools," I said. "I do consulting work, too."

Leland Albright, who was six-six but had the delicate hands and face of a pianist, stood. "Goddamn it, *that's* why you're here. Ava and the twins want you to work on me, don't they?"

"They what?"

"You heard me. And there's not a damn thing you can tell me about our Peace River holdings I haven't already heard."

I said, "Sorry, are you talking about the Peace River as in Central Florida?"

"As if you didn't know. You're leaving. You gave me a bullshit line, pretending you only came to see the island."

"Leland," I said, "I've never met your wife or your daughters. Calm down, and tell me what you have against biologists."

People who inherit wealth assume everyone wants something, so they construct shields, and Albright was embarrassed to have been caught with his down. "You just admitted you live on Dinkin's Bay. I know Ava took the twins to a party there last night. They didn't get back until almost sunrise. Now you expect me to believe you've never met? That's a tiny little podunk marina. I've seen it. How dumb do you think I am?"

I said, "Okay, I understand now. I thought it was my charm that got me in the door."

"What's that supposed to mean?"

"You want to pump me for details about the party last night, isn't that why I'm drinking your beer? But you got the wrong guy. I wasn't there. If your wife and daughters met somebody at the party, it wasn't me."

Albright tried to hang on to his anger but couldn't convince himself I was lying. His eyes moved to the fire, where a third woman had joined Tomlinson, a taller blonde. She was standing close enough to drape an arm over my pal's shoulder.

I asked, "Your wife's name is Ava?"

Albright, staring at the two of them, said, "Not if I catch her screwing around again. I know how she is when she gets a few drinks in her. Fashion models are experts at getting what they want."

"I've heard the rumor," I said.

"Me, too, but I married her anyway. You should see her in a bikini—when she bothers to wear one. That party last night, I figured it was okay as long as the twins were along. Tricia has a wild streak, though, plus they're suddenly like the Three Musketeers—the same fitness teacher, the same interests. So who the hell knows?" Albright watched his wife move her hand to Tomlinson's hip. He made a faint grunting sound as if suffering a stomach cramp.

"They can really set the hook deep," I said. For an instant, Hannah popped into my mind, and the sleek runabout owned by the Brazilian.

"If we're dumb enough to swallow it," he responded, and reached for his glass but decided against it. "You're divorced?"

I shook my head. "Only because I've never been married. I have a son and a daughter, so I understand that part."

"Do you get along?"

It was an awkward subject. My young daughter lives in Europe with her golf pro mother and female lover—a tennis star who doesn't need a racket to break balls. My teenage son attends boarding school in South America. He and I had argued during our last few phone conversations. Recent e-mails had gone unanswered. I was concerned by rumors he was smoking grass and hanging out with counterculture college types, but my son has a mulish contempt for advice. So, for Albright, I put a cheery spin on the truth. "My kids are great, but their mothers are the independent types—in other words, they don't want me around. The woman I had dinner with last night says I'm not ready to settle down."

My host began to loosen up. "She was using reverse psychology. Women are experts on everything but themselves."

I didn't agree with his cynical tone, but said, "Sounds like you're going through a rough patch. Your third marriage?"

"Third and last," Albright replied. "Manipulation is their specialty. Ava, she and the twins sit around giggling until I walk into the room. My own daughters. Last month they maxed out a credit card at some meditation retreat in Asheville, then gave me the silent treatment when I asked Ava, What the hell?" He looked out the window. "Now she shows up with two . . . *guru* types. See how she's hanging all over your long-haired friend? What do you expect me to think?"

I said, "She can't be much older than your daughters. I'm surprised they get along."

Albright, eyes fixed on his wife, didn't seem to hear. There were long seconds of silence, then he asked, "Is your friend screwing her? I know how fast gossip spreads at a small marina."

I said, "Nope. He is definitely not."

Surprised I didn't dodge the question, Albright sat back. "You sound pretty damn sure for someone who wasn't at the party."

"The one with the hair is Tomlinson. He told me they all had some fun last night, but as a group. Nothing physical. Not with your wife or daughters."

"You actually asked him?"

"We're old friends."

"He could have lied."

"It wouldn't be the first time," I agreed. "He knew I wouldn't come if that's what was going on. But I believe him. The other guy I just met, but I don't think you have anything to worry about. His name's Duncan Fallsdown—a Crow Indian from Montana."

I expected skepticism and got it. "Are you the religious type? Or just have higher moral standards?"

"I'm careful. I wanted to know what I was walking into. I've got no interest in showing up on some private island owned by a pissed-off husband."

There was a hole in my story. Albright sensed it and looked at me over the rim of his glass. "Ava said he's not charging for this drum nonsense. But I've got to ask myself why an Indian from Montana puts on his tom-tom act for free . . . and why a biologist decides to tag along."

It was time to level.

I told him about the stolen carvings, then shared what Fallsdown had explained to me in the lab. "Tomlinson met your daughters a month ago. They mentioned your family has owned phosphate mines for a long time, so he invented a reason to come here. Apparently, people in your industry keep track of artifact collectors because they're a pain in the ass—always trespassing and digging without permission. The serious ones, according to my Indian friend, will do damn-near anything, even apply for jobs, so they can hunt after hours. It was a long shot, but Tomlinson operates on instinct. Fallsdown asked me to talk to you, find out what I can, while he does his show. That's the real reason I'm here."

Albright said, "I knew you were working some kind of angle."

"There's nothing tricky about the truth," I replied.

He was still watching his wife through the window. "Shamanic drum ceremony, my ass. I figured those two for dopers, guru freaks, who want to get into my wife's pants. Or my daughters'. Now you tell me this crazy story."

"A cold trail, you've got to start somewhere," I said.

"Cold is right. My family got out of the phosphate business twenty years ago." The man confirmed my surprise with a glance.

"I didn't know."

"My father thought Johnnie Walker Black was a better investment. Second generation, just like the book says."

I said, "Now I understand why you're reading it, to get the Albright legacy back on track."

"Out of the toilet, more like it."

"Sorry to hear that," I said, "but maybe you still have access to someone's list of artifact hunters. That could help."

"I doubt it. Tell me more about these carvings. What makes your friend think they're in Florida?" Albright was interested but didn't want to show too much.

"I asked the same thing," I said. "They were stolen from tribal land back in the nineteen seventies."

"That's fifty . . . almost sixty years ago."

"I know, it sounds like a wild-goose chase," I said. "But not when you think it through. Collectors network, and they tend to hold on to their best stuff. They also know what other collectors have or what buyers want. What's the point if you can't make someone in your peer group envious? A list of names, especially collectors from twenty years ago, could put Fallsdown on the right track. Why not?" I placed my beer on a woven elephant doily. "It might be fun to help a tribe in Montana solve an old mystery."

I smiled, Albright didn't. He retreated into his drink—yes, a troubled man. A crumbling marriage, financial problems, and now he was sitting with a stranger, fielding questions. It was an uncomfortable situation, and I understood why. Even twenty years ago, phosphate mining was reviled by environmentalists. Those in the industry have learned to tread carefully when it comes to dealing with the public—especially nosy biologists.

Finally, he said, "People don't realize how much work goes into making it in the phosphate industry. My grandfather started Mammoth Ridge Mines back when they dug the stuff with shovels, not draglines. Nineteen seventeen."

Mammoth Ridge—maybe that explained the maharajah-and-elephant décor.

I said, "He had to be a very smart, tough guy. Obviously successful if he bought an island and built a house like this."

Albright motioned across an expanse of tile toward a hall. "There's a whole room full of photos and old records, if you really are interested. You'll have to dust them off. The twins won't go in there. They say the photos make them nauseated. And the only history Ava cares about is the kind that makeup won't cover."

"Your daughters are thirty-some years old?" I asked.

My tone gave me away.

"Kids mature slower these days, I agree. The year after they graduated, they married brothers who'd inherited a bundle. An Oregon family, Apple software. They both divorced about the same time, too—eighteen months later—and came home to Dad. Not literally, of course. They bought a beach house on Siesta Key. Esther is good with money."

"I wasn't criticizing," I said.

"Of course you were, and you're right. Thank god, my stepson is starting to come around. If it wasn't for him, I think I'd just say to hell with it. Let all the spinning plates come crashing down and move to Costa Rica. I hear it's nice down there, maids and a staff for next to nothing."

I knew the answer before I asked him, "Is Ava your stepson's mother?"

Disdain confirmed that she was not. "My second wife, Madison. Her husband was killed in a skiing accident. Owen, my stepson, was four when Madison and I married, then she got pregnant with the twins. She was unusual . . . the finest *person* I've ever met. Mattie, everyone called her."

Albright's reflective tone, the way he withdrew into his head, told me his second wife was dead. I said, "Sounds like quite a woman."

"Not beautiful in the regular way, but it didn't matter. We liked the same music, and she read the classics to me at night. Mattie loved this island—went clear to Morocco to furnish the place. Could hang with the boys when we went tarpon fishing, too. You ever been to the Temptation on Boca Grande? She'd sit right there at the bar and hold her own with the fishing guides."

Albright's eyes found a rectangle on the wall, where, for a time, paint had been shielded from sunlight. "Her portrait used to hang there. The older Owen gets, the more he reminds me of Mattie."

Photos from a previous marriage seldom survive a new wife, but I had to say something. "It's good that you and your stepson are close."

"We're not, but we at least get along," Albright said. "It's not easy on kids when their mother remarries, especially when new babies show up. Owen and I hardly spoke once he hit adolescence. And we had a hell of an argument when he insisted on taking back his father's name. About a year ago, though, I helped him out of some trouble, now he's working for me on a new project that could—"

Albright blinked at the glass in his hand and decided he'd said enough.

I took a chance. "You can stop worrying. I'm not interested in your Peace River property. No . . . you said 'Peace River holdings,' so maybe you're thinking of developing, or going back into the mining business. If you are, good luck to you and Owen. That's not why I'm here."

Albright wanted to believe me but used a wry tone to test further. "A biologist who doesn't think the phosphate industry and Big Sugar are part of the Evil Empire? Come on, Ford, be honest."

"What does one have to do with the other?" I asked. "The only thing sugar produces in Florida is pollution and political hacks."

"Most people group them," he countered. "I wanted to see your reaction."

"I'm not most people. I'm not up on the latest studies, but I've read that phosphate is doing a better job of containing wastewater and reclamation. Personally, I think the mines look like hell, and they've probably done more damage than anyone realizes. But I also know there's a need for phosphate. No, more than a need—phosphorus is essential. Every life-form has to have it or it dies. The stuff can't be reproduced artificially, so mining is a necessary option." I stood. "If you're done testing me, I'd like to see that room with your grandfather's photos."

Albright, for the first time, appeared interested in what I had to say. "Do you mean that?"

"Sure. I like history."

"No, about phosphate mining."

I said, "Of course. Phosphate depletion in the soil is the main cause of crop failure worldwide. A lot of people would be starving if Florida didn't export it as fertilizer."

He asked a few more questions before he said, "When I tell my daughters that half this nation would go hungry—other countries, too—they just roll their eyes." He hesitated. "Are you really a biologist? They might listen if you told them what you just told me."

I said, "Mostly, I'm a realist who believes that idealists have more fun, so why bother your daughters with the facts? But if you think it would help, sure, I'll talk to them."

The man seemed relieved our sparring was over. "Then I guess I wouldn't mind looking for a list of old artifact collectors—but, I'm warning you, it's a waste of time. A couple of carvings stolen years ago? That's as pointless as . . . well, looking for ghosts or buried gold." Albright said it in an offhanded way but awaited my response.

I said, "You sound like a man who's dealt with treasure hunters before."

"I have."

"Is this another test? Why would treasure hunters bother someone in the phosphate business?"

"Stories, legends," Albright said, still feeling me out.

"Like what?"

"Name it. Back when I was in college, they'd come to the mine with some BS story about fossil hunting, but they were really after anything left behind by the first Spaniards. Ponce de León's sword— that was popular for a while."

"A five-hundred-year-old sword?" I said. "That's stretching things."

"Or De Soto's gold crucifix—crazy stuff. I'm not making this up. A couple times a week, I'd get a phone call, or we'd catch someone trespassing."

"Why? Your draglines had to dig down thirty or forty feet to get to the phosphate beds. People actually believed pirates or Indians would bury something that deep?"

Albright studied me for a moment. "Have you ever toured a mining operation?"

"No, but that's what I've read."

"You should. I can arrange it. Then you'd understand the attraction. Sometimes these guys would *claim* to be after treasure but really wanted high-end fossils—a pristine saber cat's skull or mastodon tusks. Blue ivory is worth more than gold—damn near anyway." He saw my confusion. "Because it's so rare. That's the color it turns, bluish black. Think of it as Ice Age ivory. Tusks taken from live elephants are called blood ivory. It's been banned worldwide. But that hasn't stopped the Africans and Chinese, of course. Ice Age ivory is still legal if it's found on private property."

On the mantel was a carved elephant; elephants were embroidered in the rug. "You know a lot about this. Is it because of the company name—Mammoth Mines?"

Albright laughed. "You have no idea . . ."

Apparently not. "Did I miss something?"

"Forget it. Sort of a family thing, and it's a long story. Back to what I was saying . . . When our mines were operational, we got all kinds of stories about why people wanted to dig. Fossil clubs could be fun—kids, the look on their faces when they found something. The real pro bone hunters, though, they were a whole different animal."

"There's a fine line between fantasy and obsession," I said, then used Fallsdown's story about a mastodon graveyard as an example.

"I've heard that one, too. Right out of a Tarzan movie." He sat back, as if deciding something, then finally spoke. "You're right."

"About . . . obsession?"

People screw up, I'm no exception, so why add to our misery by belaboring it?

Irrational, Ford. You can apologize tomorrow.

End of temper tantrum, beginning of a pleasant ride home. I checked the gauges, placed a night vision monocular—a MUM-14 made in Arizona—within easy reach, then nudged the throttles up to 4000 rpm. It was a black June night, the breeze heated by mangroves, but not strong enough to stir the stars over which my boat skimmed. To the west, a quarter moon was setting beyond the Intracoastal Waterway, a line of robotic flashers, red, white, and green. Gasparilla Island pulsed with micro towers. In the black void that was Boca Grande Pass, boats pursued tarpon, their stern lights mimicking slow meteorites.

I banked south toward Sanibel, my attitude improved. It got better when, on the console, my cell phone blinked: a new text from Hannah:

If you're not stranded, you better have a good excuse for not answering.

The woman was mad because she was worried about me. I grinned. The pleasure I felt was mildly perverse, but there it was. The right thing to do was call. The wrong thing to do was show up unannounced at Hannah's dock. That would be a new low in dumb, even for me.

Use your head.

I did. I backed the throttles and slowed. Ahead was Useppa Island, a ghost town of foliage and dark houses in June, but a few lights showing on the highest mound. Sulfur Wells, where Hannah lived, was only two miles east, a halo glow above the mangrove gloom. I pictured the woman alone inside her little cabin cruiser . . . Hannah's long legs, her black hair mussed from reading, the fine angularity of

"About collectors. We kept a list of names. The kooks, the harmless ones, and another list of guys who'd cut your throat. Bone hunters—some of them are no better than street thugs. One of our night watchmen was hit in the back of the head so hard, it was a year before they took him off life support. My dad sold out not long after he was attacked."

"Because of what happened?"

"That, and some other things. It played a role."

"Did they catch the guy who did it?"

"They never arrested anyone. My grandfather was also shot at a couple of times. Back when the mine was open, I got more than a few threatening calls. That's why I don't believe anyone's story if it has to do with fossils or artifacts." He sipped his drink.

"If that's a warning," I said, "relax. I've got photos of the pieces in the boat. I'll get them."

Albright motioned for me to stay seated, went to a desk, and returned with a legal pad. "A rough sketch will do."

"Why? I can be back in five minutes."

"Humor me," he said. "It's my way of confirming if a story's legit or not."

"Nothing I can draw will prove that," I said, but gave it a shot. When I was done, I handed him the pad. "There were two carvings, very similar, made of black soapstone. They have ceremonial value to a member of the Crow tribe. This isn't about buried treasure."

Albright studied the sketch and seemed satisfied. "The bullshitters always added artistic touches—probably because they made it up in their heads as they went along. Shading, lots of swirls. Didn't matter what they claimed to be after, I could always tell. This is more like a schematic." He looked up from the sketch. "Are these owl faces? You're no artist, by the way."

I said, "Thank you. Charmstones, is what Fallsdown calls them. Were you serious about me visiting a phosphate mine?"

He replied, "Possibly," and set the notepad aside. "Why did your Indian friend send you? He could have come up here and asked me himself."

Through the window, beyond the columned terrace and in firelight, the three blondes were dancing in a line, their shadows huge against the trees. Tomlinson had the drum now. Duncan Fallsdown, hands on hips, was staring up at the house—possibly seeing my silhouette.

"Because my Indian friend is smart," I replied. "*You* be honest, Leland. Would you be more likely to talk to someone like me or to a couple of long-haired drum gurus?"

FOUR

IT WAS ALMOST TEN-THIRTY WHEN I SAID GOOD-BYE TO ALBRIGHT AND THE drum partiers and returned to my boat. I planned to drive straight to Dinkin's Bay but looked at my phone to discover a text Hannah had sent two hours earlier:

Is your prop okay? Call if you need a tow.

I grimaced. No mention of the Brazilian, of course, but Hannah and her visitor had obviously witnessed my boat snag the crab trap. Which meant they had also watched me go over the side into the water, had seen me fumbling and thrashing, in a hurry to cut my propeller free, so I could sneak away.

Embarrassing. Proficient watermen pay attention. Adult males don't spy on women they are dating—or *had* dated.

What to do?

For starters, I chastised myself with descriptive names but kept my voice low—until I was in open water, where I shouted, *"Dumbass!"* I got no argument from my roaring engines, so yelled it again, and added a directive so impossible that even I had to crack a smile.

her face, and a weighted decency about her that was real, like an aura—but it was a weight she could toss into a heap, along with her clothing, when we were alone, the two of us, in a bedroom.

At least give the lady some warning.

That was a must. So I called and said, "I'm in my boat off Useppa," when Hannah answered.

"I was worried about you."

"You deserve an apology," I said, then explained I had detoured past her dock earlier hoping to say a quick hello, not to spy. It was one of those gray lies that nags at the conscience, so I added, "It won't happen again."

"Marion," she replied, "the Coast Guard makes up boating laws, not me. It never crossed my mind a man like you would spy." There was a pause. "What time is it?"

The relief I felt was tangible. "Early enough to say hello," I said, and soon pushed twin throttles forward.

THE CHANNEL INTO SULFUR WELLS is a minefield of rocks and thin water, so a careful approach is required. Even so, Hannah didn't poke her head out of the cabin until I was tying up.

"No need to get out," she said softly. "Mosquitoes aren't too bad tonight. We can talk on the dock."

On the phone, she had sounded warm in a sleepy sort of way, the Southern rhythms of her voice an invitation. Now she was guarded. I asked, "Is something wrong?"

"Of course not." Hannah looked shoreward, where an old Cracker house, windows dark, was elevated on a shell mound. Then whispered, "For all I know, Loretta's on the porch with her binoculars. She pretends they got lost, but I know where she hides them."

Loretta was Hannah's mother, an invalid since her stroke but still a spunky woman. Even so, the dock extended two hundred feet into the bay and was screened from the house and road by mangroves. No one else around in this isolated fishing settlement, so prying eyes weren't the problem.

Hannah's uneasiness remained a mystery until I talked myself onto the deck of the vintage Marlowe that is her floating home. *Esperanza*, she had named the vessel, in honor of a legendary fishing guide, a woman who had lived on nearby Tarpon Bay. I sat on the little yacht's transom. Hannah stood facing me, barefoot, wearing jeans, plus a robe pulled tight despite a night so warm that air molecules, laden with water, dripped from the cabin roof. Mosquitoes had found us, too.

Finally I said, "If you want me to leave, just say so."

"It's not that. I thought we were having a nice conversation."

We were, but one-sidedly. I had described Albright Island and the museum of photos I'd seen, photos that tracked the history of phosphate mining in Florida. But I had yet to open the bag I'd brought aboard, photos of the two owlish-looking stone artifacts therein.

I bloodied a mosquito on my hand, swatted a dozen away from my ears, and said, "It would be cooler in the cabin. Hannah, I can *hear* the air conditioner."

She pulled the robe tighter around her neck. "Marion . . . we can't."

That's when I understood the problem but feigned innocence. "Can't what?"

"You know what happens when we're alone."

I swiveled my head for effect. "We're alone now, aren't we?"

"You know what I mean."

"We were alone last night after dinner and nothing happened."

She responded, "Only because I drove my SUV and I wouldn't unlock the doors when we said good night."

That was true, but I pressed ahead. "I've got pictures of the stone carvings." I picked up my canvas case, which had a shoulder strap. "I was hoping to get your opinion. Some say they resemble owls."

Hannah liked owls, often spoke of a great horned owl that lived in the oaks behind her mother's house. Profanity, on the other hand, seldom escaped her lips, but she came close, saying, "Daa-darnn it, Ford. If I let you inside the cabin, those pictures had better look like owls, not arrowheads."

"They do."

"You've got to *promise*."

"Yes . . . owls," Hannah admitted when we were below in the coolness of the cabin, Fallsdown's photos spread on a settee table of oiled teak. She had finally released her choke hold on the robe, her long, sun-dark fingers free when she picked the photos up one by one to examine them.

I said, "Tomlinson claims the charmstones are actually people who've turned to stone. He says the Crow Indians call them Little People."

Hannah's eyes drifted upward. "The Indian fellow, Duncan, does he believe that?"

"No, but he plays along. There's a close-up in there that shows the eyes and what sort of looks like a beak. Could be owls. What do you think?"

Hannah leafed through the glossies. I stood behind her, playing the role of a disinterested observer. After a while, I leaned against the bulkhead so that our faces were cheek to cheek. When I did, her hands gradually began to shake. I pretended not to notice and moved closer, close enough that our thighs touched. Upon contact,

Hannah's breathing changed. My lungs felt the weight of her presence and my breathing changed, too. Dopamine, released by the brain, fuels what is known as sexual tension. Spell it *dope*amine and never in history has a chemical been more accurately named.

"Marion . . . ?" She said it not looking at me, her question also a warning.

I put my hands on Hannah's waist, an invitation to face me, but she resisted.

"We . . . can't. We . . . We agreed we're going to date other people."

Gently, gently, I tried to turn her. Finally, Hannah pivoted and squared her shoulders, nose and lips a few inches from mine. "We promised we wouldn't."

Through a misty tunnel, all I could see was the woman's dark eyes, the angularity of her face. Pheromones, neural sensors—*something*—fused, and our bodies abruptly collided, lips seeking. We parted for an instant, then collided again. But then she put her hands on my shoulders to ensure distance and said, "Marion, *please*," a woman who was weakening but serious.

I stepped back and tried to blink the fog away. It took several seconds to regain control. Somehow, I had dropped my bag on the floor, scattering two Fenix flashlights and a notebook. Kneeling to retrieve the stuff allowed me to break eye contact. "Sorry," I said. "Geezus . . . I was way out of line."

Deafened by a pounding in my ears, I heard Hannah mutter what sounded like, "Pointless . . . you can't be trusted . . ."

From my knees, I could only reply, "You're right."

When I looked up, though, I saw that I was wrong. Hannah's robe was on the table, and her face was obscured by her blouse, which she was stripping off, her movements heated but sure, a woman who seldom went braless but was braless now above a rim of blue jeans when her face reappeared. Through pouting lips—or swollen lips—Hannah slung the blouse away and scowled. "Damn it, Doc, I *told* you this would happen."

The lady extended her hand to help me to my feet, so we started our night together on the floor.

THREE A.M. BIRDS TITTERED in summer darkness until the boo-boo-booming of a predator silenced all but the water slap beneath the cruiser *Esperanza*'s hull.

"An owl," Hannah murmured, "that's exactly what I was thinking about. This very instant. Now there he is."

"You've seen him?"

My chest was a pillow. I felt her nod. "On the mound behind the house. He stands about waist-high, I swear." When my chest bounced a couple of times, Hannah scolded, "It's *true*. Did you know he ate the neighbor's Pekingese?"

I said, "Why don't you come home with me? I have a dog of my own to check."

Fingers tapped my hand to encourage patience. "I couldn't resist seeing those photos. You knew it, didn't you?"

"I'm manipulative. Always a little surprised when it works, but, yeah, I was hoping." I raised my head. Gray porthole curtains revealed Hannah's face in profile. "Are you sorry?"

"*Hush.* If Indians in Montana think owls are special, maybe the Calusa did, too."

The Calusa were indigenous people, contemporaries of the Maya.

Centuries ago, they had built ceremonial mounds of shell along Florida's coast, including the mound behind the house where Hannah's mother lived.

I said, "I'll make pompano for breakfast. We can go for a run first. I'll serve you pompano and eggs in bed."

A long finger drew circles on my hand. "That's sweet. I was talking about owls. At first, it didn't make sense those carvings being in Florida. Now maybe it does. Charmstones, you said. Or did you make that up?"

I started to reply but was preempted. From a distant tree, the great horned owl thrummed again: *Boo-boo-boom.*

"See?" Hannah said, sounding sleepy but excited. "Like he's telling you it's okay."

My chest bounced until her finger became five ready fingernails—a gentle warning.

"I wasn't laughing *at* you," I said.

"It's okay if you were. I know you don't believe in things, spiritual connections and all. But sometimes you have to wonder." A hint of concern . . . or was it disappointment? Then I was reminded that Hannah seldom missed church when she added, "Reverend Nyman doesn't give sermons, he just talks like a regular person. That was his topic on Sunday."

"Spiritualism?"

"Not the way you mean it. No wonder either—Tomlinson could make a person gun-shy. He takes it way too far sometimes."

An opportunity to blame Tomlinson was so seldom offered by a woman, it took willpower to ignore. But I used it as a segue. "Tomorrow, I was going to drive north with Tomlinson and the Montana guy, but we could take my boat instead. Come with us or I can drop you here." I had already told her about Venice, fifty miles up the coast, where, according to Fallsdown, there was a flea market frequented by an antiquities dealer.

"I'm glad you're helping your Indian friend," Hannah said. She yawned and stretched, the porthole showing her breasts in profile, an undulant lift of hips . . . a glimpse of pubic hair. "Wish I could go, but I've got a fly-fishing trip in the morning."

All evening, I'd been wanting to ask about the man from Brazil and this was my chance. "One of your regular clients?"

"Yes."

"Do I know him?"

"Why's it matter? Don't be nosy."

"I was just making conversation."

"No you weren't."

She was right, of course, but I said, "I can't think of a more innocent question: How was your day? Catch any fish? It's the sort of thing people say, Hannah. Christ."

"Please," she said. "No need to swear, sugar," and returned to massaging my palm.

Sugar. It was an endearment Hannah seldom used, yet I felt a sudden claustrophobia along with a pointless jealousy. "I withdraw the question," I said.

"Don't be mad. Those two weeks you disappeared in Venezuela—once I knew you were safe, I didn't ask for details about who you saw. Lots of attractive woman down there, I'm sure, but not a single e-mail. Or why you came back with that cut on your face." Her fingers detoured to explore the faint scar . . . raised her head to kiss my cheek, then settled back, hair warm against my chest.

"I was working in a remote spot," I explained, although *dis-*

appeared was more accurate. The Venezuelan Guardia—special police—had been after me, so I had vanished into the rainforest—four days on foot to the Colombian border.

The sudden stillness of Hannah's fingers expressed doubt and prefaced what came next. "I'd rather not ask you than risk hearing a lie. And the way our relationship is, it's none of my business anyway."

A door appeared in my mind. Open it, Hannah would be there, waiting, the two of us joined, obligated to speak honestly about our lives. I couldn't do that—not yet, probably never—but I attempted to explore what lay on the other side of the door.

"Ask away," I said.

"You don't mean that."

"Try me."

Stillness . . . more doubt, so she chose a playful escape. "Did you hear about the party last night—those women skinny-dipping at Dinkin's Bay? Jeth told me. All blondes, he said. I figure they must've been pretty because he stuttered so much."

"I was at dinner with you," I pointed out.

"You must have heard *something*. I wonder what it would be like . . . you know, swimming naked with a bunch of strangers?" Her musing tone caused the churchgoer in her to add, "Not that I would do such a thing. Well . . . unless you were there . . . or . . . or maybe someone I felt safe with."

"That's not exactly comforting," I responded. "What time's your charter in the morning?"

Hannah yawned again, a neural reflex that signaled more than sleepiness. Then kicked the cover off her legs and lay naked. "I've got to be up at five, so you should probably go." There was a pause. "But not just yet . . . okay?"

Fingers slid from my hand, fumbled with the bedsheet, then began a gentle, probing search to confirm my answer. But I stopped her. I was annoyed by her scolding certainty and peeved at myself for feeling so spellbound in this woman's presence.

"You need your sleep," I said.

"You're serious?"

"Occasionally."

She sat up. "You *are* mad."

"Mad about *you*," I corrected. Then kissed the lady good night, got in my boat, and ran backcountry to Dinkin's Bay, where my dog was waiting, golden-eyed and alert.

"It's four in the morning," I told him.

The dog acknowledged me with an indifferent sniff, a single wag of its tail, and grunted for permission to swim.

"Let's go for a run first," I said.

FIVE

AFTER TWO HOURS AT A FLEA MARKET OFF ENGLEWOOD ROAD, AND BEFORE WE interrupted a burglary in progress, our cab abandoned us in downtown Venice because Tomlinson hollered, "Stop, Kato, stop!" as we passed a sno-cone vendor.

At that moment, a man carrying bolt cutters and a gun was casing a house a few miles away. A glassy, summer Friday can drift us toward disaster as surely as a waterfall.

"You scared the driver," I told Tomlinson, pocketing my billfold.

"Not if he waited to get paid," he argued. "That's *happened*, man. Cabbies hit the accelerator before my butt's off the seat." Yellow hibiscus shirt and thongs flapping, he went to get his sno-cone. I turned and walked the other way. Fallsdown, I assumed, would follow one of us.

He didn't. When I looked back, he was entering a shop that promised *Fine Shark Jewelry*. Not unusual in Venice, known as the "Shark Tooth Capital of the World," but unexpected. At the flea market, Fallsdown had gotten a lead on an elderly antiquities dealer—just a name, not an address—but the man from Montana had seemed intrigued. So I found a bench and waited. Watched the passing of pretty ladies, who scented the air with boutique incense. One after another, they reassured me that walking out on Captain Hannah Smith last night was the manly thing to do.

Soon, while Tomlinson lapped at his sno-cone, Fallsdown reappeared. He was folding a piece of paper, his expression optimistic—or so I thought. But then said, "Nothing here. Might as well head back," and asked me, "How far to the marina?"

Osprey Nest Marina, where I had tied my boat, was about ten blocks north.

"What about the old dude collector?" Tomlinson asked. We had been given the name Finn Tovar.

Fallsdown, already walking—but in the wrong direction—said, "He died last week. The lady in the store's been in business fifteen years and she knew the man. Didn't like him, but she knew him."

"Has his collection already been sold?"

Fallsdown held up the folded paper as if it were a prize. "That's what we're going to find out." Then added, *"Perfect,"* as if the universe was unfolding as he'd expected.

He knew what he was doing, apparently, so I fell in line, the three of us walking like ducks, east, for five hot blocks, before I finally asked, "Where are we going?"

"I told you," Fallsdown replied over his shoulder, "to the marina."

I stopped. "You're going the wrong way."

"What?"

I said it again.

"What?"

I waited until both men turned before asking, "Take another look at that paper. I thought the lady gave you an address."

"No, just a name. We're looking for a tour guide, some local who hangs around a bar near where we left the boat."

"You *need* a tour guide," I said. "The Gulf of Mexico is *that* way. The marina is another ten blocks north."

Fallsdown said, "You're shitting me."

Tomlinson tried to reassure the Crow medicine man. "Don't worry, Dunk, you just need to brush up on your Indian skills. I'll help you, brother."

Fallsdown asked, "Do you remember me ever getting lost back when I was a drunk? I don't."

Perfect, I thought.

A WHILE LATER, Dunk regained some of my confidence when a man who resembled Mick Jagger, but with braided pirate hair, said, "I'm part Indian," and Dunk replied, "Which tribe? Sicilian or whitefoot?"

Up until then, I'd been ready to pull the plug. There are worse ways to waste a day than gunkholing the Gulf Coast, but I'd had enough. We'd found the tour guide, whose name *was* Mick-something, at a tiki bar on the water. Osprey Nest was a nice marina—orderly docks, with a fueling station and a patio restaurant. A busy place during high season, I guessed, but quiet on this June afternoon, where Mick, a shirtless man drinking beer and smoking a pipe while in full lotus position, did not inspire confidence. Yes, he knew a relics collector by the name of Finn Tovar, but I was restless. Work awaited me at the lab. I was irritable from lack of sleep. So I had wandered off to check my boat but returned just in time to hear the tour guide's claim and Fallsdown's response.

"Whitefoot?" Mick asked. "Never heard of that tribe, man. You're trying to be funny, right?"

When Dunk told him, "They're part of the Fawnee Nation," I decided it was getting interesting and moved into the shade to listen.

Mick asked, "Faw-nee?" Then got the joke. "Oh . . . *phony* nation," and decided to ride with it instead of taking offense. "No, but I know what you're saying, there are so many fakes out there, man. See, I'm one-quarter Cherokee. My mother's side. That's why I hit it off with Old Man Tovar. It's where my talent for finding things comes from." After a glance in my direction, he relit the clay pipe in his hand—*puff-puff-puff.* A mixture of tobacco and weed, the smell. Then continued talking.

"The old man was a bastard—he'd say it himself, 'I'm a ruthless bastard'—but Finn trusted me. We did a lot of hunts together. Once, these three dudes were bird-dogging us, heard we'd found a very hot spot off the Myakka River. So what's Finn do? Doubled back and slit their tires. That didn't—what do you call it?—*deter* them, so next time Finn set what he called a werewolf wire. You know, a wire stretched neck-high? One schlub was bleeding pretty bad, but, of course, we were all trespassing, so they couldn't call the cops. Finn, he'd say, 'In the bone biz, you need balls or you end up bones.'"

When I took a seat, Mick stared at me, and asked Tomlinson and Dunk, "Is he a cop?"

"My pal's cool," Tomlinson said.

Mick accepted that. "No offense, mate."

"I took it as a compliment," I replied, which he decided was another joke and laughed. "Funny bunch, you guys. Yeah, but *seriously* . . . The Brown Shirts arrested thirteen collectors a while back. Something like four hundred felony charges, man. Confiscated all their shit. Like, perfect—I mean *perfect*—Clovis knives and arrowheads. Tools of this semitranslucent coral you would not believe. One poor schlub they got was in his seventies, spent his life bone hunting. They took a giant condor skull he could have retired on. His whole collection of shark teeth and shark points"—Mick used his hands to indicate size: three to six inches—"and they put his ass in jail."

Tomlinson explained to Dunk that Brown Shirts were "Swamp Cops," or Florida Fish & Wildlife officers, and that Florida's first people had worked shark's teeth into hunting points, "which," he added, "provides a beautiful integration of paleontology with archaeology. Don't you agree?"

Dunk replied, "Last thing I want to do is talk to a cop," then they discussed ancient tools made from shark teeth while my attention abandoned the conversation. It was because of the way Duncan had said *talk to a cop*.

A troubling possibility entered my mind. After three years in state prison, was it possible that Fallsdown was still on parole? If so, leaving Montana could put the man behind bars again. I've done far worse in my life than aiding and abetting a felon. That wasn't the problem. I liked the guy. He had come to Florida on a quest that was admirable in a clumsy Don Quixote way. Maybe a phone call or two could make it right if he had skipped without permission. It depended, of course, on how forgiving his parole officer was.

When I returned to the conversation, though, and tried to exchange eye contact, Fallsdown swung from me to Mick, the tour guide, and asked, "How much do you charge?"

"Hundred bucks an hour to look for shark's teeth. To see what's left of Finn's collection? Well . . ." Mick pretended to struggle with the quandary, then decided, "Ah, what the hell. You're a brother Skin, so . . . so let's say two hundred for the afternoon?"

Getting to his feet, Tomlinson said to me, "Hope you don't mind, Doc. We volunteered your boat." Then hesitated. "You're carrying cash, right?"

At about the same time, a thief carrying bolt cutters and a gun was entering the house once owned by another violent man—Finn Tovar.

HALF A MILE OFFSHORE, Snake Island and the Venice Pier behind us, Mick, in teaching mode, told me, "Stop, I want to explain something."

I shut down, and drifted, while learning that five million years ago, when the Florida peninsula was twice as wide, an archaic river had vented here from a shallow inland sea—thus the shark's teeth.

Mick's story varied from what I'd read, but it was close enough. I started the engines and steered south while he hollered an addendum: "That inland sea is where they dig phosphate now. For millions of years, bones stacked up there. But we don't find teeth like we used to. It's because of beach reclamation. They covered Venice Beach with tons of sand."

Then, a few seconds later, he pointed toward the airport and informed us, "You'll get a kick out of this—that's where three of the nine/eleven terrorists learned to fly. One was a pretty cool operator. He came to my yoga class, showed up every Tuesday . . . almost." As an aside, in his dreamy, stoned way, he explained to Dunk, "Yoga has a lot in common with our ancient ways. Equality, you know? The oneness of all life."

Dunk, straight-faced, said, "I didn't know ragheads were into equality."

"Rag-whats . . . ?" Mick asked.

To Tomlinson, sitting beside me, I leaned over and said, "I want that asshole off my boat."

He gave me an *OK* sign and said into my ear, "Mick has the keys to Tovar's house—it's only a mile down the beach. He keeps a bike there, so I figure he's got permission."

I didn't like it. Rather than taking charge, I said, "He'd better." Then moved on to my concerns about Duncan, saying, "Is there a chance he jumped parole?"

Tomlinson shrugged. "I can't ask. It's not the Indian way."

I said, "Yeah . . . much smarter to let him go back to jail," and bumped the throttles up to 5000 rpm, a blur of white sand to our left. Two miles later, Mick hollered, "That's Finn's place," and told me to pull up on the beach.

The Gulf was calm, so I did. It was an isolated stretch of sand and foliage, a single orange roof through the palms. A big chunk of property in an exclusive area—the violent antiquities collector had been a wealthy man. The spot appeared safe enough until my friends and the tour guide filed through the door into Tovar's house. By then, the thief had filled his bag and wanted out.

Unfortunately, I distanced myself from the expedition by staying on the boat. A bad bilge pump was my excuse.

THAT'S WHAT I WAS DOING, lying on my belly, arm deep in the aft access port, when I heard the distant whap-whap of what was probably a screen door but could have been Mick, our stoned leader, hammering off a lock.

I raised my head, but the view was blocked by two black engine cowlings, so I returned to work. My boat carries four high-speed pumps, a redundancy system for running wide open in heavy seas. Using the braille system, I was testing the float switches on each pump when, a minute later, I heard a faraway siren . . . then another siren much closer.

No need for concern. Venice is a low-crime area, but heart attacks and head-on collisions are indifferent to geography and the sunniest of days. The combination nagged at me, though. I couldn't convince myself. What if the house was equipped with a silent alarm and police were on their way? Fallsdown, even Tomlinson, might be cuffed and taken to jail.

Damn it.

I got to my knees to seal the access port, which is when I heard a man yell, "Hey . . . you! I'm a cop—I need your boat."

Was he talking to me? Yes—a nervous man in blue sweats, mid-twenties, head shaved, with a goatee. He had crossed the beach unheard because of the sirens and stood at the water's edge, yards away. Undercover cops sometimes wear jogging suits, but their heads do not swivel frantically when commandeering a vehicle. Nor do they carry a duffel bag in one hand while aiming what looked like a .22 pistol at the face of a surprised citizen.

That would be me.

I said, "If you're in trouble, this is the worst possible way to handle it. What happened back there?"

The man splashed toward the boat, pistol elevated. "Shut up and do what I tell you."

"Do you want me out?" I was hoping he did.

He swung the bag aboard, needed both hands because it was heavy. "Start the engines," he said.

That told me he wanted a hostage or was unfamiliar with boats. I scanned foliage beneath the orange roof, sirens louder now. The whap-whap I'd heard could have been his .22 pistol. Tomlinson, Dunk, or the tour guide might be lying in pools of blood. The possibility converted my surprise into anger. Even so, there was not a damn thing I could do for my friends that police and EMTs couldn't do better when they arrived.

My heart, which had been thudding, began to slow—symptomatic of a change in my attitude. Decision time: Throw myself over the side, swim beneath the boat and take the guy under before he climbed aboard? The move risked a bullet before our watery wrestling match.

No . . . the image of Tomlinson or Fallsdown wounded or dead demanded a cleaner, sharper response.

I made my decision.

Rather than pull the stern anchor, I tossed the line free, eager to put a few miles of water between my boat and any beach-walker witnesses.

"Hop in," I told the man.

SIX

I'VE KNOWN GOOD ATHLETES WHO HAD THE PHYSIQUES OF McDONALD'S CLERKS. A couple of all-American wrestlers so mild-mannered, so shy, they would have looked right at home stocking shelves at Kmart. Gauging ability based on size is typical of our culture, but unwise, naïve—dangerous, too, in a violent situation.

Like now. My boat had been commandeered by a man who was unimposing, even clumsy when he'd tumbled aboard. But so what? A heavy duffel bag and a gun proved nothing. He could be a skilled burglar . . . or a psycho killer with a new trophy to add to his collection.

Something he could also add were my billfold, my phone, and a fine Gerber multi-tool he'd pocketed after ordering me to empty my pockets on the deck. Clumsy or not, the man was careful. Which is why I was thinking, *Pick your move. Make it clean, something you can explain without ending up behind bars—or dead.*

Standing at the controls, I considered options while we cruised at thirty knots toward an empty turquoise horizon. My abductor faced me from the other side of the windshield, his knees on a cooler. It gave him a clear view of what lay behind: Venice Beach, Manasota Key, the coastline shrinking, but no helicopters or boats in pursuit. He kept the pistol pressed to the Plexiglas, a profile view, his hand flat over the weapon to brace himself against the mild dolphining of waves. But he used the weapon for emphasis whenever he yelled to be heard.

He raised the gun now, asking, "Can this boat make it to Mexico?" The windshield became an aiming post for his cheap revolver, the kind sold in pawnshops. The cylinder was loaded, but at least one chamber was empty, possibly two. The weapon had been fired.

Yucatán, Mexico, was four hundred miles away, which I communicated by shaking my head, then held up a hand until he angled the pistol away. I tried reason. "What happened back there? It can't be worse than what you're doing now, but I won't press charges if you talk to me—and give me my stuff back."

The man looked south where two boats, in tandem, cruised the beach, then north where another boat was exiting Roberts Bay. Wiped a hand over his bald head and muttered, *"Shit."*

"Take it easy," I told him. "There's not a boat around that can catch mine. If police saw you get in, they know that, so they won't try."

It wasn't true, but it earned his attention. "Yeah?" He considered the B-Impact boat's stealthy coloring, the electronics and oversize engines, wanting to believe, but he didn't. "Doesn't feel like we're going that fast."

"You want to attract attention?" I asked, touching the throttles. "We can. You should be worried about helicopters. That's what they'll send. Use a laser that transmits our GPS coordinates, but they'll keep their distance if they know you're armed."

He licked his lips and sniffed, "Cops are the least of my worries, man," but his eyes moved from the console to the sky.

I kept talking because it's easier to kill a stranger. Told him I was willing to help but needed to understand the situation. Then shared an ironic truth I couldn't entrust to a friend—or even a woman I might be falling in love with.

"I've been chased before," I said. "You're going about this all wrong."

He looked at me, really looked at me. "That's bullshit. What did you do?"

I smiled a grim smile but only replied, "We should have headed into the backcountry. Some creek with mangrove cover so we can lose a helicopter if that's what they send."

Pistol sights found my forehead. "Hey, goddamn it, I asked you a question."

I waited for the barrel's angle to change before I answered, "Police wanted to arrest me for murder. No . . . not arrest me. They would have questioned me first, then shot me. Newspapers would have said they *tried* to arrest me."

"In Florida?"

"No. This was a few months ago in another country."

"Where?"

"South of here. The name doesn't matter."

"Arrested for *murder*?"

"An assassination, is what they called it, but the same thing."

The pistol, in profile, returned to the windshield. *"Christ,"* he said, worried about it, then asked, "Did you do it?"

Ahead, I could see a color change, water translucent green, now that we were two miles offshore, the murk of mangrove rivers and nutrient crude thinning. I also saw a Styrofoam ball in the distance—a trap marker, blue crab, or a marker forgotten by a stone crabber. The ball would be attached to a hundred feet of nylon rope and a heavy cage. I steered toward it, turning the wheel gradually, while I answered, "It doesn't matter. What I'm telling you is, I've been through this."

"Did you do it or didn't you?"

I looked at him and said, "They were convinced. Same difference."

Color was fading from his face. "Jesus Christ," he said. "Are they still looking?"

"Of course. It's a capital offense." Then asked, "Did you shoot someone? Or just rob a house?"

For a moment, he came close to answering. The moment passed, and he vented his frustration by yelling at the sky, "Son of a bitch! Out of all the boats in Florida, I've got to pick one owned by a goddamn wanted killer." Flipped his middle finger at clouds, then looked north. "Then you better not let them catch us. What about Tampa? It's only an hour by car. How long in a boat?"

I found the starboard trim tab with a finger, getting ready for what came next. "Too far," I said, then lied, "but Saint Pete's just up the beach. You can see it from where you're standing."

My abductor was on his knees, not standing. I wanted him to get to his feet and reach for a starboard handhold—a finesse that might be less time-consuming than snagging a crab trap. He shielded his eyes to see. "Where? That's bullshit. Saint Pete's way the hell north of here."

"Right *there*. Are you blind?"

Then he did it—he stood, balance unsteady—which is when I made my move. Before his hand found a support, I trimmed the boat's starboard chine deep and buried the throttles while spinning the wheel hard in the opposite direction. Engines cavitated . . . deck bucked like a trampoline . . . the man bellowed, "Hey!" Then he belly-skidded along the starboard tube for an instant and tumbled overboard.

If the pistol went flying, I didn't see it, yet I spared him from the propellers by turning immediately to starboard. If I'd known for certain he'd shot my friends, it might have been different, I might have increased speed as I circled back and hit him again while he floundered on the surface. Coast Guard investigators are good at their jobs, but I had just staged an "accident" scenario that kills boaters year after year. Usually, the passenger falls off while pissing, then becomes an unintended victim when his catcalling buddies return to fetch him.

A dozen variations of that scenario were still possible as I slowed and turned. Who would investigators believe? A dead criminal or his frightened captive? Never mind the thousands of hours I have logged at a helm.

I wasn't sure Tomlinson and Dunk had been shot, however. So I idled toward him, yelling, "Show your hands!"

He did—not because I demanded it but because jogging suits absorb water, and my abductor was fighting to stay on the surface. Like a dog learning to swim, his arms flailed, pistol on the bottom by now.

"Asshole. You did that on purpose."

I checked the GPS while he hollered threats and paddled toward my boat. We were 2.1 miles off the beach, close enough to see Finn Tovar's roof of orange tile; to the south, a ridge of silver roofs, houses built shoulder to shoulder. We weren't close enough to hear sirens . . . or had the sirens stopped?

Stopped, I decided. Two miles and a mild shore breeze separated us, but sound carries over water. What had silenced the sirens? A corpse or two might be enough to turn an emergency into an academic recovery. The temptation was to return at top speed and find Tomlinson. I couldn't call him. My phone and wallet were soaking in my abductor's blue jogging suit . . . or drifting toward the bottom.

I thought about using the VFH radio, then decided, *Not yet.* Call the Coast Guard and I would have to either rescue the man or kill him before a chopper was scrambled from Tampa. Go off and leave him, he would drown, and that risked dealing with paperwork and questions later.

An alternative popped into my mind.

In the stern locker, I keep a spare anchor that's attached to a buoy the size of a volleyball. I use it when tarpon fishing—a rig I can jettison before a tarpon strips my reel, then retrieve later. No big deal if I lost it.

I decided to risk losing it now.

Engines in neutral, I gathered buoy, line, and anchor and dumped it all over the side . . . watched the buoy flutter as the line unpeeled. Then I backed the boat away from the approaching swimmer to send him a message.

The man looked at the buoy, then at me. "Hey . . . what are you doing?"

I continued backing.

"Hey, goddamn it. You can't leave me out here."

Yes I could. I'd found the buoy on the beach, the anchor while diving—neither could be traced back to me.

"That'll float you for a while," I called. "Maybe someone will come by."

"Are you *crazy?*"

I answered that by asking, "Remember what I did in South America?" then put twenty yards between us before switching off the engines.

I wanted to see what was in the duffel bag he'd brought aboard. Even if I learned nothing, it would give my abductor time to panic. When he did, I would demand information—along with my wallet, phone, and multi-tool. My phone was in what some PR person deemed a "waterproof" case, which meant it was probably ruined by now.

If it still worked, a call to Tomlinson would decide whether I left my abductor way out here to drown.

THE BAG WAS BIG, constructed for military deployment. Roomy enough for four Pelican cases. I ignored the man's pleas while opening the first case. Inside were dozens of gigantic shark's teeth, some mounted for display, most thrown in by a burglar who was in a hurry. They were remnants of extinct monsters, sharks that could swallow a great white in a gulp. The teeth were fossilized blue-gray ivory, some bigger than my hand.

Think of it as blue ivory—Leland Albright's words.

No doubt now that the late Finn Tovar's house had been robbed.

I opened the second case, then the third, noting the contents in a rush: bones and prehistoric skulls, arrowheads of volcanic black and blazing orange or coral pink—hundreds of them—and a serrated dart, eight inches long, notched for a spear. When I saw that, my hand moved involuntarily to my chest. It was the barb of a prehistoric stingray retooled as a weapon. Lethal, as I knew too well.

I sealed the cases one by one, wondering if I should bother opening the fourth. Police would confiscate the stuff anyway, and it had been ten minutes since I'd left Tomlinson and Fallsdown. I had to make a decision.

"Keep the shit, we'll make a deal." My struggling abductor, thirty yards away, had changed tactics and was trying to negotiate. He had the buoy clutched to his chest but was running out of steam.

I ignored him until he added, "The gold alone's worth twenty grand."

Gold?

I opened the fourth case. It contained several sealed display boxes. I peeked into a few: a silver bar encrusted with coral . . . two coins of gold, their archaic crosses struck off-center—doubloons from Conquistador times. Something big wrapped in plastic: an elephant tusk, mammoth or mastodon. It had a polished blue-black density when touched. The thing was heavy, almost a yard long.

Splashing to stay afloat, the man yelled, "I know where we can sell that shit, too!" while my brain cataloged the items as *Spanish Contact portion of the Finn Tovar collection.*

But I was wrong. When I opened the smallest box, I knew it— after recovering from my surprise. Looking back at me was an owl's face, its eyes rimmed with white as if once set with pearls.

Most definitely not Spanish.

My abductor had gone after the most valuable artifacts first and he had used this case. Items were more carefully packed, each pro- tected by bubble wrap, including the small rosewood box in my hand.

I cleaned my glasses, removed the artifact, and set the box aside. Came damn close to smiling when I looked closer. Photos taken de- cades ago had not captured the pearl sheen around the eyes nor the black glisten of soapstone. The carving possessed an ancient weight when held in my modern hand. But it was only three inches tall, not six as Fallsdown had told me.

Hypnotic, those stony eyes. I had to look away to wonder, *Where's the second owl?*

I hurried through the rest of the items, but it wasn't there. So I returned the carving to the little box, slipped it beneath the console, and repacked the duffel bag. Maybe my abductor knew the answer, so I started engines and idled toward him.

Soon, he was clinging to the side of the boat. I had my wallet, my Gerber, and cell phone, too, which still worked, just as advertised.

Phone in hand, I told him, "If you lied to me, I'll leave you out here."

I had asked the obvious questions by then.

"I *believe* you," he said.

Maybe it was something he saw in my eyes when I punched in Tomlinson's number. While the phone rang, the man tried to pull himself into the boat. When the call went to voice mail, I stepped on his hands until he yelped and fell back into the water.

"My friend doesn't answer," I said, looking down. "What happened to him, Deon?"

That was his name, Deon Killip—probably fake, but I had filed it away. Criminals under duress often use the name of an accomplice.

"How should I know, man? Yeah, okay, I robbed the damn house. But I didn't shoot anyone—I swear."

Prior to my call, he'd claimed he had permission to enter Finn Tovar's house.

"Keep talking," I said.

"But I never fired that gun. I told you, it was some other dude.

The guy shows up out of nowhere wearing a ski mask. Carrying a pistol. He shot at *me*. Would'a killed me. That's why I had to get away from the beach."

I didn't believe him. Mick the tour guide wasn't the ski mask type. Plus, Mick had been shirtless, wearing baggy shorts that couldn't conceal a weapon. Tomlinson and Fallsdown were automatically eliminated.

"That's your second lie," I said. "What happened was, three men showed up and surprised you. You panicked. Two were friends of mine, so I'm not going to ask again. Who did you shoot?"

His confusion appeared genuine. "*Three?* I heard footsteps upstairs, but I was already on my way out. My bike was hidden in the trees and that's where I was headed when this dude in a ski mask steps out. Like, waiting for me, you know? The asshole *shoots* at me. Then I hear sirens. I figure shit's about to really go down, so I took off, hoping he would try to cut me off at the road. When he did, I circled back to the beach and saw you."

A burglar, hoping to escape with a heavy duffel bag, would not arrive on a bicycle. Strike three.

I did a slow scan—no boats around—then told Deon, "Lose the sweatsuit. You might make it to the beach."

When my propellers were clear, I turned the boat and didn't look back.

HALFWAY TO THE BEACH, my cell rang. It was Tomlinson. He talked for two nonstop minutes, and answered one question, before I interrupted, "There's something I have to do. Call you back."

Deon Killip—the man's real name, it turned out—was bawling when I dragged him onto my boat. "The next time you talk to someone like me," I suggested, "don't say 'bike' when you mean 'motorcycle.'"

"Awful," he gasped. "I thought sharks would bite my legs off before I drowned. Thought I was gonna die for sure out here, man."

"You still might," I said.

In the cooler, buried in ice, were bottles of beer. I opened a Kalik and fit it into Deon's shaking hand.

"Now," I added, "is when you tell me *everything*."

SEVEN

WHEN I SPOTTED TOMLINSON, HE WAS WANDERING THE BEACH THREE MILES
south of the late Finn Tovar's house—he, too, had done some running from a man in a ski mask.

"Heard some shots, looked out the window, and there he was,"
he had told me on the phone. That's as far as Tomlinson got before
I had interrupted and turned the boat around to retrieve Deon.
Half an hour later, when I called him back, Tomlinson offered his
approximate location, but added, "Can't talk right now. I'll fill you
in on the way to Dinkin's Bay."

There was no sinister message in his reply, but I'd rocketed along
the beach anyway, searching. Now I understood. My hipster pal
had taken solace in the company of three women, all carrying bags
and tiny shovels, all dressed in swimsuits designed to cover, not reveal. Modest, middle-aged ladies who were so busy digging, I was
almost to the beach before their male companion noticed. I watched
him hug the ladies one by one before he got in the boat, then waved
good-bye while I backed away.

"They're in their bittersweet years," Tomlinson observed, when it was safe to speak. "Sweet enough to want more and too old for bitterness if they make new mistakes. *Fun*, when they're that age. We exchanged cell numbers. Lillian—the stocky brunette?—she's a doll."

"Where's Duncan?" I asked.

"With me until we heard sirens, then he disappeared. Mick, who knows? He went out a window. I don't think he actually had permission to be in the house."

"What a shocker," I said. "Does Dunk have a cell phone?"

"It's one of those disposable phones that migrants buy. I left two messages but kept it short. I didn't want to burn all his minutes."

"We're not leaving without him. Ever cross your mind he's handcuffed in the back of a squad car while you were hunting seashells with your new girlfriends?"

"*Shark's teeth,*" he corrected, and produced a handful from his pocket. "They were everywhere, man. Never seen anything like it." Then shook his head. "The sirens were probably an ambulance or firefighters. Maybe cops, but just a coincidence. They stopped a few blocks away. Scared the hell out of the guy in the ski mask—or maybe he actually was chasing me. That's what I thought, anyway, for the first quarter mile."

On the beach, the ladies were still watching us, so I steered farther offshore before shutting down. "We're staying right here," I said, "until we hear from Duncan—or you give me a good reason."

Tomlinson eyed the duffel bag that contained the four Pelican cases, but minus one little wooden box. "You're the one who ran off and left us, *hermano*. Where'd the bag come from? The guy in the ski mask?" My friend's expression changed. "Geezus . . . don't tell me you killed the guy, Doc."

I said, "I didn't see anyone with a ski mask."

"Yeah? Well, we sure as hell didn't leave Dinkin's Bay carrying a bagful of camera cases. I'd remember that."

I pushed the bag away with my foot. "We're not leaving without Duncan. Tell me what happened."

Tomlinson's Buddha eyes accused *You did something*, but he said, "Dunk is a Yavapai Apache, for heaven's sake. Stop worrying."

"He said he was Crow."

"Ask him about it when you see him. Dunk's probably halfway to Sanibel by now."

"Atlanta, more likely, with his sense of direction," I said. Then stifled my Christmas Day eagerness to show off the owl carving by insisting, "Tomlinson—*talk*."

The story he told matched details in Deon Killip's story, plus filled in a few holes. Deon claimed to be a full-time bartender and part-time burglar—a drug addict, too, which I assumed because of his constant sniffing. He'd overheard two customers talking about Finn Tovar's death and a treasure in antiquities in Tovar's home that had yet to be inventoried before probate.

The customers were attorneys, Deon believed, or at least successful businessmen from the way they had dressed and the twenty-dollar tip they'd left.

He'd heard the men say that the court had sealed Tovar's house with padlocks because the man's enemies started filing claims against the estate the day after Tovar died. The violent antiquities collector, according to Deon, had also been a lifelong thief. Thief, as in digging on phosphate company land, but also thief as in *thief*.

"The old man lived alone in that big house," my abductor had told me. "I checked around. No one knew for sure what was in there, but there were a lot of rumors. I tracked down a maid he'd fired—she hated Tovar. Nice old lady living in this trailer park, trying to support her daughter's babies. She described what sounded like a false wall downstairs—he'd slapped the shit out of her just for being in the room. I don't think she believed I was an undercover repo man. That's what I told her, but it didn't matter. We worked out a deal."

Deon claimed he'd told no one about his plan to rob the house—a claim I doubted. He was a drug addict who lived with his stripper girlfriend. Same when he swore he'd found the .22 caliber pistol behind a false wall where Tovar had stashed his most prized artifacts.

"What's that tell you?" Deon had rationalized. "The shit's stolen. Otherwise, he'd put it in a bank. The maid said Tovar had a big safe upstairs. But, no, he *hid* this stuff. A whole roomful. I just took a few pieces."

Their stories meshed. Tomlinson finished his account, saying, "I figured the guy in the ski mask was SWAT team—black Ninja clothes. That he was after Mick or some hidden meth lab. Didn't matter when he started shooting. Man, we were so *out of there.*"

Tomlinson looked at the bag again and said, "Your turn, Doctor Ford."

It was three p.m. Inland, anvil clouds were gathering heat and moisture—a couple of hours before the first boom of thunder would chase us back to Sanibel. I started engines and idled toward shore to give myself time to think.

"This is *me* you're talking to," Tomlinson pressed.

I remained cautious. "When you were in Tovar's house, did you or Duncan touch anything? Or leave anything behind?"

"My ass puckered when I heard shots. So I *almost* left something, but just a false alarm."

"This is important, stop screwing around."

Tomlinson gave me his *Okay, Teacher* look while opening the cooler. "One of us could've touched the door, maybe, on the way out. But I don't think so. It was wide open and that's the way we left it." He pawed through the ice. "Hey . . . you already drank two beers? The six-pack of Kalik was for me, man."

I said, "If Duncan tries to hitchhike, police will pick him up. I think I was right. I think he jumped parole. Why else would he take off on his own?"

"It's what a medicine man does," Tomlinson said, miffed about the beer Deon had drank. "He'll change shapes—shape-shifters can fly when they need to. Or buy a bus ticket. No . . . What I think is, Dunk will go to the closest lodge. So stop worrying."

"Lodge?" My mind had to shift gears. Brighton Indian Reservation near Orlando was the closest, but that was seventy miles east. "Police will spot him on the highway," I said.

Tomlinson popped one of the remaining beers, tilted the bottle back, and used the back of his hand as a towel. "Cop's would'a had to be damn quick on their toes to catch him before he got to the lodge. We passed one on Venice Avenue. Dunk saw it. Didn't you?"

"Saw what?"

"A lodge, man."

"In Venice?"

"Right there in front of your eyes."

I have learned to disengage when conversation with Tomlinson becomes cryptic ping-pong. It's his specialty. He enjoys the game too much. So I opened the electronics cabinet overhead and pretended to fine-tune the Doppler weather radar—a storm building over Myakka, which was phosphate country . . . another storm east of Englewood, but still plenty of time to get home.

Finally, Tomlinson lost patience and explained, "A Masonic lodge. Dunk's a Freemason—a lot of Skins are."

"Why didn't you just say so?"

"As if you'd believe me."

"With good reason," I said, which sucked me right back into his game.

"Believe what you want. You've never wondered why Mohawks fought the British? They were Masonic warriors just like Ben Franklin and Paul Revere. Near Sedona, the rez there, a lot of Skins are in the Brotherhood. Wisconsin—the great Sauk chief, Black Hawk, was a Mason. Red Jacket in New England. When Lewis and Clark crossed the Rockies, more than one unsuspecting Skin greeted those white bastards with a Masonic handshake. So it only makes sense that's where Dunk would go."

This was said to reassure me about the fate of our Crow or Apache friend from Montana—or was it Arizona?

I gave up. "Let's review here. The house you broke into was robbed. You do understand that?"

"*Robbed?*" he asked.

"Shots were fired. Judges don't like it when firearms are used during the commission of a felony. Valuable property was stolen, so it's grand theft. Someone saw you leave that house—the guy in the ski mask, if no one else. If police find fingerprints, they'll match them on a computer. If they . . . no, *when* they question Mick, the magic tour guide, he'll tell them about you and Duncan. See why I'm concerned?"

Tomlinson appeared confounded until his eyes found the duffel bag, then they zoomed in on me. "Jesus Christ, Doc. You hijacked the robber and took his swag. *Then* you killed him. I was right from the start."

No . . . I had struck a deal with Deon Killip and dropped him a few miles north on Turner Key, where his stripper girlfriend had relatives.

"Call the Masonic lodge in Venice," I said. "I'll explain on the way."

No answer at the lodge, but Tomlinson's phone buzzed an hour later off Stump Pass, south of Englewood Beach.

"What's your twenty, Magic Man?" he asked, grinning. It was Fallsdown. I slowed, preparing to turn around, but Tomlinson waved me onward.

"Let me guess," I said. "He's in Key West, not Atlanta."

Tomlinson covered the phone. "Dinkin's Bay—Dunk had to stop at the 7-Eleven to buy more phone minutes. Should I tell him what we have?"

By then, I had unboxed the owl charmstone but hadn't shared all the information with my pal—nor would I until I decided on a next move.

"Let's surprise him," I said.

I SPENT THE NEXT DAY, Saturday, expecting a knock on the door and a refresher on my Miranda rights. I had hidden the bag, minus the charmstone, deep in the mangroves on the western fringe of Dinkin's Bay, but was still uneasy.

A close inspection of the duffel bag's contents would have to wait until I deemed it safe.

Tomlinson and Fallsdown didn't know what I'd done but must have shared my uneasiness. They had avoided the lab and kept a low profile.

In the afternoon, my cousin, Ransom Gatrell, stopped to say

hello. With her cinnamon skin and Bahamian accent, we are an un-
likely family, but Ransom is my closest relative and among my most
trusted friends. She was leaving for Key West that night. We had a
good talk. She offered some insights into Hannah's behavior, then
shared a few details about her own love life that caused me some
brotherly uneasiness, the woman was so succinctly graphic.

"Never seen a man so fast to embarrass," she said more than
once, although her intonation varied with her laughter.

I shared a few secrets with her, too, but of a less intimate nature.

Leland Albright called as Ransom was leaving and hinted again
at his offer of a consulting job. "Don't tell me you're not qualified,"
he said. "I did some research on you. Tomorrow, I'll show you what
an old phosphate mine looks like if you're willing to discuss a business proposition."

In the morning, he wanted me to come to his home in Sarasota
and we would drive to his mining property together.

I told Albright, "Let me think about it," and walked Ransom to
her car.

His offer was tempting. Tomlinson and Fallsdown were going to
a Lakeland gun show in the morning to search for more relics dealers. Duncan was delighted to see the little stone owl but was pressing
ahead with his search for the second carving. I had been dreading
the trip to Lakeland. In a building full of right-leaning gun advo-
cates, Tomlinson would require careful monitoring—or a gag. Leland's invitation would spare me all that . . . *if* police didn't arrive
and recite my Miranda rights, then lead me away in cuffs.

I spent late Saturday with old baseball buddies, then worked
with the dog on blind retrieves using hand commands, which he
often ignored in favor of shorter routes. The early, wakeful hours of

Sunday morning were spent thinking about the duffel bag hidden out there in the mangrove darkness.

What exactly had I taken from Deon, the petty thief? Valuable, no doubt, but how valuable? Sooner than later, news about the robbery of the late Finn Tovar's house would get out. The aftershock I expected would be proportional.

Someone would come looking.

EIGHT

SUNDAY MORNING, AT LELAND'S HOME IN SARASOTA, THE SHAKE-UP I ANTICI-
pated arrived with the mildest of tremors. I was wandering toward
the backyard where, behind a courtesy fence, an unhappy wife swam
nude, when my phone chirped with the link to a newspaper story.

The interruption spared me the charms of Mrs. Ava Albright—
momentarily.

VENICE POLICE INVESTIGATE

Police investigated a possible break-in at 50 Sand Lane,
Caspersen Beach, yesterday. Officers reported a padlock
had been cut, and interior water damage caused by recent rain. The investigation was in response to a complaint
by the estate attorney representing the late Finnlund J.
Tovar, a longtime Venice resident and well-known paleontologist.

PALEONTOLOGIST? I had researched the man. Finn Tovar was to paleontology what Murf the Surf was to gemology—a driven amateur who, unlike the diamond thief, had been shrewd enough to avoid jail.

I continued reading:

> According to police, robbery was a possible motive, although the residence appeared to be intact. Pending an inventory of Tovar's possessions, the investigation will remain open. A representative of Viz-Watch Inc., which installed a security system in the home, was unavailable for comment.
>
> Mr. Tovar, during his career as a paleontologist, is credited with discovering the carapace of the largest prehistoric turtle on record, and the skull of a unicorn-like animal that went extinct a million years ago and was thought to be unique to the Florida peninsula.
>
> The subject of criticism by Native American organizations, Mr. Tovar withdrew his collection of indigenous artifacts, but his reconstruction of a mastodon skull and a saber-toothed tiger remained on display locally until he was diagnosed with a brain tumor a year ago. Scientists worldwide considered Tovar an authority on Florida mastodons and mammoths. Both prehistoric animals are related to elephants . . .

I REREAD THE PIECE, wondering if AIM, the American Indian Movement, had been involved with the protest. Fallsdown and Tomlinson had, as expected, gone to Lakeland, but would be back by sunset for the marina's Sunday shrimp roast. I would ask them about it when we compared notes.

The theft had not been discovered—a relief. That gave us some time. If the news story had been different, my next move would be to call a cop friend in Tallahassee. That would happen, but not yet.

On my phone, I typed a quick reply to Ransom, who'd sent me the link, and walked toward the backyard. To my right were oak trees and a sweep of asphalt where my old truck sat ticking in the morning heat. The Albright residence—a secluded acreage off Bee Ridge Road—was not as grand as their island mansion and much newer. A Deco ranch-style structure that rambled. No one had answered the front door. Odd—but I was ten minutes early. The back patio was the logical alternative, so I continued along fence and shrubbery, my thoughts on Finn Tovar.

Violent temper aside, Tovar had been an interesting man. It takes more than a Ph.D. to excel in the field sciences. He had possessed talent, there was no denying—a rare blend of instinct and expertise. He had eclipsed the achievements of many academics, but along the way he had made enemies. Among them was a maid he had slapped. It was the maid who had given Deon Killip the security code to Tovar's home. But had she also sent a gunman to rob the petty thief? A maid willing to take risks to secure a bigger chunk of the prize had cunning. She would know more about Finn Tovar than she had told the petty thief and drug addict. Was it worth a return visit to Venice?

I was considering logistics when I heard a woman's voice call through the foliage, "Is someone there?"

Mrs. Albright—that's the way I thought of her after exchanging only a few words at the drum ceremony. I'd been right. Breakfast on the patio had emptied the house. I stopped and replied through the shrubbery, "It's Marion Ford. Your husband is expecting me."

"Who?"

I said my name again.

"Oh . . . I remember you. *Doc.* Sure! Hey—I could use your help with something, Doc. The gate's at the back, come on around."

I found the gate, entered, turned . . . and there was Ava Albright, naked, floating, small-breasted and buoyant, in a gel of turquoise, her blond hair pinned primly, her body a paleness of refracted angles, white, brown, and pink.

"I can't reach my mimosa," she said, an intentional parody of a pouting vamp. Then stood to show off her body and laughed, "*I'm joking.* My glass is on the table—don't be shy. We're practically nudists around here."

I said, "You should post a warning sign."

I turned, exited, closed the gate, and walked to my truck. Gave it some time before trying the front door again. Leland Albright, red-faced, loomed over me. "What the hell do you mean surprising my wife like that?"

"Is that what she told you?"

"I came out on the balcony as you were leaving."

"Then you know I didn't surprise her," I said. "And you know your wife liked it, too."

Albright slammed the door in my face.

I leaned against my truck and waited. Two minutes, I allotted, then two minutes more because I wanted the list of old-time relic hunters he had promised. When I heard the ascending verbal punch and counterpunch of an argument, though, I drove away. An angry man can be won over. A man who has been humiliated cannot.

Space and time are required before he can reappear in his old familiar role.

Leland Albright had more backbone than most. I was on Bee
Ridge Road, driving east, when he phoned. I saw the name and answered, "Leland, sorry about that last crack. You didn't deserve it."

"Ava knows exactly the buttons to push," he said, sounding
hoarse, a man who'd been yelling. "You're right, Ford. She enjoys it.
Where are you?"

I told him, "Not far. Want me to come back?"

"No . . . I've still got a few rounds to go with Ava. If she'd just
admit what she does! Christ, she claims I'm imagining things. From
the pool, she invited you in—I could swear I heard her say your
name. *We're practically nudists, Doc.* That's what she said, isn't it?
Or . . . maybe I am crazy."

The man had called to make amends but was now drafting me
as a witness. "We'll make it another day," I said.

"Wait. You can still drive to the phosphate mine. You don't need
me. Owen will meet you there."

Owen, last name Hall, was the stepson. That had been our plan:
take Leland's SUV inland to a section of land north of the Peace
River the family owned and where Mammoth Ridge Mines had
started.

"Your stepson won't mind?"

Leland answered, "He does what I tell him," but heard his own
phony overconfidence. He exhaled, frustrated. "Sorry. She's got me
off my game."

"They do it to us, we do it to them. The human comedy, it's
called."

"The way Ava does it isn't human," was the reply. A coldness

79

there he tried to cover by adding, "Owen's a good kid. If anyone can get you into Mosaic on a Sunday, it's him."

Mosaic was the largest mining company in the state and an adjunct to our plan. If we could get through security, that was a bonus. If not, nothing lost. Albright still owned a square mile of Florida—more than six hundred acres. It was challenge enough for one afternoon.

Yesterday, when I had returned Leland's call, he'd been more specific about his job offer. "I want an analysis of water quality in our quarries—we have three lakes. And please don't say you're not qualified."

On the Internet, he'd found papers I had written on the effects of water turbidity on sea grasses and filtering species, another on tunicates containing high levels of a toxic algae known as "red tide." Nutrient pollution, I had concluded, was sometimes a contributing factor.

Albright had shared my study on manatee deaths as they related to red tide with his daughters. "Believe me, your opinion will carry some weight with those two. You understand the importance of phosphate. Tomorrow, at the property, I'll explain *why* I'm considering the mining idea."

I had used Albright's list of relic collectors as a bargaining chip. Which was why I was in Sarasota, a phone to my ear, listening to the man vent about his wife's behavior. I felt badly for the guy, but I also wanted that list, so I dropped a hint, asking, "Did I give you my e-mail address?"

Leland, weary of it all, said, "I shouldn't be dumping all this on you. Don't worry. Owen will give you an envelope. A partial list is in there, plus some information on mining . . . Ford?"

"Yeah?"

"Sorry about what happened. I don't care anymore what Ava thinks. But my daughters—well . . . If you're willing to keep an open mind, there's a check in the envelope, too. I don't expect you to work without a retainer."

I said, "Let's see how it goes," and signed off.

At a Burger King, I turned around and took I-75 north to the Fruitville exit, which was all the Sunday interstate traffic I could handle.

IF THE THIRTY-FIVE-YEAR-OLD STEPSON, Owen Hall, couldn't dissuade two drunks shooting turtles with a rifle, what were the chances of him charming security at a billion-dollar phosphate operation?

Not good.

That's what I was thinking, sitting passenger side in a Jeep, while Owen tried to reason with two men of similar age who weren't to-tally shit-faced but close enough. Weekend drunks can be stubborn. It wasn't going well—and even worse for the three or four turtles that lay bloody on the shore.

Owen and I had entered the property via a dirt road, between Bradenton and Sebring, into acreage laid waste by draglines. The land was growing a new skin of pines, palmettos, hat-rack cypress, too, on scars left by a hundred years of abuse. A washboard of fur-rows and high ridges aren't native to the Florida geoscopy. Nor are rectangular lakes and a sand dune the size of an Egyptian pyramid. The dune—that's where we'd spotted a red Dodge Ram. Then we'd heard rifle fire—two overage fraternity types, a case of beer between them, at the water's edge killing turtles.

"Stay here," Owen said, unbuckling his seat belt. "I know those guys."

I replied, "Take your time," and opened the oversize envelope he had presented me. Inside was a check for ten thousand dollars made out to *Sanibel Biological Supply LLC*. There were also mining statistics and a stack of vintage photos that tracked the history of Mammoth Ridge Mines. But no list of artifact collectors gleaned from records of the now-defunct company. An innocent oversight—I hoped.

Down an incline, fifty yards away, Owen was making progress with the drunks. The drunks were laughing, but still in possession of a loaded rifle. I returned my attention to the envelope.

Fifty pages of stats—I set them aside because the old photos were more fun. I shuffled through several: Leland's grandfather, circa 1900, shovel in hand, smiling up from a crater—his Albright genetics towering over a team of workers. A one-room store, Hooker's, in nearby Fort Meade, where a shed of white clapboard was the first Albright home. Photo by photo, shovels gave way to steam engines on rails, then a larger dragline afloat on a canal of its own making.

The grandfather, Henry Leland Albright, was assembling his dynasty.

The status of Owen and the drunks de-escalated into a private conversation while I browsed. It was impolite to intrude, so I skipped ahead through the decades, but refocused when, instead of men and mining equipment, I came to a black-and-white photo of an . . . elephant?

Yes, an elephant. I turned it over. On the back, in elegant script, was written *Barnabus, 1938 HLJ*.

HLJ was Henry L. Albright. *Barnabus*, I decided, was the elephant's name. But why a photo? Puzzling until I remembered the obvious: Ringling Brothers and other circuses have wintered in Florida for more than a century. The founder of Mammoth Mines had bought Barnabus, a mammoth Indian elephant, as a mascot.

Correction: *Elephants*. Henry Albright had owned two . . . no, three elephants. Photos from the 1950s told me the family had accumulated at least five of the animals, including a young male.

Had the tradition continued? I kept looking. It would explain why Leland had found my question about elephants an amusing understatement the night we'd met.

Instead of more elephants, a photo of an Egyptian-sized sand dune caught my eye. I was sitting near a dune of similar size. It took a few seconds to factor in erosion and wind-seeded foliage. The Jeep, I realized, was parked where a photographer had stood in 1945. A few photos later, I saw . . . snow skis in Florida . . . ?

Yes . . . a party of bobby-soxers and GIs on leave had once skied down the sand mountain in front of me. *Slalom Beach*, written in pencil. After their descent, skiers had cooled themselves in the lake. The lake appeared silver in several photos but was a milky turquoise when I reconfirmed landmarks.

The Albright family and friends had enjoyed a century of fun on this property, judging from what I saw. An idea popped into my head: Instead of mining for phosphate, why not stock the lake with bass and turn the acreage into a green retreat for tourists? Keep the wooded lanes, restore the creeks, but lose the erosion and exotic plants. Albright was a businessman, though. Because I am not, I got out, found a tree, and contemplated the merits of the idea while I urinated.

Midstream, I heard Owen holler, "Hey, *don't!*" For an absurd moment, I thought he meant me. I was grabbing for my zipper when a bee buzzed overhead in synch with a rifle shot.

Not a bee . . . a bullet. I'd damn near been shot.

An awkward moment later, I saw Owen trying to wrestle the rifle away from the drunks. I sprinted downhill, yelling, "Which one of you idiots did that?"

Surprise. The men didn't realize the Jeep contained a sizable passenger. No . . . a misread on my part—they'd thought Owen was alone. It was in their cloaked exchange as much as their eager denials. As I drew nearer, apologies replaced the denials, but then beer courage took over.

"It was an accident," one of them said—a lean, good-looking blond guy. "Lighten up."

"Yeah, man," the other said. "Get over it."

In some, fear sparks anger. Count me among them. Owen had the rifle. I yanked it away from him, popped the magazine and skipped it into the lake. A .22 hollow-point was in the chamber. I cleared the chamber and hurled the rifle into the water, too. It spun like a baton but made a more satisfying splash.

The drunks managed eye contact when I faced them. "Now I'm over it," I said.

"Goddamn, Orville. Who is this jerk?"

Orville, a variation of the stepson's first name, Owen. I asked him, "These are friends of yours?"

I had spooked him also, but he covered it by becoming business-like. "Doctor Ford is a hired consultant, and I don't blame him one damn bit. So both of you leave . . . *now.*"

When they balked, Owen tried to mediate, saying, "Look, guys . . . we'll find the rifle—probably won't even need tanks. Don't make me call the cops."

They were three men, similar age, good teeth and tended hair, Owen, with olive eyes and skin, standing with two upper-class scions, Yankee stock, out for a beery Sunday. The three men were friends, I realized. Proof was provided when the good-looking blond guy said, "Don't forget what we talked about . . . *Owen*."

A private message had been delivered, that was obvious. The men left, their red truck fishtailing.

"You trust them as dive buddies?" I asked.

The stepson, who Leland claimed was *starting to come around*, replied, "Not anymore."

NINE

INHABITANTS OF STONE . . . BONE FRAGMENTS EVERYWHERE . . .

I didn't realize we had been walking and driving over Florida's petrified dead for nearly an hour. Looking down was all that was required. Soon, it would become obvious . . .

Right now, though, I was preoccupied with Owen's uneasiness. I had behaved like a loose cannon—in his mind, at least—and I wanted to make amends. So, once again, I apologized for losing my temper, but this time offered to go back and dive for the rifle. "It's the least I can do for friends of yours. How deep is the lake?"

Owen had the Jeep in four-wheel drive. He noticed the photos on the seat and referred to them, saying, "I'm surprised Leland included those. No one's allowed to dive that lake . . . or any of the others—there are two more."

I allowed my attentive silence to ask the obvious.

"It's a respect thing. His father drowned here. I'm not sure which lake. That was twenty . . . I can't remember how many years ago. It was long before he met my mother. People sneak in, of course. Christ, trespassers are our biggest problem."

I recalled Albright saying that a drinking problem, coupled with the murder of a security guard, had caused his father to close the mine. Owen knew that, no doubt, but it was not a subject a stranger could broach. So I said, "You invented that story about coming back with tanks."

"I had to tell him something."

I shrugged. "Then it's good-bye, rifle."

Owen had been stony serious but cracked a smile . . . then couldn't help laughing. "The look on their faces. My god! Actually, pretty funny, when you think about it."

Rather than spoil it by saying the bullet had passed within a foot of my head, I laughed.

"I didn't expect that from a biologist."

I had to explain it some way. "I have no idea why I did that. Too many movies, I guess."

"Shock, probably. Harris, the one with blond hair, he didn't know you were up there. We graduated South Florida together. Harris was a crazy man back in the day, but he's calmed down a lot. A damn good diver, he really is. The other one, I don't know him that well."

It was Harris who had warned, *Don't forget what we talked about . . . Owen.*

Another impolitic subject—for now anyway.

"You do a lot of diving together?"

"Not lately, Leland keeps me so busy. Harris, his family used to be in phosphate mining. Now they're partners in a couple of dog tracks. Harris and I used to work at the tracks. We'd drive to the Keys on our days off, Palm Beach sometimes."

We talked about diving for a while, then dog-track racing. Owen explained, "We used to hit Vegas once a month, but I finally got smart and stopped the whole gambling thing. Gambling is for losers. No one ever wins."

He said the last part by rote, as if he had memorized it to convince himself. Leland had helped Owen out of some legal trouble, I remembered. Gambling, even as a hobby, is expensive. As a habit, it's a bottomless pit.

"I bet a couple of trifectas once," I told him, "but what I really wanted to see was the dogs catch that damn mechanical rabbit."

The stepson laughed, starting to feel better. He located a hidden pack of cigarettes under the seat and didn't seem to mind when I refused one by saying, "As long as the windows are open, your secret's safe with me."

We drove to the back side of the sand pyramid, got out, then viewed another quarry. I opened my LaMotte test kit and took water samples. Used a spectrophotometer and filter flasks to take samples back to the lab. Because he asked, I explained what I was doing: a chromatograph test for volatile organics and pesticide analysis. The spectrophotometer was for inorganic compound identification.

"Phosphorus flowing into the Glades and the Gulf is the big concern," I said. "The flasks are for membrane filtration. Get samples under a microscope, I'll look for fertilizer overload and coliform bacteria."

"Coliform?" Owen said. "That comes from human feces. You don't have to worry about that here."

"It can, but I'll check for all the pathogens—microbes, bacterium—a long list. Pathogenic stuff indicates degraded water quality. You have to ask yourself what happens if this quarry floods into the Peace River or the Myakka? You probably know that a phosphate dike broke a few years back. The runoff damn near killed those rivers, and we still don't know what damage it did to Charlotte Harbor and the Gulf. Problem is, the sugar industry causes so much pollution, it's hard to say who's to blame."

Owen handled that okay. Nearby was a ridge that was eroded but provided a vista. He parked the Jeep. I followed him uphill, the crunch of fossils and bone fragments still unnoticed beneath my feet. By then, he was calling me Doc instead of Doctor Ford, which seemed to make it easier for him to recite straight from the phosphate industry manual.

"Did you know it takes one ton of phosphate to produce enough phosphorus to grow a hundred tons of wheat? Corn, any grain, even pasture grass for cattle. Crops won't grow unless we keep mining to produce fertilizer. That's what most people don't understand. Leland says you're up on the latest studies, though."

My reply had a warning edge: "He's wrong about that. But I do know that bullshit doesn't flow uphill, and mining creates a lot of toxic waste. So you can skip the sales pitch. It would help to know what kind of project you have in mind."

The stepson didn't handle that as well but dealt with it. "Did Leland tell you the project is confidential?"

"They always are," I said.

"As long as you understand. The news media hates phosphate mining, so we can't let it get out until Leland makes his decision. After that, we would hire a PR firm to smooth things over."

"Sounds like quite a project."

"Not by industry standards. Florida's two biggest mining companies want to lease this land. With new technology, they think they can make it pay. The lease would run for fifteen years, and that's the best part, in Leland's mind. At the end, they would have to do a total land-water reclamation project. Companies are required to by state law. Leland cares—he really does. Sometimes I think he imagines he's his grandfather. Like a debt he owes the family because his own father didn't . . . Well, he let the business go to hell, to be honest."

The ridge where we stood was as rugged as a moon crater. Brazilian pepper, melaleuca trees, and other exotics had displaced native oaks and cypress. The lakes where I had taken water samples were clear but appeared lifeless, silent as alkaline soup.

"This is what reclamation looks like?" I asked. "No wonder your stepsisters have a problem with it."

Owen had referred to the twins as recovering mall girls, but as a joke. Now he took Leland's side. "That's what Esther and Tricia can't seem to understand. Six hundred and forty acres in this tract, and it hasn't been touched since the equipment was pulled out more than twenty years ago. Reclamation laws didn't come along until later. Before that, a mining company could trash a place and just go off and leave it. Things are different now. Leland—his company—would be paid royalties based on production, sure. But this land would be returned to the way it was a hundred years ago. That's what I meant when I said he cares."

In my mind, I was weighing the enormity of such a project against the likelihood of results beyond a cosmetic cover-up.

I was dubious. Owen sensed it, so he suggested we visit an area under restoration by the phosphate megacompany Mosaic Mining. "Thing is, Leland needs to make up his mind. The adjoining tracts south of here are owned by two other parties, and Mosaic, or the other company, want the whole parcel. The industry has to move south or die."

I asked, "Are you and the other owners competing for the same contract?"

"No, the companies want all three or none—that's the way they're playing it now. One section is owned by Harris's family—not the entire acreage but the mining rights, which comes down to the same thing. The other owner . . . I probably shouldn't say this, but he's a lunatic. Maybe you've heard of him. Monty Mondurant?"

I said, "I would've remembered a name like that."

"Vandar is his actual first name, but he goes by Monty. He's from Morocco. You've really never heard of the guy?"

The way Owen said it gave me the impression he was eager to discredit the man. "Tell me about him," I said.

"Monty is a walking freak show. When he lived in Beverly Hills, he was in the entertainment news a lot. Claims he's related to the royal family, and he dated a famous singer, plus a bunch of actresses. Huge family money, but Monty can't stay out of trouble. He had to leave California, then they ran him out of Palm Beach, too, he's so . . . well, offensive. I'll put it that way."

"You've met him?"

"Yeah, and twice was enough. In Palm Beach, the night his mansion burned down, his neighbors were actually chanting 'Burn, Monty, burn.' Can you imagine?"

"You're saying they torched the guy's house?"

"No . . . no one would believe that. Burglars did it, supposedly. But that's what his neighbors were chanting. There're about a hundred videos on YouTube." He gave an odd look. "You don't have the Internet?"

"Friends tell me I need to get out more," I said. "Is Mondurant's property as big as this one?"

"No. The mining companies don't bother with anything less than two square miles, which is twice what we have. Harris's family has rights to about four hundred acres, and Monty—or his family, more likely—he owns a little over two hundred." Owen pointed to a corridor of trees. "The property lines join along what used to be a creek that runs to a pond on the south edge of our property. The old Albright family ranch is there—or what's left of it."

"Vandar Mondurant," I said, making a mental note. "What's Harris's last name?"

"Sanford, but don't worry about him. The Albrights and the Sanfords go way back. I'll explain more on the way to the reclamation project. I think you'll be impressed."

I followed Owen down the ridge, the ground beneath my feet oddly resonate. That's what drew my attention. The sound. Indian shell mounds have a similar resonance. Finally, my eyes began to pay attention. I noticed what was beneath my feet.

MIDWAY DOWN THE HILL, I stopped and knelt. Imbedded in marl was a giant shark tooth similar to those stolen from the late Finn Tovar.

"Keep it," Owen said, unconcerned, but then turned. "Wait . . . let me have a look. Those things are everywhere but the quality varies."

I handed it over and, for the first time, really focused on what I had believed to be sand and rubble. Rubble took shape and revealed that the ridge was composed of bone fragments. I saw another tooth, and a round white rock that turned out to be a whale vertebra. It weighed a couple of pounds when I hefted the thing. Under my foot was a delicate jaw with teeth. Nearby was a slab of brown, curved, the length of a boat rib. Again, I knelt.

"That's a fossilized manatee rib," Owen said, distracted. "Or could be camel; they're common. Mammoth bones and giant sloths, too, but those are bigger. Fragments are tough to identify."

I kept my response light. "You're a collector?"

"I've never met anyone in the phosphate business who wasn't at least interested. Can't help yourself. When I was in college—this was way before Leland hired me—I'd come here. Now, to help with upkeep, we charge fossil clubs a group rate, but I never leave them alone. A guy told me this little stretch was the bend of a prehistoric river. River bends are always good places for fossils."

The curve of the ridge, I noticed, continued across the property lines. There it gathered a bristle of trees and followed the remnants of a creek.

"Some fossils must be valuable, huh?"

Owen said, "Hardly ever," but a little too quickly, and resumed his inspection. "Pretty nice megalodon tooth. Serration's not bad. The bourlette's mostly there, but the point's broken off. The shark probably attacked something when he lost this tooth."

I said, "I doubt income from fossil clubs could even pay taxes on a property this size."

"Leland raises cattle, too—the ranch is over the next ridge." Owen talked about cattle for a while but felt more comfortable discussing sharks. "Cool thing is when you find meg teeth near whale ribs that still show serration marks. The same teeth that killed the whale, see what I mean? Florida was underwater back then, so no dinosaurs, but there were still monsters here. Megalodons were as big as Greyhound buses. You ever see a great white?"

Rather than pressing him about property and income, I described my first encounter with a great white shark while cage-diving off South Africa.

Owen asked knowledgeable questions about diving, then handed me the tooth. "Anything else you find, feel free to keep. On the way, we'll stop at the ranch."

"Do you raise anything but cattle?"

"Yeah—something that'll surprise you. The property manager lives nearby, but he's pretty old, so I won't bother calling. Just a quick stop and you'll understand why the twins are against mining this place."

An elephant—that's what he was talking about. A suitably mammoth-sized old bull named Toby—and plans the twins had commissioned for a facility that would care for elephants when circuses were done with them. They had commissioned the plans three years ago, according to Owen, but new interests were weakening their resolve.

I stood at the fence—four thick cables that sizzled and popped with electricity—and watched the animal while Owen walked away with a phone to his ear. I've seen elephants in the wild, so the circus variety always strike me as tragically misplaced. Toby had a lot of space, though. His own chunk of land separated from cattle grazing in the distance. Like all domestic elephants, he was Asian. Like most bulls in captivity, he had been castrated—shortly after birth, Owen said. What made Toby unusual was his fully grown tusks.

He was a survivor. Toby had outlived two generations of Albrights, as well as Henry L. Albright's original pack of five, and was now grazing alone at the edge of a pond—a circle of black water ringed by cypress trees and cattails. Orienting myself, I guessed this was the pond that was connected to the dried-up creek we'd seen earlier.

Owen returned and told me the basics: the electric fence was high voltage but low amperage, not lethal, yet a barrier to Toby, who weighed about ten thousand pounds and was fifty-eight years old.

Interesting. Even a five-ton animal, with tusks as thick as my legs, can appear damn-near cuddly. And Toby did—until I noticed his sharp old eyes tracking us from a hundred yards away. He didn't approach, but he didn't miss anything.

"I'm surprised he doesn't come begging for food," I said. "Is it because of the fence?"

The electrified cables, the way they sizzled, were intimidating.

Owen replied, "All Toby knows how to do is eat and shit, so, yeah, I suppose so." He said it with an edge that told me he wasn't fond of the animal.

The fence was solar-powered—high-tech, in contrast to the gate chain, which made a medieval clatter when Owen unlocked it to check something inside the pasture. He didn't like being in there with Toby, even at a distance. I noticed that, too, but understood. Elephants are social animals, so a lonely old bull might be prone to erratic behavior. No herbivore on earth is better equipped to kill.

"You can see the position Leland's in," Owen continued when we were back in the Jeep. "Taking care of elephants is part of his family's . . . I forget the word. *Tradition*. But more than that. Henry L., the grandfather, he knew the early circus owners. They trusted him when an animal needed a home. That's how it started. Sure, Leland would like to provide a place for unwanted elephants. Who wouldn't? But there's already a place that does the same thing only a few miles north of here."

That was news to me. "I'm surprised I don't know about it. What's it called?"

"Florida Elephant Rescue Center, but there's no sign on the road. It's privately funded, and they don't want visitors. Supposedly two hundred acres, and a staff. The circuses chip in, and some animal rights groups. Can you imagine the cost? Toby alone runs us almost fifty grand a year."

"A few miles? I would've passed it."

"No, the entrance is fifteen miles or so by road, but the property lines connect not far from this ridge. That's the twins' backup plan. Donate Toby and all the land to the rescue center."

I said, "Just give it away, huh? What does Leland's wife say?"

Owen stiffened while his face attempted neutrality. "You'd have to ask Ava. Cash flow is what the company needs right now."

"I thought she sided with the twins," I said. "That's what Leland told me."

"She . . . Ava . . . well, I'm not going to get into their personal life. But I respect Leland enough to notice this decision is affecting his health. The elephant thing is just crazy, if you ask me."

I said, "The twins want all six hundred acres?"

"As much as they can get. Doesn't faze them that Leland has already set aside this spot until Toby dies—it's in the contract if he signs with the mining companies. You know, four or five years down the road, then they can bring in the equipment. But commit the whole property to rescuing circus elephants?" Owen shook his head at the absurdity of it. "That would cost millions. I have no idea what Leland's monthly nut is, but it's got to be huge. Leasing the property is the only solution. Think about it—total restoration once the mining companies are done. It would solve all his problems."

I was being pressured not only to accept the consulting job, I realized, but also to provide a favorable water analysis. So I switched to safer topics, and waited until Owen dropped me at my truck to ask about the missing list of collectors.

"Almost forgot," he said, then, after searching his briefcase, added, "I must have left it at Leland's office."

TEN

Frustrated, Dunk came into the house, saying, "What I hate about sobriety is there's no reward for beating your head against the wall."

It was an hour before sunset, and I could smell charcoal burning—Mack, Jeth, and the guides were preparing for the weekly shrimp roast. Tomlinson and Dunk had stopped to use the phone in the lab, and also to compare notes.

I asked, "What's the problem?"

"Rachel says we might have the wrong carving. And she has to have *both* stones, not just one. Personally, I think she doesn't want me to come back—afraid to die, in other words."

Rachel, the aunt in Montana.

"It's like waiting to breathe," Tomlinson observed.

"Dying?"

"Not drinking," Tomlinson said.

"Oh . . . and that. When I called, Rachel was in bed, with tubes in her arms and nose. I held the carving up so she got a close look.

'Too small, even for the Little People,' she says, then tells me, 'Besides, the owls separated are like half of a soul.' That's what Rachel believes—without the owls, she'll die without a soul."

Little People. He was using the term more frequently.

Dunk continued, "For the pain, she had a local Skin make a poultice of mescal buttons and bugleweed, as if herbs are going to help. What am I supposed to say? Always a drama queen, that Rachel."

Tomlinson suggested, "Tell her *eat* the buttons," while I pointed out, "Dunk . . . The woman *does* have pancreatic cancer. Go easy on her." Then sat back and processed what I'd just heard. We had left Fallsdown alone in the lab, with the desk phone and the polished artifact box nearby, but he was obviously exaggerating details of the call. Claiming to see his aunt bedridden with tubes, showing her the owl carving—it all had to be a medicine man fantasy. Fallsdown, I decided, wasn't as cynical about spiritualism as he pretended.

Fine. No reason to challenge the man. I said, "At least she heard your voice. When you described the owl, that had to make her happy."

"Why would I describe it?" Duncan placed the artifact box on the table and looked at me. "We used your Skype account. I assumed it was okay. The computer was on."

I started to say I didn't have a Skype account—even the thought of Skyping made me wince—but trailed off when I sensed Tomlinson's uneasiness. I said to him, "Please tell me you didn't."

"Doc . . . you're trained in the sciences. Name a safer way to have sex with strangers—or a loved one. I realize you're on Hannah's kimchi list right now, so I did it for you. There are a lot of quality women out there with laptops."

I stood, and said to Duncan, "Think about Skyping your probation officer next."

I walked away. The fossils I'd brought from Mammoth Ridge were in a bag—several meg teeth, plus a sheet of paper containing a twenty-year-old list of collectors. I handed Duncan the list as I passed by, headed for the door. "It only goes back to the nineteen seventies, but we might be onto something."

"Albright gave you this?" He was holding the list at arm's length, a man who needed reading specs.

"I had to drive clear back to Sarasota after I'd toured the mine. You'll recognize one of the names."

Fallsdown said, "I bet I can guess," and he was right. Years ago, in pencil, the name Finn Tovar had been circled, and two words of warning added: *Contact police.*

I said, "Look for yourself," and reached for the door.

Tomlinson asked, "Where you going?"

From a shadowed corner, yellow eyes flashed when I replied, "Try not to do anything abnormal for the next few minutes, okay? The dog wants out."

It was an excuse. Mentioning Skype, then Hannah, reminded me I had vowed to leave my cell phone off until sunset. That was still an hour away. Hannah and I had spoken only once since Friday night— she had called *me*—but I was beginning to weaken. Hannah, of course, would have attended church earlier in the day and might be in a forgiving frame of mind. It couldn't hurt to check messages.

No messages from Hannah, though. I understood why when, from the dock, I saw her skiff pulling away from a custom Lamberti yacht that, even at auction, would have gone for a million-plus. She'd had a charter after church, apparently. Her client, a Brazilian Johnny Depp, was smiling down as she waved good-bye, the Brazilian in jet-set white after a hard day's fishing, Hannah in khaki, shirt sleeves rolled to her elbows, and wearing a visor.

To the dog I said, "She won't look this way because she thinks I'm watching. Want to bet?" Me, an expert on trickery, predicting the behavior of an unpretentious woman.

Wrong. Hannah's eyes found my house, then located me. She smiled, and turned the boat in my direction.

"See why she pisses me off sometimes?" I asked the dog, who trotted away, more interested in mullet spooked by a circling osprey. I added, "I'm an idiot," just before the dog vaulted into the water.

When Hannah was close enough, she removed the visor and smoothed her hair back. "You must've left early this morning. I looked for your truck on my way to church."

The stubborn cynic in me vanished. "You did?"

"I saw Mack. He invited me to stay for the shrimp roast tonight. But I thought I'd check with you first."

"I should have invited you myself," I said. "I spent most the day at an old phosphate mine. The fossils I found, you won't believe. Come up for a drink?" Before she could refuse, I added, "Tomlinson and Duncan are inside."

She gave it some thought, uneasy about something. "I need to shower and change before I'm fit to be with people. Alberto offered to let me use his guest suite—just for cleaning up, of course. Not for the night."

Alberto the Brazilian, she meant, on his roomy, custom yacht named *Seduci*.

I said, "How thoughtful."

"He's just a client, Marion. But, yes, he is a thoughtful man—and a very good flycaster."

Alberto, whose real name was Vargas Diemer, was more than just an avid fisherman. He was a scalp collector, when it came to women—a charming, ruthless cockhound. Impossible, though, to explain how I knew so much about an international miscreant—not to Hannah or anyone else.

"How about I promise to leave you alone and you change in my bedroom?" I suggested.

She replied, "Or there's another option. Rhonda and Joann are spending the night on that big Sea Ray at the end of A dock. Their air conditioner went out on *Tiger Lilly*, and the owner—what's his name again?—he said it was okay. Rhonda invited me."

She was talking about Mike Westhoff's sixty-foot *Playmaker*. Mike, a good guy, was out of town for a few weeks, but his boat was moored a little too close to *Seduci* for comfort. I said, "You'd have more privacy here, and you know where everything is."

Hannah and I talked for a while about fishing, then returned to the subject of where to shower and change. She was letting me convince her when Tomlinson, who looked shaken for some reason, appeared above us on the deck. "Uhh . . . Doc, I just got a phone call, pretty bizarre. Got a sec? In private."

"Not now," I warned.

Hannah, concerned by Tomlinson's manner, pushed her boat away. "Marion, find out what's wrong. I'll see you at the shrimp roast."

"HE GETS PISSY FOR A LOT OF REASONS," Tomlinson told Duncan, trying to regain his composure, "but jealousy's on the taboo list. If he owned a TV, I'd blame it on Spock."

As in *Star Trek*.

Tomlinson had caught me peeking out the window to check on

Hannah and the Brazilian. They were sitting with wine, or possibly champagne, the two of them on a balcony aboard his cavernous yacht of white.

"Jealous, my ass. I can't think of a sillier waste of time," I countered—a denial that was a rare mix of dishonesty and truth. It returned my attention to the problem at hand. Tomlinson had received an anonymous call from a man who knew I had taken the duffel bag from Deon Killip. *Deon*—the caller had used the petty thief's first name.

"Go over it one more time," I said. "The man's exact words."

Dunk asked, "Yeah, how did he know about the duffel bag? We haven't told a soul—*I* haven't, at least."

A more significant question was *How did the caller get Tomlinson's cell number?* but I let my pal chew at a strand of hair while he dealt with the insinuation. "Who would I tell? Man, you think I'd compromise a sacred mission by blabbing?"

"He wouldn't do that," I agreed. "Our tour guide from Venice might have. Did you give Mick your contact information?"

Tomlinson shook his head. "Never had a chance."

I said, "I took the bag from . . . yeah, his name is Deon. Deon doesn't know who I am, though. Or how to get in touch. So let's take this apart one piece at a time and try to figure it out. Think hard, details matter."

"Word by word, you mean."

I told Tomlinson, "As close as you can."

"Okay. I'll rewind the whole conversation—a minute or so, we talked, no more than three. Give it a sec, okay?"

Fallsdown said, "I've seen him do this before," and moved closer to watch.

Tomlinson pressed his palms together, sat straighter, and let his eyelids droop. A meditative posture. Several long breaths later, he spoke in present tense, and projected himself onto a screen: "Phone rings—a blocked call. That alone is exciting. I leave Dunk at the table while a man's voice says, 'I know where you live.'

"I say, 'So do I!' being funny.

"He says, 'Dinkin's Bay, Sanibel—what's that tell you?' He sounds aggressive; a tough guy talking from the side of his mouth. You know . . . disguising his voice.

"I say, 'Tells me it's shrimp roast night and someone's hungry. Either that or Ol' Saint Nick's still got his chops. That you, Santa?'"

Tomlinson's eyelids fluttered, remembering there was no more joking after that. His voice alternated, gruff, then normal, playing both roles.

"'Listen up, you long-haired turd—I've got a message for your buddy.'

"'Who *is* this?'

"'We want our shit back. How'd you like a rag stuffed down your throat, gas on the rag, then I light it? Or some night alone on your boat? That's what's gonna happen if you don't convince your friend. You got a piece of paper handy?'

"'No paper—I was on the deck by then. So the guy says, 'You're a ladies' man, I hear. Picture your face burning from the *inside*. Might improve your memory. Tell your buddy, the hard-ass nerd with the boat, the same could happen to him. You ready yet?'

"'Ready?'

"'The duffel bag, dumbass. Directions. I want you to write down where you're gonna drop that bag tonight.'

"All these things were going through my head . . . Some crank? No . . . this dude is f-ing nuts. The SWAT guy, black ski mask, he pops into my mind. I almost tell the guy, 'Fire away,' you know, meaning I'm ready to make mental notes, which I realize, just in time, will only piss him off more. So I start to say, 'Hey, we can work this out—'

"He says, 'Damn right, we'll work it out. Tape your hands behind you, light the rag. Air in your lungs turns your head into a furnace. Now, listen up! What's your buddy's name?'"

Tomlinson stopped, battled to get his breathing under control— more angry than frightened, it struck me—while Fallsdown and I waited to hear the rest, the Crow-Apache giving me a look that read *This is serious.*

I got up from the reading chair and put my hand on Tomlinson's shoulder. "Take a break."

"I didn't tell him your name, Doc. There aren't many things in this world I hate, but bullies are at the top of the list."

I waited for Tomlinson to rub at his eyes before saying, "I hear flashback mode makes a person thirsty. I'll get you a beer."

When I returned, he asked, "You think it was the dude in the ski mask? You didn't see him, I know, but by his whole approach?"

Fallsdown said, "He's military, from the way he talked—'Listen up'—and he called you a hippie. No, he said *long-haired* something. Same thing. I'm thinking that's who it was, Ski Mask. Fired two shots from a combat stance—a double tap, we called it in the Marines. A black revolver that looked bigger than it sounded."

Fallsdown, wearing a Harley T-shirt, the sleeves cut, had tats on his arms—animistic symbols, mostly—and one *Semper Fi* that revealed his military background.

I thought back to the sharp whap-whap of what I'd thought was a hammer or a door. "You think the weapon had a sound suppressor? That means it was either stolen or the guy has a federal license."

"Couldn't tell from the angle I was standing. Today, at the gun show, I saw some suppressors smaller than I remembered. Could be. But I'd be guessing. And on a revolver?"

Tomlinson muttered, "Gun shows. I was lucky to exit that freak palace with my scalp." He eyed Fallsdown. "No offense, my brother."

"None taken, kemosabe."

Tomlinson smiled. "I forgot, the Lone Ranger never rides alone. Didn't that movie suck?" Then felt the need to explain to me, "Dunk's a kidder."

I tried to get back on topic, but Tomlinson kept talking. "If anyone knows my adopted name, it's Duncan. He gave it to me—Tenskawatawa. Which means *The Prophet*. That was after my first sun dance. Remember those girls from Nebraska, Dunk? Hard to believe the two of us would one day be downing cotton candy at some Nazi gun show."

The gun show—I had already discarded it as a contributing element but now reconsidered, while asking Tomlinson, "Did the guy on the phone tell you where to drop the bag?"

"You're not mad I didn't deny having the stuff? I told him it couldn't be tonight, that the bag was safe, but banks aren't open on Sundays, which he didn't believe—about the stuff being in a bank, I mean."

I avoid lying to friends but had claimed that on Friday I had called a banker friend and rented a safe-deposit locker. "Just paraphrase the details," I suggested.

"Well . . . that's when he threatened me again. Said to keep the cops out of it. And don't try contacting Deon. He meant for you not to contact Deon and was really pissed I wouldn't narc out your name." Tomlinson looked beyond me, past my telescope and short-wave radio, to a desk where maps and charts are kept rolled. "Wait, I'll show you where the drop's supposed to be."

He returned with NOAA Chart 11426, Estero Bay to Lemon Bay, a big stretch of coastline south of Venice.

I said, "Okay . . . so he's a military guy who knows the water—or a weekend boater with a Special Forces fantasy. What time is this supposed to happen?"

"Between midnight and one," Tomlinson answered, spreading the chart on the table.

"Tonight?"

"Yep. He wants us to drop the bag and leave. No violence, he promised—as long as we're not there when his people arrive. The way he said it, I got a real sensory hit—like we're the thieves and he's a cop. By then, my brain was working again."

"His people," I repeated.

Dunk, bending over the table, asked, "Where is the place?"

Tomlinson used a finger to circle an island named Cayo Pelado. "Northeast of Captiva, in a little bay. It's uninhabited, mostly mangroves, but there used to be a fish house way back. Water's too thin there for a sailboat. Doc knows the area better than me."

"It's been a long time," I said, while Tomlinson moved to give me a better look. The island, Cayo Pelado, bordered Bull Bay, east of Boca Grande, and was west of Burnt Store Village—only seven miles northwest of the Albright Island.

Interesting, but that's all. Snatching at a conclusion in advance of data is a dangerous shortcut. Coincidence, when twisted to resemble evidence, can hang you. However, there was a another seductive tie: *Pelado*, in Spanish, meant *bald*; *hairless*. Around the time of Ponce de León, shell peaks on the island would have appeared skull white—

mounds built by a warrior tribe that had killed more than one Spanish explorer.

There was another link: By 1960, uninhabited Cayo Pelado had
become a favorite target of relic hunters. The attraction wasn't just
the shell mounds; it was the exploits of a pirate, José Gaspar—a
popular figure in the Florida narrative.

Tampa's annual Gasparilla Festival celebrates Gaspar. The names
of islands map his cut-throat daring. Woman prisoners were isolated on nearby Captiva. Joseffa Island was reserved for a great
beauty of the same name. On Cayo Pelado, Gaspar's gold, silver, and
emeralds were buried. The location was confirmed by dozens of
self-published books and a million restaurant place mats. X marks
the spot if you are in search of pirate treasure.

Trouble is, José Gaspar never existed. He was the invention of
a young publicist, G. P. LeMoyne, who, in the early 1900s, gilded
history with pirate tales to promote real estate. Good for tourism but
ruinous for a small uninhabited island. A group of treasure hunters
had even floated in a bulldozer and damn near leveled the highest mound there. Cayo Pelado was now off-limits, but that hadn't
stopped the digging.

I interrupted Tomlinson to explain this. He understood. "Exactly
the sort of drop spot a treasure hunter would choose," he said.
"Mythos versus reality, man. Buffett didn't write 'Cheeseburger'
about Cabbage Key, and the fictional José Gaspar is still every archaeologist's nightmare. The dude who threatened me obviously
doesn't know his history."

Dunk said, "It's up to you guys, but I don't like it. Whoever called
doesn't have any leverage. What's he gonna do, tell cops that people
he wants to rob didn't show up?"

Tomlinson countered, "But he knows where we live. He knows what Doc's boat looks like, too—described it as *stealthy*. What he meant was, we're both easy to find."

That struck a nerve. I said, "The tour guide knows my boat. Are you absolutely certain you didn't give Mick your number?"

Tomlinson was fuming, still going over the conversation in his head, but finally replied, "No way. Ski Mask—if it was him—got my cell from someone else."

Deon Killip, my abductor, hadn't looked inside my billfold when he took it, so didn't know my name. I was certain of that.

I asked, "What about the gun show?" It was a stretch, but maybe someone had overheard the two talking about the duffel bag or my Brunswick tactical boat.

"Never seen so many polluted auras in my life," Tomlinson said. "The bastard could have been there watching us the whole time."

Dunk disagreed. He explained that he had done most of the talking, but not a word about me. The two of them had focused on exhibitors who sold rare coins and the like. It was too risky to loose Tomlinson in an arena of gun fanciers where, within minutes of entering, he had insulted a vendor who was selling ABU GHRAIB K-9 UNIT T-shirts.

"The caller said my boat was *stealthy*," I repeated. It dawned on me then. I pushed away from the table. "Tomlinson, those three women you met on the beach? Call right now and check—this guy found one of them, I think."

My pal, who is flighty but smart, clicked on the linkage. "Shit, you're right. The ladies and I traded numbers—now that bastard is tracking me. I've got to call Lillian." He rushed to the door.

I used Dunk's disposable phone to dial Deon, my abductor, while

Tomlinson returned to his sailboat to search for a card the ladies had given him.

Deon answered tentatively, saying, "Yeah?" then lost it when he heard my voice. "You got my ribs broken, man! Stay away or I'll go straight to the cops. I swear to Christ I will, 'cause I'm safer in jail."

End of conversation.

When Tomlinson returned, I could tell from his face he had lost the woman's card. "The man who threatened you got to Deon, too," I told him.

No need to add upset by mentioning broken ribs. I had to get ready for tonight—just me, alone, I had already decided, but Tomlinson took some convincing. "Those women are my responsibility," he said. "I want a piece of that jerk."

I nearly smiled. "A *piece* of him? What do you have planned—cast a voodoo hex, then scalp the guy?"

Fallsdown interceded by telling me, "Years ago, I saw our skinny friend here back down three Black Panther smack freaks—nothing in his hands but a broken bottle and roach clip. Maybe he's changed, Doc, but don't sell him short."

I said, "You're serious?"

Tomlinson muttered what sounded like "Best clip I ever owned," while the man from Montana took the side of reason. "On the other hand, if Doc knows the water better, the decision is up to him. You've got to respect that, Tenska." Using his sun dance name to urge tolerance.

Tomlinson, frowning, said, "Okay, Doc, it's your call. But Ski Mask isn't the only one who knows how to track people. Dunk, you and me are driving to Venice in the morning—to find Lillian and the other ladies. After that, who knows?"

I was seeing a new side of a man I thought I knew well—not a bad thing.

I told them, "I've got to get my boat ready, so take off."

The truth was, I had to retrieve the duffel bag and move the contents to a new spot.

ELEVEN

AT TEN P.M., BENEATH A WAXING MOON THAT WOULD SOON SET, I LEFT DINKIN'S
Bay. The shrimp roast was still going. A party guitar and laughter
cloaked the noise of my engines, just me alone in my Brunswick
Tactical, and it was impossible not to notice that Hannah's skiff had
been moved to an inside dock . . . or see the porthole glow of the
Lamberti's master bedroom cabin.

She would be in there with the Brazilian.

Grow up. Hannah knows what she's doing.

Bullshit, I informed my left brain, and was doing forty knots by
the time I exited the bay.

To keep it legal, I switched on running lights. Thirty minutes
later, still under way, I switched them off. Cayo Pelado had yet
to emerge from the mangrove horizon, but I didn't want to risk
being spotted—a concession to the chance my adversary was as devious as I.

It's the way my mind works. How would *I* do it? Well . . . if I
wanted to ambush someone, I would arrive an hour before the des-
ignated time. Tomlinson had been ordered to drop the bag between

midnight and one. It was now ten-thirty. If ambush was the plan, I would be positioned and waiting when my target arrived.

But what if I was convinced my target had been bullied into actually dropping the bag? Well . . . I would spook him away from the drop zone with a deadline—one a.m., in this case—but wait until just before dawn to retrieve the bag. Even cops on a stakeout might abandon the area after seven fruitless hours. Mosquitoes are ravenous in the mangroves of Charlotte Harbor. It would be a miserable wait.

Was my adversary armed? Was he intelligent? Variables that must be anticipated, but, to me, there was a more interesting question: Was the man a sloppy pretender? Or was he my covert equal?

We would find out.

Westward, Boca Grande Pass was a corridor of black stars. Slack tide had vanquished tarpon fishermen. I maintained boat speed while adjusting the MUM's night vision monocular over my left eye. When I switched it on, the starry corridor was fired by new galaxies. Moonless night became high noon through a green lens.

I fine-tuned the focus, then touched a directional switch on the boat's console. Overhead, a spotlight flashed on. It provided a bright pathway, but the beam was invisible to all but me. It was a tactical infrared Golight that lanced three miles ahead.

Above the helm was a cabinet: my boat's electronics suite. A single switch darkened all screens but one dedicated to thermal imaging. Body heat, engine exhaust—a robotic eye on the radar mast was a man hunter. Hide yourself in foliage, even shallow water, the eye would track your beating heart.

My adversary might be smarter, stronger, better armed. But was he as devious?

Not likely.

IT WAS AFTER ELEVEN before I found a suitable stakeout spot, switched off the engines, and settled back to wait. My adversary was late—or so I believed.

In fact, he was watching me. Didn't matter that a bank of mangroves screened my boat from the island of Cayo Pelado, a hundred yards west. Didn't matter I had a clean view of the drop spot, as well as two primary entrances to the bay.

Nothing EVER goes as planned is an old special ops maxim. I should have it tattooed on the back on my hand.

A fog of mosquitoes descended while I reveled in my cunning. I slapped and tried household spray, then got serious. In the forward locker, in a Ziploc bag, was a mesh jacket reserved for emergencies. It has a beekeeper's hood, and the fabric, which hangs on me like a tent, is impregnated with chemical repellant.

I put it on. Mosquitoes retreated into a silver whining aura around me. I resumed my watch.

Over the next half hour, I heard the distant passing of three separate boats . . . or was it four? No movement in the bay, though. I began to suspect my adversary was incompetent if ambush was his plan. By midnight, I felt sure of it.

My attention wandered. The struggle not to imagine Hannah curled naked in the Brazilian's bed was finally lost.

Earlier, I had made an appearance at the marina shrimp roast. She had intercepted me, smiling, long-legged in her breezy tan dress, saying, "Tell me about the fossils you found."

I'd replied, "They're in the lab. And there's something else I want to show you—you'll be amazed—but it has to stay confidential."

I was referring to the contents of the Pelican cases, which I had

retrieved from the mangroves. The invitation had been sponta-
neous, a generous breach of security protocol that Hannah failed to
appreciate.

"Marion, are you saying you trust me? Or warning me you
don't?"

Maddening, this woman.

Then later, when the dog materialized from the bay like the
Hound from the Black Lagoon, Hannah said, "I worry about a gator
getting that poor thing. Shouldn't you keep an eye on him at night?"

Didn't faze her when I pointed out, "You don't have a problem
with *me* swimming at night. Besides, I think you have it backward.
I haven't seen an alligator around since that dog arrived."

A joke.

Not to her . . .

"You could at least show some concern. Retrievers are such handsome dogs—not that he looks like a Lab or the others. Be a shame
to lose him, Marion. He's so smart, the way he minds. I suppose
you know folks are starting to wonder why he doesn't even have a
name."

The dog's previous owner had named him Sam, after some silly
Disney movie, possibly *Savage Sam*, about the son of Old Yeller,
which is why I never used it. No need to share that with Hannah,
so I said, "As long as he minds, he doesn't need a name. And it's not
because he's smart. His IQ is about average for a dog, I think. Not
as smart as, say, some of the herding breeds, but he pays attention."

"That's a mean thing to say about your own dog."

I was perplexed. "It was a statement, not a judgment. The dog's
fairly well trained, that's all I meant."

"But he only minds *you*."

"Yeah . . . ?"

On cue, the dog had banged me aside to get to Hannah and placed his head into her fawning hands. Hannah, falling for it, had purred, "Sweet thing, you deserve a name, yes you do. Been out there swimming with sharks and alligators and god knows what else. No one around who seems to care what kind of creature grabs you."

Trying to protect Hannah, I said, "He's getting your dress dirty. You'll have to wash your hands, and the stink's hard to get off."

Hannah didn't want protection, which she communicated by saying to the retriever, "*Stink?* . . . Hear your owner? That's like saying bay water stinks. Sweetie, you smell *good* to me." The dog, eyes closed, had moaned his appreciation while Hannah continued, "Personally, I like the name Ranger, but Tomlinson says that's not very creative on my part. He's probably right. Mack thinks something literary would be good because of Crunch & Des."

She was referring to the marina's black cat.

Then, a second later, she had rebuked me, asking, "Marion . . . is this a tick on his neck?"

No—a scar, but the Brazilian had beckoned Hannah away before I could prove my innocence.

Damn it. Why was I sitting in a boat out here alone, battling mosquitoes, while a woman I cared about was being seduced by a playboy scalp hunter? Jealousy, I rationalized, had nothing to do with what I was feeling. I simply wanted to stop a friend from making a mistake. Or was I already too late?

Twelve-fifteen a.m.

I was freeing my boat from its bushy hiding place when reason kicked in. Of course, it was too late. Furthermore, it was Hannah's decision, not mine.

I returned to my seat and regeared into tactical mode. If my adversary didn't show by one a.m., I would leave—but not before.

TWELVE-FORTY A.M.

A thought: I was on the eastern side of the island. What if my adversary had anchored and hiked across Cayo Pelado from the west? All that remained of the fish house were pilings. Tomlinson had been ordered to tie the bag to one of them. My adversary could be deep in the trees, waiting.

I used night vision and the infrared spotlight to probe the area—something I had already done a dozen times. Beneath a shelf of mangrove branches, three pilings appeared on the screen. Their barnacle necklaces were a reminder the tide was ebbing. I scanned again with thermal imaging . . . saw the chunky signature of what was probably a feral hog, rooting among trees . . . I saw blobs of furry body heat, foraging on an exposed bar: raccoons.

I was reluctant to move but would soon have to because of the falling tide.

Bull Bay is a tricky area. Over eons, its islands have separated in apparent randomness that, even by day, resemble fragments of an exploded iceberg. From the air, the shaping influence of current and wind are discernible. At sea level, though, chaos reigns—unless you are a waterman with local knowledge.

As I'd told Tomlinson, my local knowledge was rusty, and I didn't want to be stranded by the tide. So I waited only a restless few minutes before I untied my boat, pushed free, and started the engines. The bug jacket wasn't needed while under way, so I stowed it. Velcroed near the steering wheel in a holster was my 9mm SIG Sauer—another emergency backup. I returned the gun to its padded case but left the case unzipped on the console.

Fear of an ambush was no longer in my mind. There were now two probabilities: my adversary would appear shortly after one a.m. or he would arrive at dawn to collect the bag. Anticipating both, I had devised a finesse that didn't require a confrontation—or even my presence.

It did, however, require the duffel bag.

I opened the console, hefted the bag onto the deck, and idled toward the drop spot. I had already looped a rope through the duffel's nylon handles. Lashing a forty-pound bag to a piling would be awkward and I didn't want to waste time. The X spot, a trained sniper would call the pilings—an intersection the quarry could not avoid.

It was a shiny stainless hook that put me on alert, a hook that had been augured into the foremost piling. My adversary had been here first . . . might still be here, I realized. It was a revelation that caused a beat of indecision. Should I bury the throttles and duck, hoping crosshairs weren't already locked on me? Or deliver the bag and hope that would pacify him?

Too late to turn back now, I decided.

I swung the boat around, bow pointed at the closest exit, before maneuvering closer. When the piling was within reach, I used one hand to transfer the bag—and that's when a spotlight from the trees found me, the man behind it shouting words I could not hear over the sudden twin roaring of my engines.

I EXITED THE BAY doing a serpentine thirty knots, then opened the throttles, still afraid to raise my head above the console. Waited until Cayo Pelado was a mile astern to stand and reassess. My adversary had been deep in the trees—a wild hog, I'd thought—but that

119

meant he would have a long, clumsy hike to his boat. In fact, I could probably intercept him there, where his boat was anchored, on the western side of the island.

No . . . that wasn't the way to handle it. My adversary had no reason to follow me and I had nothing to gain by forcing a confrontation.

I had already contrived a better alternative: in the duffel bag, superglued under a flap, was a transponder. Its frequency had been entered into my GPS radar system earlier. I could track my adversary, if I wanted, but that was unnecessary—better to wait until he had reached his destination.

Made sense. Outside the country, I make up the rules as I go, but I was in Florida, where playing loosey-goosey with the law might put me in jail.

Time to reassume the role of the good citizen that I pretend to be. I had postponed my call to a cop friend in Tallahassee. In the morning, though, I would make that call. I would provide the duffel bag's final destination and explain what had happened—most of it anyway. My friend might also have a lead or two that could help Fallsdown find his tribe's stolen property.

First, I wanted to confirm the transponder was working. I checked gauges—oil and water pressure: normal—then switched on the GPS radar and punched in the tracking code.

Blip . . . Blip . . . Blip . . .

"Hello to you, too," I murmured. The duffel bag and my adversary's boat were between Cayo Pelado and Devilfish Key, two miles behind. Would he steer north toward Venice or circle east toward Albright Key? The opportunity to find out was too tempting to resist. I dropped the B-Tactical off plain and waited in darkness, watching the screen.

Blip . . . Blip . . . Blip . . .

A red pixelated circle was my adversary and he was gliding south toward me . . . traveling at a high rate of speed.

"Fast boat," I said, while I switched on thermal imaging. Then added, *"There* you are."

A mile and a half away, his engine exhaust cast a fiery wake. Very soon, he would turn east if Albright Key was his destination . . . or he could continue on toward Burnt Store Marina . . . or bank northeast into the mouth of the Peace River. Phosphate country.

Blip . . . Blip . . . Blip . . .

None of the above. My adversary continued south toward me. Strange. Presumably, he had ties to the Venice area. Why south?

I found out. His boat was equipped with a spotlight. He switched it on: The beam was invisible to my right eye but dazzlingly bright through the night vision monocular.

"Damn." The driver was using tactical infrared—proof that a covert equal was tracking me. A fellow devious bastard.

I switched off thermal imaging and the Golight to reduce my heat signature. Should I take the SIG Sauer from its padded case and wait to meet my adversary? Or outrun his boat?

I ran.

TWELVE

TWO FAST BOATS WERE CHASING ME, NOT ONE. FLYING AT FIFTY KNOTS ACROSS thin water didn't permit a glance over my shoulder, but the radar screen confirmed it was true. The pixelated red circle had been joined by an anonymous green blip.

Don't be there when my people show up, the man had warned Tomlinson.

I had assumed it was a purposeful lie. Now I wasn't so sure. Worse, the anonymous boat was closing the distance between us, only a mile behind. No doubt the driver had a night vision system, maybe thermal imaging, too, because I was running without lights, invisible even to roosting pelicans that flushed as my boat screamed past the northern rim of Pine Island. To the south, a mile-long shoal—Jug Creek Bar, some called it—guarded a narrow channel. I hoped to lose the boats there.

First, though, I had to pay attention and not plow aground myself. I no longer had a spotlight to guide me, but the monocular I wore was passive night vision—no infrared signature. It allowed my left eye to convert darkness into eerie day.

I spotted the channel. It was marked by a picket row of red triangles and green squares. *Red right returning* is the old sailors' maxim. That's what I did, kept red triangles to starboard and followed them into the creek, a mangrove opening not much wider than a cave. On thermal imaging screens behind me, I felt sure, I had disappeared.

No time to risk a glance astern. My trackers would figure out what I'd done. They also would follow the markers—I hoped. I also hoped they were unaware of an unmarked exit from the creek that was like a back door. *Take the bait.* If they did, I would soon be in open water while they zigzagged toward the creek's terminus, the pretty little fishing village of Bokeelia.

A lot of boats were moored at the marina there. Once my adversaries figured *that* out, I would be gone. But my timing had to be perfect. Exit the creek's back door too soon, they would see me before they had entered the creek by the front door.

I slowed to cruising speed, a change of pace that allowed a troubling thought to nag at me. Mangrove channels are dangerous. Jug Creek is among the most dangerous in Florida. Lots of blind switchbacks, sharp turns where innocent boaters have been crushed by the hot rod types. It was after midnight, but it was still possible that some unsuspecting fishermen were anchored ahead, hidden by mangroves. I pictured it: my adversaries running two fast boats in blind pursuit . . . shouted warnings unheard . . . carnage after a collision.

Lose my pursuers only to read about more Jug Creek fatalities in the news? I couldn't do it.

Damn damn damn.

Change of plans. Ahead, to the right, was an opening in the mangroves—the back door exit from the creek. I turned, slowing until I was safely through the cut, then crossed Burgess Bay doing fifty. I emerged, expecting to see my pursuers north of the shoals about to enter the channel. Instead, I saw a blue strobe light—a police boat traveling fast.

I checked the radar. No doubt that the red pixelated circle carried the flashing blue lights. Ahead of it was the anonymous boat, running lights out. His thermal imaging had already spotted my engine heat. Both vessels were changing course, their bows soon aimed at me.

I maintained speed and turned southwest, wondering, *Why are police chasing me?*

True, I had been too busy at the helm to do a visual check; the blue strobe could have followed me across Charlotte Harbor. I remembered Tomlinson saying he'd gotten a sensory hit from the man on the phone, sensed he was a cop. However, I also remembered Deon, the petty thief, yelling *"Police!"* then commandeering my boat.

Any civilian can purchase a blue strobe. There were only two other possibilities: either I'd stumbled into a legitimate sting operation or my adversaries were crooked cops.

A sting? Absurd—I couldn't construct a scenario to explain it. On the other hand, the bad guys were not responding like bad guys. The threatening caller knew where Tomlinson and I lived. If he was a crooked cop, instead of giving chase he would go straight to Dinkin's Bay and intercept me there.

A spooky possibility came into my head: Maybe the man on the phone, my true adversary, had done exactly that. He could be at the marina right now, carrying gasoline and a bundle of rags. Or ransacking my lab in search of the stolen relics.

My boat's top speed is sixty-five miles an hour. I toyed with the trim, seeking maximum efficiency, then activated all four bilge pumps. Water is heavy, and I wanted to jettison unnecessary weight. I had to get home fast without those two boats tailing me.

A decision was required. On a rhumb line, Dinkin's Bay was fifteen miles to the southwest, but a direct course was impossible—islands and shoals lay between. The safest route was via the Intracoastal Waterway, its blinking markers just ahead. A riskier route was backcountry: a slalom course across a plateau that, on this falling tide, would soon reveal grass and oyster bars that could rip the bottom out of any vessel drawing more than a foot of water.

The most dangerous course was my best hope, I decided. This wasn't Bull Bay. Here, my local knowledge wasn't rusty.

Off Captiva Pass, in shallow water, stand a cluster of fish houses built in the early 1900s. I steered toward them and switched on the radar long enough to confirm I was still being chased. The lead boat was only eight hundred yards off my stern—one hell of a fast boat. The trickiest stretch lay ahead, but water west of the houses was good. I had a minute or so before reaching the point of no return, so I tried raising Tomlinson on the radio. Aboard *No Más*, he monitors channel 69—tasteless VHF humor he can't resist.

No response. I fumbled with my phone and tried calling. Voice mail.

Imagining his sailboat ablaze was a futile distraction to be shoved aside and that's what I did.

Time to concentrate. I reduced speed by half. I secured loose items on the console and confirmed the ignition kill switch was hooked to my belt. Water temp was up a little, but that was okay. I banked to within throwing distance of the fish houses and ran parallel them, their tin roofs black beneath a gray flotilla of clouds. Somewhere over the Everglades, lightning flickered. A freshening rain-wind cooled the air.

Now I was also racing a thunderstorm, but it was the least of my worries.

The first of several hazards lay ahead. A shoal joined the fish houses. It ran north-south, then broadened to intersect with a larger shoal that ran east-west. The junction was interrupted by a trough not much wider than a gate. Thread the gate, a channel lies on the other side. Miss the gate, any craft larger than a canoe will be left high and dry at low tide. Sometimes a stake marks the opening. Tonight, the cut was marked by glassy water on both sides. Easy to read if you know what you're looking for.

I hit the opening at a good angle and felt the Brunswick settle into what was the channel—but a narrow channel. So far, so good.

Ahead were hillocks of oysters, one bar partially exposed, the other hidden. Between the bars was a winding gutter that ascended after a few hundred yards into another shoal. Without risking a glance behind me, I weaved my way through the bars, engines trimmed until I cleared the shoal, then I used a heavy hand on the throttles.

A quarter mile later, I switched on the radar. Among concentric circles was the anonymous green blip. The blip was stationary, as if it had hit a wall. I watched the second boat—a pixelated red circle—veer west to avoid colliding with the lead boat . . . only to be stopped by an unseen oyster bar.

Success.

I was off Hemp Key when it happened, but watched the screen for another two minutes before dropping off plain. By then, the boats were so far away, I saw only the flashing blue strobe.

My ego intruded. Why not circle back and ID the boats from a distance? It was a dumb excuse to gloat before a storm dumped rain on my pissed-off adversaries. Even so, I was giving it serious consideration when I saw a rhythmic glitter approaching from the north.

What the hell?

It wasn't a boat, but was too low on the horizon to be anything else. Or was it?

A helicopter is what you should worry about, I had told Deon, my would-be abductor. *They'll hit you with a tracking laser.*

That's what I was seeing: an aircraft flying low, rocketing toward my grounded adversaries. Its running lights were tilted at the angle of a scorpion's tail.

A helicopter. But would it hover over the blue strobe or come straight for me?

Waiting to find out wasn't an option. I had told Deon, *You're going about this all wrong. Find a creek with mangrove cover.*

That's what I did: pointed the B-Tactical inland toward Demere Key, where the cry of honking peacocks followed me south. The course change allowed me to keep an eye on the helicopter. It had settled over the blue strobe but was climbing now, the aircraft suddenly linked to the water by a searchlight. The beam became an elastic tether. The tether stretched two hundred feet into the air, then the copter angled south, skating a white wafer of light across the water as it gained speed.

Police were after me, no doubt about it. What agency, and how I had been lured into a sting, didn't matter, but the motive did. Something else: if my adversary was a crooked cop, the chopper would fly directly to Dinkin's Bay.

Or would it? The chopper began a low-level search, a methodical grid based on radar contacts and my last-known heading. I kept a wall of mangroves between us, hopscotching between unnamed islets. I followed the Chino cut, wound my way behind York Island, then crossed open water to Dinkin's Bay with a heavy southeast wind pushing astern.

The last leg was the most unsettling because it was open water. The crossing required the leisurely speed of a drunk puttering homeward, while, two miles north, the helicopter drifted toward me, undecided, then peeled away.

It was a little after two a.m. when I reached the marina basin. No sign of fire or recent chaos, and the Sunday shrimp roast party was long over. I plucked a celebratory beer from the ice but then returned it unopened.

Lights in the Brazilian's bedroom were off now, but Hannah's boat was still moored in a slip nearby. Extra lines had been added, I noticed.

Hannah, or the Brazilian, had anticipated the squall that was following me home.

THE NEXT MORNING, after sunrise, I put away *The Journal of Morphology*—a good article by Dr. Phil Motta on scale flexibility of black tip sharks—and decided a tough workout was the rational way to deal with the irrational emotion that had kept me awake most of the night.

First, I returned to my boat and checked the GPS locator: some-one—a smart cop, possibly—had found the transmitter in the duf-fel. The transmitter had been disabled—the last marked location was the bar where the two boats had run aground.

Question: Why had I been targeted by a sting operation? I settled on three possibilities: 1. Police had used a badass relics dealer to lure me—a fellow dealer—into a trap. 2. The drop had been sabotaged by a third party—*possibly* a crooked cop. 3. The badass dealer, once the relics had been confiscated by police, could prove he or his boss was the rightful owner.

There were variations on each theory, but the last two were the most plausible.

The puzzle wasn't enough to shield my thoughts from Hannah, though, so I jumped off the dock, swam toward Woodring Point, then did pull-ups on the bar under my house.

Still not enough, so I went for an early-morning run. Put the dog on a leash, and we jogged double time along Tarpon Bay Road, where, at the Periwinkle intersection, something happened that fi-nally displaced jealousy—a van ran a stop sign and damn near hit us both. *Would* have hit me if I hadn't dived for the bushes.

Unbelievable. Sparse traffic on this Monday morning, no one around but early customers breakfasting at the Over Easy, where, it is true, the smell of bacon had diverted my attention.

The van stopped. I calmed myself, expecting the driver to apolo-gize. Instead, a florid-faced man screamed out the window, "You stupid son of a bitch. Watch where you're going."

My disposition changed. I asked him, "Do you have something against runners, pal? Or just suicidal?"

"I've got a crowbar in here, asshole! I'll use it."

Before I could respond, the man sped away, driving a blue soccer mom van with out-of-state plates I should have focused on but was too stunned by the absurdity of what had just happened.

To the dog I said, "The guy runs a stop sign—hell, I could be bleeding in the ditch right now—then yells at me."

The dog was used to our workout routine. He could smell the nearby Gulf of Mexico, knew there were birds to flush and dolphins to chase. He had already dismissed the affront as an insignificant lull in one hell of an exciting life.

Not me. I watched the van splash through puddles and turn left into the beach-access parking lot a quarter mile away.

"Bastard didn't use his turn signal either," I pointed out, then commanded the dog, "Come on."

A quarter mile in two minutes is a comfortable pace for me, but we covered the distance a lot faster than that. The parking area was screened from the road by foliage, which was unimportant because I had no interest in surprising the guy. All I wanted to do was . . .

What? Put him on the ground and choke him? Give a lecture on driving etiquette? Truth was, I didn't know. Never in my life had I fallen victim to that apex stupidity known as road rage. Now here I was about to go toe to toe with a stranger who claimed to have a crowbar.

In my current humor, the stranger would need more than a crowbar.

"They could be loading me in an ambulance right now," I reminded the dog. "What if I'd been some kid on a bike? Damn it, the guy needs to be straightened out."

A seventy-pound retriever that seldom strains at the leash is a rarity, so I noticed when mine tried to tug me away from trouble and toward the beach.

I pulled harder, and there it was: a blue van jammed between two compacts, the man who had threatened me just about to open the door. Chunky man in his thirties or forties—prime age for macho posturing—so I watched, letting the anger inside me build. The driver's face was still flushed, his expression impatient, when he yelled to someone, "Goddamn it, I told you to ride up here, you . . . *idiot*!"

A classic example of the abusive bully—Finn Tovar incarnate had been served up by fate for my analysis . . . or as a deserving punching bag.

I looped the leash around a *No Parking* sign, told the dog, "Stay," and started toward the man as the van's sliding door opened with a hydraulic whine. Unexpectedly, a woman in nurse's scrubs stepped out. She carried towels, a plastic bag, and a spray bottle. The man had yet to get his door open. When she attempted to help, he screamed, "I can do it myself!"

Finally, he did. The steering wheel, as I could see, was equipped with a hand brake—no foot pedals required—and a driver's seat that responded to another hydraulic whine. I retreated while the seat tractored the man, who was legless, clear of the doorway.

The nurse handed him a towel and the spray bottle. Only when she went to fetch a wheelchair from the back did I notice the purple heart on the license plate.

I turned away before the man, who was weeping with rage, began to clean himself with the towel.

WITH THE DOG SWIMMING HARD TO KEEP UP, I jogged the beach to Knapps Point and tried to catalog all the petty so-called indignities I have tolerated over the years.

On the highway: Many a fast driver had speared a middle finger at me and my old truck. Slow drivers clogging the passing lane had done the same. In bars: I had ducked loud drunks and walked away from the taunts of a few. The toughest to ignore were men big enough to present a challenge. Decline to engage a smaller man, you are less likely to be labeled a coward.

Either situation not a problem for me, usually. Most of us acquire a mix of wisdom and confidence that insulates our ego from unhappy strangers and their behavior. I had dealt with these indignities by using a technique that was instinctive, but Tomlinson has refined it and given it a name: the Spam File Method, he tells his Zen students. A tailgater blares the horn while passing. A drunk hollers an insult. A neurotic's insults are a cry for attention but also invite an angry response. Fail to engage and you risk the *I should have said, I should have done* replays that make it hard to sleep.

Nope—all pointless tangents, a waste of energy that derails us from what Tomlinson calls "the forward flowing harmony of life." It is healthier to retool and implement a new system of response behavior. The technique requires a quiet corner and mental imaging. Here is how it works: Isolate the insult or incident, then seal it in a bag and drop it into a spam folder. Hit the cerebral *Delete* button and it vaporizes. Repeat as needed. The process doesn't erase the memory, of course, but it does add a cheerful distance between reality and random adolescent bullshit.

Tomlinson tells his Zen students the method requires practice, yet it came naturally to me—until recently anyway. What had caused me to snap and chase down a blue soccer mom van? Why had I embarrassed Owen's friend, Harris, by hurling his rifle into a lake?

At the Island Inn, I turned around, signaled the dog to change course, then mulled it over for a hard mile and a half of beach.

Hannah was the obvious scapegoat, but I couldn't let myself off the hook that easily. Reality-based people—which I am, I'd like to think—don't search outside themselves to place blame. Hannah's decisions were her own. If I was acting out my anger, the problem was me, not her. It was a personal lapse that required mending.

To instruct and illustrate, I did a Tomlinson and rewound recent events into future tense: Instead of chasing the blue van, I punch the guy through the window when he threatens me. Headlines announce *Biologist Assaults Legless Veteran*. Or the legless vet isn't legless. I break his nose or he cracks my spine with a crowbar.

Why? For what good cause? There was none. Better to disengage and drop the incident into the spam file.

Recently, I'd read about a young man who had treated his new girlfriend to seats at a Mets game. Their second date. Because, on that sunny day, he wore a Yankees cap, two drunks heckled the couple for six relentless innings. When they threw beer on the girl—a girl he had hoped to impress—the young man decided he had to do something. He stood, confronted the drunks, and his skull was crushed when they knocked him over a railing.

Rewind and change the choreography: The young man risks the label of cowardice by signaling security . . . or he knocks the drunks over the railing, then he is hauled off to jail.

Credit the young man's courage and blame the drunks, blame the lapse in security—both deserve it—but courage is a quality that merits a good cause, not the random intrusions of strangers.

At the beach-access parking on Tarpon Bay Road, I turned in, hoping to introduce myself to a stranger who was an expert on the subject.

The blue van was gone, though, and with it the chance to retract my angry questions: *Do you have something against runners, pal? Or are you just suicidal?*

It would be a while before I could drop that one into the spam file.

THIRTEEN

I WAS FINISHING AN HOUR ON THE PHONE WITH MY COP FRIEND FROM TALLA-
hassee when I saw Hannah coming up the steps. Had I not encountered the crippled vet, I might have been frostier, but he had put
pettiness into perspective. But what do you say to the woman you've
been dating after she has awakened in the bed of another man?

I tried a bland, "Hi. Too rough to fish this morning?"

Hannah, coming through the door, said, "Quite a storm last
night, huh? We're hoping the wind lays down by this afternoon."

We're hoping—her budding affair with the Brazilian had become
a Deep South contraction.

"Probably made it tough to sleep," I said. "All that lightning and
rain."

"No, I'm getting used to sleeping on boats. I like it. That rocking
motion, you know? *Esperanza* rocks even more, but his boat's a lot
bigger. Three times as long, I'd say, and twice the beam."

Was she baiting me? No . . . Hannah was actually talking about the Brazilian's yacht, said it in a levelheaded way, an unpretentious woman who was making me aware of a reality: Relationships change—*deal* with it.

Okay, I would. I had always admired Hannah's honesty, and it was hypocritical to fault her for it now. So I offered the lady coffee and a chair. She accepted both but balked when I suggested she follow me from the lab into the house.

"Coffee requires boiling water and that's where the stove is," I explained patiently.

Hannah, wearing fresh gray shorts and a blue blouse, sleeves rolled, looked at me, meaning *That's where the bed is, too.* "I'm comfortable here," she countered.

I said, "Believe me, being alone with you isn't going to be a problem."

"Hah!" she responded. "I fell for that the first ten or twelve times, and I don't trust either one of us. I would like to see those fossils you mentioned. We were hoping you'd stop by this morning and show us."

"We," I repeated.

"Yes. And there was something else . . . The thing you weren't sure you could trust me to see. That's why I came here alone."

"The only reason, huh?" I said.

She cocked her head at me. "Marion . . . have you been working with chemicals? I know you don't sniff glue."

Fascinating. In the space of a few sentences, the woman had flattered me, insulted me, and convinced me that she was nuts. "Milk and sugar, right?" I said, reaching for the door.

"I need to show you how to make sweet tea one of these days," Hannah replied.

I crossed the breezeway, paused to watch the retriever climb the stairs, a coconut in his mouth. "She's all yours," I told him.

The dog dropped the coconut, shook a haze of water off his back, then picked up the coconut.

"You're right. It's safer swimming with sharks."

From the lab, Hannah, indignant, called, "What's that supposed to mean?"

I replied, "You'll understand when you see what he's got in his mouth." A nonsensical lie that I left my ex-lover to ponder.

IN THE GALLEY, I lit the stove and was debating whether to fetch the valuable relics from their new hiding place when the phone rang. Tomlinson.

"You found the ladies already?" I asked. Worried about Lillian and the others, he and Fallsdown had driven to Venice, but they had been gone less than two hours.

"No, but I found Mick. And Dunk finally got ahold of his probation officer. Which do you think would be better for him, crossing the border into Mexico or into Canada? At first, I told him Canada, thinking more Skins lived up there. But I—"

"Tomlinson, have you lost your mind?"

"I know, I know—I entirely forgot the whole Mesoamerica civilization. Geniuses, those Aztecs. I think it's because Mick has me so spooked. Ski Mask, according to him, was just another Harley gangbanger until he took a spill, which—"

I interrupted. "I told you to stay away from that guy."

"Can't do it," Tomlinson said. "You didn't hear some of the truly ugly shit he said to me. A man who takes advantage of three sweet women? Let me finish: After the gangbanger wrecked his Harley, he went entirely psycho when he saw what road rash had done to his face. Permanent variety."

I said, "What did Duncan's probation officer say? No, wait—is Mick there?"

"I can get him."

"Hold on! Does he know Tovar's house was robbed?"

"Interesting you should ask. That's what Mick wants us to do— go back to that guy Finn's place and check it out. He suspects something's up, but, no, otherwise not a clue. Mick knows Ski Mask wants our ass, though. *If* Ski Mask is the guy he thinks he is."

I had already told Tomlinson about last night's debacle but hadn't mentioned I was going to contact my cop friend in Tallahassee. I now knew that an anonymous caller had tipped off Florida Fish & Wildlife officers—it was their boats and a sheriff's department chopper that had chased me—but the cop and I had spoken in strict confidence. Not even Tomlinson could know—or people a lot more competent than a Harley gangbanger would be after my ass.

My theories about the sting operation had been trimmed to two: the drop had been sabotaged by a third party or the badass caller worked for someone who, once the relics had been confiscated, could prove ownership.

I said to Tomlinson, "What I think you should do is leave before there's more trouble. And, for god's sake, get this probation thing straightened out. Where are you?"

"At the marina where you tied the boat. Mick thinks he knows who's behind all this. Finn Tovar had a blood feud going with another bone hunter. Dates back thirty-some years. Everybody hated Tovar, but this particular dude made a pile of money somehow.

He's got the cashola to hire Nazis like Ski Mask to do his dirty work."

"Would you please stop calling him Ski Mask," I said. "What's the biker's name?"

Tomlinson hedged, which made me suspect he was working on a plan of his own, so I insisted, "Tell me the biker's name, damn it."

"But Mick's not sure Ski Mask is the gangbanger with the scrambled brains. Even if he is, Mick won't tell me. The man's a tour guide by profession, which, as a private sector type, you can understand. He expects to get paid—but twenty percent off because he claims to be part Indian." After a long silence, Tomlinson asked, "You still there?"

How does one disengage from a phone conversation without hanging up? I said, "I suppose Dunk is sitting under one of the chickee huts so he'll be easier for police to spot. Did he tell the probation officer he's in Florida? Probably even mentioned he's staying at Jensen's Marina."

"*Possibly*. They're both Skins, and it's not the Indian way to lie. On the other hand, his probation officer is also a Freemason, so there could be some wiggle room. Depends if Dunk dropped any of the code words—but that's something I can't get into. Wish I could. Doc . . . you know Masons aren't allowed—"

I cut in. "Don't even say it." He was about to urge me to come to a lodge meeting by claiming he couldn't invite me.

He said it anyway. "We're not allowed to ask people to join. The first move is entirely up to you. But, man, it hurts not to be able to share stuff that's very ancient and cool."

"We'll talk about it after you and Dunk get your butts back to Sanibel," I told him. "And don't trust Mick. Where is he? Right now, he could be selling you out to the guy who threatened to stick a gas rag down your throat."

"That one's a sickie," Tomlinson replied, more serious. "Even on the phone, I could smell demons in his voice. Someone like him feeds on inflicting pain. You could plant belladonna in his breath and the stuff would grow."

Yes . . . I was sure of it now: Tomlinson intended to find the man on his own.

In the background, I heard Fallsdown talking. Tomlinson covered the phone, then returned, saying, "Lillian, remember her? The sweet, sort of pudgy brunette? Dunk just found out she lives at the beach. After that, Mick's trying to arrange a meeting with Tovar's blood feud enemy—you know, look the devil in the eye. If it happens, I'll tell the dude he can have what's in the Pelican cases if he produces the other owl charmstone. Or both charmstones, if you found the wrong one. Is that okay with you?"

No—and not just because his plan was so damn dangerous, although it was. "Do me a favor," I said. "Stop whatever it is you're cooking up and come straight to Sanibel."

"Can't do that, man."

"Damn it, Tomlinson, the stuff in that bag isn't ours to trade."

"But, Doc, I'm scared for those ladies. Three sweeties, and they obviously have no problem talking to strangers. One of them had to give the sicko my cell number. I can't just go off and leave them."

Now, in the background, I heard heavy thumping music over the growl of engines and Fallsdown saying what might have been: "Hey . . . you think *maybe*?"

Tomlinson answered, *"Shit oh dear,"* then in a rush told me, "Motorcycles, Doc. This might be the asshole who threatened me."

He hung up.

THE TEAKETTLE WAS WHISTLING. I poured water over ground beans from Cuba and watched coffee drizzle through a filter before I redialed Tomlinson's cell. I got voice mail.

"Druggie lunatic."

"Everything all right?" Hannah was standing outside the screen door.

"I'm worried," I said.

She entered and closed the door with the care of a nurse entering a patient's room. "I know. I wish you'd tell me about it. Did you and your son have another argument?"

I said, "He won't answer my e-mails, let alone answer a phone, but it's not that." I took a moment to clean my glasses. "It has to do with Tomlinson and Duncan—but this is strictly confidential, okay?"

Hannah's jaw flexed as if she'd been slapped and she came toward me. "Marion Ford, if you say that to me one more time!" She didn't stop until her toes were almost touching mine.

"You'll do what?"

"Why ask me such a . . . *Oh!* You make me so mad sometimes."

Hannah is a sizable woman, and I was looking straight into her dark, astute eyes, irises flecked with gray and gold beneath a cornea that sparked. The air she had displaced while crossing the room regathered: a girl scent of shampoo and cotton, momentarily warm, then warmer. Or maybe it was just that we were standing so close. Pheromones began intermingling, dopamine reserves were alerted, ready to drop the floodgates at the first brush of skin against skin.

She felt it, too, and stepped back. "Of course you can trust me. Yesterday, Tomlinson was so upset, I knew there was something wrong."

The analytical nerd in me wondered if Hannah had been eaves-dropping but then credited her instincts instead. I said, "It has to do with the owl carvings. There's a guy in Venice—crazy, apparently—who threatened Tomlinson, but he and Duncan drove up there anyway. Just now, on the phone, Tomlinson hung up so fast, I'm worried the guy found them."

Hannah said, "Why in the world would anybody hurt someone as gentle as Tomlinson?"

"The charmstone—the carvings—they're valuable," I told her.

"Then call the police."

Before it escaped my mouth, I deleted the word *confidentially*, then explained, "I can't. Duncan skipped probation when he came here from Montana. They could arrest him. Tomlinson might be a suspect in a house burglary, too. He didn't do it, but this guy—the crazy one—might have seen him leaving the house that was robbed. Something else: There's a slim possibility the guy's a cop himself."

Hannah's expression read *This is insane.*

I said, "You asked."

The woman's mind went to work on the problem while she poured coffee and added sugar. "Where was Tomlinson calling from? Venice, I know, but where in Venice?"

I told her.

She snapped her fingers. "I'll call the marina. If there's a fishing guide around, he might recognize my name. I'll ask him to check on two friends of mine. Professional courtesy."

It was true Hannah's reputation as a fishing guide was growing. She had appeared on the covers of two magazines; the best photo-graph had Hannah looking into the camera but also *through* it, late sunlight bronzing one side of her face, water turquoise beyond her blue-black hair. The photo captured a Barbara Stanwyck duality: the competent woman outdoorsman who was not beautiful but handsome in a way that intimated sensuality, plus something deeper available behind those dark eyes of hers. Intimidating but sexy. A friend of Hannah's, a famous photographer on Captiva, had taken the shot.

I made coffee for myself, opened the door for the dog to come in, then opened it again and let the dog out while she made the call. No fishing guides present at Osprey Nest Marina, but a genial employee told Hannah three motorcycles were still in the parking lot.

After getting Tomlinson's voice mail again, then trying Dunk's number, I asked her, "Do you know anything about the Freemasons? There's a lodge nearby and they're both members."

She replied, "When my Uncle Jake was buried, it was a Masonic funeral—kind of strange, because he never said anything about it. Do you want me to call information?"

I said, "Worth a try," and soon dialed the Masonic lodge in Venice. The call went to voice mail, but then a man picked up. I told him I wasn't a Freemason, then explained why I was calling.

"I can get you the number for Venice police," he offered.

I put him and his fraternity to the test. "Police might get the wrong idea and detain my friends. One of them's on parole—a good guy, a Crow Indian from Montana."

I expected a panicked excuse, then a dial tone, but the man asked, "What lodge do they belong to?"

"I have no idea."

"How do you know they're Freemasons?"

If the man was expecting some mysterious code word, I disappointed him. "Because they told me," I said.

He thought about that, but not for long. "My truck's outside. Tell me their names and what they look like—what they're driving, too." When I finished, he asked, "Should I call you back at this number. Or is there a better one?"

"Wow," Hannah said when I was done. "I think there was a lot my Uncle Jake didn't tell me. Marion . . . I'm thinking the same's true about you."

Eye contact again; pheromones scattered, then vectored, a brief intermingling that I stopped by reminding myself, *She slept with the Brazilian last night, for christ's sake.*

I replied, "I don't belong to any fraternal organizations."

"Would you tell me if you did?" Hannah waited while her eyes searched my face for some sign of trust.

I decided to provide it and backed away, saying, "I've got something I want to show you," then went out the door and down the steps, trying to breathe normally.

The dog, still carrying the coconut, followed me from the breezeway.

FOURTEEN

THE BEST TEMPORARY HIDING SPOT IS A PLACE NO THIEF WOULD BOTHER searching because who in their right mind would hide valuables there?

Under the house, next to the pull-up bar, is a shed. The door wasn't locked because there is no lock. Last night, before leaving for Cayo Pelado, I had emptied the Pelican cases and stacked the artifacts inside among paint cans and brushes. Then I had seeded the cases with fossils I'd found with Owen, plus some ambiguous ballast stones, before loading the duffel bag onto my boat. On the phone, my Tallahassee cop friend had commented, "That stuff in the Pelican cases didn't fool our people for long . . . but they gave the bag man high marks for knowing the water. One question, Doc: Was it *you*?"

That's when my friend and I had negotiated our pact of confidentiality.

While Hannah waited, I made three trips up the stairs, arms loaded, while she *ooh*ed and *ahh*ed in wonder. She said the fossils and Spanish coins were interesting, pronounced the coral arrowheads

"Beautiful," and she had a professional appreciation for the giant shark's teeth.

The owl carving, though, Hannah loved. She cupped the stone in her hands while examining the mastodon tusk. "I've never seen anything like that. How old, do you think?"

"Dates back at least ten or twelve thousand years," I said. "People were living on the Florida peninsula by then. They hunted mastodons and mammoths, which were similar but different animals. Or the tusk could be more than a million years old, I don't know. Mastodon fossils are rarer, I assume because there were fewer mastodons."

I carried the tusk to the scale and weighed us both. Hannah followed but stopped as we neared my closet-sized bedroom. She was waiting when I returned.

"A yard long and almost forty pounds," I said. "A few years back, there was one stolen. I was thinking this might be it, but that one had primitive carvings on it."

"Carvings of what?"

"Thatching, sort of lacework lines, from what I read." I held the tusk away from me and squinted but needed a magnifying glass— an inspection I would save for when I was alone. "Tomlinson doesn't know but I'm turning all this stuff over to the authorities when the time's right. But not the owl. That stays with Duncan unless I hear differently."

Hannah placed the owl in its rosewood box, then skated her fingers over the mastodon tusk. "It's so smooth, and sort of elegant the way it's curved," she said. "Like blue glass. Shiny, almost wet-looking."

I considered Hannah's blue-black hair, enjoying the way it flowed, heavy and soft, to her shoulders. "Not blue. The fellow who owns the phosphate mine described the color as 'Ice Age ivory.' I just realized it's the same color as your hair." Looking into her eyes, I added, *"Beautiful.* You're right."

Pheromones that had been pinging around the room returned with magnetic accuracy. Hannah pushed her hair back, as if the room was too warm, and asked, "Can I . . . hold it?"

A deep breath was required before I replied, "Of course."

The weight of the tusk required a clumsy nose-to-nose handoff. My fingers, acting independently of my brain, brushed the sides of her breasts in the process. While I apologized, my hand found the fleshy curve of her hips and pulled the woman closer. A minute later, the tusk was in the reading chair, and Hannah was pulling my shirt over my head while I battled the buttons on her blouse.

The floor . . . again . . . ?

No, like sensible adults, we groped our way through the door and collapsed the bed frame with our weight when we hit the mattress.

It didn't matter. Fog once again encased us, two dopamine-soused primates blind to all but skin on skin, mouths joined, my hands coaxing her body into a frictionless readiness, while her fingers stroked and teased to encourage full male participation.

Hannah, once the lines of modesty have been cut, is set free, un-leashed. The chaste churchgoer becomes feverish. And she sounded feverish when she wrestled me atop her and whispered, "Don't stop."

I hesitated, remembering, *She slept with the Brazilian last night.* Not only was the man a scalp hunter, he traveled internationally— no telling who or what he might have passed along to this trusting woman.

Feeling a little feverish myself, I tumbled off the mattress and lunged for the dresser, where, months before, I had hidden a box of condoms.

"Why . . . What are you doing?" Hannah sounded dazed.

"Protection," I said. "Damn it—I thought they were in the sock drawer."

"Protection . . . from what?"

I was tossing underwear and folded T-shirts aside. "Maybe Tomlinson took them, that bastard."

"You mean a *condom*?"

"A whole new box. It hadn't even been opened."

Hannah sat up and blinked her eyes, disoriented. "Why do we need a condom?"

"I don't like them either, but . . . damn that guy."

"Marion? What are you saying to me?"

"That he uses everything I own, doesn't bother asking either."

"Not about him. I'm talking about us. You said you had a blood test. And I didn't go on the pill just to make my breasts bigger. Have you . . . Has something changed?" She pulled the sheet over her hips and waited.

In the bottom drawer I keep slacks and dress shirts, clothing seldom worn. I knew I hadn't hidden the condoms there, but my drugged-out, inconsiderate pal might have—if he'd left any. Still searching, I explained, "Hannah . . . darling . . . I know who you slept with last night. It's none of my business, I haven't pried. But safe sex is smart." I glanced to see how that went over.

Not well. Hannah's face was coloring, and she had pulled the sheet to her neck. "Is that what you think of me?"

When responding to denial, I remain cool, rational. "It's him I'm worried about, not you. You see the Brazilian as a good-looking guy with lots of money. Fine. But I know things about him you don't."

"You think I would do that *for money*?"

"Of course not. I was trying to be objective—see the physical attraction through your eyes."

A different tone came into her voice. "I don't need help from a man who's *half blind* to tell me what I see."

My glasses—she had a point there—I wasn't wearing glasses. Find them, the box of condoms might appear. I said, "Hannah, let's be adults about this." I pointed to the bedstand. "Do you mind handing me those?"

"*Yes!* For your information, I slept aboard Mike Westhoff's Sea Ray last night. The mates' quarters, because Joann and Rhonda slept in the master suite. Which I told you *yesterday*." To herself, she added, "Money—what does he think I am?"

Uh-oh. A man standing naked, only seconds after delayed penetration, looks ridiculous enough. I turned my back and began closing drawers. "Well . . . I remember you saying it was a possibility, but—"

"I bet Tomlinson heard me. *He* listens. Are you saying you didn't get my note either?"

"A note?" I stood, a T-shirt in one hand to shield myself. "I didn't see any note. Wait . . . If you gave it to *Tomlinson,* then—"

"Stop blaming that poor man! Last night, I left it on the counter next to the sink. It was after midnight, in a place you'd see it when you came in. You didn't notice I cleaned up around the dog's dish and filled his bucket? I didn't want you to worry. In the note, I invited you to breakfast, thinking it would be nice for Rhonda and Joann to see the fossils."

Deliverance. Finally, it all came together and provided me a way out. I backed through the door, then rushed to the counter. Over the sink, I'd left the window open a few inches. The counter was still wet from last night's rain. Hannah's note was dry, though, when I found it between the fridge and the counter.

"Guess what I found," I said with a smile, coming through the bedroom door. "The wind blew it on the floor before I got home."

Hannah, unimpressed by my deductive powers, continued buttoning her blouse and told me, "Put some pants on, for heaven's sake."

I knotted a towel around my waist instead. "Don't you get it? I made an unfair assumption, I admit. But it was based on the only information I had at the time. This wouldn't have happened if the wind hadn't picked up. So, when you said *We were hoping* in reference to the fossils, it was only logical for me to think you meant the Brazilian, so—"

"Please stop," Hannah said. She wasn't angry now, just hurt. "We can't let this happen again. I mean it this time. I want you to promise."

I said, "It was an innocent mistake."

"Promise me," she insisted.

I cleared my throat. "I can't do that, Hannah. It's not what I want."

She looked up, shorts buckled, her expression serious. "Marion, I was awake last night when you got back and tied your boat. Worried sick because of that storm coming, and there you were, dressed like—I don't know—a commando, I guess. And wearing some kind of gadget over your eye." She stepped closer. "Look . . . my Uncle Jake was a detective, Tampa police. I *know* what a gun case looks like."

When I attempted to explain, Hannah held up a hand and kept talking. "In April, when you went to Venezuela, I read about the fighting there. A war almost started, and one of the head people was killed—assassinated, they said. Something to do with a drug cartel or a revolution. It was on the news. You told me nothing happened while you were there. But I'm not stupid."

I told her, "I was in a remote area without TV—"

"Let me finish," Hannah said. "There's something else I never asked about: My Uncle Jake used a special kind of oil to clean his weapons. Hoppe's Oil, same as you. The night you left for Venezuela, I recognized the smell in your lab, a kind of fruity odor. Jake had scars on his body, too, from a shooting and lots of fights."

Hannah, not looking at my chest, straightened her collar and adjusted her belt, while I said, "Okay, your uncle and I had some things in common, so what?"

"I wouldn't bring it up if we could behave like friends. But we can't. And I don't want to fall in love with a man who keeps secrets."

"We all have secrets, dear."

"We don't all live secret lives," Hannah said, facing me. Then asked, "Do you?"

"*Yes.*" The word slipped from my mouth.

She didn't expect that—nor did I. But now it was out there, no taking it back. I said, "Have a seat for a minute. I've got something to tell you."

"My lord, Marion, I guess I better." Sounding a little spooked, she sat on the bed while I explained.

"The mastodon tusk and the owl—all this stuff—I took it from a man who robbed a house near Venice. That was on Friday. Last night, I went out, hoping to eyeball the guy who had threatened Tomlinson. The crazy guy, not the robber."

"Then what? I don't understand why someone like you would take such risks. You were carrying a gun!"

"I walked into a sting operation. I'd been set up."

"You did what?"

"The legal owner must have tipped off police. Or someone torpedoed the crazy guy. I can't think of another way to explain it."

Hannah took a deep breath, then said again, "But you were carrying *a gun*."

"I had no intention of using it. I outran their boats. When the timing's right, I already told you, I'll turn everything over to the authorities."

"Are you telling me you're not a criminal?"

"That's right."

"But you stole those things, you just admitted it."

"I said I *took* them. I didn't say anything about stealing."

"If you're not a criminal, then you . . ." She combed her hair back, confused. "Do you work undercover for the police? No . . . you robbed a man. Taking's the same as stealing, I don't care what word you use. And it doesn't explain Venezuela. Or the way you were dressed last night when you docked." She reviewed for a moment. "What was the thing over your eye?"

How far was I willing to take this? I had already shared too much. "Tonight, I'll show you. Hell, you can borrow it—an inexpensive night vision scope. You'll see thousands more stars. There's nothing sinister about that. Hannah, I'm trying to be honest with you here."

"There's a difference between being honest and being open. Jake sometimes went to South America. Police undercover work, I always figured, but now I have reason to believe he might have done smuggling on the side. Either that or he was a spy. Marion, I can't picture the CIA hiring a man like you, so there has to be something you're leaving out. I'm going to ask you one simple question: Are you smuggling drugs to make ends meet?"

I felt a crazy smile appear on my face. "Honey, I'm the guy who won't even smoke marijuana. Are you serious?"

"My Uncle Jake wasn't a drug user either, but all the similarities worry me." She sighed, uneasy about something else, and finally said, "I feel awful about this. I've been snooping. I . . . I did a background check through our agency's computer. You were born in Florida and you've lived in this house for more than ten years. Other than that, there's next to nothing about you in any data banks I could find. Oh—and that new boat of yours cost as much as some folks pay for a house, but your tax returns claim—"

I was smiling when I interrupted, "You have every right to check on a man you're dating. I expected you to. Hannah, look"—I took her hands in mine—"I don't cheat on my income tax and I'm not a drug smuggler."

Gently, she pulled her hands away. "Then there's something you're leaving out. Just *tell* me."

I couldn't do that. On the other hand, I knew Hannah Smith. She has the sensibilities of a mermaid but the instincts of a shark when it comes to deception. One more lie would be the end of us. No doubt in my mind about that, so I said, "For now, you have to trust me. It won't always be this way."

Shaking her head, the woman turned and exited the bedroom. I hoped she would busy herself brewing tea while I dressed. She had barely touched her coffee. Instead I heard the screen door open, then close softly—a courtesy that spared me a parting rebuke.

I felt a sickening tightness in my stomach. Seconds later, though, she returned to the door and said through the screen, "I'm sorry I lost my temper. I don't make friends easily, Marion. I'm not quick to give them up either."

I was smiling again. "Come inside and finish your coffee."

Hannah moved her head side to side slowly, a thoughtful but determined *No*. "Tonight maybe, but I want to think things through. And I'm not coming back here alone—I'm serious about that."

"Would it be better if I asked Tomlinson to stop by?"

Hannah muttered something, then said, "If it's okay, I'll bring Rhonda and Joann. I'd like to look at the stars through that night scope thing. My friend Birdy Tupplemeyer also. She called and wants to do something tonight—but you don't have to worry about her."

"I'm not a drug smuggler," I said again.

Hannah, her eyes soft, looking into mine, let that go unchallenged. "I don't want us mad at each other, Doc. But it can't be the way it was."

When we were alone, she seldom called me Doc, but that was okay. I had kept the best megalodon teeth I'd found with Owen, plus a few other good pieces that I could show her friends.

"I'll make mojitos and lay out some fossils, too," I said.

Birdy Tupplemeyer, a high-octane redhead, was a cop, worked for the sheriff's department, but I wasn't going to blow it by questioning Hannah's judgment.

SHORTLY AFTER HANNAH LEFT, the man from Venice Masonic lodge called. "I'm at the marina, but your friends aren't here. Heard from them yet?"

"No," I told him. "What about the motorcycles?"

"There were only two, not three, so maybe one left before I got here. The dockmaster saw your friends get in a car and follow both motorcycles out of the parking lot. A fellow who does shark tooth tours was in the backseat, a local named Mick. You said they were driving a white Chrysler?"

"A rental car. I don't like the idea of them following motorcycles. Maybe I should call the police."

The man, distracted for a moment, spoke to himself, saying, *Is that smoke . . . ?* He sniffed the air, then got back to me. "Don't worry about the fellas on the motorcycles, they're both members of our lodge."

"You smell something burning?"

"Someone getting their charcoal going, probably. We've had a lot of rain."

I asked, "How do you know the two bikers belong to your lodge?"

"Because the dockmaster is a member, too. He's trying to get one of them on the phone right now, but motorcycles are loud. It might be a while. In the meantime, I can keep looking if you want. Up to you." The man hesitated. "How serious is this?"

I was unconvinced that membership in a fraternity guaranteed that one of the bikers wasn't the crazed Harley gangbanger. I said, "I've met the guide, Mick. Do you know him?"

"Only by reputation," he replied. "So I guess I just answered my own question. Yeah, I should keep looking and . . ." Another distracted pause before he said, "Hmm, okay . . . I know where it's coming from now."

"What?"

"Last night, a house on Caspersen Beach caught fire. This wind must have stirred the smoke up."

Phone to my ear, I walked toward the lab, then returned to the window, saying, "My friends might have gone to Caspersen Beach with Mick. Was it the house owned by Finn Tovar? Tovar was a—"

"I know what Finn Tovar was. No, the owner was a widow, used to own a jewelry store here. She died in the fire."

"A *woman?*" I said. "Was it arson? Do you know her name?"

The man became guarded. "Why are you so interested in Finn Tovar? No . . . don't bother. I'll have one of the brothers ask your friends. They're obligated to tell the truth. I've heard some things—about the fire—but what I heard isn't official, so I can't give out any names. But how does a house fire concern you?"

Venice Masonic lodge also had members who were firefighters, I guessed. I was explaining that Tomlinson was searching for three women he had met on the beach when the man got another call. "Have to take this," he said. "Your friends will be in touch soon." He hung up.

I had failed to ask the man's name, I realized, and my phone was beeping. Tomlinson—just as the man had predicted.

I answered, saying, "Where are you? Get in the damn car and drive straight to Dinkin's Bay."

Tomlinson, however, was in the middle of a meltdown. "Doc, it happened, man. There's blood on my hands again. I led the devil to Lillian, that sweet lady's house, and he—"

I said, "I was afraid it was her. I just heard about the fire."

"From who? Lillian's house, I'm standing at the edge of the drive. You can't even tell except for a window upstairs where the siding is scorched. What I can't help picturing is—"

I told him, "Get in the car. Once you're on the interstate, we'll talk." Tomlinson had to snap out of it. There was a chance the man who had threatened him was somewhere nearby, watching. If he was also the arsonist, he was a killer.

My pal couldn't stop. "Poor little Lillian. I'll have that freak's head for this, Doc, I mean it. I can't help picturing how scared she would've been, a rag jammed in her mouth. The way her eyes must have looked when he—"

"Stop it," I said. "You don't know that's what happened. Put

Dunk on the phone and go start the car—lock the doors, too." When he protested, I said, "You're putting the other women in danger just by being there. Is that what you want?"

Tomlinson said, "No . . . but give me a few minutes. I'll have Dunk call you back."

TWENTY MINUTES LATER, Fallsdown, unperturbed, told me, "I can't talk any sense into him. Our friends here say the fire was—well, I can't tell you what they said. But there's no proof the woman was murdered. Now Tomlinson's looking for the other two women—and the guy who did it. He's as mad as I've ever seen him."

I asked, "Is Mick with you? What about the guys on motorcycles?"

"Give me a sec." I imagined Fallsdown putting some distance between himself and the others before he resumed. "Mick said for three hundred bucks he'll set me up with the biggest relics collector in the state. Same person Finn Tovar had a feud going with. He wants me to meet him tomorrow at a spot this guy is supposedly working. Just me."

"Setting you up might be exactly what he's doing," I said.

"Our friends don't trust Mick either and they *know* him. I'm going anyway."

"Offer him six hundred," I said, "but I want to come. If Mick balks, offer him more—but not much more. That would make him suspicious. Don't worry about the money. I'll cover it."

"Up until now," said the man from Montana, "I thought you were the rational type. Next, you'll be volunteering to go on spirit quests."

"Where are you supposed to meet Mick and this blood feud guy?"

Fallsdown had been given only the route numbers of an intersection, inland Florida, between Bradenton and Sebring, an isolated area. When he finished, I said, "With your sense of direction, you'll be in Georgia by nightfall. You need me."

Fallsdown responded with a pretty good Tonto riff: "White brother have something up sleeve. Or maybe he catch fever from sacred fossils."

Good. I hoped he believed that.

"Finding those shark teeth was like finding King Tut's tomb," I agreed. "I know the area you're talking about."

Yesterday, in Owen's Jeep, I had crossed the same intersection. It was only a mile or two from a sandy ski slope and the quarries owned by a defunct company, Mammoth Ridge Mines.

Fallsdown said, "Mick told me to bring a mask and fins because we're gonna stop at some river. At first, I didn't know what he was talking about."

"He expects you to dive with Tovar's old enemy? Or just the two of you?"

"I'm not sure. Then Mick got around to money. How much would I pay to get the carving back? Either that or, if this big-time collector can produce the carving, I'll need something extra special to trade. Plains Indian period, he hinted at Hopi ceramics, and mentioned that a Skin—meaning me—could make a lot of money as a supplier."

"You have access to burial sites," I said. "I hope you used it as leverage."

"Back when I was drinking, don't think I wasn't tempted to get into the business. But piss off the Little People . . . ?" He chuckled, and left it hanging.

I said, "Let's play along. I've got extra snorkel gear you can use."

Fallsdown replied, "At Deer Lodge prison, snorkeling was more of a nighttime elective."

He covered the phone and hollered something, then returned. "I better grab Tomlinson—he's chanting in some weird language and wandering toward the dead woman's house."

FIFTEEN

THAT NIGHT, AFTER RHONDA, JOANN, AND BIRDY HAD SATED THEIR APPETITE
for fossils, mojitos, and astronomy, I escorted them to the marina,
saved my warmest hug for Hannah, then jogged back to the lab. I
put the mastodon tusk under a microscope for the first time.

I was interested—no, eager—because, using only a magnifying
glass, I had made a discovery just before the ladies had arrived: Eons
ago, a fellow primate had etched his personal nightmare onto the
tusk. A Paleo hunter had carved what appeared to be a serpent's
head with fangs . . . *something* that so scared him, he had put down
his club and summoned the first primal stirrings of the artist within.

In the field sciences, the payoff isn't money. It's that exquisite moment of anticipation that separates discovery from revelation. This,
potentially, was one of those moments. Across a distance of ten
thousand years, a man or woman had sent a message. What was it?

The tusk was too big to view under a standard lab instrument.
Recently, I had bought an inexpensive digital microscope by Ce-
lestron. It was handheld, but also had a mounting vise. Plug the

scope into a computer, and unwieldy subjects were instantly transformed. The sandpaper skin of a hundred-pound hammerhead became a crystal forest of articulate denticles. Tap a computer key and the image was saved.

I carried the tusk from its newest hiding place—a cabinet—and placed it on a towel next to the monitor. Got the goosenecked lamp positioned just right and touched a switch . . . fiddled with the microscope's focus, then switched to low power.

Stunning—no other way to describe what I saw.

My god . . .

Because Tomlinson wasn't around, I summoned the dog, saying, "You've got to see this."

The dog opened his eyes long enough to yawn and went back to sleep.

I was looking at the head of a saber-toothed tiger in profile, not a snake. The cat's jaws were thrown wide, fangs curved, and long enough to appear venomous. The artist had used flint or shell or a shard of coral—two tools: one pointed to trace the outline, another that was sharp enough to bite into ivory. He had made some false starts at the base of the tusk. The microscope revealed where he had applied too much pressure and his hand had slipped, the gouges tracking always to the right.

The artist had been left-handed.

Was that unusual? It would be interesting to discuss with a Paleo sociologist, if such an expert exists. One thing for certain, this was not the work of a beginner. The lines were spare and masculine, one graceful curve adjoined to another, yet they evoked emotion—power, predation, fear.

The artist, who was a hunter by necessity, was also aware that to this apex predatory, he, on his two slow legs, was easy prey.

"A saber cat," I said aloud. Leland Albright had called the animal that when he had compared the value of fossils to gold. And it was Dunk Fallsdown who had told me the value was maximized if the fossil had been *worked* by Paleo man.

"This thing's worth a mint," I said to the dog, placing the microscope on the desk. "Definitely a petroglyph—a faker would have made it obvious. Archaeologically, this could be priceless. Depends on when it was carved. If it was thirteen thousand years ago, it's still a great find, but not earthshaking. Fourteen thousand years is the magic number."

I looked at the retriever for a moment, then explained: "The Bering Strait was still underwater fourteen thousand years ago. That's key. It means that Asiatic man first arrived in the Americas by way of Polynesia—Thor Heyerdahl proved it was possible. And there's an archaeological site near Tallahassee where artifacts already suggest that people arrived on the Florida peninsula before the Bering Strait existed. Or . . . was it fifteen thousand years ago?"

The dog grunted, meaning he had to use the mangroves or he wanted a quieter spot. I let him out, sniffed the air for rain, then returned to the computer. I saved a dozen images of the petroglyph, then disappeared into an Internet abyss. I read a paper on the Tallahassee dig site, then a newspaper article about a mammal bone that also bore a message from Paleo man.

By Cara Fitzpatrick

PALM BEACH POST STAFF WRITER

VERO BEACH, FL.—For nearly three years, an artifact that might be the oldest piece of artwork in the Americas lay under the sink of an amateur fossil collector's mobile home.

It was pure luck that [he] noticed it at all.

Cleaning his fossils one day last year, the . . . Vero Beach man spotted a small carving on a piece of mammal bone. The image looked like a mastodon, a prehistoric cousin of the elephant.

If authentic—and a team of scientists at the University of Florida believes it is—the carving would be thousands of years older than Stonehenge in England, the pyramids in Egypt, and Florida's Everglades . . .

Already, one anthropologist involved in studying the artifact has dubbed it the "oldest, most spectacular and rare work of art in the Americas."

But scientists fear the rare artifact may be lost to public view forever. [The owner] plans to sell it at an auction, much like any private art collector might sell a Picasso . . . The auction, which hasn't been scheduled, is being advertised online.

THERE WAS A PHOTO of the carving: a mastodon in profile, humpbacked, with short thick tusks. Elegantly simple, the lines spare.

The same artist? The odds of one frightened, observant person threading a hole twice through a thousand centuries were not good. Still, it was pleasant to muse over the possibility, and it underlined the importance of getting the tusk into the hands of experts.

And I would.

I searched for results of the auction. In my mind, there was nothing sinister about the Vero man's decision to sell—he had health problems, and a Social Security check was his only income. Who could blame him for not donating a godsend?

Nothing on the Internet, though, about the sale—if there had been a sale.

I soon found out why. Auctioning Native American relics had been banned by the U.S. in the 1990s. Most European nations had honored the ban.

France was an exception. Paris became the marketing ally of relic traders worldwide. In 2013, France's right to sell artifacts, and its refusal to reveal the names of sellers and buyers, was challenged by the Hopi Indian tribe of Arizona. The tribe filed suit against a Paris auction house to stop the sale of seventy ceremonial masks—kachina masks, some two hundred years old, carved from wood and still brightly colored despite their age.

French courts took the side of French auctioneers. Not only were the masks sold, the Hopi tribe wasn't even provided with the date and location of the auction.

France. Maybe the lucky man from Vero had sold the Paleo carving there. One thing I knew for certain: If a stolen tusk bearing only simple thatch designs had been worth a half million, the bone petroglyph he'd found was worth two times, ten times, as much. More, possibly. No telling.

I stood and looked at the length of ivory with new appreciation. As I did, I wondered about the neighbor Owen had mentioned, Monty Mondurant—Vandar, his real first name—the Moroccan. France colonized Morocco. French is the country's second language. If Mondurant was actually related to Moroccan royalty, he would have powerful friends in Paris. What bothered me was Owen's eagerness to discredit the man. His comments had had a scapegoat quality, and it all seemed to fit too neatly.

I did a quick computer search on Mondurant and wasn't impressed by what I found. He was a publicity hungry ne'er-do-well who had failed at or destroyed everything he touched. According to a recent magazine blurb, he was now living in Spain with an actress "protégée."

The rarity of the tusk eclipsed my interest in the Moroccan. Then Toby, the last Albright elephant, came into my head. He and mastodons shared common ancestry, so I compared the two animals. Toby's tusks were of a similar girth, although longer, and it was possible that, in Toby's massive brain, genetic memory retained an image that had also survived the Ice Age. Carved somewhere deep within might be the memory of Paleo man as seen through a mastodon's eyes. The reverse image of what the ancient artist had captured: a strange-looking primate on two frail legs, a spear in his hand.

If true, the image would trip all the ancient alarms: *Danger. Crush or flee.*

Fanciful, but I remembered Toby's saucer-sized eyes, the sharp look of appraisal as I had approached the fence, the subtle way those eyes had tracked Owen after he opened the gate. The elephant hadn't survived six decades of captivity by being inattentive.

I stored the digital microscope in its box and got out my camera bag. Using a full format Canon 5D and a 24mm lens, I took wide-angle shots of the tusk. I switched lenses and attempted a macro close-up of the petroglyph. Sometimes a good lens can see what the human eye cannot.

But not in this case. The carving of the saber-toothed tiger remained elusive.

That was significant. Unless Finn Tovar had used a digital microscope, the saber cat might have escaped him, too. Even through a good lab glass, the petroglyph was indistinct, so it was possible he hadn't noticed.

I wanted to believe that. A message from the Ice Age had been sent. I wanted to be its twenty-first-century discoverer.

While printing photos of the tusk, the phone rang. Dunk calling from his cheap 7-Eleven cell phone.

"YOU GOT BACK IN ONE PIECE?" I asked him.

It was nearly ten. Dunk and Tomlinson had kept me updated on events in Venice until their rental car was safely on Interstate 75, heading south.

"I just dropped our pal at Dinkin's Bay," he told me. "You haven't seen him yet?"

"No. How long ago?"

"Five, ten minutes. He didn't have his key or lost it, I don't know, but he said he was going to climb over the gate. If he doesn't stop at your place, he probably went to the nearest bar. He's taking that woman Lillian's death pretty hard."

My mind was on the meeting Dunk had arranged with the *blood feud collector*, as Mick described him. I asked, "Are we still on for tomorrow?"

"It took some doing," he said, then explained that Mick didn't want me along, I looked too much like a cop, but he had finally settled for the promise of eight hundred in cash. "Is that a problem?"

"That's fine. Do we meet him in Venice or at the intersection?"

"He's driving. You'll pay him when we get there. The guy—the blood feud guy—has people working a section of river not far from where we'll meet. Mick wouldn't say much about that, only that the sun needs to be high or there's no visibility underwater. So we're meeting at high noon. Don't forget your snorkel gear."

I said, "He's worried we'll be wearing a wire. That's why he wants us in the water. I'll bring extra stuff for you."

"Hell, I can't even swim good, but Mick doesn't know that. Oh—here's what I wanted to tell you: Just before we got to Sanibel, I got a phone call. It was the thief you took the duffel bag from, but he hung up, then called back a minute later. That's how I know it was him."

"Deon Killip?"

"Yeah, Deon. You called him from my phone last night, so he expected you to answer. That's why he got scared the first time."

"What did he say?"

"He wanted to speak to you, but I wouldn't give him your number. Which really pissed him off. That's when he finally told me his name. Said he wanted you to call him right away. He sounded wasted."

"Anything else?"

"Well . . . that you're a total cop narc asshole, which got a laugh from Tomlinson. I had it on speaker. If you want to call him from my phone, I can turn around. Seven-Eleven only carries twenty-dollar SIM cards, but I should still have a few—"

The phone went dead. *Minutes* is what Fallsdown had intended to say.

I went to the window expecting to see Tomlinson on the walkway or at the marina getting into his dinghy. Neither. On the bright side, Hannah's skiff was gone, and the Brazilian's sleek runabout was where it was supposed to be, suspended from its hoist. The combination provided me some adolescent comfort.

Rather than call a drug addict thief from my cell phone, I used the office phone, dialing star 67 first to block my number. When Deon picked up, I asked, "Who told you I'd be off Cayo Pelado last night? The biker who broke your ribs? Or the maid?" I was guessing, but it got a reaction.

"Cayo *what*? Jesus Christ, how many people you got in on this? The number you called from yesterday, some douchebag answered. And today two guys showed up in Venice asking questions. Were they cops?"

I replied, "Is that what Mick the magic tour guide told you?"

Another startled pause from Deon. "Hey . . . I don't know anybody named Mick—but you just convinced me. You are a cop. With the feds, I bet. Dude, let's drop the bullshit."

I was right about him knowing Mick. But was Tovar's former maid involved? I asked about her again, adding, "You want something or you wouldn't have called. Maybe we can work out a trade."

Deon, getting desperate, said, "Stop screwing with my head, man. If you're with the feds, hell, I'll cooperate. Really."

"I'm listening," I said.

"I mean it. I had a buddy, the feds gave him a whole new identity, haven't heard from the man since. But first, I've got to live long enough, right?" Nervous laughter, then, speaking confidentially, he said, "I need that shit back, man—no joke—or they'll kill me."

He had called hoping I was a federal agent, I realized. I asked, "Who's *they*?"

"Kiss my ass. Like, *tomorrow* I need what was in those cases. Aren't you listening? I'll sign papers, take a lie detector. I had no idea what I was getting into, man. Please—I'll give the stuff to this guy, then you can pick it up later when you arrest him. You've got to do this for me first." Deon was losing it, but then his brain sparked and he caught himself. "*Whoa*. Hey . . . if you're really a fed, why'd you have to ask who wants the shit back?"

I said, "Does it matter? I've got what was in the Pelican cases.

You don't. I'm willing to part with some of it, but when we had our little talk you gave me a fake name for the maid—I checked. And who was the guy in the ski mask?"

"Oh . . . Christ," he muttered, "you're *not* a fed."

"Doesn't mean we can't work something out," I told him. I suggested he go to a motel for the night, then tried to press for more information.

Deon had already cut free of the conversation, though. Speaking to himself, he said, "I am so screwed," and hung up.

HALF AN HOUR LATER, Tomlinson, instead of being flustered and in a funk, came through the door acting like his old self. "I've never heard this dog bark, have you?" he asked, scratching the retriever's ears. "Probably because of the throat injury, but it could be he's waiting for the right moment. I'm trying to learn patience from him." He cupped the dog's head. "Aren't I, Mr. Flamingo?"

The dog pulled away, stared at a lamp, and sneezed.

Flamingo . . . Matecumbe . . . Largo . . . Tomlinson had tried several experimental names, seeking a geographical fit. We had found the dog a few months ago lost in the Everglades, traveling south toward the last inhabited spot—an outpost named Flamingo. In Tomlinson's mind, he would have continued onward, swimming across Florida Bay to the Keys. I'd had to pry the teeth of a decomposing boa constrictor out of the dog's neck.

I said, "Flamingo might be the worst name ever." When I said it, however, the retriever snapped to attention.

"I'll be damned," I muttered.

"Aren't we all?" Tomlinson said, suddenly despondent again.

"First time in my life I actually wanted to kill someone. Ski Mask—the crazy Harley gangbanger. I'd bet they're one and the same. So, after Dunk dropped me at the gate, I did a power meditation, just me and the stars trying to get my humanity back on track."

He reached to pet the dog, adding, "It's a classic Buddhist koan. Does a dog have Buddha nature? Doc, the reality is, we're all part wolf. It scared me how fast I reverted."

The dog, who dodged Tomlinson's hand, smelled of fresh mullet and mangroves, and he was dripping water on the floor. I shooed him outside and used disposable automotive towels, not a lab towel, to mop up. The nearest washing machine was at the marina and I was tired of making trips.

"I'm sorry about Lillian," I said.

He replied with a *Me, too* shrug. "A Masonic brother found the names of the other two ladies and I called them. They're fine, thank god. I'm still waiting to hear how Lillian died. How it happened, or whoever did it, that won't change anything. For Lillian's sake, I'm trying to move on."

"That's not the impression I got from Duncan," I said.

"I know, I know . . . But between the Venice exit and Tuckers Grade, I said prayers for Lillian's safe transition. I feel better now. God calls us all. How's it go? *The wise and dumb and the very well hung.* I'm taking a *Live in the moment* approach. If Ski Mask stuffs a rag down my throat, I'll simply disappear before he lights the match."

I removed my glasses and cleaned them. "Are you okay?"

"A little thirsty, that's all." Tomlinson selected a graduated beaker from the shelf, went out the door, and returned with a bottle of twenty-one-year-old El Dorado. With reverence, he poured 250 milliliters of rum over ice. It was a recent preference, drinking fine rum from a beaker of borosilicate glass, laboratory grade. Twenty bucks apiece, those beakers cost me, but no point in warning him again.

"Duncan says he put the phone on speaker when Deon Killip called," I said. "Give me your version of the conversation."

No new details, so I told Tomlinson, "I've got something to show you. It'll cheer you up. While I get it ready, you can explain why you're acting so weird."

Looking through the screen door, Tomlinson fixated on the retriever. "Strange that he never even woofs. Just sort of grunts when he's gotta piss. Did you get those tests back yet?"

The dog had been raised in Atlanta, I'd discovered, by a hunting trial enthusiast who had also been a noted geneticist. The dog's oddities—not barking was only one of them—had piqued my curiosity. So, a week ago, I had sent off blood and hair samples, interested in the DNA results.

Tomlinson was buying time, though, so I said, "He can damn sure growl. And you're dodging the question."

"*Okay.* The problem is Mick. I've got a full read on him now."

My pal was serious. I mounted the digital microscope on the table and listened while he explained. "Part Indian, my ass—he has a lowlife pirate streak in him. That's why I want Mick to believe I'm a harmless flake. He won't let his guard down if he thinks I'm tricky. Before we left, I sold him a dime bag of Seven Mile Bridge at a discount. That should grease the skids."

"Sold him dope," I said.

"*Weed.* When will you ever learn the difference? My own special hybrid. Two tokes, you're over the hump and walking on water." Tomlinson plopped down at my desk, holding the beaker in his hand as if it were a brandy snifter. "Live the part, don't play it—the

Strasberg approach to acting. At the drum ceremony, Ava and the twins were convinced I was a flake, too."

It is not unusual for Tomlinson, who is an unorthodox character, to veil himself in the caricature of what people believe him to be. Typically, he does it to entertain or charm. He becomes the cheery butt of his own jokes; the drug-numbed jester who welcomes mockery with feigned confusion and a humility that, in private moments, he will confide is a test of his own Zen Roshi training.

I carried a bottle of water to the desk and sat on the folding chair. "It's better than wanting to murder someone. But where're you going with this?"

He asked, "What's your read on Ava?"

I hadn't mentioned our brief re-meeting at the Albrights' swimming pool. "Promiscuous," I said, then told him what had happened.

Tomlinson wrestled with something—possibly the desire to ask if the woman's breasts were real—but stayed on topic. "There're a few dark souls who go through a greed incarnation. Only manipulators use sex as a weapon. With Mick, greed's behind his whole *ancient calling* act. A gift for finding arrowheads because his ancestors speak to him—*please.* And he claims he killed mastodons in a previous life. All total bullshit. That's the sort of paranormal gibberish that no thinking person would fall for—but a lot do."

I had to take a sip of water before saying, "Yes, I suppose you're right."

"Dunk, of course, was onto him from the start. Doc?" Tomlinson hunched forward in the chair. "Remember Mick saying he teaches yoga? Actually, it's more of a fitness thing, Brazilian yoga or aerobics yoga. He's just a trainee. But here's the interesting part: Ava told me she and the twins did a yoga retreat in Asheville a while back."

"*Meditation* retreat," I corrected. "Leland mentioned it. They maxed out his credit card."

"Yoga, mood rings, mediation—to a suit like Leland Albright, it's all the same. Trust me, this is my wheelhouse. Today, I put it together, but I played dumb and let Mick lecture me on the subject. It's one of those franchise deals—Brazilian yoga, Jazzercise, cross-training. It's all similar. Lots of sweating to loud music. Mick's on the lowest rung at the Venice studio. But the regional manager is the head yoga stud, which is based in Sarasota. He was the headliner at Asheville. A franchise gig—a chain owned mostly by French and Saudis. See the connection?"

I liked the direction this was going. "Does it have to do with Paris auction houses? I was just reading about that. Or something to do with the Muslims who took flight training in Venice?"

Tomlinson tugged at a strand of hair while his expression read *Someone's a little slow today.* "No. Umm, I'll take it a step at a time. Ava and the twins attended the gig in Asheville—an obvious link. The head yoga stud also visits his franchise studios and works with new teachers—a link with Mick. But it's more than that. Mick can't say enough about this yoga teacher guy. He was almost an Olympic gymnast, a real motivator named Enrique Jones. You're a jock. Ever heard of him?"

"I don't follow the sport."

"Well, Enrique likes to talk—especially about his female students. According to Mick, screwing students is one of the perks. The yoga stud—Enrique—he uses it like a carrot to his male trainees, who, in fact, are just salesmen. Like a pyramid scheme. He charges them a fee but keeps the fire burning with stories about his sexual conquests."

I said, "I see where this is going now."

"That's right. There's a rich Sarasota wife who's crazy about Enrique. Supposedly wants to leave her husband, and bring along a ton of money, if Enrique will just say yes. Enrique is no gentleman, Doc. Told Mick that she's a *oral savant*. And he used her first name. It was Ava."

I said, "She's promiscuous, I told you. But I don't see Ava walking away from Leland's money for a yoga instructor. This guy wants to marry her?"

Startled by my naïveté, Tomlinson made a fluttering sound through his lips. "Dude, a yogi-gymnast can blow himself. Why the hell would he? No . . . Greed, that's the connection. Turn it around. Mick tells Enrique there's money in rare fossils. Enrique knows Ava's husband owns a phosphate mine. Then Mick brags to Enrique about how much Finn Tovar's private collection is worth. Ava wants in on it, or maybe Mick and Enrique work out their own deal. There are a lot of scenarios."

I asked, "You're saying it was the yoga teacher in the ski mask."

"No. Mick would've known, and he's not that good an actor. With Enrique, it's more about sex. He bragged about doing the mother-daughter thing, but the Sarasota mother doesn't know."

I said, "You mean, Ava doesn't know?"

"Yep. He's screwing one of the twins, too. Cockhounds like him make even me cringe. Leland Albright and I didn't exactly hit it off, but I feel sorry for that man."

We talked for a while longer before I told him that I was meeting Mick tomorrow, just Duncan and me, no one else. Tomlinson understood but wanted to know, "How are you going to handle the magic tour guide?"

I said, "He thinks I'm a cop, so Duncan will do most of the talking. I'll be the negotiator, though, if this collector can produce the stone owl."

"That's not what I mean. Mick sees himself as the high mystic of bone hunting. You've got to play to his ego. He's the expert, you're the student." Tomlinson's expression urged *Pay attention*, then he added, "You have to convince him you've got a bad case of fossil fever. Like you've decided *My god, Mick's the teacher I've been waiting for*. Play it straight, he won't give you the time of day."

"I'm not much of an actor either," I said.

"His ego will take care of that. Put your brain in wind tunnel mode and let Mick's bullshit blow right through you. I'll be sending you good vibes from Sarasota." He gave it a few beats before adding, "I'm having lunch with Ava."

That was a surprise. In response to my accusing look, Tomlinson said, "I'm not that low. You told Leland I haven't touched her and I won't. Information is all I'm after. Ava sees me as a harmless, charming goof."

"It's the charming part I'm worried about," I told him.

He finished his drink and placed my twenty-dollar beaker on the desk. "I'm a social scientist, don't forget. Today Mick had no idea my questions were classic personality probes. You ask a person *Are you honest?* he'll say yes, which is meaningless. But combine it with opportunity: *If my Crow Indian friend has artifacts to sell, could you find a buyer?* See? Plausible temptation has to be introduced to make an accurate assessment. That's straight from the Minnesota Multiphasic Personality Inventory."

I said, "You asked Mick that? I already know the answer."

"Which is why I didn't bother asking," Tomlinson said. "On the phone, I asked Ava and she said maybe."

"She admitted it?"

"Could be she was playing the role of the bad girl, although I doubt it. Ava's greedy. At the drum ceremony, after a few drinks, she complained about the prenup she has with Leland. If she maxed out his credit cards, could be she's squirreling away cash. But she would need a really big score before she drops the hammer on a wealthy husband."

Impressed, I tapped my bottle of water against the beaker. "Welcome back, Dr. Tomlinson."

Tomlinson's Nordic eyes were sharp and mildly predatory. "They suspect we have the missing relics, *hermano*."

"Mick said that?"

"No, Ava—it flowed from her thoughts right into my head. There's a reason she invited me to her house for lunch tomorrow. Doc . . . I'm going to find who's responsible for what happened to Lillian. There's more to this than some whacked-out Harley cowboy."

His mood began to soften, which promoted me to say, "You don't know for sure Lillian was murdered."

"She was; I could smell it in the smoke. But that's not the only reason. You never sat with Duncan's aunt and watched a Montana sunrise. Rachel was lionhearted in her day. Now she knows she's in for a long, cold trip if she doesn't get her packing done. She needs those owls."

He glanced at the digital microscope. "You were going to show me something."

I lifted the mastodon tusk from the cupboard and placed it on the desk. "A message from the Ice Age," I told him.

Tomlinson managed a smile. "Really? I haven't heard a word from those folks in years."

SIXTEEN

AT NOON THE NEXT DAY, IN THE PALMETTO HEAT OF INLAND FLORIDA, MICK
swung a machete, tossed a branch aside, then turned his ear to the
sky. He listened for a moment before asking, "Was that a trombone?
Or maybe a Jet Ski?"

An elephant is what he'd heard, Toby trumpeting somewhere
to the north. I had suspected we were near the Albright property
but had no idea it was that close. I hadn't told Fallsdown about the
Albright family pet, so kept it to myself. "It could have been. How
many people are you expecting?"

Mick, who'd already made it clear he didn't trust me, said, "You
ask a lot of questions."

Rather than remind him *I also paid you eight hundred dollars*, I
followed Tomlinson's advice from the night before. I said, "Sorry.
Duncan warned me about that."

Behind me, I could feel Fallsdown listening.

Mick said, "About what?" then asked Duncan, "What did you
tell this dude?"

I said, "I found my first megalodon teeth a couple of days ago.

That's no big deal to someone like you, but I'm a little overeager. Dunk told me to keep my mouth shut, that I could learn a lot."

"That's true." Mick turned to Duncan. "You gave him good advice."

I said, "The teeth and some other fossils are in the car, if you're interested. And this big whale vertebra, really incredible. Plus, some manatee ribs."

"*Dugong*, not manatee," Mick said, then shared his irritation with Fallsdown, who was clearing his throat. "Are you sure this guy's a biologist?"

"He's got a nice setup," Dunk replied. "Lots of aquariums. I've been in his lab."

"His *laboratory*?" Mick chuckled. "A biologist who doesn't even know the difference between a modern manatee and dugongs from the Pliocene. That's what a college degree will get you out here." Chiding me, he added, "They're the same genus, *Sirenia*, but totally different animals. Where'd you get your diploma? I've met a lot of preppy so-called paleontologists, biologists—the whole list. Get you guys out in the field, you're clueless."

I reminded myself of Tomlinson's advice: *Put your brain in wind tunnel mode and let Mick's bullshit blow right through you.* Which is why I replied, "*Sirenia*—sure. Sirens, mermaids on the rocks. The Latin root. I should've known."

Mick, wearing a backpack larger than my dive bag, fanned a haze of mosquitoes from his face and continued toward the creek. "You're in my dojo now. Finn couldn't stomach *classroom cowboys*—that's what he called people like you. And this collector you want to meet, he's *almost* as good as Finn was." He hacked a few more limbs before curiosity got the best of him. "Where'd you find the meg teeth?"

I had been undecided whether to admit I knew Leland Albright.

If I did, I wanted to observe Mick's reaction but spoke to his back anyway, saying, "I know a guy who owns an old phosphate mine near here. His stepson took me around."

"Sure you do. What's his name?"

When I told him, the magic tour guide stopped as if I had said a magic word. "You mean Albright as in Mammoth Ridge Mines?"

"Leland Albright. I'm doing an assessment of his property. It's business, so I can't say much else."

"Mr. Albright wants *your* expert opinion?"

"Water quality, not fossils." I forced a smile into my tone. "It's not likely the subject of fossils will come up, but I was going to ask anyway. Would you mind if I contact you? I'm sure Albright's company would pay a consulting fee."

Mick's ego unfurled like flower. "He let you on the property?" When I nodded, he became deferential. "Well . . . you couldn't find anyone better. How much are we talking?"

"That's up to me," I said.

Duncan, who was smiling, stopped to retie his shoes so we could walk ahead in private.

I continued, "On consulting jobs, fees vary. You probably know this, but the contractor—that's me—he gets something for his trouble if he hires an expert from another field. Whatever you bill hourly, I would add a percentage and pass it along to Albright's company." I lowered my voice. "But that's strictly between us if it happens."

Mick liked that. "Hell, just smart business. Sure . . . occasionally I provide expert advice if the money's right. But let me get this straight. You're talking about *the* Mammoth Ridge property—just north of here? They closed down years ago."

I said, "I spent almost three hours touring the place Sunday."

"No shit?"

"Strictly between us," I said. "When I go back, it would be nice to have an expert along. Leland Albright—have you met him?"

"Of course. Well . . . not actually, but I'd like to."

"That's who hired me. What I'll tell Leland is, I need unlimited access to the property. If he says okay, you're in. But you can't wander off by yourself. I'm serious about wanting to learn how to bone hunt."

Mick talked about his respect for professionalism, then asked me, "Aside from meg teeth and the dugong rib, what did you find?"

I let a whiff of fever creep into my voice. "Enough to get me hooked. This ridge the stepson showed me, it was pure bone. Fragments, mostly, and that was the problem. I didn't know what I was looking at. Megalodon teeth everywhere. A whale vertebra, of course, I recognized. With someone like you, though—"

"The key," Mick said, "is training all the senses to find bones, not just the eyes. Describe the ridge you were on. I've heard rumors about a spot there—Finn got a hard-on just talking about it. Christ, but it couldn't be the same place." He touched a meg tooth that he wore as a necklace on a gold chain.

I explained that the area was the bend of an ancient river and, presumably, draglines had created the ridge. "Below the ridge was what might have been a creek until it was drained by digging. I could tell by the tree line. Oaks, I think, grew along the bank."

"What color were the leaves?"

"I don't know . . . sort of reddish, I guess."

"Those were *swamp maples*," he corrected, but was getting into it. "Did you see any really big bones? What you thought were dugong could have been points off a mammoth rib. Or mastodon, but they're rarer."

I let him watch me think back. "Yeah . . . now that you mention it, maybe I missed something so damn obvious—"

"*What?*"

"Fossilized wood—that's what I assumed it was. Do you ever find petrified tree limbs?"

"Jesus Christ," he muttered. "Was there a lot of it?"

"I don't know. I kicked some aside. But, like I said, I'm new at this."

Mick's eyes, dulled by smoking cannabis all morning, sparked. He waited until Duncan had caught up, then went into lecture mode to hide his excitement. "It's a learning process. Me, I'm different. I was born with a gift and I thank God every day. Finn recognized it; used me as a tool, but also as a teacher. Old Man Finn's ego"—Mick's machete severed the top of a bush—"You would not believe what an asshole he could be. But Finn *knew*. The bones either speak to you or they don't, and there aren't many like me. Doesn't mean you can't learn. What I tell students is . . ."

While Mick lectured, I looked back at Dunk. His expression told me *Well played.*

Soon, Jet Skis: a two-cycle whine on the sudden musk of fresh water. The creek, framed by foliage, appeared: a slow-flowing stream, amber-glazed rocks, banks eroded naturally, but also in huge chunks that had been cut away by digging. Man spores, too: bottles, plastic, a flattened beer carton seeded in raw earth. This was no virgin spot. Pirate fossil mining had been done here.

The Jet Skis closer now, Mick said, "That's them." Then turned to Fallsdown and got serious while he lit his pipe. "The blood feud guy I mentioned, he's not coming. Finn hated him, and vice versa, so I wasn't surprised when he backed out. Instead, he's sending his grunts to get a feel for what you might have to offer. Stay cool, okay? I've never met the people he's sending."

Fallsdown, wearing jeans, long sleeves, and a red neckerchief, was sopped with sweat, not cool, but had no problem staying composed. "Why not keep it simple? I could meet the guy at a Starbucks instead of humping our asses through a mile of mosquitoes."

A quarter mile, more like it. Our rental car was parked off the road on a survey lane, Mick's truck behind us. I had left the car's doors unlocked—for a reason. I suspected we were being set up and had laid a trap of my own.

Mick asked, "You want the truth about why we're here?"

To me Dunk said, "The Fawnee brave has forgotten the Skin code of honor."

"Like I would lie to you," Mick laughed, striking another match. "Here's the deal: River bottoms are public land. It's illegal to collect artifacts from a place like this. The man—don't even ask his name—he needs something on you in case you turn against him. See? That's why his feud with Finn was never settled. They're both assholes and they both had enough to hang each other, so it would've been mutually . . . What was that Cold War term?"

Two Jets Skis skidded around the bend. Mick finished, but I wasn't listening. On the lead ski was Harris Sanford, the good-looking blond guy I had embarrassed in front of Owen by deep-sixing his rifle. Behind Harris was a man wearing a Harley vest, sleeveless, and a helmet with a tinted face shield. It wasn't Harris's beer-drinking buddy from Sunday. Too muscular.

The psycho biker, possibly.

Dunk was thinking the same thing. So was Mick, suddenly so nervous he dropped his pipe while his eyes focused on the guy. Finally, dismissive laughter, and he retrieved his pipe, saying, "Lighten up, boys. No steel hook, and he's not wearing gloves. The gang-banger I warned you about lost his left hand."

Dunk, unconvinced, replied, "Ski Mask, yeah. I remember he wore gloves. But the way he handled his weapon wasn't a guy with a hook."

Mick said, "Not a hook—pinchers on a cable, more like a crab," speaking in confidence from the side of his mouth while he waved at the Jet Skiers.

I was in the trees, watching, waiting, when a third Jet Ski appeared: a woman, a shorty wet suit protruding from her shorts, yellow neoprene, short dark hair, her body skinny enough to need warmth on this hot afternoon.

The woman and I made eye contact—her reaction was mild disapproval.

When Harris recognized me, a stronger reaction.

AFTER GLARING AT ME ONCE AGAIN, Harris said to Mick, "The more you talk, the less sense you make. Have we met?"

For emphasis, his helmeted partner revved the engine while his Jet Ski pissed an arc of water onto the opposite bank. The woman flanked them but stayed out of it. Mounted on the skis, I noticed, were coolers, supplies, and miniature cameras on the handlebars—waterproof GoPros.

Mick had greeted the trio by introducing himself, but Harris was playing dumb. So Mick tried again, saying, "Quit screwing around. I've been in the biz twenty-some years, mate. You're saying you never heard of me?"

The passenger seats of the vehicles were heavily loaded, equipment covered by tarps, but Harris replied, "Not a clue. We're just out for a nice ride."

"Get him on the phone," Mick responded. "He told me to be here."

"Buddy," Harris said, "I don't know what you're talking about." He looked at his partner; the helmeted man stiffening, alert for whatever came next.

I slipped past Mick, saying, "I'm the problem," and spoke to Harris: "Sorry about the other day. I didn't know you and Owen are friends. No hard feelings?"

Over the aggressive thrum of an engine, Mick, who was confused, asked, "You know each other?" Then said to Harris, "This guy's cool—a newbie. Dude, if the man didn't trust me, we wouldn't be here. So let's break out the tools and bag some bones." When he added, "I'll personally vouch for this guy," I made a mental note to thank Tomlinson for his advice.

Harris dropped the act. "Sure, I've heard of you—you're the stoner who hustles tourists, seeds beaches with throwaway meg teeth." He motioned toward me. "What? You think that asshole's just another one of your Buckeye fossil hounds?"

Mick's smile vanished. He looked at me, and took a step to distance himself. "What about him?"

Harris said, "As long as a tourist has money, huh? You didn't bother to check the guy out, did you?"

"Well . . . but I asked around. Right from the start, that's what I suspected. Is that it—he's a cop?" Mick moved another step away.

I thanked my own good judgment when Harris said, "He's a state-licensed biologist, you dipshit. The owner of Mammoth Ridge Mines hired him to write a report on their property. I don't know why you guys are here or what you're expecting . . . Christ. But the man you mentioned—whoever that is—he'll think you're a goddamn idiot."

Harris, who had already appraised Fallsdown, included him, finally saying, "Tough luck, chief." Then signaled his partners to follow, and the Jet Skis screamed away.

Mick watched, saying, "Flaming asshole!" then turned to me. "*Harris*—is that what you called him? I wasn't even told the guy's name . . . as if I give a damn now."

The truth added to my credibility, so I explained how Harris and I had met but played down the heroics. "Maybe it was a pellet rifle, but it sounded louder," I said. "Guns, who knows? So I threw the damn thing as far as I could."

Dunk caught my attention to warn *Don't overdo it*, then he said to Mick, "All that really matters is I get my tribe's stone carvings back. This collector you're talking about, instead of jumping through his hoops, why not introduce us? Or at least tell me his name." To me he added, "They planned to video us taking fossils. You notice the cameras? I don't trust them already."

Mick was still festering over Harris's insults. "Ask any bone hunter in the South, they know my rep. What a prick that guy was."

"Duncan has a good point," I said.

"Preppy assholes," Mick said. "Finn was right, the man—this bigtime collector, supposedly—he hires know-it-alls, amateur punks. Did you hear how he talked to me? I'm booked every afternoon this week—fossil clients who pay top dollar. In one day, I could put my hands on bones those three clowns couldn't find in weeks. Even then, they'd screw it up." A detail popped into Mick's head. "Harris— what's his last name?"

"Sanford," I said. I was hoping to catch Mick off guard. I did.

Instead of showing surprise, though, Mick had to think back. "Sanford . . . Yeah, I've heard of them. There were some Sanfords involved with mining way back. Harris Sanford, huh? Makes sense—a spoiled rich brat whose daddy made a bundle off raping the land. But what was he doing on Mammoth Ridge property?"

"Harris and Albright's stepson were college buddies," I said. "That's why I apologized."

Mick accepted that. "Screw him. Passive resistance is part of yoga discipline, but I would've broken the sucker's nose if he'd said one more word." He crouched, as if sitting on a chair, palms out, then did a kung fu sort of thing with his hands. "It's not like you lied to me. A biologist. You were right up front about that. And so what?" His brain switched gears. "Hey . . . Since we're here, let's crunch some bones anyway. That's why you're paying me. And don't worry—I'm still willing to help out on that Mammoth Ridge project."

I said, "Thanks for being so understanding."

Fallsdown gave me another cautioning look and slipped between me and Mick.

That was okay. My mind was on an envelope I had left in the rental car, doors unlocked. I had studied a map and knew the closest boat ramp was five miles downriver. If someone robbed the car, I wanted to know where to intercept them. But Harris had come by Jet Ski. Skis didn't require a full ramp.

When I asked Mick about it, he said, "There're a couple of put-ins close to here that FWC cops hardly ever patrol. Why?"

I said, "Just curious," then told Dunk, "Stay here and spot for Mick. I forgot something."

Jogging, I returned to the car.

SEVENTEEN

OLDER MOTORCYCLES AT IDLE MAKE A RESPIRATORY RUMBLE, A SLEEPING dragon rhythm, almost stalling, then snorting when the carburetor revives itself with a gulp of air.

I knew our car was being robbed before I exited the trees.

I carried a stainless .32 caliber Seecamp—a miniature pistol, four inches long, but loaded with Hornady hollow-points, 60 grain. I slid the weapon into my front pocket and parted the bushes. One man, his butt in the air, was leaning into the backseat, where I had placed an envelope containing photos of the mastodon tusk. Not the magnified shots of the petroglyph, just wide-angle shots that showed forty pounds of black ivory.

The photos were bait—give the blood feud collector a reason to negotiate for the owl stones but not reason enough to murder me in my sleep.

The robber wore jeans, boots, a tattered black shirt, and a motorcycle helmet. But I couldn't see his arms until he stood, his back to me, an envelope in his bare right hand and an oversize glove on his left hand. I suspected who it was but knew for certain when he removed the helmet and turned to open the envelope in better light.

The Harley gangbanger wasn't as disfigured as I'd imagined. Asphalt had taken his left ear and scraped flesh from his skull, but surgeons had done a good job. They had pulled the skin together into a hairless sheen that showed only on his cheek and as a bald patch above the left temple. Scars that warranted a second look but not the instant horror, say, of third-degree burns.

Facial scarring, however, is not a reliable index of brain damage. Psychological scars are phantoms. An angry, legless man had recently proved it. Around the biker's neck was a tubular scarf—an emergency mask—which suggested his ego had yet to accept his injuries. I watched for a while before making a move.

The biker had lost teeth, too. With incisors of white resin, he snared the glove off to reveal two stainless hooks that were spring-operated pincers. He extended his arm, the pincers opened. The inside edge of one hook was sharp and he used it to slice the envelope. Then he closed the pincers by retracting his arm.

A shoulder harness, which I should have noticed, became visible beneath the shirt. The pincers were adjoined to his wrist by a quick-release socket of stainless steel. Like a rechargeable drill, maybe other tools could be attached.

I watched him go through the photos, biting his tongue as he concentrated. A bland, bony face, curly hair, and sharp, mean eyes. Not an athlete, but not much body fat either. A loser since birth, I decided, who had to do something to make a living.

I also decided, *What the hell.*

Walking toward the car, I spoke. "Can I help you?" It is a question commonly asked by robbery victims. Otherwise, the noise of the motorcycle would have cloaked my approach.

Or maybe not. The Harley gangbanger didn't lift his eyes from the photos when he said, "I was beginning to think you was just one more scared civilian. How long you been there?" Jaw damage caused him to speak from the side of his mouth; distinctive, like a hick farmer chewing a straw and discussing the weather.

"Long enough to call police," I answered.

"Go ahead. I'll tell my side, then listen while you explain about owning pictures of a stolen mastodon tusk. I want that shit back, by the way—the ivory—all of it." Head down, the pincers moved to the scarf and squared it over his nose before he looked at me.

"Sun cancer's a bitch," I said.

"Then you die," he answered, a smirking tone. He slid the envelope under his shirt, turned and faced me, a bandito sizing me up from behind a mask of red. It was a while before he spoke. "The way Deon talked, I expected some great big dude who was born-again hard. Them glasses—you remind me of a pharmacist I had to visit for personal reasons. I figured him for a dick smoker, not the type would leave a man offshore to drown. Did you?"

"Did I what?"

"You know, really do that? Deon, he said three or four miles from the beach, you left him out there to drown. Didn't even look back. That there were sharks everywhere, but you didn't give a shit."

Brain-damaged—a glassy look in the man's eyes; mean but not stupid. And he sounded eager to confirm the petty thief's story. Hopeful, even. I pictured him breaking Deon's ribs, kicking Deon while he was down, to extract the truth about a story he wanted to believe was true. Now the biker was asking me.

I stopped five paces away, a safe distance between us while I humored him. "I thought he'd shot two friends of mine. Turns out it was you with the pistol. Were you in the Army or Marines?"

"No kidding?"

"About Deon, you mean?"

"Come on, pard. *Tell.*"

"You really expect me to admit it?"

The biker made a cackling noise from behind the scarf. "Hell, man, you're safe with me. I love a good story. You ever watch that Mel Gibson flick about them Aztec Indians, the way they'd cut people's heads off? Which is cool if you've got a big audience, but not as cool as leaving a whining piece of shit out there to drown. That shows creativity on your part."

He used his good hand to make a beckoning motion: *Tell me the details, man.*

I said, "Let's put it this way: If I did something like that, it would've been less than two miles offshore. And I didn't see any sharks. But then went back for the guy when I found out he wasn't the shooter."

The biker said, "You *would've* left him, though." That hopeful tone again.

I said yes because he wanted to hear it.

Laughter; threw his head back and had to restraighten his mask. "That is so goddamn outlaw, man. Just left the dude. I figured the asshole made it up. Last Friday, right? Just before the old ladies saw you in that fancy boat, you and your hippie friend."

"The afternoon you showed up wearing a ski mask," I added, "but the house had already been robbed."

"Ski Mask?" He was a pretty good actor, the way he shrugged it off. "That don't compare with the way you handled your situation.

You in a hot rod boat; Deon so far offshore, he can't even see the damn beach." The biker coughed and cackled but showed some manners by touching the pincers to his mouth. "Okay . . . what about the sweatsuit part? Deon claims—"

I said, "Over a beer sometime, I'll tell you the whole story. Right now, I'm more interested in why you're robbing my car."

"Come on, I gotta know. Deon says the guy—you, I'm starting to believe—Deon says he's drowning, he's begging, but you look down and say, 'Dude, your choice, I can shoot you in the head—or lose the sweatsuit, maybe you'll make the beach.'" The biker sobered. "Did you really say that?"

A scene from a movie was running in his head, I realized. Brain-damaged. Or maybe he'd always been a man-child who saw Hollywood's stone-cold killers as heroes.

I was done playing along. "On the boat, I wasn't carrying a gun." I touched a hand to my pocket to indicate I was now. "How about we save the war stories for later?"

Snap. The biker's eyes changed. He extended his left arm to open the pincers and clacked the steel tines like teeth. "I ain't Deon, cowboy. I admire your style, but don't push your luck."

"Then let's talk about you," I said. "You threatened my friend on the phone but didn't show up Sunday night. Or tell me about the woman who died in the house fire."

"I did *what?*"

"Did you stick a rag in her mouth?"

I was fishing. He knew it but let the truth slip anyway. "Hell, man—now you're blaming me for some old woman who fell asleep smoking weed." His indignation was an admission—that's the way he'd done it, gotten Lillian to smoke something—but then dismissed it all, saying, "The hippie—yeah, I know who you mean.

Thompson . . . Tomlinson . . . something like that. The gas-rag-in-the-mouth thing really got to the ol' boy. About wet his panties."

The biker's snorting laughter caused something in me to snap. The temptation was to put him on the ground, tag him, bag him, then leave him for the vultures in some high, distant tree.

The biker sensed it, was spooked for an instant. But then fed off what I was feeling and piped it back at me. "Know why your hippie pal was so scared? 'Cause I love watching people's face light up. You can't fake love—*can you*, hoss?"

I had to take a slow breath. "I waited for you off Cayo Pelado until one. If you don't know how to run a boat, I'll be happy to give you a private lesson."

The biker enjoyed that, understood it was a threat. "And leave my ass offshore, I bet." He wagged his steel hooks at me—*Behave yourself, man*—and walked toward his motorcycle, saying, "Style! That's what I'm talkin' about." Then stopped, as if he'd left out a detail. "Oh . . . I meant to ask: What do you think of that elephant?"

The man's brain jumped around, but how did he know I had been to the Albright ranch? Or maybe he had heard the elephant's trumpeting. Either way, I wasn't going to buy into it. I said, "No idea what you mean."

"Really? You will, hoss, you will. Black ivory's worth a shitpotful. But blood ivory's worth more—even if it takes ten or twelve rounds in that big ugly bastard's head. What I'm asking is, do you have any good contacts in China?"

When I didn't respond, he laughed at what he read as my confusion, but, in fact, it was contempt.

"When you see Mick," he said, turning toward the Harley, "give him your phone number. We'll order some pitchers, just you and me. Be a honor to face a man with style, then see who walks away."

He was leaving? I didn't believe it. I palmed the pistol while he opened a saddlebag and stuffed the envelope inside; expected him to turn, a weapon in his hand. Instead, he donned glove and helmet, straddled the bike, and booted the kickstand free.

"*¡Vaya con dios!*"

He actually yelled that, riding away.

I memorized the license number and dialed my cop friend in Tallahassee. No answer, so I left a message saying I had information on a woman who had died in a house fire. Then added a description of the Harley.

TWO OF THE THREE JET SKIS HAD RETURNED, the woman in her yellow shorty neoprene standing with Fallsdown, Mick in the water, while the man who'd worn a helmet waded his ski toward the opposite bank.

"Shelly, meet Doc Ford," Fallsdown said, after he'd asked me in private, "Is everything okay?"

When I extended my hand, the woman ignored me by scowling at Mick, only his fins showing on the water's surface. So I said, "Are we keeping you from something?"

She didn't appreciate that. "How obvious does it have to be? I have only two weeks a year off. I was just telling your friend that I paid Harris in cash for this trip. Now he's gone off and left me with his assistant."

"I didn't know he was a guide," I said.

"Harris is the best. In April, we did the Myakka River—unbelievable. This is my third trip. But he has a thing about outsiders. So now, of course, he's too mad to work."

"Because of me," I said.

"I don't tolerate men with a temper," she warned, meaning Harris had told her about me splashing his rifle. Then she banished me by speaking only to Duncan, saying, "I've been looking forward to this dive since May, now I've got to share the water with three strangers. You seem like a nice guy, but we've got to be careful because of the idiotic laws when it comes to fossils."

"Only two divers, not three," Dunk replied, and managed to sound both wise and empathetic. "I'm not going in."

"Really?"

"Nope. I live in the Rockies, and Florida is a whole different deal. The water here isn't comfortable. It's . . . earth-colored, not clear like in the Rockies."

Earth-colored? My god, he was playing a role, the noble red Indian. I was tempted to explain to the woman *He can't swim*, but I had been dismissed from the conversation.

"That's thoughtful," Shelly said to him, "but not necessary. Why don't we buddy up?"

Arms folded, the man from Montana studied the river, which was an amber gel making a slow glide seaward. "I'll stay here as your spotter. Not far is a golf course. We passed it. There was a sign that warned about alligators."

The woman laughed. "You are so sweet. But that was Arcadia or Venice—thirty miles from here at least. Look, I was being bitchy. Sorry, or . . . Hey, are you worried about me?"

Fallsdown used his wise-old-Indian smile and said, "Women who travel alone are hard to come by. While you swim, I'll stand watch."

Oh brother. But it was working. Shelly excluded me by moving closer to Duncan so they could talk. Fine, I was all for it. Dunk liked what he saw in this thirtyish woman who was athletic, thin as a marathoner but attractive, a nice face framed by short brown hair, her shorty wet suit promising good things if Shelly unzipped it and stepped into the shower.

"I'll find a nice meg tooth for you," she told Duncan. "It's so rare to get a chance to dive a spot like this."

"That would be *perfect*," the man from Montana replied, then pointed. "Hey . . . look."

Mick, wearing a mask, was standing, water up to his chest. He spit the snorkel from his mouth and held up something long, black as a tree limb but curved delicately as a scythe. "Rib bone," he hollered to Fallsdown. "Mastodon or mammoth—this is in our blood, man. Didn't I say I heard the bones calling?"

Harris's partner, on his Jet Ski, shook his head, disgusted, then turned an ear skyward—Toby, a mile or more away, trumpeting again.

Dunk looked at me, his expression asking, *Wouldn't Tomlinson love the timing?*

But not Harris's partner, who'd heard elephants before. Toby, or the elephant rescue facility, both of them close enough. He had used ropes to secure the stern of his Jet Ski to the opposite bank and was just finishing. Downstream, chunks of earth had been gouged from the bank. Now I understood: Harris's group used the skis to dredge soil away and expose fossils buried beneath tree roots. The man's vehicle was tatted NASCAR-like, *Sea-Doo GTX*, a muscle machine propelled by impellers that jetted water with the force of a fire hose. I wondered how effective it was as a cutting tool.

Very effective. He started the engine . . . gunned the throttle while ropes strained . . . revved it higher, and soon, behind him, the riverbank began to melt away.

"Is this standard?" I asked Shelly over the noise.

"If you knew anything about rivers, you'd understand that banks erode—every year, it's a natural cycle. This just speeds up the process."

"That's a lot of silt for a creek this narrow," I replied. "Have you ever seen a toilet back up?"

Shelly didn't appreciate that. "Do you get some kind of weird kick out of ruining my day? If you don't like it, leave."

My pal, the noble redskin, played both sides by observing, "Rivers find their own path."

Geezus. I waited for Shelly to gather her mask, fins, and weight belt and leave before telling him, "You should contact the Actors Guild and get a card."

Fallsdown kept his eyes fixed on the woman. "I've been a member since *The Horse Whisperer.* What do you think of Shelly? I really like her legs and that cute little chin of hers."

"You've been in movies?"

"Redford believes I'm the hereditary medicine man of the Crow Nation. But three years in the joint knocked me off the A list. I like her body, but there's something not quite right about her . . . I don't know—her behavior, I guess. Something."

"She can't stand me. Or, are you asking if she's onto your act?"

Duncan said, "I give people what they want. Sometimes it makes them happy to play along. Besides, what makes you think I'm acting?"

"From your wise-old-Indian bullshit," I replied, which made him smile. I was about to tell him about my confrontation with the biker, but he suddenly got serious.

"I saw something out there, Doc."

I said, "On the other side? It was probably a feral hog."

"In the water. Big, too. It surfaced just before you got back." His eyes left the woman long enough to explore downstream. "Fifty meters or so, but it could have been a log, I guess. It came up, then went under."

"What color?"

"Blackish . . . dark green, maybe. Too big for a fish. Or maybe not."

Because of the Jet Ski's dredging, the creek was beginning to boil with vegetation and silt, the surface brown as coffee, while, upstream, the water maintained its rum clarity. I said, "Some of those pools look deep enough, it could have been an alligator gar. They get to three hundred pounds. Lots of teeth, but they're harmless. Or even a manatee. Are you really worried?"

Duncan said, "It looked more like a damn snake. Sort of humped its back when it went under."

I took off my glasses; checked on Mick, who had deposited the mastodon rib on the bank and was diving again. Shelly, adjusting her mask, was shuffling backward, water to her waist. The Jet Ski's scream mimicked a chain saw. The noise added chaos and a sense of danger. No point in mentioning Florida's problem with exotic snakes—ball pythons and other constrictors, some twenty feet long, even waterborne anacondas.

Duncan asked, "Are there alligators this far north?"

He missed the irony when I replied, "Only the ones that survive." I took the little pistol from my pocket, tilted it to show a round in the chamber, and handed it to him. "Keep a watch behind us, too. The psycho biker made an appearance."

Dunk understood. "Did he find the photos?"

"He took them. Mick set us up."

"Are you sure?"

I said, "I'm not worried about it. Whoever's in charge knows we have the tusk. Or soon will. He'll keep his people on a leash until we make the trade."

Fallsdown, folding his arms again, said, "If Mick makes the owl stones angry, the Little People will tear him a new asshole. Or I will."

I smiled. "Hollywood is missing an angel," I told him, then got in the water.

EIGHTEEN

UNTIL A SNAKE GOT ITS MOUTH AROUND MICK'S WRIST, THE MAGIC TOUR GUIDE was at his ingratiating best. An overeagerness to please is a red flag, but neither his yoga training nor twenty years dealing with tourists had taught him the first tenet of infiltration: Only whores and amateurs tumble eagerly.

Mick started on the wrong foot at first by instructing Shelly on breath control. "Slow down. How much lead you wearing? Doesn't matter 'cause in a wet suit it's never enough. So what you do is . . . *Here.*" He handed her a chunk of rock. "Use this as an anchor. And never search an area any wider than your shoulders. One square foot at a time, then move another foot or two."

Irritated, Shelly told him, "This is *so* not my first fossil dive—back off." A slap with a mall girl sting that didn't connect when she followed Mick's advice, then surfaced with a megalodon tooth bigger than her hand. She whooped and called, "Alfie! See this? *Alfie!* The best spot ever!"

Alfie—the man sitting aboard the Sea-Doo GTX—looked only slightly less bored when he responded, "Need your dive bag?"

Even Alfie began to soften when Mick helped him re-anchor the ski at a fresh spot downstream and said, "That virgin bottom belongs to you and Shelly, man." Meaning he would dredge new territory while Alfie put on a mask and had first pick of the fossils he had sluiced free.

Mick did it, too: revved the engine with the abandon of his psycho Harley associate while the GTX bucked and strained against its ropes. The magic tour guide was no stranger to bone hunting.

I swam upriver, no longer concerned about what Fallsdown had seen. It was that damn Jet Ski. Noise is an effective weapon. Noise is to the twenty-first century what cigarette smoke was three decades ago—a menace to all, including the minority of abusers. I've yet to meet an angler who didn't dread the sound of Jet Skis. I'm no different.

In the river's deep pools, though, was refuge. Mick had been right about buoyance even in this mild current. I'd brought a belt strapped with twenty pounds of lead, but it wasn't enough to keep me on the bottom. So, after rationalizing I would have done it anyway, I found a chunk of limestone and banged my way along the bottom. It was like floating over Mammoth Ridge as seen through an amber filter: stubs of black bone, petrified oysters, globs of ancient dung that had been compressed into rock, and shark teeth everywhere. A shark produces thirty-five thousand teeth in its lifetime, and megalodons had thrived in Florida's inland sea.

The fossil fever I had faked became a mild reality—out of character, so I imposed a limit of only two prime specimens to take home. Three meg teeth later, I increased the limit to six, but then dumped all but one tooth to prove I'm a choosy hypocrite.

Fifty yards from the other divers, the creek narrowed, then widened into a switchback, a cove that was shaded by oaks and Spanish moss. The drop-off beneath the bank was deeper than expected. I was making my third dive when the ski went silent. Soon Mick swam up beside me.

"Mate, you've got a good eye for water," he said. "In the shallows, the shit we find has been banged around by the current. A spot like this could be the real deal. Not just because it's deep. Understand why?"

Maybe. Florida sits on a volcanic base that connects Florida with Africa. Piled on that is limestone three miles thick, which is covered by a veneer of soil and foliage. Occasionally, an underground river surfaces through the limestone: a spring or bottomless lake.

Mick explained it differently. "Some river switchbacks are prehistoric watering holes. Ever see documentaries on Africa? A place where animals and the first people came to drink. Rare, but they exist. Finn called places like that time tunnels. You know, tunnels that lead down, not up into space."

The tour guide was a good diver, I had to give him that. Careful with his fins rather than screwing up visibility. The spot had hard bottom. It wasn't an archaic well, but Mick surfaced with a crocodile jawbone . . . No, from a whale with a crocodilian head, he decided, when we waded to the shallows. "See how this tooth's triangulated? Six prongs—a yoke tooth, it's called. What'd you find?"

What I had *seen* was a flint or chert spearhead lying near a fossil that resembled a loaf of sliced bread and was just as large. It took willpower to leave the spearhead untouched, but seemed okay to have a look at the fossil.

"This is from a mammoth," Mick said, holding the thing in both hands. "A grinding tooth. Has a higher crown than a mastodon.

Nice find, mate." He offered it to me, and I could see him thinking: *The guy's an undercover cop if he doesn't take it.*

I dropped the fossil into my net dive bag, which was clipped to my belt.

"Only one meg tooth?" he asked, seeing the bag.

"This damn mask," I said. "The eye doctor changed my prescription. Everything else I found was either chipped or I didn't know what the hell it was."

Mick wasn't sure he believed me but moved on to what he really wanted to talk about. "Are you serious about that mining property? I'm booked every afternoon this week, but we could go mornings—or at night. I like night diving."

I said, "I'll call Albright when I get home. But I won't mention you. If someone sees us on his property, then I'll explain."

"As your consultant," he said.

"Sure. How about this week?" I replied—ingratiate myself to the ingratiating tour guide and Mick might reveal the name of the collector who was paying him.

"Tomorrow morning's good," he said. "Bring dive gear—tanks if you have them."

I wasn't expecting that. "If you're thinking of the creek I told you about, it's dry. I didn't say that?"

We were standing near a bank walled with deadfall and palmettos; moss, green on rotting logs, moss-draping shadows in the trees. Mick took a look downstream to confirm the others couldn't see us. As he did, the Jet Ski started and began dredging again, but farther away. He removed one fin, then the other, and felt it was safe to speak in a normal tone. "Finn used to hunt the Mammoth Ridge property. I don't know what happened, some sort of trouble, but he wasn't allowed back—this was before my time. One of the quarries there he claimed was the real deal. A watering hole before the drag-lines got in."

"A prehistoric watering hole," I said. "That had to be twenty years ago if the mine was still operational."

"It was. There were security guards, so Finn had to be careful when he dug there—always at night even before the trouble happened. For some reason, he stopped doing that, too. Which never made sense if the place was as hot as he claimed."

I was thinking, *Maybe Finn Tovar killed the night watchman*, so nudged Mick along. "What do you mean 'hot'?"

"Incredibly rich, man. Mammoth and mastodon ivory. At Finn's house, I was going to show you and Dunk this tusk he found there. Has to weigh fifty pounds."

Actually, forty pounds, but should I admit it? No . . . If the blood feud collector was smart, he would dismiss the tour guide as a bad risk. Mick would never hear about the photos the biker had just taken. I said, "Wouldn't you love to find a spot like that?"

A dreamy stoner smile as he replied, "Whoa—black ivory worth half a mil—probably more these days. And Finn found a bunch of it. You didn't wonder how he could afford a beach house?"

"Half a million dollars, huh?" I said, then played dumb by mentioning the stolen tusk I had read about, the one that had been insured. He didn't let me finish.

"You don't have to tell me—it had like this simple thatch sort of decoration. Mate, what you've got to understand is there's not an important find I don't know about. Finn's tusk, the one I wanted to show you, fifty pounds of mastodon ivory—if it had been worked by Paleo man?" His wagging eyebrows read *Name your own price*.

To me, that suggested Finn hadn't noticed the saber cat petroglyph. He would have bragged about it to his favorite pupil. I said,

"You just convinced me," then hesitated, as if thinking it through. "But wait—it's been a long time since Tovar dived Mammoth Ridge. It could be cleaned out by now. I'd be risking my job."

"You saw the lake?"

"*Three* lakes. They all looked man-made. I wouldn't know where to start."

Mick's expression read *I do*, but he said, "I mentioned Africa? There are these watering holes where elephants go to die. Some think that's a fairy tale, but Finn was smarter than any three men with diplomas. Think about it." He pointed a finger at the massive tooth in my bag. "There's your proof. A mammoth or mastodon gets old, he loses his teeth. Same with elephants. What's an elephant going to do when he's dying and can't chew? He's gonna find a spot with water and the easiest food. It's not about being some mystic sacred spot where elephants go to die—although I have my own thoughts about that. They draglined a time tunnel at Mammoth Ridge, that's the only explanation. Know what Finn called the place? It was a deep spot in one of the quarries. He called it the Ivory Pot."

I wasn't going to let myself tumble easily. "It's been twenty years," I said again. "I might lose my contract if Leland Albright finds out."

Mick waved the name away as if unimportant. "He's totally out of touch. Let me tell you something." His voice became confidential. "A buddy of mine's screwing Albright's wife *and* his daughter. What do you think of him now? And his son's a gambling junkie— Albright doesn't know about that either. Or maybe I'm thinking about the stepson, the one who showed you around the Mammoth property. Mate, no offense, but you're such a straight-acting dude, an old man like Leland Albright, he'll believe whatever you tell him."

I remembered Owen saying *Gambling is for losers* in a way that had the flavor of a mantra. Maybe it was true: Owen was a gambling addict. The gymnast yogi instructor was Mick's informant, as I already knew, but it was still necessary to ask, "Who told you this?"

"I've got my sources, man."

"I hope you're right. My only fallback is a job for someone named Mondurant. It would pay a lot less than Albright. You ever hear of the guy?"

Mondurant the name got no reaction, just Mick's impatience. "Twenty years, that's how long I've been in this business. Stop worrying."

"Yeah, so we dive and find nothing but get caught. Then what?"

Mick, getting excited, said, "Not if we find the Ivory Pot. I'm the only one Finn told about it, and what's down there is worth a . . ." He took a breath to calm himself and started over. "Let me explain how the business works. Most quality ivory comes from Russia, up near the Arctic Circle where it's still frozen. That's why it's in prime condition. Florida's different. Word would have gotten out if there'd been a major find in Florida. It hasn't happened, man. I'm an expert—you either trust me or you don't."

I said, "It's tempting."

Mick sensed I was weakening. "Look . . . there's not a bone hunter in the world who wouldn't give his left nut to dive those lakes on Mammoth Ridge. Me included. You've got the magic ticket, man. Don't blow it, okay?"

I wrestled with the decision but didn't overdo it. "Under one condition. Fallsdown's a nice guy and all, but I want him out of my hair."

"What?" The tour guide tried to sound indignant. "Dunk and me are brothers, man. I thought you were his friend."

I said, "Then put him in touch with your boss. Or tell me the man's name. Dunk can't even swim, for christ's sake, so it's better to let him and the collector make their own deal."

Mick, for once, didn't tumble easily. "Can't do that, mate. Not because of Dunk—business is business. But it's like the drug biz, man. We never share names."

I held up my dive bag. "If your boss wants incriminating video, I can hand Dunk this. I understand needing leverage, but, look, I'm not going to risk my job and then split three ways."

The tour guide's opinion of me changed. "Goddamn, Ford, that's nasty. You've got the makings of a real bone hunter, I'll say that."

"It's a win-win," I said. "Duncan gets his sacred carving, or whatever it is, and I get to learn from an expert. Think about it."

The tour guide did while he stroked his chin. My back was to the trees. He faced me. He started to debate the pros and cons, but then his eyes vectored in on something beyond my shoulder. He grinned. "Damn right, I'm the expert," he said. "Turn around and tell me what you see. The bones, they speak to me, man."

Protruding from the bank, amid vines and rotting wood, was the nub of something that resembled a stick of charcoal. A bone of some type. And Mick was right: I would have never noticed.

As he sloshed past me, I told him, "Watch out for poison ivy."

The man laughed to remind me *You're in my dojo now*, and was still grinning when he got to the bank. "Another mastodon rib. What'll you bet?" and then he looked at me while he hunkered down and reached for the bone.

Only I saw what happened next. A chunk of rotting wood came to life near his wrist . . . a sudden coiling of scales that struck, mouth wide, while I hollered, *"Snake!"*

Too late. Rows of needle teeth had already locked into Mick's flesh.

Mick yelped and yanked his arm away, extracting a five-foot reptile from the vines; the snake in kill mode, biting harder, or its teeth had snagged in Mick's wrist. He made a gagging sound and spun with such force that he launched himself backward, and the snake ripped free, spinning boomerang-like toward me.

Slow motion, it seemed—even my poor vision discerned dung-colored scales, the pale latticed underbelly, and one round black eye as the reptile revolved at speed toward my face. Still wearing fins, I could only fall sideways.

I felt a whip-stinging weight hit my shoulder as I went down.

NINETEEN

"COTTONMOUTH!" MICK YELLED THE WORD OVER AND OVER. *"GODDAMN SNAKE* bit me!" He was applying pressure with his left hand, blood dripping from his fingers.

Downriver, the Jet Ski made an indifferent whine. From the trees came the sound of a big man crushing branches—Duncan Fallsdown on his way to the rescue.

I was more interested in the snake. Where was it? I rinsed my prescription mask and put it on.

The snake surfaced. I backed a step. Cottonmouth moccasins can strike underwater or atop it. This snake fled, though, and I watched it carving giant *S*'s on the surface as it traveled a straight line toward the bank.

"I need some help here, man!" Mick, going into shock, appeared pale.

"Hang on," I said. I removed my fins and started toward him while still watching the snake.

I'm no herpetologist, but it's dumb to live in Florida without knowing the basics. Cottonmouth moccasins—which are pit vipers, although seldom aggressive—swim with their heads high out of the water. Very high, a forty-degree angle or more. As a warning, they often open their mouths wide before striking—a white telltale bloom I would have noticed before it struck. No guarantees about that, however, which is why I paid attention.

Common water snakes swim and behave differently. They can be surly, aggressive animals that bite, and keep biting until they decide you're too big to eat. Nonvenomous but lots of teeth. Unlike cottonmouths, they swim low in the water with their head level to or on the surface.

I watched the snake exit onto the bank. That told me what I wanted to know and I decided to take advantage of the situation. Taking Mick's arm, I asked him, "Is the bite throbbing? Do you feel a burning sensation?"

"*Yeah* . . . goddamn hurts, man! Where the hell did he come from?"

People in shock are easily manipulated. I said, "How about nausea? That's usually a first symptom."

"Oh man . . . I feel like shit."

"You'll probably have to vomit soon," I said—a subliminal nudge.

A minute later, Mick groaned, leaned over the water, and coughed until he did vomit.

Fallsdown appeared from the trees, caught his foot on something, and stumbled down the bank. It gave me the chance to help him up while I whispered, "Just a water snake—play along."

His eyes posed a question: *Are you sure?*

My eyes locked into his and I nodded but said loud enough for Mick to hear, "A cottonmouth bit him, I think."

Fallsdown was a quick study. "Holy Christ!" he responded. "Are they bad as a rattler?"

"A big one," I said, "so maybe worse, but it could be a dry bite. I haven't checked yet."

Mick made a sobbing sound. "Goddamn cottonmouth bastard!" and he allowed me to take his wrist while he instructed Duncan, "Call nine-one-one—I'm hurt bad, brother."

Duncan patted his pockets, then asked me, "Doc, where's your phone?"

I was studying the wound. Blood dripped. I used my T-shirt several times. Water snakes have curved teeth that are short but sharp as needles. They angle toward their throat, which is why the snake couldn't let go. The underside of Mick's wrist was perforated. The teeth had gouged two wide, convincing holes.

"Fangs got him near a vein," I said, then asked Mick, "Do you have a weird taste in your mouth? You're probably starting to feel dizzy."

He spit and licked his lips. "Shit yeah, like I'm gonna pass out." He looked downriver and hollered, "Call for a medevac!" then muttered, "Goddamn Jet Ski," because he knew that Shelly and Alfie couldn't hear.

I asked Duncan, "What do Indians do for snakebite?"

The man's blank expression requested guidance, so I added, "The suction method and ice don't work. Is there something traditional we can try?"

"Poultice," he answered immediately, assuming the role of a Crow medicine man. "Sit him down. Let the river clean the wound while I grab some moss."

Mick yanked his arm away from me. "Moss? Are you out of your mind? I need a fuckin' doctor!" Then screamed for a medevac again before stumbling toward shore, where he'd left his fins. He intended to swim for help.

Fallsdown wrapped his arm around the man. "Whoa . . . calm yourself. Doc? Help him sit, and wash it out good. We'll do this the old way."

"My arm's gonna turn black, you idiot," Mick shot back. "I could die—call nine-one-one."

Duncan took Mick's face between his hands to make him focus. "Until help gets here, you need to trust me. Do what I say. Take a big, slow breath, then let it out."

The tour guide tried to wrestle away, but Duncan held him in a bear hug and made him do it. Stood there looking into Mick's face while Mick took several deep breaths—no theatrics about Falls-down's concern—then helped him sit, Mick resigned and calmer while shock settled in.

I took over while Dunk scrambled up the bank and disappeared. I checked Mick's pulse, then, against my better judgment, washed the wound in the river because I'd been told to do it. I don't find humor in scaring people, but if it won the tour guide's trust, or caused him to feel indebted, the ploy was worth a try. Mick had set us up, after all, to be robbed by a brain-damaged biker.

One thing for certain: The tour guide was scared. He went on a talking jag, hyperventilating again and speaking way too fast.

"A medevac chopper, mate . . . I've got to get to a hospital . . . Shit, can't believe this is happening."

I tried to calm him, but he wouldn't shut up.

"On Discovery Channel, I watched a whole thing on snakebites. My arm . . . it's gonna swell up and turn black because it's, like, *rotting*, man. And . . . they'll have to cut my arm off before the venom gets to my heart. Then I'm really screwed—but only if I don't die first." He almost chuckled at that, but panic returned. On impulse, he sucked at the fang marks and spit. Did it three times, then looked at me, eyes wide. "Oh my god. Why'd you ask me about a funny taste?"

We all know the taste of blood. Mick had just set himself up. I replied, "*Metallic*, is how some of the victims describe it. Or *minty*. It's one of the symptoms in the literature about pit vipers."

He groaned, his face chalky, and tasted his lips. "Metallic . . . oh god. That sonuvabitch really got me good."

It gave me an opening to ask about the psycho biker, who already had a hand missing, but I resisted and let him ramble on about losing an arm, and necrotizing flesh, then he got back to snakes, groaning, "Damn . . . I've seen a million cottonmouths. Had my head up my ass as usual. Showing off to impress you . . . Man, why am I such a loser sometimes?" That sobbing sound again.

I felt a wisp of guilt, so told him, "We all think we're losers occasionally," then stood because Dunk had returned. He had a glob of moss in one hand, a bouquet of tiny purple flowers and what looked like miniature carrots in the other.

I didn't like the way this was going. There are too many dangerous plants and flowers in the Sunshine State. I'm familiar with only the most common—lantana, manchineel, a few others. The man from Montana was about to risk actually poisoning a guy who, at the worst, might suffer an infection.

"Don't get carried away," I whispered when I intercepted him.

"Arrowleaf violets and snakeroot," Fallsdown responded, and held up the flowers for me to see. "How's our patient doing?"

"He'll be fine if you don't kill him with that crap."

"Not a chance," he confided. "In prison, the books on ethnobotany were in the herbs and spices section." Which sounded like a joke until he added, "Except for the moss, the same plants grow in the Rockies." Then gave me a *Can't hurt* shrug and went to Mick without waiting for my okay.

I watched Duncan sniff the wound, then say, "Let me smell your breath."

Mick exhaled. "Metallic, huh?"

"Good weed, more like it," was the reply. "I think my Fawnee brother has gone and pissed off the Little People."

"The *what* people?" Mick sounded weaker but compliant.

Fallsdown turned to me. "Doc—hike back and call an ambulance. Just in case, okay?"

Twice, I checked over my shoulder for a secret signal to cancel the call, but the Crow or Apache medicine man was busy chanting. Using the moss, too. He had Mick's wrists clamped between his hands.

The last time I looked, Mick was chewing something. He also began to chant.

AN HOUR LATER, by phone, Tomlinson asked me, "Why did the crazy biker threaten to kill the elephant?"

I hadn't yet mentioned what the biker had said about how Lillian had died. Instead, I was listening to Tomlinson tell me about his afternoon with Ava Albright, but a faint trumpeting had nudged us off topic.

I said, "I'm not sure, but the biker's mean enough to kill animals just for fun. You're right, I think he was the guy wearing the ski mask."

I was in the rental car, air on low, while Dunk, Mick, and Shelly stood in the heat watching the ambulance pull away. Mick, a bandage on his arm, waved. He had declined a ride to the hospital, said he felt fine . . . no, had said he felt *reborn*, which had caused the EMTs to roll their eyes. After checking vital signs and treating the wound, the medics hadn't pressed the issue beyond what protocol obligated them to tell their semi-stoned patient, who didn't appear to be in danger.

Now some color had returned to Mick's face, but he still looked shaken when he turned and followed the others from asphalt into shade. Dunk conversed with Shelly—no surprise—but Shelly was more attentive to Mick, the fossil savant, who had recently been wounded in battle. Her motive was obvious: Mick was her key to fossil greatness.

That morning, I had packed sliced mangoes and grilled fish in a cooler. The cooler was open on the seat beside me. I took a bite of a snapper-mango sandwich, and told Tomlinson, "I wish you could see this. The great Chief Fallsdown is hitting on the woman I mentioned, but she's more interested in your stoner buddy. Ask Dunk about Shelly when we get back."

"No thanks," Tomlinson said. "Not after five hours with Ava. I've had it up to here with women. She pulled her swimming pool act again."

"I warned you," I said.

"You would have been very proud."

"I bet. What did you find out?"

"That there are too many Avas in this world and not enough Lillians." Tomlinson had sounded upbeat until he said that, but then rallied, asking, "After seeing Ava in the flesh, you mean? I found out I'm still a breast man, God help me. Last year, it was noses and dimples. But I'm not hung up on the consistency thing."

I said, "That's not what I meant."

"I know. My friends in Venice still haven't heard anything about how Lillian died. You should warn Leland about the biker. Did he threaten to kill the elephant for his tusks? Or was it more an extortion thing?"

From Tomlinson's phone, in the background, a bell tinkled; a child's voice spoke of hating papaya. I asked, "Where are you?"

"Just leaving a juice bar, downtown Sarasota near the bookstore. Mack wouldn't loan me his Lincoln, so I now have to wait for my radiator to cool."

I wasn't surprised to hear that his van had broken down.

He added, "It'll be hard to say good-bye to the ol' Magic Bus, but I think it's time for new wheels. I'm considering an almost cherry GTO."

Tomlinson's VW van, with its "Deluxe Swiss Alps Touring package"—a fridge and an automatic pop top—didn't fare well in hot weather. The Electric Kool-Aid Love Machine, as it was also known on the islands. I suggested, "Try something from the current century," then asked about Ava again.

"She and I had an interesting talk once she finally put on some clothes. That's why I wouldn't feel right about calling Leland. I'd be forced to lie."

I asked, "Since when has force been required?"

"Sure, go ahead, make jokes, but Ava is nothing to joke about. She wants two things from me. One is to convince the twins their father should cash in on the mine."

I asked him to repeat that before remarking, "That's a switch."

"Not really. Ava has been manipulating the daughters all along. That's what I think, anyway, which wouldn't be that hard."

"Esther and . . . What's the other one's name?"

"Tricia and Esther. Esther is more levelheaded, but they are identical twins. They're the kind of girls who think they can save the earth by cutting back on air freshener and donating to PETA. Smart, but they're not devious, so they still buy Ava's act—but not enough to manipulate their vote. Ava's counting on me, just like Leland's counting on you to write a rosy report about the water quality."

"Squeeze play," I said.

"Ava did her damnedest to score, that's for sure. When I didn't hop in the pool, she had a backup plan all ready—a yoga mind-link thing that involved a blindfold and touching hands. Talk about God's little morality tests. It's a way of swapping polarities, she said, but then pretended to see images projected from my hara. Take a guess at what she saw."

"Projected from your navel?" I asked.

"Close enough. She claimed to see stolen Spanish coins and the other stuff in the duffel bag. Didn't come right out and say what they were. It was more like one of those old-time séances. She stumbled around, describing the mammoth tusk, and I was tempted to say, *Yes, yes! That's the gigantic dildo on my boat.*" He made a snorting, laughing sound. "But nothing about the saber cat glyph, Doc. I dreamt about that carving last night."

I said, "Ava knows you're a sucker for metaphysics. That's the angle she's taking."

"Of course. She sized me up at the drum ceremony. But also because of my book—which the twins love, by the way. Tricia and Esther can both quote whole passages verbatim. Or so they claim. How would I know?"

Tomlinson's *One Fathom Above Sea Level*, written between shock treatments and hallucinogenics, was still paying him royalties, plus perks in the form of female groupies.

I watched Duncan, Mick, and Shelly file into the trees, returning Shelly to the river and her Jet Ski, while Tomlinson told me more about his yoga mind-link experience. I could picture him and Ava near the pool, sitting in an air-conditioned gazebo with yoga mats and candles to cover the smell of marijuana. Ava wearing a flimsy beach dress over a bikini while Tomlinson, blindfolded, played along by clinging to the last thread of what, in him, passes as morality.

"With Ava, it's not just about sex. It's about assembling Ava addicts to do her heavy lifting," he said. "The yoga stud, Enrique—Ricky, she calls him—he's on the team, but I'm no longer convinced they're a pair. Just the opposite. She doesn't give a damn about Ricky. A woman like Ava would go after a real power player. I think there's someone else."

He knew about the other landowners—the Sanford family and the Moroccan—and I asked if he had slipped their names into the conversation.

Tomlinson said, "Of course. Monty Mondurant has been in magazines, so he would be her obvious choice. Ava lit up when I mentioned him, but only because she was hoping for an introduction. Because of my book, she thought I might know the bad boy neighbor she's read so much about. The stepson steered you wrong there, Doc. Monty never comes near Central Florida. It's just raw property his family owns."

In my head, I replayed Owen talking about the starlet-loving Moroccan. *Burn, Monty, burn* was from the Internet, but Owen's contempt had had a personal edge. Maybe I had been right: Owen had offered me Monty as a red herring.

I said, "Ava could be a better actress than you think."

Tomlinson asked, "How much power does the stepson have?"

"None that I know of. Did Ava mention him?"

"*Owen*—that's his name? She said he was trying to straighten himself out, that's all. Not enough to activate my censors. I'd bet I'm right about Monty. She'd love to meet the guy. From what she said, the head of the Sanford family is an attorney in his seventies. Too old for her, I think."

"Harris Sanford isn't," I said. "He's another possibility. But don't count the yoga instructor out yet."

"That's why I'm going to overnight in the van," Tomlinson said. "There's a twenty-four-hour Walmart not far from Hooters I've got my eye on. I'm meeting Ava for Ricky's power yoga class in the morning. Later, the twins want to have drinks by the pool."

As he spoke, Duncan appeared in the side mirror with his new best friend, Mick, who had the keys to his truck in hand.

I warned Tomlinson about solo riders on a Harley, then added, "With any luck, Dunk and I will meet a major player tonight. But first, we're going to check on the elephant—if Leland will give me the combination."

TOBY WAS GRAZING in a grove of stunted citrus near the pond that, to Mick, was more interesting than an elephant standing a hundred yards away. He walked down to get a closer look through the electric fence that separated him from the water and Toby.

I thought, *He never stops hunting.* Mick's life combined fairy tales with addiction—the search for time tunnels, or what Finn Tovar had called the *Ivory Pot*, which was a lake, not a three-acre pond, that Mick was studying.

Duncan waited until we were alone to tell me, "I had a talk with Mick on the drive over." He had ridden with the magic tour guide. I had driven the rental.

"Did he open up?"

"Turns out that Mick's only contact is the biker. Quirk or Quark's his name. He doesn't know the actual collector—he lied to us about that. We only had a couple minutes, so maybe I'll find out more later."

I said, "Mick didn't react when I mentioned the Sanford family or the other property owner's name. What happened to his blood feud story?"

"That part's true. Tovar had a feud going with almost every collector in the state—including Leland Albright's father. That doesn't mean his father was a collector. All the mining tycoons hated Tovar."

"Mick's a con man, we knew that going in," I said, then asked, "The psycho biker's name is Quirk?"

"Maybe Quark. He's not a bad guy—Mick, I mean. When you left to call the ambulance, he admitted he's Irish with some Italian, not a Skin. But he's a believer now."

"A believer in what?"

"You wouldn't be interested. It was a ceremony I did back at the river."

I said, "Good thing it wasn't a real cottonmouth."

Dunk raised his eyebrows. "You're positive it wasn't? The bite had a weird smell." He sniffed, as if remembering, and said, "Musky— even worse than that damn elephant." He looked across the pasture, where, a hundred yards away, Toby grazed and used his ears to swat flies.

I smiled until I realized the man from Montana wasn't smiling— part of his medicine man routine, but I couldn't be sure. He was watching Mick get as close as he dared to the electric fence, then cup hands around his eyes, Indian style, to block the late-afternoon sun.

Dunk asked, "What's he looking at?"

A big chunk of inland Florida is what I'd been looking at: cypress trees on knobby muscled trunks, limbs moss-heavy, shading the pond. An abandoned barn on the other side of the pond and hump-backed cattle grazing on a far ridge. Then a wheat-tan savannah that tied a mile of blue sky to trees in the distance, and white birds feeding. It could have been Africa. Only a CBS storage building inside the fence interrupted the vista. A large building with green steel doors and a double garage.

Our tour guide, though, was focused on something else, because he stood and stiffened like a pointer, then waved us over. Not frantic, but serious.

When we got to him, he asked, "Is that a big tree stump or a pot?" He pointed toward the abandoned barn.

"A pot?" Fallsdown asked.

"For boiling things; a cauldron, you know, like witches use." Mick strained to see what I'd thought was a tractor tire or a barrel near the barn. Hard to make out from a distance because, in late-afternoon sunlight, the object lay among weeds in eastern shadows. He said, "I'd swear that's not wood." Then, getting excited, he reached for his pipe and matches. "If that's not a tree stump . . . Jesus Christ, guys . . . this could be the place."

Dunk spoke to me, asking, "What's he talking about?"

I had a guess but waited.

Mick said, "I need to get closer," and hurried along the fence, as if that would help.

It didn't. The fence consisted of four parallel cables strung post to post on yellow insulators, but spaced far apart, ten feet high. The cables were coated with white synthetic for visibility, plus orange caution signs that warned *Danger.*

It was an electric fence that was solar-powered; high voltage but low amperage, Owen had explained, so it wasn't lethal yet would still zap Toby—or anyone else—with a hell of a shock. At the gate, which was chained with a combination lock, there was a dedicated breaker switch.

Mick began to pace, his eyes fixed on whatever it was he thought he saw. "What would happen if I tried to step through the fence?" he asked. Then changed his mind because of the sizzling sound the cables made. "Or I could pull my truck up, stand on the bed, and jump over."

"How would you get out?" Dunk asked.

Mick said, "Damn it," then looked to me. "You could make up a story and ask Mr. Albright for the combination to the gate."

I had called Leland from the car about the gangbanger's threat to shoot his elephant. The property manager was in poor health, Leland had told me, so he'd been happy to give me the code to the front entrance a quarter mile away. Asking to enter a pasture with a ten-thousand-pound elephant, though, might be a different story. On the other hand, I had been here before. I had seen Owen look under a solar panel before opening the gate—a new lock, he had said—so maybe someone had written the combination on the post.

Duncan asked Mick, "Why's it so damn important to get in there? That elephant sees us. Elephants kill people. I've seen it on the news."

Toby had wandered closer. He was snatching wild sugarcane out by the roots and looping it into his mouth after tiring of guavas among bare citrus trees. Castrated or not, he was in his territory. Big flat eyes never left us.

I said to Mick, "What do you think you see?"

Sharing information wasn't the bone hunter way, so I knew he was trying to construct a believable lie. After a few seconds, he reconsidered, and addressed Fallsdown. "That was some pretty heavy shit you laid on me back at the river. *You* know what I mean."

I certainly didn't, and Duncan only shrugged.

Mick said, "Okay—but this is between us. Ford's already heard some of it. There was a place Finn talked about. I pictured a big lake; a spring that had been dug into a lake for phosphate—that's the way he described it. Which could have been to throw me off, which was just like Finn. But there was this one night—he'd had some wine—he told me about a landmark. A great big boiling pot, he said. A pot that weighed at least two hundred pounds, otherwise someone would have carted it off. I never forgot that because that's what he called the lake: Ivory Pot. He found a fifty-pound tusk here, if this is the same place."

The man from Montana and I exchanged looks. We had held that exact tusk, although Mick didn't know it. Fallsdown had seen photos of the saber cat petroglyph, too. We both knew its value.

Mick stood on his toes for elevation. "Doesn't that look like a big boiling pot to you? Turned upside, see the way it curves?"

Dunk, wanting to believe, said, "Gold miners are like that, close-mouthed bastards. I don't think I've ever seen a two-hundred-pound boiling pot . . . But, yeah, I guess it could be." Then thought for a moment. "What about the elephant?"

"Before electricity," I reasoned, "they used cauldrons to boil sugarcane into molasses. A tractor tire, is what it looks like to me. Now . . . Well, the size is about right."

Mick was convinced. "If Albright will give you the combination, I'll risk going in there."

I also wanted to believe in the Ivory Pot—embarrassing to admit but true. Sometimes our hunter's instinct takes over. Mine was now arguing with my own good judgment. "There might be another way," I said.

Mick brightened. "Then what are we waiting for, mate?"

The analytical nerd in me responded, "There are legal considerations."

"And that elephant could crush us like a grape," Dunk added.

I walked to the solar panel. On the post, written in pencil beneath the bracket, were four numbers. End of argument.

I said, "I suppose it wouldn't hurt to take our snorkel gear and do a bounce dive—*if* the combination works."

Mick was so excited his hands shook when he lit his pipe. Cannabis smoke trailed me to the gate.

When the lock popped open, Duncan asked again, "What about the elephant?"

TWENTY

WHAT *ABOUT* THE ELEPHANT?

Mick paid no attention to Toby as he jogged ahead of me and found a cauldron the size of a truck tire rusting in the weeds. He squatted and tried to lift the rim. "Can't budge this bastard," he hollered.

The analytical nerd in me did double duty: watched Toby and noted that, even before electricity, there was a lot of sugarcane in Florida, which meant there had been thousands of rendering pots. No guarantees this was the right one.

"Two or three hundred pounds easy," Mick called.

I shushed him. "Keep your voice down."

On the other side of the pond, the elephant chewed and watched. Then he began to sway, shifting his weight from side to side. Nervous behavior I'd witnessed in Indonesia and Africa. Duncan, standing outside the fence, was doing something similar, shifting from one boot to another. He had been relieved when I'd told him to stay where he was, just be ready to open the damn gate if we had to run.

"Mate"—Mick was grinning again—"this could be the most amazing day in my life. First, I think I'm gonna die from snakebite. Then I stumble onto the freakin' Ivory Pot."

He sounded feverish, not high. Then became a Mick Jagger look-alike, as he stripped off his shirt and flung it aside: a bony man with braided pirate hair, a meg tooth dangling from his neck. But there was a bandage on his wrist that proved, when the fever was on him, he was careless enough to get us both killed—if Toby didn't kill us first.

I placed my dive bag on the cauldron while Mick hurried to the edge of the pond. Toby, a football field away, pivoted slightly to watch. Then squared his ears when the tour guide yelled, *"Shit!"* and jumped back from the bank.

Snakes, two big ones, skated onto the water, their heads swaying like cobras as they swam. Cottonmouths, no doubt this time. The elephant saw the snakes and lifted his trunk in a warning display, tusks like marble spears. He lifted a rear foot while his ears slapped flies.

"Not so loud," I told Mick.

The tour guide looked like he was having another meltdown. "I don't want to get bit again . . . those sonuvabitches. But, man . . . I can't pass up a chance like this."

I said, "Snakes are the least of our worries," while I scanned the perimeter—clumps of cattails, cypress trees, and lilies—a couple of gator slides, mud vents that angled into water—while, on the surface, the snakes were still gliding toward the opposite shore.

I decided it was time to pull the plug. "We're leaving. We'll walk to the gate together." Then added, "No matter what happens, *don't run.*"

Mick agreed, at first, but then fever took control. Fossil

addiction—I had underestimated its power. He mumbled to himself, then finally said, "Can't do it, man. I told you, I've dived with thousands of moccasins, never had the first problem. I might not get this chance again." He had packed his gear but emptied the bag on the ground.

"We're leaving," I said.

"No. I'll do a quick look-see. You can stay here. Really, I don't mind."

Mick didn't want me in the water, I realized—the fever in him talking, a fever that included greed.

I said, "Hang on a second and let's see what the elephant does. He doesn't like snakes."

"He saw them?"

Toby still did. Or could smell them. He had elevated his trunk like a periscope and was scouting the air. One cottonmouth had submerged. When the second snake disappeared, the elephant's head bobbed a few times, then he trumpeted a flatulent *All clear* signal—at least, I hoped that's what it meant.

The animal returned to grazing. I walked to the bank, telling Mick, "You've got an open wound. Let's see what we're getting into first."

The tour guide understood, but reluctantly. "Yeah, take a look and see how clear the water is. Could be gators, too—always give them at least ten minutes to surface. That's what I do."

It wasn't just water clarity and alligators that worried me. This might not be a natural pond. Man-made water holes, even big ones, become cesspools if not connected to an underground spring or a creek. Cattle dung, fertilizer, decades of carrion and waste are cumulative. Elephant spoor—a distinctive musk—was also in the mix. It was a hot afternoon in June. In the muck of overheated lakes, bacteria thrive. Filamentous amoeba can enter the nostrils, or a cut, then burrow into your brain. Even the young healthy ones can die within a few days.

I was wearing boat shoes but didn't remove them before I waded out to my thighs. Mushy bottom. Water was cooler than expected— a good sign. It suggested fresh water was flowing in from underground, but hard to judge the water's clarity, because of the sun's angle. I took another step and the bottom disappeared beneath me—a better sign.

Sculling, I immediately checked the elephant. He didn't like snakes but appeared indifferent to swimming primates. Toby was a full-grown Asiatic bull but was near the end of his years, I rationalized. He had also been castrated, according to Owen. A tragic but common precaution. Testosterone and a chemically charged cycle called *musth* make bull elephants dangerous in the wild and deadly in confinement.

Male elephants have no scrotal sacs, so visual confirmation meant nothing. I checked anyway and decided it might be okay. I stuck my glasses in my pocket and called to Mick, "Toss my mask."

The tour guide already had his fins in hand and was approaching the water, but warily. With all the foliage, another snake might be waiting.

"Wait until I see if it's worth diving," I said.

Mick was torn but did it anyway.

I use a heavy U.S. Divers tri-view mask, reconfigured with prescription plates and a mounting platform for night optics. The thing hit the water like a rock. I intercepted the mask underwater, cleared the glass, then jackknifed and let the weight of my legs push me down. Like the river I'd dived earlier, the water was tannin stained but even darker. The bottom—wherever it was—was black.

I stroked with my arms. Midstroke, a tree limb appeared, and I buried my face in silt when attempting to dodge it.

I surfaced, grabbed a breath, jackknifed again and angled toward the middle of the pond. Below me, black water gave way to fragments of gray. Rocks . . . or a ledge. I swam toward the color change. Fins would have covered the distance easily, but I was wearing shoes so used a mild dolphin kick.

Visibility improved. Pressure on my ears told me I was about ten or twelve feet deep. As I approached, instead of surfacing for another breath, I went more slowly to conserve air. It was because of what I saw: a limestone shelf, objects protruding from it. A large jar, maybe, near a shaft of waterlogged wood.

Or was it wood? No . . . a tree limb is seldom curved like a scythe.

When I was close enough, I grabbed for a handhold. The rock ledge broke away. No . . . a piece of roof tile, it appeared to be. As the chunk swayed toward the bottom, I grabbed at the ledge again. This time, limestone withstood my buoyancy. When I plucked the large jar fragment from the muck, a cloud of silt bloomed around me, so I waited. That's when I felt an odd percussion banging at my eardrums: *THUMP-A-THUMP . . . THUMP.* Several refrains in the space of seconds.

A big bull alligator calling, possibly—I had seen their mud paths. Even a choir of bullfrogs could produce such a sound underwater. Impossible to identify the source *if* it was an animal. At night, beneath my stilthouse, pistol shrimp no bigger than my pinky crackled like gunshots.

Silt caused my other senses to sharpen. Beneath my fingers, limestone vibrated, too. Limestone is skeletal matter compressed with sand. The image of bone china rattling in synch with a big man's footsteps popped into my head. That's when I knew.

Toby was lumbering toward the pond.

Instinct told me to surface and get the hell out, but the jar frag-ment had hooked me. It had the heavy feel of pottery. Once the silt cleared, the long rib-bone-looking object I'd seen might be close enough to grab. The piece of what could be tile also deserved in-spection. In my two dives combined, I'd been under less than a min-ute so still had some air. How much ground could a sixty-year-old elephant cover in thirty seconds?

A lot, it turned out. When I finally surfaced, Toby was in a stomping rampage at the water's edge, and Mick was on the run . . . sprinting toward the gate. Fallsdown was there, waiting, while also waving to me and yelling what sounded like, "Get your ass out of there!"

Impossible to hear because of the elephant's wild trumpeting . . . or to even make sense of what had transpired. The elephant wasn't chasing Mick. Not now, he wasn't. The animal was focused on a clump of cattails near the abandoned barn . . . No, something hid-den in the cattails that lay between me and the gate.

I sidestroked to shore, carrying the jar fragment and what I'd thought was a piece of tile but *wasn't* tile.

I watched the scene unfold. Toby, ears spread wide, charged the spot again and again while cattails thrashed. Then he reared on hind legs and slammed his feet down—a thunderous sound accom-panied by more trumpeting.

Whatever was thrashing in the cattails ceased its thrashing. Yet, the elephant wasn't satisfied and his rampage continued. Beneath the flesh and muscle of five tons, the earth registered his seismic weight. Cypress leaves twirled to the water's surface.

Scary. No wonder Mick had left his dive gear and ran. Too late for me, however, to slip past Toby without being seen, but . . . maybe he would allow me to circle the pond instead of passing between him and the barn.

Keep the water between us—that's what I did. Eyes fixed on the elephant, I slipped what I'd found into a bag, collected Mick's gear, then backed along the bank in the opposite direction. No problem until I reached the fifty yards of open ground separating the gate from the pond and the storage building. That's when the elephant used his tusks to prod at something in the cattails, then turned and squared his body, his full attention on me.

Silence. Not a sound from Fallsdown or the tour guide, who, until then, had been calling advice. I would have ignored them anyway. For several seconds, the elephant and I exchanged eye contact, then he snorted and ambled toward a spot that would block my escape.

I reversed my course. If Toby charged, I would spend the night in the pond. Not a pleasant option because of the snakes and alligators, but better than being stomped to death.

But Toby didn't charge. Nor did he block my escape. The elephant turned his butt to me . . . jettisoned a mountainous pile of dung . . . then lumbered past guava trees and citrus to graze, once again, on wild sugarcane.

WHEN THE GATE WAS PADLOCKED, I stood and watched Toby feeding. There was a lazy rhythm to his movements. Sniff . . . gather stalks into a bundle . . . then swing the bundle, roots first, into his mouth.

"Sugarcane," I murmured. I was wondering how many years the Albright elephants had been penned on this acreage. No connection with what was in my bag, but it might explain a two-hundred-pound cauldron.

Mick, jabbering away, didn't hear; Fallsdown misunderstood. "They're *cattails*, not sugarcane," he corrected. "When that alligator crawled from behind the barn, that's where the elephant caught him. Just as you went under. Scared the hell out of my Fawnee brave here."

Mick heard that but waited for me to ask, "How big was the gator?"

"That's not what scared me," Mick said. "He was only a six-footer, but Jumbo there would've done the same to a twenty-footer. I thought the bastard was coming after me. Screw the gator. I'll take a gator anytime." He smacked his pipe against his hand. "Goddamn it, I wanted to be the first to dive this spot."

What I'd thought was flooring tile was in my bag with the jar fragment. Both were obscured by fins and dive gear. I opened the bag and handed the flat object to Mick, saying, "You're too late."

I had found a dive slate—a sort of underwater clipboard, but erasable, with a pen attached on an elastic cord. At the top was a mesh tab and a tiny compass.

I said, "This didn't belong to your buddy Tovar. Divers don't carry slates if they're diving alone. So at least two divers were here—and recently."

It took the tour guide a while to process. "Shit . . . it looks practically brand-new. Did you see anything else?"

"A lot of mud," I answered, which was accurate but not the truth.

Mick sensed it. "Yeah? Be straight with me, man. You wouldn't be here if I hadn't told you about the boiling pot."

I shrugged the way people do when they've lied and aren't going to talk. "I was only under for a couple of minutes."

His eyes found my mesh dive bag. "Then what's that—a piece of an old jar? Might be Spanish, mate. Let me take a look . . ."

Before he could bend down, I blocked his way and said, "That crazy biker you warned Tomlinson about? I caught him robbing our car, and he said to give you my phone number. You set us up, Mick."

The tour guide's reaction: guilt, contrition, then a slinking eagerness to please. "But that was before Dunk saved my arm—maybe my life. I was going to tell you . . . really."

Fallsdown and I exchanged looks while Mick added, "You saw ivory down there, didn't you? Now you're looking for a reason to cut me out of the deal."

I said, "What I'm looking for is a reason not to feed you to that elephant. Why are you and the biker working together?"

"*Working?* No . . . the dude is crazy, man. He showed up in Venice maybe two weeks ago and he's already beat the shit out of half a dozen guys. What was I supposed to say when he told me to keep an eye on you two?"

"Showed up from where?"

"Like, I'm gonna ask? I don't know, someplace out west with the cactus. He calls people *cowpoke, buckaroo,* shit like that. Nevada, someone said; one of the cowboy states." Mick turned and appealed to his Indian brother. "Talk to him, Dunk. Something changed in me back there at the river; you know it. And the three of us had an agreement."

I said, "*Had* is the operative word," then signaled Fallsdown to leave, saying, "You mind starting the car? It'll be an oven in there."

The good-cop medicine man walked away, which made Mick nervous. He loaded his pipe and avoided eye contact until I spoke. "You might be right about this place."

"Yeah . . . ? Then you did see ivory."

No, I had found the tip of a curving rib bone too big and heavy to dislodge from the mud. A prehistoric elephant, or whale, but said,

"Duncan might trust you but I don't. Duncan doesn't dive. That's what I want to talk about."

A glow returned to the tour guide's eyes. "Then he doesn't need to know. What did you find down there?"

I said, "Without me, Leland Albright won't let you through the front gate. Were you telling the truth about being booked all week?"

Mick appeared lost for a moment, then said, "Oh, fossil trips—yeah, every afternoon. Old clients of mine, plus Shelly asked if she could—"

"I'm going with you," I said. "Duncan can come along, but we keep this between ourselves."

"Come as part of my group?" he asked. "No, you can't do that. They're paying for a private trip. But if you mean when we come back here to dive—"

I stopped him with a hard look. "I don't care what they're paying you. Figure out a story. Before I let you dive this pond, you're going to show me how bone hunting is done."

TWENTY-ONE

I GOT MY FIRST LOOK AT A CHUNK OF SABER CAT SKULL THE NEXT DAY. MICK AND his clients were diving a branch of the Myakka River southeast of Sarasota. It was a ribbon of water that passes beneath the interstate where I-75 makes a sharp east-west jog. The clients, which included Shelly, were frosty, although she took the time to wave at Fallsdown, her wise Native American protector. When she did it, we both noticed the waterproof camera strapped to her wrist.

No Jet Skis on this trip. Just a muddy lane, a long walk, and heat.

"Try not to piss off my paying customers," Mick instructed me, then took Duncan aside, probably to complain about my bullying.

I told him, "I'll stay downstream." It was my way of avoiding Shelly and three men who Mick claimed were serious collectors. Also, basic diving courtesy. Silt, disturbed by sloppy fin work, does not flow upstream.

I carried my bag toward the sound of interstate traffic and found an opening in the bushes two hundred yards away. Not far enough for good visibility because of the divers upstream but okay for a creek that was only waist-deep and fifteen yards wide. Water was bathtub warm, foliage dense in this space between subdivisions, and only a mile from one of Florida's busiest highways.

Contrary to all rules, I swam southwest with the current. I expected nothing. The topsy-turvy randomness of good luck favors irony and the stupid. The combination made me a favorite to find something.

I did. After twenty minutes in the water, I drifted around a bend and saw what might have been a cement block elevated above the muck. Flat on top. I fanned some mud away. An eye socket as big as my fist stared back. I fanned harder. A broken yellow fang appeared. The fang was a foot long, not counting the missing tip.

Startled, I drifted seaward to let the silt clear, then stood to orient myself. What the hell had I found—a prehistoric snake? That's what it resembled. Then I remembered the mastodon tusk. I had made the same mistake viewing the petroglyph under a magnifying glass. A saber-toothed tiger, jaws thrown wide, resembled a serpent's head in midstrike.

"Holy shit," I said, then returned to the spot.

I didn't touch the thing. I used my hands to fan mud and do some dredging. My excitement survived a minor disappointment. Only half of the saber cat skull remained, although it was so flat, I went back and forth about whether it was actually feline. No, not feline . . . *Smilodon* was the genus, as I knew from researching the petroglyph. Two or three varieties of giant cat had roamed Florida's peninsula. If it was *Smilodon*, this had been a fully grown adult. An animal that weighed half a ton and was capable of snapping the head off Africa's largest lion of today.

The fang convinced me. It was long, symmetrical, and bowed by evolution into a perfect killing spike. Not yellow, as I'd thought.

The ivory had weathered like meerschaum. The top layer was the color of fine leather. Interior layers were amber. Where the point was broken, dentine revealed rings like a sapling that had been sharpened into a spear, then fired for strength.

I didn't see all this in one viewing. It took two dozen dives. On this trip, my weight belt carried thirty pounds of lead, so staying under wasn't a problem. The problem was visibility. After each dive, I had to wait for the silt to clear. What I'd found was so remarkable, I became impatient with water clarity. I wanted to memorize each detail. Why the hell hadn't I brought a camera?

Wait . . . I did have a camera. The case on my cell phone had been water-tested by Deon, my would-be abductor. I'd left the phone inside my shoes a quarter mile away.

First, I marked my discovery. Only the inexperienced believe submerged objects are easily refound. On both sides of the skull, I snapped tree branches, then located an opening downstream. I marked that spot, too. I was wearing dive booties, not ideal for rough terrain, but I jogged anyway and soon returned, my phone in camera mode.

I took dozens of photos. The whole time, I had to battle a voice telling me *Take the skull, you'll never find another.* When good sense refused, the voice goaded *At least hold the ivory fang in your hands . . .* Then amended *No—take the damn thing; lock it away for the wakeful hours. Who will know?*

Even the analytical nerd in me wanted to side with temptation. Ice Age fossils, genus *Smilodon*, are the rarest of the rare. Auction value of a broken killing tooth? Twice my annual income . . .

Monetary value, however, didn't compare to my desire to hold the saber cat's fang in my hands. The fang was an evolutionary masterwork. To me, its existence represented a powerful concept. By design, it was a vindication of killers who kill to benefit their species. The ivory's purity of purpose touched a personal chord.

Close-up shots of the fang—I took several. Was so preoccupied I didn't notice I had visitors until a man's loud voice called, "What did you find?"

Upstream, Shelly and one of the men were watching. A guy in his fifties, fit, wearing a camo dive skin, mask, and snorkel tilted on his head. His question sounded more like an accusation. Same with the look on Shelly's face. I had intruded on their private hunt. They were worried I'd discovered something they might have found.

The perfect lie popped out of my mouth. "Cottonmouth," I said, pointing at the spot. Kept my voice low, as if I didn't want to spook what lay beneath the water.

Shelly, sensitized after yesterday, took a step back, but the man was unconvinced. "You're taking pictures of a goddamn snake?"

I touched a finger to my lips, then waved to summon them closer. "Big one on the bottom. You can see his head sticking out from a rock."

Shelly said, "That's just stupid," and turned to go.

But the man noticed the branches I'd snapped as markers. "Snake, huh?"

I told him, "Look for yourself," while I unclipped the dive bag from my belt and pretended it needed repositioning.

The bag was empty.

The man's eyes moved from my dive bag to the branches, then to me. He didn't believe my story. But finally said, "Mick wants to see you," then followed Shelly upstream.

The analytical nerd in me counseled: *If you don't take the saber cat skull, that asshole will.*

RIDING SHOTGUN IN THE RENTAL CAR, Duncan driving, I swiped through photos on my phone. A couple of okay shots, but none that did justice to a skull that was an evolutionary masterpiece.

Dunk had been talking about Mick, convinced that he was on our side now. Said our guide had spent the night at a motel because he was afraid of Quark, or Quirk, the gangbanger. Said Mick would move in with a buddy, if needed, and was no longer answering Quark's calls. Privately, Mick had given me the biker's cell number on a matchbook. Swore he would find out more about the mysterious collector because he was eager to dive the elephant pond. Then Duncan, after driving in silence for a while, surprised me, saying, "Hate to lay this on you, but I think Shelly's a cop."

I concentrated on my phone, asking, *"Shelly?"* Then switched from photos to recent messages.

"She shoots a hell of a lot of video. You notice? And she doesn't come back with that many fossils. Just enough, seems to me, to convince the others she's trying. But it's more of an attitude thing."

I said, "She avoids me, that's all I know."

The man from Montana gave me a look, then said, "I noticed." And let me wonder about that before adding, "I was thinking of asking her out. Now I'm not so sure."

"Your loyalty is appreciated," I said wryly, then changed the subject. "I had a friend run the crazy biker's license and I just heard back. The plate was stolen yesterday. More likely, the night before, but that's when it was reported. I'd bet he's using a fake name. Who the hell names a kid Quark?"

Fallsdown said, "I think that's right. Or Quirk," and took his eyes off traffic long enough to see I was reading text messages. He told me about some strange fake names he'd heard in prison, asked about Tomlinson, who was still in Sarasota, then said, "At this next spot, watch how she behaves," back on Shelly again.

Mick and his group were caravanning north toward the Manatee River, a little creek east of Bradenton. We lagged far behind. There was a reason, but the man from Montana hadn't asked why I'd insisted on being the last to leave the river. He'd probably assumed I had to make a toilet stop because I'd headed for the bushes when the others were gone. Or maybe he was holding the question in reserve for later.

I wasn't concerned. It was a little after two, on this muggy afternoon, with clouds. Time enough to make another dive and be back at Dinkin's Bay before sunset to compare notes with Tomlinson.

Duncan used his blinker to pass a line of eighteen-wheelers, then signaled again to return to the slow lane—a probationer mindful of driving courtesy. He said, "I like her eyes. And she's funny—a sense of humor is important. The way she plays off my medicine man act, I don't know, just the right touch, mostly kidding around but not. She knows I have fun with it, too. Like we're enjoying a private conversation the whole time nobody else can hear."

I asked, "Does she know you jumped parole?"

Duncan winced and said, "Geezus, you gotta bring that up again?" and used his blinker to pass a Winnebago. After thinking it through, he decided, "Yeah . . . maybe I shouldn't ask her out. If she's a cop, the odds are about fifty-fifty she'd put me in jail before I got her into bed."

I said, "Don't underestimate your charm. I'd make it seventy-thirty. Either way, she looks like the type who'd put you in handcuffs first."

Dunk said, "Hmm . . . think so? Then I will ask her out."

Shelly, I had to agree, used her camera a lot—but, at least, didn't have a GoPro strapped to her head like the two divers who were already in the water when we arrived. Another group had beat us to the spot, Mick explained, but there was plenty of room. When Alfie, the Jet Ski operator, appeared, I understood. Alfie's boss, Harris Sanford, wasn't around, so he and Mick had apparently worked out some kind of deal.

I spent forty minutes in the water, which I figured was the minimum required not to attract suspicion. Because Duncan was busy charming Shelly, it was another half hour before we packed up and left.

The man from Montana thought I was behaving oddly and finally said something as we banged toward the highway. "Do you have a guilty conscience? Or just afraid I was enjoying myself too much?"

I didn't have an excuse ready but came up with one fast. On the computer, I had mapped Florida Elephant Rescue—the two-hundred-acre facility Owen had told me about. A section abutted Mammoth Ridge property, which was only a few miles inland. I told him I was in a hurry because I wanted to have a look before it got late.

"They don't allow visitors," I said, then added, "But if there's no gate, maybe we'll see some elephants before they run us out."

Duncan found that odd but remained neutral. "You're a real curious guy, know that?"

"Curiosity is healthy," I told him.

"Doc," he said, "that's not the way I meant it."

TOMLINSON, AT THE COMPUTER, opened my photos of the saber cat skull, and said, "I wouldn't put off warning Leland. After two days with

Ava, I think he's about to have his balls handed to him. Or worse—if I could think of something worse."

I was using a siphon hose to vacuum a hundred-gallon tank, the tank cloudy with sand, while miniature stone crabs threatened me from their enclaves. I kinked the hose, then decided I needed to hear more before imposing on Leland, a man I barely knew. "I haven't cashed his check, but he's paying me for water analysis, not family counseling," I said. "So far, I've heard the ugly part. Get to the dangerous part."

The ugly part was Tomlinson, Ava, and the twins drinking mimosas by the pool after yoga class that morning. The over-thirty daughters in black two-piece swimsuits, Ava in a beige thong bikini; a relaxed group who'd already shared an hour of sweating to hip-hop yoga. Tricia, the one who Tomlinson said had a dark side, had become more animated when their instructor, Enrique, showed up uninvited.

"Ricky, they call him," Tomlinson said. "I got the impression he knew Leland was gone, but he didn't expect anyone but Ava. The house has a five-car garage. I'd ridden with the twins and they'd parked inside."

That's how it started. Tricia and Ava had something in common that only Ricky knew—along with a bunch of locker-room buddies between Orlando and Naples. Three drinks into the impromptu party, Ava had become suspicious of her stepdaughter's behavior. Tricia responded with innuendos of her own. Ricky sat back and enjoyed himself while their catty exchange escalated into a yelling match. The argument got out of hand, and Ricky had fled when Ava snapped and exited the kitchen, screaming threats and carrying a knife. Tricia had stomped off, too, leaving Esther to shepherd Ava inside after asking Tomlinson to roll a joint . . . or did he have a few Xanax?

"If that's not dangerous enough," my pal said, "let me tell you about the stepson."

"Owen," I said. "Does Ava refer to him as 'my stepson'?"

"Wait, I'm not done. Owen went through a twelve-step program—gambling. Alcoholics can be forgiven, but gambling debts don't go away. Owen is a sports junkie. Did you know that?"

"I suspected," I told him, "but I wouldn't believe much of what Ava says."

That was only part of what my pal thought was a dangerous mix. Tomlinson has his oddities, but he is perceptive and pays attention. He had gleaned enough from the twins, the odd dropped remark, and from family pictures inside the house, to suspect that Owen, Ava, and Harris Sanford were closer than anyone knew. Possibly had a secret agenda.

"The mysterious power player could be Harris," Tomlinson said. "You said he was good-looking."

"Athletic, blond," I said. "But she already has that in the yoga instructor—doesn't matter what color his hair is—a young guy tucked away. You know what I'm saying?"

"That's why I'm wondering if it could be Harris's uncle. I'd discounted the guy because of his age. Dalton Sanford. He's the seventy-some-year-old attorney I mentioned. Dalton is partners in an Orlando law firm that has branch offices, including one in Venice. Esther and Tricia worked there during college. I don't know if the firm represents Finn Tovar's estate but wouldn't be surprised. I think Leland's so wrapped up in family problems, he doesn't see the big picture."

Tomlinson reflected for a moment. "Funny, huh? Just because Dalton Sanford's over seventy doesn't mean that he has outlived his tallywacker. Ava could have her sights set on an older, wealthier husband."

"How do you know Dalton has money?"

"Men like Dalton always do," Tomlinson replied.

I used my lab apron for a towel and hung it on a hook. "I'll give Leland a heads-up, but not over the phone. I'll call and see when he's free."

I did, left a message on Leland's cell, then resumed cleaning the last of twelve tanks while Tomlinson rehashed the scene at the pool, then finally refocused on the saber cat photos.

It was my turn to talk about fossil diving and our attempt to get past the guard at Florida Elephant Rescue. "We could have hiked in from Leland's property—there are logging trails—but maybe another time," I said.

I was just finishing when Mack called to tell me a rental boat had come in with what might be a lionfish—a poisonous exotic that is reeking havoc in the Keys and might be working its way north.

"I have to ID a fish," I told Tomlinson.

He waved me away, too engrossed in photos of the saber cat to respond.

THUNDERHEADS RUMBLED OVER THE MAINLAND, and Mack had locked the marina gate by the time I returned to the lab. Tomlinson was still at the computer, an empty Corona bottle on the floor, a fresh beer next to him. When I came through the door, he said in an accusing way, "You shouldn't have done it, man. I'm surprised at you."

"Life is full of little disappointments," I replied. "What didn't I do?"

"You left this beautiful tiger skull out there all alone, man. How do you know the bone hunter and what's-her-name, Shelly, won't go back tomorrow?"

I hadn't denied taking the skull. I had only admitted moving it to a safer spot. He was making an assumption.

"They can look all they want," I said. Then tilted my head and sniffed. "You smoked a joint in here, didn't you?"

"Nope, on the porch. Flamingo must'a left the door open."

I almost asked, *Who?* but caught myself. "Don't blame the dog," I said. "And stop calling him Flamingo. You know better than to smoke that damn stuff here."

Tomlinson deflected that by concentrating on photos of the skull. "You're a dog person, that's what most people would guess. But secretly, you're more cat, and cats know the truth about their own. This tiger found you, man, not vice versa."

I told him, "You're high," and reached for my apron.

He sat back and touched a finger to the computer screen. "The way his fang curves just blows me away. A crescent moon, that's what it reminds me of. But there's blood on this particular moon. See the shape of the tooth, that color? Doc—you were supposed to rescue him."

I *had* rescued the skull. But Tomlinson was in the pre-stoned talkative stage and I wasn't going to discuss it. Fallsdown hadn't pried, why should he?

"It's not the Indian way," I told him.

"Sarcasm, whoa, dude. I know there's going to be trouble when you resort to sarcasm."

I put the apron on, intending to finish my cleaning, but stopped near the sink. In a lone tank was the jar fragment I'd found in the pond. Beside it was a folder I'd made, *Conquistadors/Florida* printed on the tab. The folder was open. The papers inside were out of square.

Tomlinson had been snooping. Rude, but it was no big deal, so I straightened the papers, closed the folder, and went about my work.

Last night, I had called an archaeologist friend and e-mailed photos of the jar fragment. She had tentatively IDed it as the rim from an olive vase, stem broken. Probably Spanish, possibly 1600s but maybe 1500s. She needed to consult Gainesville or Madrid. Thus the folder and my interest in Conquistadors who had not only explored Florida's Gulf Coast but had ventured inland—perhaps as far as the pond on Mammoth Mines property.

Tomlinson broke into my thoughts, asking, "Did you figure out which Spaniard belongs to that jar? I couldn't help noticing your research."

"I couldn't help noticing you left the damn folder wide open," I replied. "Why don't you take a guess? If it is Spanish, and if it dates back to the fifteen hundreds, *someone* hiked forty miles inland carrying an olive jar."

"I only skimmed through the data," Tomlinson said, "but there are only four possibilities. I mean, only four Spanish captains are mentioned. Which, of course, totally ignores all the men and slaves who actually did the grunt work. Typical of the Anglo-centrist mind-set when it comes to writing history."

I told him, "No more smoking dope in here, okay?"

He remained silent while I neatened the folder, primed the siphon, and resumed vacuuming.

Some of what my pal had said was true. History contained only the names of four Spanish explorers who had ventured into inland Florida during the fifteen hundreds. None of those men had fared well. Only two had survived to tell the tale.

I thought about it as I worked. Of those four, the most interesting—to me, anyway—wasn't the famous Ponce de León or Hernando de Soto. It was a much lesser known Spaniard who, under the guise of exploration, had come to Florida on a personal mission. He came to search for his son and also some former crewmen, all of whom had disappeared in a shipwreck off the Florida coast.

Pedro Menéndez was the explorer's name.

Because I have a son, Menéndez's story was compelling. But there was another link that struck a nerve: Captain Menéndez had sailed to Florida carrying a letter of marque. The letter was a legal document that governments still have the power to issue—as I knew from experience. It granted Menéndez the right to "mete out judgment" to anyone he deemed a threat to his country or to his cause.

Any and all threats to your country or your mission was a phrase more familiar to me.

A letter of marque was a dangerous tool in the hands of an angry, driven man. Menéndez was both. As a young officer, had been tortured in a French prison, and he had described natives of the Bahamas as "the most wretched and godless savages on earth."

By the time Pedro Menéndez's ship arrived in Sanibel waters, the loving father, the loyal naval officer, had become a stone-cold killer.

The click and whirr of the printer interrupted my thoughts. When I looked, Tomlinson was using a magnifying glass to inspect a glossy of the saber cat skull. He went over it carefully before he spoke. "When you put your hands on this, what did you feel?"

"The skull?" I said. "It felt like bone."

"Come on . . . You know what I'm asking."

I played along. "Take your pick: I felt a charge of primal energy. Or voices of the first aliens who seeded Mother Earth with life. *Bone*," I repeated, "that's what it felt like. Heavier than expected because bone mineralizes over time. It's what makes fossils. Water seeps into organic tissue. Minerals crystalize within the cells and the cells harden to create a sort of stone duplicate. I looked it up."

When Tomlinson pressed about what I had felt when touching the skull, I shifted the siphon saddle, changed buckets, and carried several gallons of detritus outside, where I dumped it over the rail. Over the Gulf, fresh nimbus towers had gathered in a rumbling green mass.

Leland Albright returned my call as I was coming through the door. He sounded tired or slightly drunk. Possibly both, since it was after seven, cocktail hour, on this Wednesday evening, but no hint he was upset by today's ugly scene at the pool. He asked about water samples I'd taken from Mammoth Ridge. I told him I needed more extensive samples from differing depths. He accepted that, asking, "Can we meet tomorrow?"

I was diving with Mick's clients in the afternoon, and Leland was busy anyway. We settled on later—six-thirty at the Albright ranch.

"I'll bring my sampling kit," I told him.

I didn't risk adding *And my dive gear.*

TWENTY-TWO

THAT NIGHT, AN OCEANIC STORM ANCHORED ITSELF OVER SANIBEL AND knocked out the power, which gave the psycho gangbanger time and privacy while he cut the chain at the marina gate and snuck onto the property.

The man had no idea how lucky—or unlucky—he was. At Dinkin's Bay, Fridays and Sundays are party nights, but Wednesdays also are an excuse for a midweek gathering. The schedule doesn't vary much. Chinese lanterns and music come on at first dark, and the socializing doesn't stop until the last beer is gone.

If not for the storm, the biker—Quark, according to Mick—might have been cajoled into joining the party . . . or he would have gotten bored waiting for drunks to leave and probably ridden his Harley home.

But there was a storm. One of those Gulf Stream flotillas that seek the heat of land for renewal. I felt the first rumbling at dusk and switched on the VHF radio to hear warnings to any boater foolish enough to venture offshore.

There would be no Wednesday-night party on this evening. That was fine with me.

I have a monkish streak. I like the solitude of heavy rain and wind, and wasn't in a party mood. Hannah, I suspected, had a date—with an attorney from a neighboring county, not the Brazilian. And I was tired of people in general.

So, great. Bring on the lightning and rain. Flood and pestilence, too, for all I cared. I had work to do in my lab. At first, I didn't even allow myself a beer but then weakened and poured a Bud over ice and carried it to the computer.

As a peace offering to my son, I wrote a long e-mail, and included photos of the mastodon tusk. I caught up on some other correspondence, including a note to my former lover, Dewey Nye, the ex–tennis pro turned golf pro.

Even added, "Give Walda my best," as a goodwill gesture to Dewey's man-phobic girlfriend, the Romanian ball-breaker.

By nine, I was multitasking. Between bouts at the computer, I had two lab projects going. I was using Tomlinson's favorite rum beakers to decapsulate brine shrimp cysts. Because my aquarium animals need to eat, it is a common chore: separate brine shrimp naupili from shells, then refrigerate. Not a complicated process, but it required attention.

I was also fine-tuning a terrarium that replicated a mangrove shoreline. Trying to anyway. Tulane University wanted twenty dozen fiddler crabs, and the order had to be filled incrementally over the next three months. That meant I'd have to warehouse specimens.

Fiddler crabs are colony animals. They dig burrows along the shore, depositing the fill as little balls outside their holes. When the tide rises, the crabs vanish into their burrows and use the balls as plugs. When the tide recedes, the males shove the plug away, then extend one oversize claw and begin to wave for female attention. Hundreds of males at the same time, all swaying in a unity that resembles the string section of a symphony. Fiddler crabs are either very easy to catch or they are damn-near impossible to catch. Thus the terrarium.

Perhaps because I was worried about my son, I soon returned to my research on Pedro Menéndez. The expedition to find his son, Juan, had not gone smoothly. The search had spanned three years and had transformed the loving father into a tyrant and a methodical killer.

On Florida's Atlantic Coast, Menéndez had executed more than three hundred people, mostly French colonists, before sailing around Key West into the Gulf of Mexico—payback for his stint in a French prison.

In a letter to the Spanish king, Menéndez described his preferred technique for dispatching justice: "I had their hands tied behind them and had them stabbed to death . . . To punish them in this manner [was] serving God, our Lord, and Your Majesty."

As a trademark touch, Menéndez had many of the corpses strung from trees with signs around their necks as a warning to anyone who wasn't Catholic.

Pedro Menéndez was on a mission. He wanted his son Juan safely home and God help anyone who got in his way. The letters of marque he carried justified his methods even as his methods degenerated into cold-blooded slaughter.

Finally, on Florida's Gulf Coast, the desperate father struck what he believed to be his son's trail. Somewhere near Sanibel, he made contact with the indigenous people. They were the same people who had built pyramids of shell on Cayo Pelado and Captiva and on many other islands along the coast. In his journal, Menéndez referred to the reigning warrior chieftain as "Carlos" to honor the king of Spain. The people, he named the "Calus."

Menéndez's big break came when he discovered that the chieftain's slaves included a Spaniard who had been shipwrecked seventeen years earlier. The Spaniard's name was Hernando Fontaneda. Fontaneda became the explorer's eager guide and interpreter, and later, in his own journal, would claim to have saved Menéndez's life at least twice.

To win Carlos, the warrior chieftain's, cooperation, Menéndez married Carlos's sister—but fell from grace when he ordered Carlos's brother beheaded. Menéndez and his men escaped and continued searching, often inland, on foot or by following rivers.

Relentless. The word fit a man and a story that, unlike tales of pirate treasure, were as real as the jar I had found and that was soaking in a nearby tank. Occasionally, as I read, I looked at the thing: a shard of gray clay, its rim black on the outside, buckskin orange within.

Pedro Menéndez might have poured wine from the jar after hiking through forty miles of Florida jungle—or used it to sluice blood off his hands.

I could relate.

THE DOG GRUNTED FOR HIS DOORMAN, so I took a break. Rain had slowed to a rumbling downpour. Umbrellas have yet to dent marina culture. Easier to changes clothes later . . . or wear no clothes at all. Standing at the railing, I whizzed off the dock. A motorcycle headlight skimmed the top of the mangroves, which should have set off alarm bells but didn't.

It was only nine-thirty. Why would a brain-damaged biker risk invading our little marina when residents were still awake?

Brain-damaged was the key anomaly, yet I ignored the possibility.

Instead of investigating, I used a towel, changed shirts, and checked messages. There were two from Mick the tour guide. He was becoming my dutiful pawn. Before I would allow him to dive the pond, I required information; the name of the unknown artifact collector was at the top of my list. There were a couple of other things he was working on, too.

No messages from Hannah, though. Better to stay busy than to ruminate over where she was, or who she was with, so I went back to the lab and did a few more rounds with the computer.

Researching Pedro Menéndez dovetailed with rivers and hydrological changes in Florida. Hydrology dovetailed with phosphate mining.

I followed that track for a while. Depending on the publication, the phosphate industry is either flooding Florida's estuaries with killer nutrients or bleeding our aquifers dry. Studies done by major mining companies, however, presented data that, while occasionally similar, offered far rosier conclusions.

One thing the studies all agreed on had become a familiar refrain: The industry had to move south toward the Peace River or die. Phosphate, like oil, is a finite resource.

Who to believe? Not since Darwin's time have field scientists been so threatened (and influenced) by the powers of righteousness— groups righteously devoted to their environmental convictions on one side, companies blindly devoted to profit on the other. Both were a coveted source of research funding.

Charles Darwin had courage enough to challenge Genesis, but

how would he have fared against politics, peer pressure, and almighty funding dollars?

Working alone beneath a tin roof during a storm is a pleasant thing. My only interruption was the dog. Every ten minutes or so, he wanted in or he demanded to go out. The dog can bang the screen door open, if needed, but he preferred that I inspect his gifts from the sea: a bucket, a chunk of wood, a mullet, a crab buoy, the rope from a crab buoy, then an entire crab trap, which he tried to pull through the door, and that's when I put a stop to it.

I banished the retriever to the breezeway and returned to work . . . until a sizzling blast of lightning killed the power. I said, *"Damn it,"* but was actually delighted. Losing the Internet was like being rescued from a ketamine drip. I had been returned by force into the realities of a summer night in Florida.

Beneath the floor, the little Honda generator kicked on; aerators in a dozen tanks continued their ozone burble. I ignored the emergency options and chose oil lamps over electric or a Coleman. *Delicious* is a word too feminine for what I felt, but pretty damn close. I found the newest issue of *Coral*, a superb magazine for marine aquarists, and carried it, plus an oil lamp, to my reading chair and plopped down.

In the subtropics, rain mimics the rhythm of oceanic waves. Lulls are troughs that escalate in volume. As waves peaked, a waterfall hammered my tin roof. During each lull, Cuban tree frogs competed with native frogs in a chorus of burps and trills that argued supremacy.

Fifteen minutes into "Nematocysts—Nature's Arrows," my cell rang.

"Damn," I said again, and meant it this time.

It was Jeth, who lives in an apartment over the marina office. He asked, "Do you know who belongs to that motorcycle blocking the gate? The headlight's off, but it's still there. If you have company, maybe ask them to move it when the rain stops, okay?"

Trying to sound patient, not irritable, I said, "If the headlight's off, how do you know the motorcycle's blocking the gate?"

"Because of the lightning. I happened to be taking a leak when they pulled up, I can see it from the bathroom. That was fifteen or twenty minutes ago, but the bike's still there."

"Congratulations on the longest piss in history," I said. "You saw two riders? You said *they*."

Jeth stutters when he's annoyed. "You don't need to be a sa-sa-smart aleck, Doc. I thought you'd want to know. I'd go check, but Janet's at her mother's, so I'm taking care of Javier alone."

Javier, age two, was named after a close friend of the marina, Javier Castillo, a good man who had escaped Cuba by crossing the Florida Straits on a raft made of inner tubes.

Feeling like the ass I sometimes am, I apologized. Jeth was doing me a favor. The gate is next to the path that leads to my house. It was odd for someone to sit there in the rain on a . . . *motorcycle?*

Finally, it hit me. I put the magazine aside and got to my feet, saying, "You didn't answer. Is there one person or two?"

Jeth replied, "It's too far to see, but"—a strobe of lightning interrupted him—"Yep, the bike's still there. Hard to tell because of the trees, but maybe two people under a poncho."

"Under one poncho?"

Jeth said, "It's not even ten o'clock. If they wanted out of the rain, why not pull into the 7-Eleven? That's why I figured you have company, so—" In the background I heard a clattering noise, then Jeth reprimanding his son. Talking fast, he said to me, "Javier just threw his spoon at the weather girl, now he's chewing the remote. Call me, okay?"

I WENT TO THE DOOR AND SWITCHED ON DOCK LIGHTS. Rain angled across the walkway, wood gleaming beneath lamplight that ended where mangroves began, shadows churning.

No visitors . . . unless the biker was somewhere on the lower deck, where the tactical Brunswick and my old net boat are moored. The toolshed was there, too, where boxes of relics—minus the priceless mastodon tusk—were hidden in plain sight, if someone bothered to look.

The Honda generator can carry a sizable load, so I flicked on more lights beneath the house and waited. No telltale thump of a man's feet, but waves banging at the pilings might have covered that.

I stepped into the breezeway and looked out to check on Tomlinson's boat. *No Más*, at anchor, was pointed into the rain, a gray husk. One frail porthole light suggested my pal was aboard, but he wasn't aboard. No dingy tethered astern. So . . . after Tomlinson had left the lab, he'd probably gone to the Rum Bar with one of his lady friends, or with Duncan, or both.

But maybe not. Maybe the crazy biker had intercepted him and was now preparing rags soaked with gas.

Moving faster, I went inside, found a flashlight, and removed the MUM-14 monocular from its case. Sanibel Island is not the sort of place one packs a gun to confront strangers, so I stuck a wooden fish billy in the back of my pants.

When I opened the door, the dog came in, dripping water on the floor. I had yet to hear him bark a warning, and his retrieving skills weren't required, so I told him, "House," meaning I didn't want him to follow. He carried a nondescript object in his mouth and collapsed near the Franklin stove that, instead of providing heat, whistled with a Gulf Stream wind.

I killed the outside lights, then went down the steps and checked under the house. Boxes that had contained megalodon teeth, fossils, Clovis points, and the little box of doubloons were where I'd left them. My boats appeared intact.

False alarm so far. Then, as I was scanning the mangrove fringe, I heard a motorcycle start. Reassuring. The crazy biker wouldn't leave without attempting to search my house. Unless . . . unless he had found Tomlinson and had decided to use him as bait.

Jogging, I adjusted the night vision over my eye and pulled the club from my belt. Ran harder when I got to the path, but the motorcycle was accelerating away, lights out, as I exited the mangroves.

A flare of red brake lights suggested only one person was aboard—male, probably. Wearing a helmet. I blinked my flashlight at him as a pointless challenge. The last thing I expected was the driver to turn around.

But he did. Threw out a leg, spun the bike, and switched his light on bright, approaching slowly at first, then faster—maybe because he recognized me. In rain and blinding light, I couldn't be sure, but I did know that waving a club at a stranger invites a visit from police. So I wedged the fish billy down the small of my back and retreated a step. As an afterthought, I twisted the headgear around to hide the monocular.

The bike stopped, the engine died, but the headlight remained aimed at my face. Then a voice called, "You son of a bitch, I knew you was here—what'd he do with it?" The man sounded rattled.

I shielded my eyes. "Do with what?"

"Are you saying you don't know?"

"Get that damn light out of my eyes," I told him. "Who are you?"

After a long look, he muttered something, then attempted civility. "Shit, hoss, I figured you had a special welcome waiting." Sounded like a farmer chewing a straw when he added, "Think she'll rain tonight?"

It was the psycho biker demonstrating his mood swings.

I reached back and rested my hand on the club. "The light—you're blinding me."

That distinctive cackle while he swung the headlight toward the gate—the chain in place but hanging at an odd angle. Helmet and poncho pivoted toward the mangroves. "A goddamn swamp like this, I'm surprised you don't got alligators guarding the place."

A strange remark. "Depends on the tide," I said. "Why are you here?"

"Is this how visitors get treated? As I was pulling up, I saw you stuff that gun down your butt—long one, like with a silencer screwed on." The headlight panned over me again, then angled toward the bushes. "And you're wearing Army night optics. Toys like that don't come with a badge." He made a whooping sound of approval, suddenly in better spirits. "Partner, I'm beginning to think you're the real McCoy."

He had mistaken the club for a pistol, which was okay with me.

"I'm not a cop, but I know their number," I said. "Answer my question."

Rain drizzling off his helmet, he replied, "By god, try to convince that idiot Deon you're not a cop. He was hoping for witness protection. Know what I told him? I told him, 'Dumb shit, feds ain't allowed to steal.' By the way, you happen to have them Pelican cases handy? I'd be much obliged."

"Is that why you called me a son of a bitch?"

"Don't get your panties in a tither, I was referring to something else. But I want them cases. Even if you'd drowned Deon to get 'em, they ain't yours."

"I can take you for a boat ride if you're interested in Deon's story."

Laughter. "Ain't you full of beans tonight—inviting me on another boat ride."

"Just the two of us," I said.

Nodding, playing the game, he studied me. "Know what I think? What I think is you're more the sport killer type. Just fancier. Where's your trained attack dog? His pelt would look good in front of my fire."

I said, "I don't know what kind of drugs you're on but a thunderstorm is bad timing. You came here to rob me, didn't you?"

He ignored that and patted a saddlebag behind him, using the glove on his good left hand. "Me, I keep it simple. A .357 Mag stainless—no rust, no fuss, and no brass to hang my ass." He hooted—a joke that rhymed—then indicated the other side of the Harley. "I got a tooled-leather scabbard I carry sometimes—a Winchester .30-30. You ever watch that ol' TV show *The Rifleman*? Big looped cocking lever, just like Chuck Connors. But Southern cops frown on a man carrying a rifle. I don't often tie her on my saddle— but should've." He let that settle before adding, "Tonight would have been a whole different story."

I didn't know what that meant, but it was a threat. Behind my back, I released the club, then showed him an empty hand by scratching my shoulder. Hand drier, I regripped the fish billy and waited.

That convinced him I had a gun. "What caliber's that bad boy? Don't be shy."

I didn't respond. The biker didn't like that but kept it going by motioning toward the bay. "The stink alone would be enough to drive me out. You really got a house in them trees? I pictured something inside the gate. Small but, you know, *nice*. That's always the problem with trailer parks and marinas—a hundred uptight assholes all have the same address."

I said, "I think you better leave before your hand starts to rust."

In a low voice, he said, "Kiss my ass." Touchy about the subject, but then switched moods and pretended to be amused. "I don't need my hands now that I got the lay of the land. You live in a swamp and I saw the hippie's sailboat. Don't get me wrong, I admire your style, but I can't say much for your taste in friends."

I said, "Why would you care?"

"His dinghy's the rubber one, right? I figured, 'cause it's such a mess—them peace signs sort of give it away. So what I was doing when you showed up, I was headed for the closest bar to find your boyfriend Thompson, or Tomlinson. Say, 'Hello, amigo,' and have a drink or two." With his good hand, he tapped the back of his seat. "Plenty of room on my bitch saddle, if you're thirsty."

Above us, a towering cloud flickered. The biker's helmet shield was flipped up fighter pilot style, dark eyes peering out, a misshapen smile. Something else: his prosthetic hand was hidden by a poncho that glistened while the rain slowed. The .357 was under there, not in a saddlebag, I suspected.

I said, "The police station is only half a mile away. If you cut that gate chain, I'll have you arrested . . . Quark."

That offended him even more. "*Quark?* Who the hell told you my name is—" He stopped. "That clown Mick, wasn't it? Him, with his big mouth. Well, that goes both ways, hoss. Guess what? Next time you scuba dive that elephant pond, *I'm there*. The ivory mother lode, Mick claims. See what I mean about your taste in friends? That deaf, dumb shit—*Quirt's* my name. I told him a million times. *Quirt,* not *Curt,* which he keeps getting wrong. And sure as hell ain't *Quark.* You know what a *quirt* is?"

I said, "You're going to tell me anyway."

"Just for that, I won't. Or call me El Sid—which is a long story. Or Reno's okay. Take your pick. They're both a lot better than god-damn *Marion.*"

He knew about the pond. He knew my name. Not good.

I said, "If your boss wants to talk, tell him to come in person," then started toward the path to my house.

"Hey!" he hollered. "Just having a nice conversation ain't enough? I left you a private envelope. It ain't my fault you live in a swamp."

I turned. "Left it where?"

"There, dumbass." He spun the headlight to where my truck was parked. An old GMC I've had for years. A little rust, but otherwise in good shape . . . until now. The passenger window was shattered and the door open. No dome light, so he'd probably used his bionic hand to break that also.

He said, "How was I supposed to know it wasn't locked?" cack-ling again, but then got dead, cold serious. "That don't make us even, slick. What I should do now is set your house on fire—and kill that goddamn dog."

Insane—or it was a line from some cowboy movie—*Shane* or *Lassie*—where the bad guy threatens the kid's collie.

A Freon sensation streamed through me, urged me to come back with a pistol and shoot out Quirt's tires. I battled through it even after rationalizing the irrational: *Convince the crazy bastard you're even crazier than him.*

No . . . that isn't the way pros handle gangbangers—especially not within throwing distance of my own home. Something else: He wanted me to do it. In some twisted way, the man was hoping to find a psycho playmate—the ultimate game: Gunfighters at high noon, the craziest one lives.

Would he really go through with something like that? I doubted it. So far, just the illusion that I was carrying a gun had made him behave.

Didn't matter because it wasn't going to happen. I walked toward my truck, kept walking even when he called, "If your upholstery's wet, I can come back with a can of gas." Then paused before what came next: "How about tomorrow night? We can cook us up some elephant steaks and chew the fat."

I was meeting Leland late tomorrow, another visit with Toby. Did he know about that, too? Quirt kick-started his Harley as I turned, left me to wonder about it when he skidded the bike around and throttled away, his right arm finally appearing from under the poncho but holding no gun that I could see.

I seated the monocular over my eye and memorized a second license plate—a different number, not a Florida plate, but I couldn't make out which state.

I checked the gate chain. Quirt had used a saw to cut one of the galvanized links . . . or a bolt cutter attachment on his bionic hand.

I called Sanibel police.

TWENTY-THREE

ON THE PHONE, I TOLD TOMLINSON, "THE CRAZY BIKER'S ON THE ISLAND. TAKE a look at the parking lot, but stay inside."

The dog wanted out again. It gave me something to do while I waited for my pal to check.

Tomlinson was at the Rum Bar on Captiva Island, at the entrance to South Seas Resort, a few miles away. There were only a few local places to choose from, and Tomlinson's VW Electric Kool-Aid Love Van would be easy for the biker to spot.

"No Harley choppers," Tomlinson reported after a wait, "but there's a table of women here celebrating some kind of reunion. Did Mr. Psycho threaten you again? He's got a real nasty tongue on him."

"He delivered a letter from his boss," I said, then gave an abbreviated account. "I got his license number. Police are watching the marina, so I'll come to the bar—if he didn't smash my distributor, too. I didn't look under the hood."

As I went out the door, the retriever came up the steps carrying what looked like the same chunk of wood, but it had gotten tangled in rope or something.

I said, "You could choke on that," and took the mess away from him. Almost tossed it in the garbage before realizing it wasn't driftwood. The object resembled a garden tool—a small rake, the kind rose fanciers use—but was too big.

The Honda generator was still firing, but I'd turned out the dock lights. I switched them on, then stood looking at the object for a moment before saying, "Maybe Quirt's not as crazy as I thought."

I was holding his prosthetic hand. The elastic harness ripped but still attached.

The retriever sat, his head tilted, while two yellow eyes awaited my decision—keep the thing or trash it? Speaking whole sentences to a dog is pointless—worse, confusing to the animal—but I did it anyway. "How the hell did you get this?"

The retriever's mouth edged a few inches closer, possibly thinking he could snatch the hand away from me while I babbled.

"Did you find it?"

The retriever's tail thumped the decking twice—a wild display of emotion, for him.

"Jesus Christ," I said, "you caught him trashing my truck, didn't you?"

The dog blinked at me before his attention shifted to a mullet that leaped into a night of rain and wind, but the wind calming.

The dog whined, his coat vibrating, while I said, "I can't wait to get those DNA tests back," then spent ten minutes going over him inch by inch to see if he'd been hurt.

He wasn't.

I left the retriever in the house, doors locked, with part of a rib-eye steak I planned to have for breakfast.

Quirt's bionic hand I placed in the toolshed.

ON MY WAY TO THE RUM BAR, I stopped at Jensen's Marina to show Falls-down the soggy papers I'd found on my dashboard, but his rental car was gone, lights in his cottage off.

I was disappointed, but it could wait. The envelope contained a typed message and the photo of another owl-faced carving. This one was different: black soapstone, but it had a triangular head crest, unlike the stones in photos Duncan had brought. The carving was lying atop a recent edition of the *Tampa Tribune* to prove its authenticity, the photo printed on cheap paper.

The unsigned note read *This was obtained legally from a Montana dealer, but am willing to trade for a stolen item that is rightfully mine. Suggest you don't compound your criminal activity. Will make contact soon.*

Articulate—Quirt wasn't the author. It was more evidence that Crow or Apache ceremonial carvings had, indeed, traveled to Florida.

Little People, Fallsdown called them, an oddity I had yet to question.

At the Rum Bar, however, Tomlinson studied the photo and felt obligated to explain, while I ordered a draft and looked at the menu. His story was so bizarre, it allowed me to obsess on Quirt's threats. Gave me time to replay how I could have handled the scene with more . . . well, style. Tell the crazy bastard, *You've got a lame horse, cowboy,* after shooting out his tires. No . . . tell him, *Reach for the sky,* then fire three fast rounds before his crippled brain realized what was happening. Use a sound suppressor—thunder would have covered the shots.

I was pissed. My truck's interior was soaked, glass everywhere.

A garbage bag and duct tape had made a poor replacement for a window.

Where's your trained attack dog? His pelt would look good in front of my fire.

Quirt had said that, too. I hadn't told Tomlinson what the dog had done, yet, was savoring the moment. The more I thought about the biker's threat, the madder I got.

"Doc . . . you don't seem to be listening." Tomlinson, perturbed by my inattention, swirled rum in a snifter. "Did you hear me?"

I lied, "Yes," then made the mistake of adding, "About what?"

"I was talking about Lewis and Clark."

"No, thank god."

"You don't have to be rude. A simple *I don't give a shit* would suffice."

Before I could say that, Tomlinson was already explaining. "Lewis and Clark were the first to document the Little People, their actual existence. The mystical components, sure, I expected that to go right over your head. I've known you long enough. But we're talking Anglo-American history here."

I told Brian, the bartender, "Yucatán shrimp, please," and returned the menu. Tomlinson, derailed by the glow of his rum snifter, added some advice. "Has your manager ever considered lab beakers? You have no idea what volumetric glass can lend to the subtleties of rum. Expensive, but, hey, scientists ain't exactly dummies."

Then continued his explanation while I gazed among a dozen TVs and finally settled on a baseball game: Blue Jays and Nationals, R.A. Dickey, the knuckleballer, pitching.

"Meriwether Lewis," Tomlinson said, "described the Little People as 'ferocious devils' with huge heads—typical racist bullshit, of course. Who's to say what constitutes an oversize head in a people who can turn to stone any damn time they choose? In fairness to Meriwether, he also wrote that they are very astute, brilliant tacticians. I'm not sure when—it had to be before 1804—but a handful of Little People killed three hundred Lakota warriors in one night. They attacked because the Lakota screwed up and tried to cross sacred LP ground."

To prove I was listening, I said, "Sacred Little People ground," then refocused on the knuckleballer, who had gotten Adam La-Roche to pop up and was now facing Bryce Harper.

"Read Lewis and Clark's journals. The facts speak for themselves. Dunk, of course, is reluctant to discuss the issue with outsiders. The Little People have a special relationship with the Crow that dates back—oh, hell—thousands of years, by the white man's calendar. There was a Crow chief named Plenty Coups. He's legendary. Supposedly, the Little People visited Plenty Coups in his dreams and entirely reshaped the destiny of the Crow people." Tomlinson's tone provided a confidential nudge when he added, "That's just a cover story, of course. I think you know what I'm getting at."

Watching Harper strike out on a third straight floater, I muttered, "I don't believe it," then asked the bartender for a list of NA beer.

Tomlinson, laughing, waited until Brian was gone to say, "*Believe it*. I knew I wouldn't have to spell out the obvious for someone like you."

Now I was completely lost. "Believe what?"

The envelope, the photo, and unsigned letter were to Tomlinson's left, drying on the bar. Using his fingers like tweezers, he lifted the photo while he buffed a spot with a napkin, then placed the photo in front of me. "I have a hunch this is really him."

I asked, "Who?"

Tomlinson eyed me as if I were a prankster. "Good one! And you're right. We shouldn't talk about this. Sacred knowledge should never be verbalized."

I signaled Brian the bartender—*Vodka on the rocks, please*—then turned in my seat. "What in the hell are you talking about?"

Tomlinson tapped the photo. "This is undoubtedly one of the Little People. But notice the ceremonial crest? It's *him*—Chief Plenty Coups, I think. Duncan's gonna freak when he sees this." He hesitated. "Now that you understand, you're probably already wondering about Dunk's current manifestation."

I said, "No, I'm wondering why I'm listening to this bullshit—and about Dunk's current location. He wasn't at Jensen's. I checked on the way."

Tomlinson was concerned. "Did you knock?"

"His car was gone so I didn't bother. What's wrong?"

Tomlinson grabbed his cell and got up. "He told me he was hitting the sack early tonight so I need to call and find out. Eat your shrimp—but save a few for me, okay?"

I CANCELED THE VODKA in time to get another beer and watched the ball game. A couple of Boca Grande fishing guides stopped to say hello and to remind me the full moon in June was only a week away.

The Tarpon Moon, local anglers call it. The best night of the year to hook one of the world's great game fish—until recently. Because of a snagging technique misrepresented as jigging, Boca Grande Pass had become a freak show of fast boats. The number of spawning tarpon had declined. Last year, during the Tarpon Moon, there were no tarpon.

The guides took a seat and we discussed it. My trips to Bone Valley had given me a new insight, which I wanted to share. For unknown centuries, tarpon have massed in Boca Grande Pass to feed and engage in a behavior not yet understood. Daisy-chaining, it is called. Packs of male tarpon pursue females in a rhythmic pattern that suggests ritual. Biologists I respect theorize that tarpon make the annual migration to meet and fatten before heading offshore to spawn.

I didn't doubt it was true. *But why Boca Grande Pass?* There are dozens of passes that link the Gulf of Mexico with brackish backwater bays. Yet tarpon always chose that single outlet to the ocean, a space less than a mile wide.

The guides listened while I offered an explanation based on what I had learned from Bone Valley.

"The Peace River flows into the bay, then exits through Boca Grande Pass," I said. "Thousands of years ago, when inland Florida was underwater, a river emptied near the same place. That's why Venice has so many sharks' teeth. Tarpon might be coded like salmon to return to the same spawning ground. Ancient behavior in an ancient species. Impossible to prove, of course, but it fits."

We continued talking until, from outside the door, Tomlinson summoned. I paid the bill before he explained, "Duncan forgot to get gas, but he's back. He says Rachel wants to talk to you. He gave me her number."

"His aunt?"

"Dunk will explain when we get to Jensen's Marina."

Actually, Fallsdown didn't explain. Sitting on the porch of his cabin, which was nearest the water, all he said was, "It's only eight o'clock in Billings. The Home Hospice nurse told me aspens are already turning, so, don't worry, Rachel's still awake."

I didn't see a connection but asked, "Why does your aunt want to talk to me?"

He considered the crested charmstone, holding the photo at arm's length, before signaling Tomlinson with a look.

"Rachel doesn't trust us," Tomlinson explained.

Say no more—I was convinced.

I carried my phone past the bait tank to the end of the dock and called Montana.

ON THE DRIVE HOME, I was reviewing my conversation with Rachel Fallsdown when I received a text from Hannah: *Are you awake?*

It was eleven-fifteen, late by her standards. Trying to hit redial, I dropped the phone. At the same instant, another call came in. Quirt had busted my dome light, so I had to pull over to find the damn thing, the phone ringing while I searched.

It took a while. Ringing stopped, the phone beeped with a message. When I checked, instead of Hannah's voice, a Sanibel detective's voice said, "Call me. We got the guy."

Quirt had been detained, hopefully arrested.

If it had been any other reason, I would have postponed returning his call. Rachel, a dying woman with smoker's lungs, had impressed upon me the brevity of life. Had reminded me that we are allowed only a finite number of screwups with family, friends, and lovers. Not in those words but from what Rachel had said, her struggle to breathe while telling the truth about how sacred artifacts had ended up in Florida.

So I called the detective first but kept it brief.

Police had caught the psycho biker on the bridge. They had arrested him for stolen plates, after a wrestling match, but had yet to confirm his identify. "Quirt Reno," he had told them, which matched a driver's license that was fake and a registration that looked phony, too.

"Until someone bails him out," the detective said, "his new address is the county jail. But, Doc, stay on your toes. He blames you for setting him up."

"I wish I had," I said, then we discussed the best time for me to stop at the station and sign some papers because I wanted to press charges.

With the crazy biker out of the way, I felt better about leaving the retriever alone at the lab tomorrow—I was diving with Mick's fossil group in the afternoon, then was meeting Leland at what he called the ranch.

It put me in a more positive frame of mind when I dialed Hannah.

"I'm surprised you're still awake," I said when she answered.

Hannah wasn't awake but said, "I'm glad you called. Do you realize we talked more when we were just workout partners, not dating?"

"I thought we were done with dating," I said, "but you're right."

"I blame myself. I've been lying here thinking about it. What I figured out is this: Sleeping with a man can funnel all the fun into the bedroom, then lock the door when you leave. The relationship gets so serious, you know? I liked the way we were before better."

I slowed for the Blind Pass Bridge, whitecaps slapping at darkness to my right. "I'm not sure how to take that."

"I'm telling you how I feel. It's not a criticism."

"What the problem might be is, sex isn't a major deal to many people," I said. "Maybe we both need to lighten up."

"I don't *have sex*, Marion. Making love, is what I call it, and it *is* a big deal. That's not going to change. But there are other kinds of closeness. Like tonight, I was tying up at the dock—this was after my late charter—and Loretta came out and yells, 'No matter what the sheriff says, I didn't do it!' Can you imagine?"

I smiled. "Your mother's a character."

"She used some swearwords, too, so right away I knew she'd done *something*. Used to be, I'd call you and we could laugh about whatever it was. Not just Loretta's behavior, of course. Whatever was on my mind. That's what I wanted to tell you. No matter what, I want to keep our friendship."

"What did Loretta do?"

I was being too literal or sounded overly concerned. Hannah explained, "It's not what she did. I miss talking. Not the serious talks—lord knows, we've had enough of those. Just picking up the phone and gabbing about things. Birdy and I, we send texts back and forth, and we talk, but it's different talking to a man. You, I mean. Not just *any* man."

"I appreciate that," I said.

Hannah yawned. "I'm being silly . . . and it's late."

I liked the way this was going and wanted to keep it alive. "It's weird you brought it up. Not fifteen minutes ago, I was talking to Duncan's aunt in Montana. She'd ask me to call. First thing I wanted to do when I hung up was tell you about it."

"Really?"

"I know exactly how you feel."

"Talking like friends," Hannah agreed, "I miss that. Did Duncan's aunt say anything about the owl carvings? The way that stone felt when I held it, I'd like to know more."

I'd chosen the wrong topic for light conversation but trusted Hannah enough to stay on track. "Actually, she told me about three stones, plus some other artifacts. Have you heard of the American Indian Movement? Twenty years ago or more—Duncan's aunt wasn't sure of the dates—she came to Venice Beach with some other AIM members on a protest bus. Something happened there that she's ashamed of."

I pictured Hannah sitting up in bed, heard the click of a light switch, serious enough about the subject not to push for a quick explanation. "What's her name?"

"Rachel. She was married but went back to her maiden name, Rachel Fallsdown. Tomlinson's known her for a long time."

"Did she bring the owl stones to Florida? I'm guessing she lost them somehow."

"That's not when it happened. Her group came to Venice to protest a collection of Indian relics owned by"—I decided to omit Finn Tovar's name—"Well, it doesn't matter, but a guy who was disliked by Florida Indians—Seminoles, Miccosukee—and I don't blame them. Rachel at the time must have had a drug problem. She didn't tell me that, I'm guessing. Somehow she got involved with the guy, this collector, and he paid her cash to become what they call a pot hunter."

"Is that like *pot hauling*? Rachel shouldn't blame herself if she needed money." Hannah was more tolerant of smuggling marijuana than most because of where she lived and how she'd grown up.

"Out west, pot hunters are people who dig up Indian relics. And, yes, Rachel did it for money. The collector put her in touch with more buyers. She sold the owl carvings and some other things to different people over the space of a few years. Then her conscience started getting to her, so she stopped and turned traditional, went back to the reservation. Duncan doesn't know she's the one who stole the carvings."

Hannah processed the obvious questions in silence. "She was right to trust you, Marion. Now she wants to make amends. I hate to ask, but how long does she have to live?"

I didn't remember saying that Duncan's aunt was dying, and it didn't matter. Hannah, with her good instincts, had figured it out. "Pancreatic cancer is fast," I said. "She's already on a morphine drip."

"Does she know you're the one who stole that owl stone back? I'm wondering why she didn't confess to Tomlinson . . . No, wait. He probably slept with her, and it's none of my business anyway. What's important is that you find the other carving before she dies. That's why she wants them, isn't it?"

"I don't think I would've liked Rachel if I'd met her a few years ago," I said. "And vice versa. She's a good person, though. She wants a clear conscience, and to do all she can for her tribe before she goes. I was struck by that—we all make mistakes. We all run out of time."

Hannah said, "Heaven knows," with a familiar huskiness in her voice that made me want to see her, not turn left at the stop sign ahead, Dinkin's Bay and my lab not far. Which she sensed. "I'm glad you told me. Maybe I can help. A private investigator is allowed computer access to files you wouldn't be able to open."

Hannah, who had inherited a part-time agency from her uncle, didn't know I had friends who worked for the world's most sophisticated spy agencies—the NSA and others. And that's the way it had to stay, but I indulged her, saying, "Sure—would you mind running a background check on a few people?"

Dalton and Harris Sanford, and Owen Hall were the names I wanted to give her.

While Hannah got pen and paper, I decided there was something I could admit. When she returned to the phone, I told her I was diving with Mick's group in the afternoon and, on Sunday, joining Mick and several other collectors at an unnamed spot on the Peace River.

"This isn't just about the owl stones, is it?" she said.

Good. She'd figured that out, too.

I replied, "It depends on what the Florida Wildlife cops find and who they arrest when they get there," and used an insider's inflection to communicate what I couldn't say.

A bad-boy glint came into Hannah's voice. "Why, Marion Ford. You never struck me as the tricky type—but, then, my Uncle Jake didn't either."

"I'm too straight, you mean."

She said, "I don't know about that, but it would be nice to believe you're not a drug-smuggling criminal."

"Believe it," I said.

"I want to," Hannah replied, then rewarded me by saying, "That leaves you with Monday open, sounds like. Why don't the two of us go fishing—just you and me?"

TWENTY-FOUR

THE NEXT AFTERNOON, AS I STEPPED THROUGH THE GATE INTO THE ELEPHANT'S pasture, Leland Albright told me, "Years ago, redneck kids lived around here and they'd shoot at him with pellet rifles. A .22, a couple of times, and tranquilizer darts. Used the poor old boy for target practice out of pure meanness."

"Tranquilizer darts?" I said. "How did kids get ahold of something like that?"

"Every cattleman in the area uses them. Shooting a steer with a pneumatic rifle is a lot easier than culling him out of the herd, then roping him. That's why Toby doesn't come to the fence for strangers. Elephants are smart."

Toby was plodding toward us but not in a rush. With Owen, I remembered, the elephant had stayed away.

It was nearly sunset. In my truck, where plywood now covered the broken window, my dive gear was still wet from diving with Mick's fossil group.

Leland commented on how vicious people could be, then said, "If it was the twins, Toby would move a lot faster. I don't get out here much. Plus, it's bad for animals to associate people with food. Try to tell Tricia that. Esther is the steady one, but she's just as bad when it comes to spoiling Toby."

It was an opening to ask about the twins. Did he know about yesterday's screaming match between Ava and Tricia? Instead, I waited while Leland unlocked the block-and-steel building I'd thought was for storage but had a little office, too. Bars on the windows beneath a metal roof painted white to deflect heat; cool inside, with air-conditioning, and fluorescent lights that snapped on.

Something else: Chipped megalodon teeth and other fossils were scattered haphazardly on the desk and cabinets as common as golf balls at a driving range. I followed him through the office into another room with a steel door that locked—two antique gun vaults and cabinets inside—then into a double garage, where there was a tractor, tools, and maintenance stuff but no scuba equipment that I saw. A pneumatic rifle, though, stood in a rack next to a medicine cabinet.

Leland noticed me looking at it and said, "The redneck kids didn't bother loading the darts with tranquilizer. They did it just to shoot at something alive out of meanness. Even if they had, Toby's hide is too thick."

On the bench was a packet of darts, needles an inch and a half long. I asked, "How does Owen get along with the elephant?"

"Okay, I guess. No, that's not exactly true. When Madison and I first married, he was only four, and he had a bad experience. Toby was just being friendly, but Owen has kept his distance ever since." Then Leland touched a button to open the garage, me blinking at the sudden sunlight. Outside, pasture sloped toward cattails and the pond, the skeleton of a barn beyond.

"When my father was alive, I stayed out here by myself a lot. We didn't get along, but I guess that's typical." He handed me the lid from a storage container. "How's your son doing?"

"Haven't heard from him," I responded, then asked, "Have you ever dived that pond?" It threw him for a moment, but then he saw me staring across the pasture.

"Oh, I forgot. You need more water samples."

"My dive gear's in the truck," I said.

Leland kept his hands busy while he told me, "That's a bad idea. There are snakes as thick as your leg down there. Gators, too, sometimes, but the gators don't last long."

"Why's that?"

"Like I said, elephants are smart. My grandfather's first one was a bull—bigger than Toby, even—this huge guy, but sweet as could be unless he saw an alligator. He'd stomp them to death. Thought they were crocs, I guess—something in their brain from way back in jungle times. Toby's the same way. They all are. Did you look at the pictures Owen gave you?"

I said, "I'm not sure what you mean," then remembered the old photos I'd looked at in the Jeep. "Oh—Barnabus, that was the first elephant's name," I said. "Him, and there were at least four others in a couple of shots. From what I know about boys—though you grew up here, Leland, and it's hard to imagine a boy not going in for a swim. What about Owen?"

"Swim in the pond, you mean?"

"He told me he likes to dive."

"Neither one of us, no way. The elephants own that pond—ask the gators," Leland replied, then closed the subject by asking why I hadn't heard from my son.

We talked about that while he did a few things, then carried what looked like a block of brown salt outside. Heavy, like a salt lick for cattle, although I wondered. Toby was waiting, but at a distance.

"He doesn't know you," Leland explained. "Those damn rednecks terrorized him for years. As much as he loves this stuff, he still remembers."

A block of molasses, is what I suspected, but asked, "Is that salt?"

Leland said, "Watch this," standing close enough for me to smell alcohol on his breath. Then used a post to shatter the block, the largest piece slipping from his hand. Said, "Damn . . ." and picked it up, calling, "Toby . . . Hey. Say hello to our visitor!"

It was a command. Twenty yards away, the elephant's head bobbed, he trumpeted a halfhearted farting sound.

Leland glanced at me for approval, then ordered, "Toby—wave!"

The elephant flapped a haze of flies from his ears and lifted one massive front foot.

"Good boy." Leland held out the block. The elephant approached, a white cattle egret settling itself on his back. "When he was younger, he could do all the tricks. Rear up on his hind legs, all the basics, but I don't make the old boy work for it anymore. You reach a certain age, you know?" The man smiled, relaxing for the first time since I'd arrived half an hour earlier.

It was after seven, the sun hot above cypress trees at the water's edge, yet the sun vanished behind Toby's gray mass as he neared. A musky pcat bog odor and buzzing flies accompanied him. His trunk, framed by ivory tusks, became a separate creature, extending, mouthing the air for taste, then swiping the block from Leland's hand and slinging it into his mouth.

Wave a magic wand and shrink yourself to the size of a chimp.

That's what I felt like, standing next to a five-ton bull elephant, when his trunk snaked toward me and sniffed my crotch.

"You're okay," Leland said, "he's harmless."

"I hope he's not looking for peanuts," I replied, "Right now, he could mistake me for female."

Introverts process humor by first inspecting it for sarcasm. A beat later, Leland laughed, patted the animal's trunk. "You wouldn't want to walk in here with a pellet rifle. That's why we have all the gates and fences and signs. Damn rednecks, but ol' Toby here has never hurt a flea." Another friendly pat on the trunk. "Have ya, big fella? Sometimes I wish you'd caught one of those brats."

I replied, "Who could blame him?" aware the elephant's saucer-sized eye, a star-black cornea linked to a brain, was focused on me. From the nearby pond floated the scent of carrion, but no vultures were feeding in the cattails. Yes, he remembered crushing the gator . . . And he remembered me.

Leland dusted his hands together, saying, "Eat the rest, old-timer," and returned to the garage. I walked backward until the elephant released me by concentrating on what was scattered on the ground.

"Cane sugar," Leland explained. "My grandfather used a great big pot to boil it down for the elephants. Now we buy it in blocks. The twins would let the old boy founder on the stuff if I didn't keep this building locked."

Another opening to ask about Ava and Tricia, but I waited. Better if Leland brought it up himself.

NO . . . BETTER TO WAIT until Leland pretended to find a bottle of Smirnoff in the office mini-fridge, saying, "Wonder who left this?"

"Maybe they left some mixer, too," I hinted.

The third in line to the Albright fortune appreciated that. "I guess the sun's over the yardarm, so why not? I've had two of the worst days *ever*." He looked up from the fridge. "You probably already heard what happened yesterday. Esther didn't tell me until late last night."

The yelling match. Yes, he knew.

Stupid to play stupid, so I said, "The scene at your pool? Yeah, from Tomlinson." The building had central air but was cooler here in the office, which was small—a desk, a file cabinet, and two chairs on rollers, vinyl on both chairs cracked. I chose the one without armrests and sat, placing my canvas briefcase beside the chair.

Leland found plastic cups and ice, saying, "Smirnoff . . . it's crap compared to Grey Goose. Stoli's okay. Belvedere's better," then poured. "What did your friend say about their argument? Esther only gave me the censored version, and I don't believe a damn thing Ava tells me anymore."

His daughter Tricia, I guessed, had refused to talk.

I said, "This is the sort of third-party situation where I've told my son never to open his mouth."

"Good advice." Leland, no longer relaxed, poured another inch into his cup, handed me mine, and sat, stretching his long legs. "But, Doc, put yourself in my place. It's not like you're being paid to breach a confidence. You still haven't cashed that check—I called today."

I tilted the ice to my lips but didn't drink. How carefully had Esther censored the truth? That's what was holding me back.

Leland said, "Jesus Christ, I deserve to know the whole story. I'm asking you as a favor. Wouldn't you want to know?"

I said, "Yes, I would," which made the decision his, not mine. I told him what Tomlinson had said minus the accusations the women had traded. "Risky to paraphrase something I didn't hear," I explained.

No need. Leland sighed, sagged back in his chair, and swallowed. Looked at the ceiling until he had it under control, and finally said, "Esther told me *without* telling me, if you know what I mean. I'd like to break that yoga bastard's neck. You ever see him? Short little shit, tattoos and a nipple ring—likes to show off his abs, Esther says. Seducing Ava is bad enough, but my little girl, too? Tricia usually has better sense."

Laughing, exhausted by it all, he exhaled toward the ceiling. "I've been paying that prick to screw my wife and my daughter. That's what it amounts to. Enrique—Ricky, they call him. Stupid me, huh?"

I said, "I don't think you told me how you and Ava met."

He replied, "What you're asking is was I drunk and the answer is no. Just . . . tired of living alone, I guess, and it's unusual for beautiful women to laugh at my jokes. That's how it started—this was in Nassau, I own a small piece of a hotel there. Ava was doing a shoot for our management company and was supposed to fly home the next day. Like they say in the movies, one thing led to another. That was . . . two years ago."

"Where's she from?"

My questions were siphoning energy from Leland's anger and he didn't like that. "You're wondering if I ran a background check, and I should've. But she moved around a lot, worked mostly for hotel PR firms, and there are a lot of Ava Johnsons in the world. What it comes down to is, I married a tramp and it's going to cost me a lot of money. But I'm done paying for her goddamn boyfriends, I'll tell you that much."

Leland, six-six but delicate as a pianist, drew his legs under him and tried to puff up like a tough guy. "What I should do is break the little prick's neck, and I still might. I could, if I got mad enough."

I nodded as if convinced. "He's not worth going to jail for," I said, then tried to switch the subject, asking about a shark tooth I was holding, but Leland remained fixated on the yoga teacher. So I returned the tooth to a cluster of broken fossils and listened.

"Know what Ricky had the gall to do? A week ago, he talked Owen into investing five grand in his franchise, whatever the hell he calls it. It's not a lot, but it's my money. Owen signed a promissory note for what's no better than a pyramid con. I found out Tuesday, and then the son of a bitch stops by my pool for drinks like I'm a clueless old fool. I canceled the deal, of course. So what's Ricky do? He sent that freak to threaten my family."

I hadn't heard that part. "This was yesterday?"

Leland said, "I assumed you knew. Some greaser on a motorcycle . . . But wait, Esther wasn't clear about that. Maybe your friend was already gone by then."

I put the cup aside. "Tricia took the car, so Tomlinson hitchhiked back to his van. What did the guy look like?"

Leland said, "That explains it," then described Quirt: a biker wearing gloves who didn't remove his helmet when he appeared at the pool gate, then came through the gate while Esther, then Ava, watched from the kitchen. Ava told the girls to go away, claimed she could handle it. But it was Esther who had confronted the man.

"He threatened to torch our house if Owen didn't pay up. Esther was shaking when she told me last night. Called her a bitch and other names—she wouldn't say what—and Ava, of course, played ignorant about the whole thing. You know, clueless about her boyfriend's gangster methods."

Rather than telling him Quirt had been arrested, I waited to see what I could learn. "Tomlinson was definitely gone by then," I said. "He wouldn't have tolerated that."

"I would hope not. The bastard comes onto my property and talks to my daughter that way. Tonight, I'll stay at a hotel or have my stuff moved to the island. I don't ever want to see Ava again. I told the twins the same thing, stay away from that witch." He stood, his drink finished, but caught himself before pouring another.

I asked, "Did Esther get his license number before she called police?"

Leland didn't wince physically, but I sensed his discomfort. "No. She . . . she thought Owen might owe him money for another reason. I didn't tell her about the promissory note."

I had been holding back, but so was he. Time to put it out there—most of it anyway—and hope for some clarity. I said, "I think we do need to talk about it," and waited for Leland to turn, his expression defensive. "I know about Owen's gambling problem. And there are some other things you should be aware of, Leland."

"Owen's *what?*" He stared at me a moment. "My personal life is none of your damn business."

I said, "I didn't cash your check, remember? I thought we were talking as friends."

"Well . . . But just because your hippie pal heard some gossip about—"

"His name's Tomlinson," I said, "and he's worried about your daughters. He says they're nice women, just a little naïve."

"Now he's a behavioral expert, too, huh? I don't remember asking his opinion."

"Leland, come on. We can talk honestly or not, that's up to you. But let me straighten you out on a few things. I asked what the biker looks like because it's the same guy who threatened to shoot that elephant out there. The description matches, and so does the torching your house part. On the phone, he threatened to use gas rags and set Tomlinson's head on fire. That was . . . four days ago. And on Saturday, in Venice, a friend of Tomlinson's died in a house fire. They don't know yet if it was murder, but, let's face it, this guy's dangerous."

Leland, suddenly nervous, said, "Jesus Christ . . . are you sure?" He reached for the Smirnoff.

"I met him. He's brain-damaged from a motorcycle wreck—or maybe was always nuts—but one thing I'm sure of, he's bad news. No . . . two things: he's dangerous and he's not working for some small-timer like Ricky. Not for five thousand, he's not. Are you saying you didn't suspect he came to collect Owen's gambling debt?"

"Jesus Christ," Leland said again and walked to the window. Stood there a while, then said, "You have no right to make accusations about my family."

"Let's hope I'm wrong. You were afraid of hurting Owen's feelings, weren't you? I can relate. Last thing you want to do is alienate a son once he starts to come around."

"My *stepson*," Leland corrected, but said it as if he'd hoped for more. "Sure . . . the gambling thing crossed my mind. But when I talked to Owen this morning, he agreed that Ricky was behind it. The kid feels badly enough about investing in that damn franchise. Five thousand is his max without getting my okay and he knows he screwed up. Personally? I suspect Ava was nudging him along. She can manipulate without saying a word—I should know."

"You didn't ask Owen about gambling debts, though."

"He's been clean for almost a year. It would have been a . . . breach of trust, I guess. But, wait a second . . ." Leland placed a hand on the chair between us. "This biker, he threatened to set your friend Tomlinson on fire? Why didn't *you* call the police?"

I didn't answer right away, so he jumped ahead. "Is there something going on between Tomlinson and Ava that you're not telling me?"

I shook my head as I used an index finger to move the stone rib, then two meg teeth, neatening them like chess pieces among the other fossils. "It's all about these," I said. "Did you find them?"

The man shrugged. "It's an old habit. If I see something, I pick it up. But what's that have to do with this crazy person threatening people?"

"Money," I said. "I understand fossil hunting, the attraction, I really do. Owen told me the same thing: Everyone in the phosphate business becomes a collector. What I'm getting at is that list of names you gave me. I didn't expect to see your father's name, but what about men like Dalton Sanford? There had to be others in his circle."

Leland's reaction: nervous, same as when I'd asked about diving the pond. "If you're insinuating I own those stolen carvings, you're wrong."

"I'm not," I said. "At first, I thought it was a possibility, thought that's why you offered me a job—to monitor my progress. People do that sort of thing. But not people like you."

"Thanks . . . I guess. But I still don't see how this is any of your business."

I had made an observation, not offered him a compliment, but let it go. I swung my chair around. "Do you want some brain-damaged hit man to burn your house down? He not only threatened Tomlinson, he threatened me. You need to wake up before this gets out of hand."

"Well . . . sure. But why bring up Dalton's name?"

I said, "Someone is paying the guy. He showed up in Venice a couple of weeks ago, supposedly from out west. Nevada, I heard, and Owen told me about his trips to Vegas. Him and Harris Sanford. So some pissed-off Vegas loan shark could be behind it. Or someone local could've made a few phone calls and hired outside help, a pro at collecting debts, but also crazy enough to kill someone. Maybe the person knows it, maybe he doesn't, but he's still responsible."

Leland didn't want to believe me. "I covered Owen's outstanding debts after he agreed to go through a twelve-step program. So you're wrong. I have no idea about Harris and don't much care. Harris is . . . Well, he's always been a bad influence."

I said, "Maybe he still is. He and Owen grew up in phosphate country and they know people in the business. I assume Ava does, too. Put it all together. The relics trade is a multimillion-dollar business in Florida. It pays in cash, tax-free. If someone wanted to make a lot of money, fossils and artifacts are a lot safer than dealing drugs."

Leland, skeptical, said, "You and the Indian, the drum shaman, you've been looking for those carvings less than a week. How do you know so much?"

I indicated the chair, saying, "Leland, have a seat. It's what *you* know that can put the bad guys in jail."

IN THE STORAGE ROOM, isolated between two steel doors, Leland opened the first antique gun vault and pulled out several drawers, which were oak and lined with gray velvet to cushion expensive firearms. Instead of guns, they contained megalodon teeth and other fossils, no apparent order.

"No one's touched them," Leland said, exhaled his relief— *Phewww!*—and stepped aside. "Look for yourself."

I did, inspected the largest shark tooth, while he commented, "I hate opening these old safes. It's been a year since I bothered. No . . . two years. We switched insurance companies. That was the last time I looked."

Leland avoided the gun vaults for the same reason he seldom visited the ranch: They reminded him of his late father. That's why it had taken a while to convince him we should open the safes. Inside was what remained of the family's relics collection.

"Which isn't much," he had warned. "My father was a drunk. I think I mentioned that. Toward the end, after he'd screwed up everything else, he sold or lost our best pieces to finance his drinking—or on get-rich-quick schemes. He told my mother that the collection was stolen, but I never believed him for a moment."

I had countered, "Don't be so sure," to tempt him.

Leland had set his drink aside, then pushed the bottle away, when I told him the house of another major collector, Finn Tovar, had been robbed.

Tovar—Albright recognized the name but didn't interrupt.

"Owen is the fourth generation," I reasoned. "A gambling habit instead of whiskey. It could be that he's dealing in relics to pay for his losses. If he is, someone else is involved—one of the Sanfords, probably Harris, not Dalton. I could be wrong about that. And . . . well, I'm wondering about your wife, too. A stranger shows up on a motorcycle and Ava says she can handle the guy? There's something wrong there."

It was enough for Leland—Henry Leland Albright III—to decide, "Well, there's an easy way to find out." Then he had led me into this room where twin antique vaults, both a faded green with bright gold leafing, were bolted to the wall.

Now, here we were, looking at several hundred fossils jumbled on gray velvet, and I felt foolish—until I reexamined the tooth in my hand.

"Owen wouldn't steal from me," Leland said. "Ava, though, she's a different story. That's the only reason I bothered opening this safe."

He reached to move me aside, but I said, "You're the expert. What do you think of this?" I handed him the megalodon tooth, then removed two more from the drawer.

"It's from a prehistoric shark, for christ's sake. You expect a guided tour now?"

I said, "Take a close look." Owen had lectured me on the importance of coloring and common flaws, such as chipped serrations and splintered enamel. The specimens I had just selected were both chipped. Five teeth and a jawbone later, Leland was finally convinced.

"Good lord . . . I see what you mean. On this one, part of the root lobe is missing . . . the bourlette is barely visible. My grandfather, even my dad, wouldn't have kept junk like this in the collection."

I said, "If you think that one's bad," and handed him two more.

Slowly, at first, Leland sorted through fossils in the top drawer, then opened the other drawers in a rush, pawing through each, before moving on. At the bottom of the safe were two oversize doors that required a key. He said, "I'm almost afraid to look," but opened them anyway.

They were empty.

"I can't believe Owen would do something like this," he said, then stood, more dazed than angry.

I asked, "What was supposed to be in there?"

"Someone took the collectible stuff and replaced it with worthless crap. But wait . . . Maybe it wasn't Owen."

"Who else has the combination?"

He had to think about it for a moment. "No one. Not the twins, not Owen, nobody. The only place it's written down is in my estate papers and they're sealed until my death."

I asked, "Is your attorney Dalton Sanford?"

The inference troubled him at first, then irritated him. "No. Well . . . Dalton was our attorney, but I moved our business to another firm after my father died."

I was wondering if Leland had changed the vault combinations, too, but asked, "What about the property manager?"

Leland said, "Old Cliff? No, his health has been so bad the last couple of years, I keep him on out of loyalty." He stared at the other gun vault, already worried. "My grandfather's most valuable pieces are in there." He turned, his face mottled. "You mind waiting in the office while I check?"

I was sitting, my canvas briefcase in my lap, when Albright came through the door. One look and I knew, before he said, "Everything's gone. Whoever did it didn't even bother with fakes in the other safe. Fakes would have been so obvious."

In my hand was an envelope containing wide-angle shots of the mastodon tusk, but I waited. "What's missing?"

"I just told you—*everything*." Which sounded condescending, so he added, "Sorry, Ford. Uhhh"—his eyes found the mini-fridge, where he'd placed the Smirnoff—"I would've never found out if it wasn't for you. Screw the dollar value, what was in there was all that was left of my grandfather's collection. Irreplaceable, some of those pieces." He started toward the fridge but reconsidered, saying, "My father, of course, pissed the rest of it away."

"The bottom of a bottle can be a long fall," I agreed.

Leland tested that for criticism, then decided, "Yeah, a hell of a waste." He turned away from the bottle and the fridge, saying, "Guess I better call Owen."

I carried my briefcase outside, through the gate to my truck, and removed unnecessary gear from my dive bag. Some of it was still damp from diving with Mick and his clients. I put the envelope containing mastodon photos in the bag, plus the spectrophotometer and some filter flasks for water samples, and left my briefcase in the truck. Leland was standing at the window when I returned.

"Did you get ahold of Owen?"

"I left a message," he replied, "but I didn't mention the safes. He'll know from my tone I'm upset, though." The man sounded exhausted, and didn't ask why I was carrying a different bag. He added, "I was trying to remember if Owen was here the day the insurance agent inventoried the collection."

I said, "Two years ago, you said. Think Owen might have memorized the combinations?"

"I'm pretty sure he didn't, but maybe. He's got a first-rate memory, that kid. His mother was the same way." He looked across the room while his mind worked at something. "The other night, you struck me as a pretty solid guy, Ford. I'm curious about something. Did you really ask your pal Tomlinson if he was screwing Ava?"

I replied, "Yes . . . but only to protect myself. When I lie, it's usually for the same reason."

Leland nodded. "Then I was right about you."

Photos of the mastodon tusk. I was thinking about them while he tried to collect himself by rehashing what had happened, then finally admitted, "I asked you to leave the room because I didn't want you to see what was inside that safe."

"I'm aware of that."

"I think it would've been okay."

Rather than ask, I said, "You can't be too careful."

"But I tend to overdo it. Having money—not that we have much left—and owning a piece of Bone Valley attracts all sorts of crazies. So, for me, it's easier to shut out everyone. I've . . . never felt comfortable around people. Which was okay until the last few years. Don't most men have friends to call when everything goes to hell? I can't tell the twins, and I sure as hell can't go running to Ava." He made a sound of frustration. "Hell . . . maybe I should have taken up golf or something like everyone else my age."

His admission had the flavor of adolescent angst, and I pictured Albright as a towering, clumsy kid, the easy target of pint-sized bullies. Because he was wealthy, his shyness would be mistaken for aloofness. Now the towering adult was still a loner and was still an easy target—an ex–fashion model was proving that.

I tried to lighten things up. "You're welcome to call Tomlinson. He's a lot of things, including a Zen Buddhist master. He'll talk you to death if he doesn't cure you first."

The man chuckled, a weary sound, without turning from the window, but then did turn and wasn't smiling. "The biker who threatened Esther, what did you mean I'm the one who can put him in jail? If you're right about Owen, I can't get the police involved."

"Put the *bad guys* in jail," I corrected, then explained that Quirt was already in jail.

"Well . . . that's great," he said, then appeared puzzled. "What's his name again?"

I told him.

"*Quirt?* That's a strange one. When this was actually a ranch, a couple Florida cowboys worked for us. A quirt is a small whip with knots tied in it so it cuts what it hits. That's what they called it, a quirt."

"The name fits," I said, "even if he made it up. Our next move—and this is just a suggestion—it all depends on what's missing from your gun vaults and how long it's been missing."

"We did the inventory less than two years ago," he said.

"I'm talking about the pieces your father claimed were stolen. Do you have a list?"

"Somewhere. I've never thrown anything away."

"What I'm thinking," I said, "is part of your collection might have been stolen twice—the second time when Finn Tovar's house was robbed. If that's true, and if your insurance company has a manifest list, it all still belongs to you. Including the things your father claimed were stolen."

Tovar—once again the name registered, but Leland let it go, saying, "Owning something doesn't mean much if I don't know where it is."

"You will if the police make a recovery," I replied.

Surprised, Leland cleared his throat but remained cautious. "But I don't want the police involved. Not if it puts Owen at risk. First, I'll sit him down and ask if he's gambling again. If so, how much does he owe? To hell with what's missing, I'm not going to send my own son to jail."

"Leland," I said, looking him in the eyes, "I know where your collection is."

He stared back, a *Who are you?* moment. "I'd like to believe that."

"It's true. Part of your collection anyway."

"How?"

"I can't tell you," I said.

"If Owen's at risk, you're going to have to do better than that."

"He's a grown man, Leland. That's all I can say right now."

Albright had already made up his mind to trust me, so it threw him. He started to say, "In that case—" but then stopped, surprised by a sudden thought. "Shit," he muttered.

"What's wrong?"

He headed for the door, saying, "I need to check on something. Stay here." Then reconsidered. "No . . . you might as well come along and see for yourself."

TWENTY-FIVE

OWEN AND HARRIS SANFORD WERE IN A TRUCK, WATCHING US, AS LELAND EX-
ited the building, and I followed him across the pasture, past the
pond, while Toby, in the citrus grove, shifted his weight from left
to right.

I didn't see or hear their vehicle. Maybe the elephant did.

Beyond the barn was a rise I hadn't noticed yesterday, a rounded
elevation that, beneath weeds, showed trenching scars as we neared.
Leland walked fast but slowed when he got to the top and studied
the area. He moved several times, his eyes snatching details from the
ground.

"Thank god," he said after a while.

"What's the problem?"

"I was worried somebody had been out here digging."

"Someone was," I said. Trench scars were as orderly as graves at
the top of the mound where weeds had taken over.

"Nothing fresh, though," he said. He took a big breath and let it
out, a man who wasn't overweight but didn't get much exercise. He

stood there, huffing after the long walk, and tugged at his shirt for air. "I was worried because of what's missing from the safes. If someone knows the combinations, they might have found out about this place, too."

"What's special about it?" I asked. Tractors had harvested sod from the area, it looked like, but years ago.

Leland walked toward the pond, saying, "I hope I'm right about you," which meant something. I watched him kick at an eroded spot, kneel, and sift through a matrix of sand and fossils. He tried two more spots, ignored a nice-looking meg tooth, before saying, "Okay . . . this is more like it." He brushed off his slacks and handed me a pottery shard, then a wedge of black glass. "Hold it up to the sun," he suggested.

Tiny air bubbles were gelled within. I said, "This was hand-blown," then examined the pottery: charcoal gray on one side, sand-colored on the other, but not thick like the jar I'd found. "Could be early Indian," I said, "but where'd the glass come from?"

He did a slow pan to the water, hands on his hips—a land baron savoring his property—while he tried to recover from his recent shock. "No one but my grandfather could have figured it out. In those days, men—the empire builder types—didn't bother with college. They learned so much from their failures, they knew damn-near everything by the time they succeeded. I've walked archaeologists through this pasture but they never looked twice."

I considered the hill's contours and referenced a map of archaic rivers in my mind. I guessed, "Was this an Indian trading center?"

"In a way. It was a Paleolithic village, and that was a primary watering hole"—he looked toward the pond—"for god knows how many thousands of years. The early Spaniards were here, too. That was the confusing part. Maybe as early as the fifteen hundreds, they had a camp here—that's based on the glass we found. It's everywhere."

Aware that my attention vectored, Leland smiled. "You like history, I could tell the night we met. Go ahead, look for yourself."

I squatted over the spot while he continued talking. "When I was ten, my grandfather brought me here almost every afternoon. Summer vacation. I'd made my parents mad, for some reason— boys' camp, that was it. I hated camp, all the bullying crap that went on, and I didn't like sports. Anyway . . . my Grandpa Henry would load up shovels and sifting screens, strung the area off in quadrants, and we did our own archaeological dig. But first he made me promise not to tell anyone and he meant it. By then, he already knew what this place was. He was another very straight guy. To him, a man's word meant something. I don't know how my father got so screwed up."

Among fossil fragments and shell, I saw more pottery and another fleck of glass, but also kept watch on Toby. If not for the elephant, I might have seen a truck slowing among trees outside the electrified fence—Owen and Harris Sanford returning to dive the pond.

Leland talked on about his grandfather, then finally explained why he'd brought me. "A lot of the pieces missing from those safes we found right here. Same with some of the best stuff my father sold off . . . or whatever the hell he did with it."

I asked, "Like what? And don't tell me Ponce de León's sword. You were testing me the other night."

"It's a way of smoking out kooks who'd kill their mothers to find what we found," he said. "Those stories are just that—fairy tales. But we did recover the hilt from a sword—no idea who it belonged to, but it could have been De León's, I suppose."

"It was in the safe?"

"That, and other things my father didn't bother with because they'd be harder to sell. Now that you bring it up, I like the idea of that rusty old thing being Ponce de León's."

"Or Pedro Menéndez," I said. "Last night, I was reading about him."

"*Exactly.*" Albright, pleased I was interested, sounded enthused. "I've wondered the same thing. Menéndez spent two or three years searching for his son and he made probes inland. There was no way of knowing who it belonged to, though, from the piece we found. Steel with scrollwork, but in pretty bad shape. We didn't find De Soto's gold cross either, but that's not the point. What we found was valuable to me. It was like solving a puzzle. Who was here? Why would a man go off and leave his sword? Like that. You know?"

I said, "Maybe the archaeologists could've helped if you hadn't steered them in the wrong direction."

He took that as a slight and walked to another spot. "I figured the first thing out of your mouth would be, 'What did we find worth selling?'"

"Or worth stealing," I said.

"I already told you that, too. Ivory from the Ice Age. Several very nice pieces." Leland noted my reaction before continuing. "Ivory doesn't hold up well in Florida unless from deep in the muck—or unless it was used as tools by the Ice Age people. I don't know why that is."

"It could have already mineralized by the time they found it," I suggested.

"An *anaerobic environment*, the books say," he replied, and used his hands to indicate the width of a trench. "We stripped away a layer at a time. Shovels; my grandfather wouldn't use a tractor. I think he was trying to build up my muscles without me knowing and I didn't care because it was so interesting.

"We figured we traveled about five hundred years for every few feet after the topsoil was cleared away. But that varied. Paleolithic tools, the really primitive pieces, were close to the water table or deeper. Stone tools, some coral spearheads, most of them very rough. My mother was furious if I came home muddy, so I brought clean clothes every day. And kept my mouth shut about what we were doing."

I probed again, saying, "I'm still surprised you didn't go for a swim."

Leland, grimacing at the pond, said, "With all the snakes? My grandfather wouldn't allow it. He saw a cottonmouth, back when the barn was still standing, he said was the size of a small alligator. I don't know how many times I heard him tell that story—a thirty-pound cottonmouth. And he wasn't a talkative man."

I didn't doubt that but doubted the story. The first Henry L. Albright, I suspected, had been as cunning as he was secretive. Giant reptiles are better than fences when it comes to discouraging visitors. I said, "You two must have been close."

"I wish to hell he was still alive. He was a tough businessman, but he lived by a code of ethics. A year later, we found the first burial, then what might have been a mass grave, and that was the end of it. For him, it wasn't about money. It really bothered him, finding human bones. He made me promise never to dig here again and keep what I knew to myself. That was . . . fifty-one years ago. Aside from Mattie, you're the first person I've brought here."

Mattie—Albright's second wife and Owen's mother.

"Why me?"

The man shrugged and gazed, hollow-eyed, at the water. *Because he has no one else,* I thought, but he responded, "I'll pay a reward if you help get our collection back. Why can't you tell me the whole story?"

I dodged that, saying, "Do some more digging, you might find even better artifacts. It's not illegal if you own the property. You're not tempted?"

"Lately, yeah, with all the bullshit at home. You know, spend some alone time out here and sift for Spanish material—that's my real interest. Possibly get a more exact date. Ivory and the burials are below water level, so I wouldn't disturb any of that. But I've read so much about amateurs screwing up important sites . . ." He drifted off again, then focused on his feet. "Most of the Spanish stuff came from right where I'm standing. Pedro Menéndez, or one of them, could have stood on this exact spot."

He'd used Menéndez to keep me interested, I guessed, but no need. "You told me the glass was everywhere," I said.

"The most valuable pieces are what I'm talking about. My grandfather had a theory. He believed one of the early captains didn't trust his crew—the men left guarding the ship—so he carried his valuables with him in a leather pouch. Then he was killed, or lost the pouch, because we found it all in one little heap about a yard deep. The pouch was long gone, of course."

He searched for a moment, then kicked at the ground. "Right about here. I sifted out every piece myself." He smiled, remembering, then realized he'd left me hanging.

"Oh! I found six Spanish coins and an uncut emerald. A beautiful thing about this big." He used a thumb and index finger to create a circle. "And also . . . Do you know what a bezoar stone is?"

I was picturing the two gold doubloons I'd taken from Deon the petty thief when I answered, "I don't think so."

"They're calcified stones from the bellies of wild goats. In those days, they believed bezoar stones could absorb arsenic from poison wine—which might be true. I found one attached to a gold chain. Only a ship's captain would carry something like that, my grandpa said. They were popular with royalty."

I asked, "It was all supposed to be in the gun vaults?"

Albright cleared his throat, the pleasant memory erased. "Nope. Like the leather bag, the stone, the emerald, the coins—lots of other nice pieces—they're all long gone. Which is why I hate opening those damn things."

He knelt and refocused on the ground, upset again. "What the hell. Truthfully, I was more interested in the old bottles anyway. Like that piece of glass. They were black unless you held them up to the sun. Or crockery that had fingerprints baked into it from some man or woman who died five hundred years ago in Spain. Not particularly valuable to your typical bone hunter but simple things that to me seemed pretty cool."

"Bone hunters like Finn Tovar," I suggested.

Leland was sifting dirt but stopped. "I was waiting for you to ask about him. If anyone has your artifacts from Montana, it's him. Did Tovar tell you his house was robbed? If he did, don't believe him."

My turn to watch for a reaction. "Tovar died a week ago. Brain tumor."

"Really?" The troubled land baron brightened. He put his hands on his knees to stand, a tall man with lower-back problems. "Finally . . . some good news. It's been a long time since I've heard that name. Are you sure he's dead?"

"I want to show you something," I said. My dive bag was behind us, and I went to get it while Leland continued talking.

"The last time I saw Tovar—he was such an offensive little prick, that guy—it was a few days before he was arrested for assaulting our night watchmen. That was twenty-some years ago. I was still in college but already working for the company." He cast a look toward the cattails. "My foreman found the guard lying down there, the back of his head smashed in. They couldn't make the charges stick, which was bullshit."

"You seem pretty sure." I was walking toward him, dive bag over my shoulder.

"What would you think? A few nights before it happened, I caught Tovar trespassing, and he threatened to kick my butt. Then threw his damn shovel at me when I didn't back down."

"Where was this?"

"There." He indicated the pond. "The shovel didn't leave a mark, so I couldn't prove it. And the guard never regained consciousness, so Tovar walked. But you know why I really think they let him off?"

I asked, "Tovar was near the pond but not in the water when this happened?"

"Yes, digging." Irritated that I had interrupted. "It's possible he got off because he was my father's sometimes drinking buddy. People wouldn't say it to my face, but that's what I heard later. The Albright name carried a lot of weight back then . . . or maybe Tovar was blackmailing him. I've always suspected that, too. Along with the booze, my father supposedly had a lot of girlfriends. Tovar was a ruthless son of a bitch. He would have used something like that or even set him up. For ten years after my father died, I expected to get an envelope full of sick nudie pictures in the mail with an extortion note."

"Leland," I said, "then it's possible he did blackmail your father. Maybe your father had to pretend the collection was stolen to cover the truth—he used it to buy his way out."

Men don't release long-held convictions easily. He grumbled something and then said, "You didn't know my father."

"No, but I'm getting a pretty clear picture of Finn Tovar. You never saw him after that?"

"A glimpse every few years, but I always went the other way. We had just that one run-in."

I placed the bag on the ground and opened it while he added, "What you said about Owen, that he might be repeating the same cycle . . . Well . . . that is possible. It really hit home."

Should I show him the mastodon photos or press for water samples first? The sun was almost down, and diving visibility was fading with it. That's what I was deciding when a couple of details sparked, then fused. I said, "Wait a minute. Why wasn't Tovar afraid of your elephants? You had several from the photos I saw."

The man was glad I asked. It allowed him to share his one small victory over the bone hunter. "Because after what happened to our night watchman, I figured out a way to stop that bastard. I had the elephants moved here. My father didn't give a damn by then, and it solved the problem."

I said, "You're a clever guy," which produced a smile that was unexpectedly shy.

He talked about how obvious the solution seemed at the time, speaking in a matter-of-fact way that introverts use to deflect attention they in fact enjoy. Then said, "Most people believe I did what I did, put up all this fencing, because of how my father died. You know, some gesture to honor his memory. But that's not true. I did it to protect what my grandfather and I found here. If I sign the mining lease, this little section will be exempted." Leland grabbed a fistful of gravel and used his fingers as a sieve while his eyes avoided the pond.

I said, "I got the impression your father drowned in the quarry by the big sand dune."

Leland didn't look up. "You heard that from Owen. That's what I want people to think," then did look at me and used the envelope I was holding to change the subject. "What do you have there?"

I handed him the photos.

Twice he mumbled, *"My god,"* as he studied the wide-angle shots of the mastodon tusk.

"Does it look familiar?"

"My grandfather found this. I'm not sure where, but the ivory we found—digging here, I'm saying—those pieces didn't compare to this one." He turned the photo so I could see it and touched a finger to the tip of the tusk. "There's a rectangular sliver missing, and the shape is exactly right. There's no doubt in my mind."

I wasn't going to tell him about the petroglyph. Not yet, but I was curious. "There's something unusual about that tusk. If the police recover it, they're going to ask. Did your grandfather mention anything different about it?"

Leland had been squatting but stood. "Don't play games. This is one of the things my father sold. How did you get these pictures?"

"Sold it or gave to an extortionist," I said. I had my snorkeling gear and water flasks bagged and ready to go. "We'll talk more when I'm done getting samples."

"You're not going in there—the sun's almost down."

I said, "I think you'll want me to, Leland. The part I didn't tell you earlier? I'll tell you now if you let me dive that pond."

WHAT I TOLD LELAND BEFORE WADING into the water was, "You'll get that tusk and part of your collection back if you help me, but think about this: Wouldn't the things you and your grandfather found be better off in a museum?"

I had spent twenty minutes explaining, so it was after eight, too late for light to pierce water, but I stripped down to shorts and dive boots anyway. Leland believed I wanted samples, which was true, but I didn't need to get wet for that. What I wanted was to see how Toby reacted to my second entry into the pond.

At least two divers had been here before me . . . possibly more, depending on how Leland's father had drowned. The details could wait. I wanted to know if familiarity altered the elephant's behavior. A big block of sugar might also work as a bribe. If I had noticed Toby's fondness for sugarcane, someone else might have figured it out, too. It was a way of attacking my own theory, which kept getting uglier: Leland's stepson, his new wife, and someone else— possibly Harris Sanford—were systematically stealing what the man was fighting hard to protect.

Challenging my own belief system is healthy. It occasionally con- firms that I'm a misguided dumbass and as lazy-minded as the next guy—not that I or anyone else has to admit it.

The process is cleansing enough.

In this case, I *wanted* to prove myself wrong. Not just because I liked Leland, although I did like him in a distant, arm's-length sort of way. I wanted my theory to collapse because, if I was right, an even uglier hypothetical slipped neatly into place: The rednecks who long ago had used Toby for target practice were in fact upper-class brats who lacked a conscience.

The elephant hadn't approached when I showed up with Owen on Sunday. On that same day, I had witnessed Harris Sanford shooting turtles because turtles were the only living creatures within range.

So I pushed ahead with my little experiment while Leland paced along the shore. Used a chunk of bamboo to bang the cattails as a warning, then used it as a probe to spook snakes lying on the bottom.

Toby watched my progress.

I was thigh-deep, getting my fins ready, when Leland's cell rang and I heard him say, "Where are you? You sound upset." Then he turned and shaded his eyes. "No, I don't see any truck," but then did a minute later, saying, "Yeah . . . okay, I see you now."

Truck? I followed his gaze to a red Dodge Ram that was greyhounding toward the gate, the passenger door opening before it stopped. It was Harris Sanford's truck. I recognized it from the shooting incident, so stood and watched while Leland said into the phone, "Hold on a second, *I* make the decisions. You don't own this place yet."

Owen, in a blue shirt, was getting out, a phone to his ear, and said something to which his stepfather responded, "This is stupid— come down here if you're that mad." Then walked away, talking, his voice too soft to hear.

The conversation went on for a while before Leland returned, tucking the phone away. He appeared nervous, a man caught in the middle, and tried to ease into an explanation, saying, "I told Owen about the safes being robbed. He's as shocked as me. And he was

already upset after seeing you in the pond and . . . Well, Christ—
how about we do this another day, Ford?"

I asked, "What's his problem?" and glanced at the elephant—
Toby, his trunk curled into a question mark, was rocking side to
side, while Harris slammed the door and joined Owen at the gate.

"Like I explained," Leland said, "we don't let people dive on the
property—even Owen and his friends. That's always been a rule, so
naturally he didn't like it when he saw you. There are insurance is-
sues, so he has a valid point—not that I'll back down on this. But
let's wait until he cools off."

"They just got here," I said. "How did he know I was in the
water?"

Leland thought about that. "Damn if I know," he said finally.
"Hang on."

He waved Owen and Harris toward us, then dug for his phone
when they didn't respond. After that, I listened to a one-sided family argument. Muck tried to suction my shoes off, water cooler than
the air. I kept my feet moving while my eyes moved from the elephant to the two men at the gate. A couple of minutes was enough
to draw a conclusion: Owen was afraid of Toby, Toby was afraid of
Harris or he was afraid of Owen—or both.

I slogged to shore and got dressed. By then the phone argument
had escalated. Leland kept his distance, mostly listening but occasionally snapping off a few words. The exchange continued as the
truck did a one-eighty and banged cross-country toward the trees,
not south toward the front gate.

Strange . . . yet it offered me hope of speaking to Owen and his
trigger-happy friend. I wanted to get a look inside the truck and see
if there was a gun rack—and scuba tanks. Both men were gam-

blers, and I was willing to bet they'd already recovered the rifle I'd thrown into the lake.

"He's a sensitive kid," Leland explained, walking me to my truck. "Like his mother. Mattie was sweet, but I had to be careful what I said. One thing I'm sure of, though, he had nothing to do with opening those safes. He wants me to get the police on it right away. That's a good sign. Tells me Owen has nothing to hide, which means you're wrong about him. The gambling, at least."

I was tempted to respond, *Police are already on it*, but didn't because of a rumbling noise coming toward us. Leland heard it, too, and turned to see a motorcycle, driver helmeted, taking his time on the gravel lane that led to the entrance a quarter mile away. The bike slowed . . . stopped, then turned around, but not before the driver waved a jaunty hello or farewell, one big black glove mimicking a cowboy hat.

I said, "Shit—that's him. Someone posted bail."

Leland didn't make the connection. "Owen must have left the main gate open," he said, then added something I didn't hear while he patted for his phone.

I opened my truck and slid my bag onto the seat. Told him, "Call the police. I want to make sure the guy leaves."

Leland still didn't understand. "It's probably a sightseer or one of Owen's friends. Let me give him a call."

I stopped Leland by taking his arm. "Damn it. That's the biker who threatened to burn your house down. Call the police."

"But you said he was in jail."

"Just do it," I said, and got in my truck.

TWENTY-SIX

MICK HAD GIVEN ME CRAZY QUIRT'S CELL NUMBER. SHOULD I CALL HIM?

No . . . but I picked up my phone anyway and noticed a message from Tomlinson. It read, in part, "I know who's responsible for Lillian's death. Call me . . ."

I'd been right. Tomlinson had been tracking the mysterious power person on his own. I couldn't call him now, but I did consider sending Quirt a text—something to taunt the man and glue him on private property before he got to the main gate.

Trespassing wasn't much of a charge, but it was a start. Another possible bonus: If Owen and Harris reappeared, it might force a confrontation between them and the biker.

I know who's paying you. A text like that might do the trick, even though Tomlinson hadn't divulged the name. *Afraid of me?* That was better. Poke the biker's ego and all his craziness might come pouring out.

I thought about it as I drove, avoiding potholes, my truck's shocks creaking on a tractor lane in need of grading. At the speed I was going, I wouldn't catch a motorcycle, that was for damn sure, so maybe sending a text was the best next move.

No need. I came around a bend and there was Quirt a hundred yards away, blocking the entrance, the main gate closed, which screened him from the road, Quirt astride his rumbling Harley. Not waiting on me necessarily, probably waiting on Owen and Harris, his arms crossed until he saw my truck. Then sat straighter—an *Oh boy!* surprise, which he signaled with another wave, his big black glove imitating a bareback rider.

I slowed and reached for my phone again, worried that Leland hadn't called the police. Quirt saw me, figured out what I was doing, and gunned his motorcycle at my truck. My window was open; plywood covered the other. The Harley's engine was so piercing, it caused me to drop the phone, downshift, and steer toward the pasture to give him room to pass.

Passing safely wasn't what Quirt had in mind. The Harley reared when he kicked it into second, then hunkered itself on the gravel while he steered straight at me, his helmet a projectile that glistened in the late sun.

A game of chicken from some old movie, *Rebel Without a Cause*, came into my mind. But a motorcycle versus a pickup? No . . . this was a test or a game. Quirt was brain-damaged, not suicidal. But if he expected me to sit there and play along, he was wrong.

I gripped the wheel, turned toward him, and hit the accelerator— which damn near caused my truck to stall. My engine recovered when I double-clutched, and my tires kicked some gravel as I shifted into second. Thirty-five miles an hour . . . forty, almost fifty. I expected the Harley to veer right or left.

It kept coming. So maybe Quirt was suicidal—but I'm not. A

few car lengths before impact, I surprised him with what driving instructors call a boot turn. I jammed the emergency brake to the floor . . . skidded . . . and turned the wheel a quarter turn, which spun the bed of my truck into the Harley's path.

Everything in the cab went flying, and I tensed, expecting eight hundred pounds of motorcycle to crash through the rear window. Instead, I felt a mild thump, and watched in the mirror as a helmeted rag doll tumbled past into the pasture. The Harley came next, its foot bar gouging a furrow as it tilted to earth.

When I jumped out, Quirt was already getting to his feet, so I checked my truck for damage as I circled around the back. The rear bumper had clipped the Harley's front wheel—the wheel still spinning even though the bike had stalled while trying to auger itself into the ground. My fender was smudged with a tire-tread tattoo but otherwise fine.

"Goddamn, hoss! Where'd you learn that move?" Quirt shouted it from inside his helmet; tried to sound impressed but couldn't disguise his rage. It was in the way he marched toward me, shoulders squared, but staying busy with something as he walked. He'd found a spare bionic hand, I realized, and it was hanging loose, the stump of his wrist showing, while he worked to reattach the thing.

He worked at it some more while yelling, "Wish to hell someone had that on a movie camera! That was James Bond material right there."

"Are you hurt?"

"Naw . . . just a temporary glitch." He stopped, adjusted a strap, and extended his left arm—*click-click*—a different attachment on this hand: snippers sharpened top and bottom like an axe. Not huge, but large enough that the man resembled a crab with a claw. "See?

Good as new." *Click-click-click*—he demonstrated again. "But you better pray to God that bike's not broke, I'll hang your balls on my mirror." He veered toward the Harley.

"We'll let the police decide," I said, and turned to search the cab for my phone.

"Now, hold on a minute! Let's you and me discuss matters before we get our insurance companies to bickering."

I ignored him until he said, "*Hey*—how about this: I'll put a bullet in your belly if you take one more step. *Asshole.* I spent the night in jail 'cause of you and your goddamn dog."

I turned. Quirt's helmet pivoted from me to his bike to emphasize his advantage, Quirt only a few steps away from saddlebags he claimed held a .357 Magnum. Plus, the rifle scabbard he'd mentioned, the butt of a Winchester, protruding from fringe work. No way I could get to his bike or my truck before he got to his guns.

He was convinced of it. I was, too.

Quirt said, "Unless you got another pistol in your butt crack, I'd advise you to take me seriously for a change. You want to guess what happened to the last man who went crying to the cops?" By habit, he reached to remove his helmet but flipped up his visor instead. The sun was behind me, below the trees. Enough filtered through to bronze the man's crushed left check. It added a glaze to his eyes.

What I wanted to ask was, *Did you bury him on Boot Hill?* but chose diplomacy, saying, "Maybe I'm overreacting. Let me help you lift that bike. It looks heavy."

He stared at me a moment, then knelt over the Harley, pulled the rifle, and shucked a round using only his good hand—did it with a flourish, something he'd practiced. *The Rifleman*, he'd said, and was right about the cocking lever, a hoop that allowed him to spin the weapon and shoot one-handed. Didn't point it at me, but close enough, the rifle angled in my direction. "Overreacted, my ass. You pressed charges against me, slick. Now you're gonna pay the price." He motioned with the rifle. "Come around to this side of the truck."

The bed of the truck was between us. I wanted to defuse the situation but not leave myself defenseless. I walked to the tailgate, no farther, and said, "You've got a right to be mad. But your boss isn't going to be happy if he has to forfeit his bail money. How much if the cops arrest you again?"

Quirt cackled at that while his attention shifted from me to the motorcycle. Finally, he got the thing on its kickstand and looked it over. A bent fender; high chrome handlebars, off square, above a black teardrop gas tank with white script: *No mercy.* I watched his bionic hand become a vise. He twisted the fender straight with no effort. Same with the handlebars. Brushed away grass and dirt clods, but not fussy. When done, he started to say, "Marion—that's a damn sorry name for anyone who stands up to piss. Why'd your folks—" but then music in his pocket caused him to reach for his phone. "I might have to take this," he said as if apologizing. "You mind?"

He steadied the bike, then checked caller ID. An awkward moment for Quirt—should he remove the helmet or put the phone on speaker? I was thinking, *If he turns his back, I'll break his neck.*

Quirt, a survivor, wedged the phone under his helmet instead. Told the caller, "I'm sort of in the middle of something, so don't talk, just listen. You didn't tell me to dress for company. Understand my meaning? So give me a few minutes—dumbass."

The phone rang again as he put it away, the same music which I finally recognized: "Flight of the Valkyries." What had thrown me was trying to match the tune with some cowboy classic—or country rap, which I wouldn't have known anyway.

Quirt, phone in hand, confided to me, "Persistent prick, isn't he?" and this time put it on speaker, saying into the phone, "Harris, you got the brains of a duck. Don't you know how to take a hint? A fella here named Marion Ford is listening to every word, so go ahead, shoot your mouth off all you want. You remember Marion—the ol' boy who took your rifle, then should've spanked your bitch ass."

The crazy biker knew about the rifle incident, too.

Harris Sanford didn't speak for several seconds. Then said, "I must have the wrong number."

Quirt jumped on that. "Don't you hang up on me, you prissy bastard. I got a question—no, two questions. *Harris?* Don't pretend you can't hear me."

Another long silence before Harris said, "Christ, I called three times. We didn't expect Ford and the old man to be here. Don't you check messages?"

"Son, on the back of a Harley Shovelhead, especially the muffler system I got—" Quirt got that far, then realized what he'd just heard. "What old man? If you done screwed up again, I got no choice."

Harris said, "Don't threaten me. Jesus Christ, why are you talking to Ford? He's the one who—"

"Threaten you?" Quirt cut in. "When I stick a gun up your ass, that'll be your first clue. I asked a simple question: How many people did you invite to this monkey hump?" Then glanced at me as if we were buddies, two good ol' boys bonded by this rich kid's stupidity. Actually covered the phone to ask me, "Can you believe this shit?"

I replied, "Leland Albright, that's who he's talking about. He owns the property."

"The head honcho, huh? Where is he?"

"About three hundred yards up the road. You'll see a black Escalade. Why not put the rifle away and we'll get this straightened out."

That ended our friendship. "Shut your damn mouth," he said, then asked Harris, "Did you bring your uncle's whatchamacallit?"

Silence, then Harris answered, "His lockbox, yeah. It's in my truck. But we haven't done the other thing yet because they were here when we showed up."

Quirt didn't like that. "Goddamn it, then get your froggy flippers on or whatever it is you use. I ain't leaving here without at least five hundred K in ivory. Or cash money, which you don't have being a worthless punk."

"You're taking advantage of something that's not my fault," Harris argued. "Why?"

Quirt said, "'Cause your eight seconds are up, cowboy," then asked, "What about the elephant? You harvested them tusks yet?"

I don't know why that surprised me. The biker had dropped enough hints.

Harris stammered, "No . . . *no idea* what you're talking about—" which pushed Quirt over the edge, him saying, "You better be up to your elbows in Jumbo blood by the time I get there. And have a chain saw primed. I want that ivory."

He slammed the phone against his thigh, the rifle slipping from under his arm before he caught it with his bionic hand. Got it under control, put the phone away, then said, "I'm startin' to hate that song," when "Flight of the Valkyries" summoned him again.

He didn't answer this time. Gave me his full attention while he limped closer, feeling the spill he'd just taken. Stopped and considered the saddlebags, wondering if a .357 revolver was a better choice than a Winchester. Decided it was but kept track of me while he made the switch. Once he had the revolver out, he checked the cylinder before leaning the rifle against the Harley. Brain-damaged but still a careful man.

"This is the last place I expected to see you," he said. His voice different, talking like a farmer, with his sideways mouth, but deep into something, his mind already made up. "You got your gun in there?" He meant my truck.

"Look for yourself," I answered. "You don't really expect Harris to kill an elephant with a .22 rifle, do you? He's the one you need to worry about. The other day, he almost shot me in the head."

Quirt said, "I heard that story. But I like the one where you left Deon out there to drown better." He used his big-barreled pistol to designate a grassy patch. "I want you on the ground before I go through that truck. You sure a pistol ain't in there?"

"I never claimed there wasn't."

"Don't get sassy. If I find a weapon—listen to me, now—if I do, I'm going to call Deon and tell him to burn down your house. He's on his way to Sanibel with high hopes for them Pelican cases. Oh— and five gallons of gas."

I thought, *Warn Tomlinson*, but said, "He won't find what you're after."

"Then he'll start a nice fire and convince the hippie. Or set the hippie on fire—I don't give a shit as long as I get what I came for."

"There's an easier way," I told him. "I'll take you there myself— but call off Deon."

"What I want is not to have to repeat myself. On the ground, goddamn it!" He waved the pistol. "Toss your wallet toward me first. And I'll need the PIN code for your debit card if you got one."

Apparently, he was going to shoot me execution style. I took my time emptying my pockets while my brain discarded one hope after another. I hadn't brought a gun, and there was nothing in my truck but a seine net, a pair of white rubber boots, and two scuba tanks, both secured in an aluminum rack. Throw a boot at Quirt and

322

charge him—that was suicide. Or sprint away, zigzagging, and hope he'd miss with the revolver before he remembered the rifle. Almost as stupid.

The air tanks provided the out I needed when Quirt, after going through my wallet, noticed them. "You're a scuba diver?"

I said, "That's why I'm here. My gear's in the cab."

"You any good?"

"Better than Harris. You can't trust him if he's going to dive that pond. How will you know what he sees and what he doesn't?"

Quirt gave that some thought. "I might be willing to postpone this thing between you and me—but it's gonna happen. I knew from day one." Then flinched, as if an ant had bitten him, scratching at something under his helmet. "Shit . . . this brain bucket drives me nuts—never had to bother with one before."

"Then take it off," I said.

He did. I watched him remove the helmet . . . scowl . . . then lob it toward his bike. Didn't look at me for a moment, then turned, letting me see his face. No mask around his neck today. "What do you think?"

"This doesn't have to go south," I replied. "The cops have you down for a stolen plate and vandalism. So what? If you shoot me, though—"

"Not that," Quirt said, "the job that asshole surgeon did on my face. When the sun's low like this, his needlework looks like seams on a football. I've been thinking about hiring a lawyer."

I said, *"Oh,"* as if interested, then used my shirt to clean my glasses.

Quirt talked while I made up my mind, asking, "Why don't you trust Harris?"

"If you met him," I said, "you already know."

"A whining little punk, yeah. I can't disagree. Him and the other one, Owen—that's his name—they're in to friends of mine, a sort of organization, for three hundred thou. Which those fools let grow into a half a mil. That's the trouble with rich kids. They don't know the value of a dollar."

"Leland, the property owner," I replied, "he was just saying the same thing." Then took a long look at the biker's face before adding, "I've heard that if you sue a surgeon for forty thousand or less, their insurance doesn't even bother fighting it. Turn a little to your right— the light's better."

"That's how this happened," Quirt said, tilting his head. "A kid in his daddy's Corvette caused me to dump my bike as he was pulling out of a Denny's. Forty thousand, huh? That ain't nearly enough." He glanced at me to warn *I'm not stupid*, then forgot he was posing and strode to my truck, pistol ready.

"Ask four million and let them pick a number."

"Yeah," he said, "and sue the kid's daddy, too. I look like a turd dropped in cat hair, but he didn't give a shit. I'll tell you this"—Quirt opened the truck and leaned inside, tossed my dive bag onto the ground, before continuing—"That accident gave me what you'd call a different outlook on life. A few years before—you'd find this hard to believe—I was quite the stud. Even did some art modeling at school. Sparks Community College, which is close to Silver Springs."

"You're talking about Nevada?"

"The Fighting Cougars, yeah. We were ranked as high as seventeen, Division II football. Point is, that art teacher didn't hire me 'cause I was a faggot. I had looks."

I was thinking, *Keep him talking until he makes a mistake.* "If you sue," I said, "the problem will be convincing a jury your financial position has been impacted. What position did you play?"

Quirt opened my glove box after checking under he seat. "Quarterback—I wasn't just another pretty face. That's something else that hitting the asphalt at seventy-plus will do. After business school, I was on the fast track, got recruited by the Plaza. That's a hotel in Vegas. I would have been a blue-chip prospect, maybe worked for the Bellagio. But then a shit sandwich appears in the form of a Corvette. This idiot hippie kid, tanked up on waffle syrup, with a full-on Denny's buzz. Two years later, I'm wearing a steel plate in my head and collecting for loan sharks. No more beauty queens fighting to tickle my pud. Instead, now what I do is, I play Frankenstein and scare the shit out of deadbeats like those two."

He stood, looked down the road, letting his anger build, his mind on Owen and Harris. Or not. I was worried the word *hippie* had connected Tomlinson with the Corvette.

"Did you date any fashion models?" I asked him, Ava Albright on my mind.

Quirt gave me that look again—*I'm not stupid*—and slammed the truck door. "I was sort of hoping I'd find your pistol. If it wasn't for them scuba tanks, I'd've loaned you mine. My rifle, I mean. Put it in reach, with you on the ground, and backed away ten paces. Ever see *A Fistful of Dollars*? Sort of like that. It's still going to happen, but let's take care of some business first." He went to the Harley and yanked the rifle from its scabbard.

Insanity . . . now he was challenging me to a showdown.

I said, "Quirt, I don't know what's going on in your head, but it doesn't make much sense to collect money from Owen and Harris, then risk it all in a shoot-out. Think about it."

"Hell, hoss, I've *done* it. You'll be my fifth notch—not that I'd notch these fine buffalo-horn grips." He held up the revolver to show me black handles on chrome.

The man was unbalanced, so I tried twisted reasoning. "This is different. For one thing, I don't owe you money. But what's really going to piss people off is if you hurt that elephant. Shoot me, to be honest, it's no big deal—the news media, I'm saying. But shoot an elephant, people are going to be screaming for your head. I'm telling you, Quirt, this is a bad idea."

He filed that away, then motioned to the hood of the truck. "You ride up there. I want your back to the windshield so I can keep an eye on you. I'll drive." He waited until he'd opened the door to ask, "Are you saying I'm crazy?"

"A college quarterback is smart enough to walk away from a situation like this. Something's not right with the way your mind's working—have you seen a specialist?"

Quirt appreciated me not ass-kissing. "Good for you. I was losing faith in your style, ol' buddy. But now I'm gonna tell you what's what. 'Bout three weeks ago, I finally found that kid in the Corvette. Who wasn't such a kid, it being six years since the Denny's incident, but he still bawled like a baby when I gave him my rifle and backed away. What I told him was, 'You get first move.' He was still bawling when he made it . . . my fifth notch." White ceramic teeth grinned while he added, "I've got me an undefeated season going."

"Your fifth gunfight," I said.

His grin widened. "Sure as hell not the fifth person I've killed. You got any idea what it's like collecting for Vegas loan sharks? Those boys are like ticks in Italian shoes."

I said, "That's my point. Your lifestyle's not normal."

Quirt extended his arm; the stainless snippers made a hedge-clipping sound. "*Normal?* Hell, I left out the best part. See, what I did was I cut the kid's trigger finger off first—but not for the reason you think. Well"—he wanted to be honest—"there's no doubt cutting his fingers off gave me an edge in a shooting contest. What I'm saying is, I *like* hurting people since my wreck. It was just my way of thanking the kid for opening up a whole new way of life."

He said it in a bragging way to conceal what I believed he actually meant. "You want someone to stop you—is that it, Quirt? If it is—"

Face coloring, he shouted, "Let me finish my story! This happened out in the desert, mid-May, not even a month ago. No one around, so I cut that boy's nose off next, and"—he clicked his pincers to illustrate—"a snip here, a snip there. Well, I just sort of lost control after that. As you can understand, that had to be my last night in Nevada. As to the loan sharks, they'll be looking for me, too."

He enjoyed my reaction—a look of disgust—and was adding gory details when we heard *pop . . . pop-pop*: a small-caliber weapon, three careful shots fired long spaces apart. It puzzled him. He reached for his phone, saying, "That dumbass Harris, he told me his daddy had a Remington big bore rifle he could use—something that could handle the job." Then dialed and put the phone to his ear.

"Shit—voice mail," he said, and tried again, muttering, "Answer, damn you."

He was dialing Harris Sanford a third time when his hopes were realized. *BOOM . . . BOOM*—the report of a heavy-caliber weapon from somewhere near the pond. A trumpeting call, more like an elephant's scream, followed. Then a third shot, *BOOM*, that chased a flock of egrets out of the sunset, a sky streaked with pink and turning indigo.

Moonrise was hours away, but it would be dark soon.

Quirt smiled and put away the phone. "Hope you're hungry for elephant steaks. Now, sit your ass on the hood like I told you."

On the wild ride to the pond, I was thinking, *He didn't make bail. The crazy bastard escaped.*

TWENTY-SEVEN

THE PASTURE GATE WAS LOCKED AS WE BOUNCED TOWARD THE ESCALADE AND red Dodge Ram parked outside the fence, no one around, so Quirt laid on the horn, driving way too fast. That's when Leland staggered out, holding his chest, the office door open behind him, garage open, the concrete building leaden against trees.

The man's shirt didn't show blood but looked wet. He'd been shot. On the hood of my speeding truck, I lay back and banged at the windshield.

Quirt saw him and locked the brakes. I expected that but still went flying from the hood, which is what he wanted. I landed on my feet but momentum tumbled me. The crazy biker was out, revolver ready, by the time I was up.

"Shitfire," he said, "them boys were supposed to be here." He reached through the window and used the horn again. Looked at the red truck, his mind on the lockbox Harris had promised, but sniffed and said, "Goddamn place stinks. I thought goats were bad." Then studied the pasture, the musk of elephant strong in the air, it was true, but Toby was not in his usual spot. "That weed-chopper sounds nasty, hoss. I bet those rich pricks locked the gate."

The electric fence, he meant, four cables spaced ten feet high. High voltage, low amperage, Owen had told me. Not lethal.

I hoped that was true, because Leland needed help. He had stumbled to one knee, blood on his face, and was trying to get up.

"The combination is under the solar panel," I told Quirt, then ran toward the fence before I could change my mind. The bottom cable was a yard off the ground, humming in synch with three cables above—a sizzling sound. With enough speed, I told myself, I could dive between the first and second cable without feeling much.

I didn't feel much . . . until my trailing foot snagged as my hands touched ground on the other side. A hundred thousand volts sparked behind my eyes . . . then it was gone . . . and I was on my feet, Leland's face dazed as I ran toward him.

"You're . . . *not burned*?" Albright, in shock, was coherent enough to call out. Then pointed vaguely at the pond and said something I didn't understand. By the time I got to him, I saw what he was pointing at: a bright blue shirt near the cattails, a human arm protruding from what might have been a body.

Owen had been wearing a blue shirt.

I told Leland, "You'll be okay," although I had no idea if it was true. I got my hands under his arms and helped him sit, then laid him on his side, fearing he would aspirate. I ripped his shirt open, Leland saying, "Hurts like hell to breathe. Harris . . . he darted us both."

The man sounded drunk.

I said, "You mean shot you." A pneumatic cattle dart would have knocked him unconscious, and it didn't explain the blood.

From outside the fence, I heard a door slam and looked to see Quirt carrying a box away from the red truck. Then he dropped the box, smaller than a footlocker but heavy. He stuck the stainless pistol in his belt and knelt for a closer look.

On Leland's sternum, a tiny black dot appeared when I wiped blood away; I found another bruised spot low on his chest, right side, that might have shattered a rib. Not holes, more like needle marks. A gun designed to dart cattle would hit with a hell of an impact, but why was there blood on his face?

I said, "Open your mouth. Did you call nine-one-one?"

Leland shook his head, mouth wide, and let me look—no obvious internal bleeding—then insisted, "I'm okay. But . . . Owen. Go check. And where's Toby? Harris shot him, too, used a real rifle."

"Are you sure you were darted?"

He groaned, attempted to get to his feet, and fell back. "The first one bounced off . . . hit bone. I pulled out the next one but got dizzy as hell. He shot Owen in the back, though—is he okay?"

He turned toward the pond where his stepson lay hidden by cattails, not moving.

I asked, "Where's your phone?"

He had trouble processing that. "Harris must have took it. Or . . . maybe in the office. That's where I passed out."

I said, *"Shit,"* then jogged toward Owen but stopped a few yards away. There was nothing I could do to help him—that's how obvious his injuries were. Harris might have darted his old college buddy, but something else happened to finish the job.

Leland was waiting for an answer when I turned, but was spared the bad news by a gunshot, then another—Quirt trying to shoot the gate open, the biker furious when he inspected the lock. He waved the pistol, yelling, "Hoss! Drag that tall bastard up here and make him open this damn thing. You hear me . . . Hey, *Ford*!"

I ignored that and was soon kneeling by Leland again, him asking, "How is he?"

"Owen's still out," I said. "We need a phone."

From the gate, Quirt hollered, "Screw the combination. How many volts you say this fence is?"

We both turned. The biker was reaching his bionic hand toward the middle cable. Leland struggled to sit up, a panicked expression that told me Owen had lied. The fence wasn't harmless, might even be lethal, which fit with what Leland had said after watching me dive through the thing.

You're not burned?

I whispered to Leland, "Quiet," then waved Quirt toward us, calling, "It didn't hurt me."

"Goddamn thing's sizzling, hoss." The biker lowered his bionic hand, threaded the .357 pistol through his belt, and stepped back. "Where'd you say the combination is?"

Leland tried to sit up. "It could kill him."

Voice low, I replied, "Good. I've got to find a phone before he kills us both. Leland, you've got to trust me—I want you to play dead no matter what happens. At least unconscious. Can you do that?" Then I yelled to Quirt, "It's high voltage but low amperage."

"What?"

I said it again, adding, "Why even bother? He already called the police. Harris shot Owen and they're both in bad shape."

"Goddamn greenhorns." Quirt stomped his boot on the ground and walked toward my truck—fleeing, I hoped.

Leland grabbed my shirt and pulled me closer. "You've got to help Owen. I should have listened to you. Harris talked him into robbing me, but now he wants to square things. Harris turned on us both. He might come back and kill my son."

"Stop talking," I warned, and forced his head back. The crazy biker, instead of leaving, was returning with his Winchester. Maybe more firepower to shoot the lock off—something that seldom works.

No . . . I watched him stride to the fence in bulletproof mode, shoulders wide, while showing his face to the world. He reached the rifle out as if to test the middle cable, then decided, *Screw it*. Used his bionic hand instead, extending his arm, pincers open, and whooped like a drunken cowboy before he clamped down hard. A fireworks of sparks . . . then a sizzling boom when the cables fell . . . and Quirt reappeared through the smoke, his face aglow in the sunset light.

The crazy biker was right about the way he pictured himself: Frankenstein.

COMING DOWN THE HILL, Quirt hollered, "*Woo-wee!* I am a miracle of space-age plastics!" Then, midstride, swung his rifle at me. "We got work to do. Is that the head honcho?"

"He's unconscious," I said, stepping away from Leland.

"I don't give a shit if he's dead. Grab his wallet."

Albright allowed me to roll him on his side so I could, then I tried to decoy Quirt by walking toward the pond. "The cops are on their way. You should cut your losses. I'll come along, if you want."

He didn't understand at first, then said, "Oh, and show me where you hid them Pelican cases. Ain't that sweet—but it won't stop Deon from doing a number on your hippie friend. I'll get what you stole anyway." Quirt was taunting me, in good spirits again. His head pivoted along the pasture until he saw one blue arm protruding from the cattails.

"Owen's out," I told him. "Harris shot the elephant, too. The elephant probably ran off and Harris went after him—into those trees, most likely."

I wondered how Leland would react to that, but I kept my eyes on Quirt. He was angling toward the open garage, the rifle shouldered, his finger on the trigger. "What, you got X-ray vision now? I ain't leaving until I get what I came for—half a million dollars' worth. That prissy bastard could be hiding."

"*Where?* Have you ever seen an elephant?"

"Seen three of 'em a couple days back; made a wrong turn and damn near got arrested. Not an inch of ivory on them, though, or that would be my next stop."

He also had encountered security at Florida Elephant Rescue.

I started to repeat my lie about the police, but he cut me off, saying, "Hey . . . look what we have here." And plucked a chain saw from the grass. Sniffed it, inspected the blade and approved, before returning his attention to me. "Hoss, I don't like the way you keep pushing. Instead of running your mouth, get your flippers on and find what's in that pond."

"What did Harris promise you?"

"Ivory, dumbass, and some other goodies somewhere hidden on the bottom. A great big bag, he said. Now, get your butt in gear while I have a look around." He placed the chain saw where it was easier to see, reseated the pistol in his belt, and continued walking.

An ambush from the garage, that's what he suspected. It was obvious from the way he hunched down, taking slow hunter strides, his attention on the open garage. He poked his head in, then disappeared. It gave me an opportunity to whisper to Leland, "Stay down. Call police the moment I get him out of here."

Seconds later, Quirt reappeared from the office doorway, hollering, "Who you talking to?" and held up a cell phone he'd found. "Is this what he used to call the cops? Slick, I believe you been lying. Makes me feel better about you being my sixth notch. No"—his eyes found Leland—"my seventh." Then smashed the phone against the wall and swaggered toward us, raising the rifle to his shoulder.

I stepped in front of Leland. "Shoot him, you have to shoot me. Then who's going to dive for that bag?"

Quirt made a snarling sound that resembled a wolf and fired over my head. Spun the rifle one-handed and fired again. This time, the bullet kicked sand near my shoe and damn near hit Leland in the head.

I jumped away, yelling, "Is this your idea of a gunfight?" then took a few steps toward Quirt, who was closing the distance.

"You still got your trigger fingers, don't you?" he cackled, and shot twice more, both slugs threading the space between my legs into the dirt—not accidental. The former quarterback was a good shot.

My instinctive reaction was to stoop. Instinct gave way to a flooding anger that leached colors from the sky and tunneled my vision. Suddenly, I could see only Quirt in his biker vest, his damaged face and eyes that glistened—a hopeful look, staring at me—while he spun the rifle to shuck another round.

Behind him was the concrete building, the garage open like a cave. He flashed a silicone grin and yelled, "You 'bout ready to do this thing?"

This was the showdown he had been wanting.

I said, "I'm done with your bullshit, if that's what you mean."

"I can see that, hoss."

"Rifle or the pistol, I don't care—throw me one. You promised me a chance."

He held out the Winchester. "You mean this?" One-handed, he

leveled it from twenty yards away, chest-high, to kill me, but let the barrel dip just before he shot. The slug skipped off something to my left and tumbled toward the water, a buzzing sound that faded.

I flinched, despite my anger, and reassessed: A short-barreled carbine. Winchester 94, a western classic, with a magazine that held . . . I didn't know how many rounds. Fewer than nine but more than five, obviously. And probably four rounds left in his stainless .357. If he wanted to shoot me, though, he would've done it.

I kept walking.

"For a big ol' nerd, don't he got *style*?" Quirt looked beyond my shoulder, and it took a moment to realize he was speaking to Leland Albright. Leland had stopped playing dead, was struggling to get to his feet, while the crazy biker, unsure he wanted an audience, watched. Then Quirt welcomed him, asking, "Hey . . . you ever see *A Fistful of Dollars?*"

Leland's expression swung a question toward me: *Why is he doing this?*

It gave me an opening.

"His brain is more screwed-up than his face," I said. "If he had balls, he'd cut my fingers off first. That's what he does. But I'm not some idiot kid."

Use an audience to manipulate behavior—an effective tactic.

Quirt's facial scars flushed white, but he regained control and pretended it was funny. Said to Leland, "Ain't he something? He left this ol' boy I know two miles offshore to drown. Sharks everywhere, but he didn't give a shit." Then leveled the Winchester again, fifteen paces away, and ordered, "Stop right there or I'll shoot your tall friend."

Leland, now on his feet, resembled a drunken crane as he staggered toward Quirt, intending to help me . . . but then surrendered and stumbled toward Owen. Quirt tracked him with the rifle until I intervened by calling, "Hey—are you backing out?" Then flipped my middle finger at him. "Cut this one off first, then give me the shot you promised."

The insult exceeded my diving skills, and I'd gone too far. Quirt appeared to shudder, his mood change was so abrupt. His voice changed as well, raspier, and oddly more articulate, the sham cowboy displaced when he said, "You don't think I know what you're doing? Psychological bullshit won't work. You just killed your buddy, Ford—one piece at a time."

He raised the rifle to shoot Leland . . . but then lowered it when Leland stumbled and fell, the last of the Albright males still far from the cattails where his stepson lay dead. Quirt, for some odd reason, saying, "I'll be damned. Look at that—ivory on the hoof."

Which made no sense until I followed the biker's gaze to the hill where a Conquistador had once camped on bones of mastodons. An elephant was there—Toby, blood sluicing from his rear quarter. His eyes were fixed on Quirt, a man holding a rifle that might have been a spear. Wobbly, obviously wounded, but the elephant's brain was still working.

The biker hooted, "He ain't what you'd call smart, is he?" Then used bionic pincers as an aiming post and almost fired his sixth round . . . but reconsidered. A Winchester packs a punch, but it wasn't elephant-worthy—not from point-blank range, let alone two hundred yards.

"We gotta get closer," he said; swung around and ordered, "Grab that chain saw or I'll shoot the head honcho. Help me harvest that ivory, I might go easier on you both."

"Chain saw," I said, already picturing it as a weapon. "If that's what you want."

TWENTY-EIGHT

WHAT WAS TOBY, THE LIFELONG CAPTIVE, THINKING?

I watched the elephant as I followed Quirt. Old black eyes tracked us, exchanging data with an ancient brain, as we drew nearer. Ears flapped, but Toby's trunk dangled like a hose; limp, not bothering to wind-scent our progress.

The animal was in trouble. Harris had shot him with at least one heavy-caliber slug, his rear quarter black with blood and swarming flies. Alert, though—*something* had to be going on inside that massive head.

Something was. As we rounded the pond, Toby made a snorting sound and lunged, stiff-legged—a warning—then pivoted and lumbered toward the trees. Not running away . . . more like he didn't give a damn if we followed. Not concerned about the fence either— he bulled right through it, cables that had lost their sizzle falling like strings.

The biker fired a quick shot that caused the animal to buck but not stumble. Then Quirt held up his hand like an Indian scout and said, "Shit, hoss . . . he's a big 'un, huh? Wouldn't matter if I did hit him—not in the ass, it wouldn't."

"He's ready to go down," I lied. "See the blood?"

"If Harris was worth a shit, he'd already be dead. What we heard back there was shots from a big-bore rifle. That's what I need to finish that bastard. Wonder where it is?"

The biker turned and motioned a warning. "You keep your distance, hear? Any closer than ten paces, I'll shoot you in the belly. Harris . . . he probably got scared and run off," then he refocused on the elephant, who was entering the trees.

I carried the chain saw by the handle—get close enough, I would throw it, then rush the crazy bastard . . . or startle him by yanking the starter and lobbing it at him. A screaming chain saw would have an effect.

Quirt's euphoria was fading into uncertainty. *Good.* Owen was dead. Nothing I could do about that. But Leland needed medical attention, and Toby might survive bullets that had missed his brain and vital organs—if I got help.

Quirt was rattled by the size of the animal. Not just rattled, he was scared. Rather than pursue, he chose to dawdle, saying, "Figured he would charge us. Like in the movies, an elephant charges, a man has to stay cool and wait for his shot. You ever seen that? That's what I would've done."

"Really?"

"Go for a clean shot to the heart. Drop down on one knee and squeeze the trigger at the last minute."

I motioned toward the trees. "Then what are you waiting on?" Said it with an edge.

"For a sport killer, you don't know shit. I grew up killing mule deer, elk. You give an animal some time before following a blood trail."

"A live coward's better than a dead hero, huh?"

Quirt made his wolfing noise again and raised the rifle. "I've just about had it with your snotty mouth. What I think I'll do is—"

"How many rounds do you have left?" I interrupted. "Maybe you forgot to count. You won't get close enough to use that pistol, and a .357 wouldn't stop him anyway. Now you're going to waste a bullet on me? Police will nail you for murder—never mind what happened in Nevada."

Quirt said, "You know that tall bastard didn't call the cops," but touched the pistol in his belt anyway and muttered, *"Damn."* Thinking about how many times he'd fired or what to do next.

I said, "How about I give you an excuse to turn around? Instead, I'll dive the pond, but under one condition . . ."

"Oh, I'm *gonna* take that big boy's ivory. Just you watch."

"Listen to me," I said. "When I surface with the bag, you put your phone on speaker so I can hear. Have them send an ambulance . . . *and* a vet. Give the location. I'll swim the bag to shore, but you have to leave your weapons by the gate. After that, you can be on your merry way."

My reasonable offer registered in Quirt's brain as a challenge.

"I ain't scared, dumbass—or are you worried about that poor ol' elephant?"

I was more worried about Leland, who was on his feet again and searching among the cattails for Owen. Quirt followed my gaze and aimed across the water but then remembered he was low on ammo.

"What we're going to do is," he said. "As of now, you're leading the way. I'll follow *you* into the trees. If that big bastard charges, you better hope I get a clean shot—and don't tell me you never saw it in a movie."

Minutes later, crossing the knoll where a Conquistador had camped, a man's howl spanned the distance.

No point in looking back.

Leland Albright would be standing near the son he'd never had.

WALKING FAST, I descended the hill and didn't slow until tree shadows cooled the air: moss-draped oaks, some cypress, the canopy dense enough to choke undergrowth and dilute sunset into dusk.

Quirt, lagging yards behind, hissed, *"Hold up."*

I did, transferred the chain saw to my left hand, then waved him ahead, saying, "Here's his trail." I kept going, worried the biker might shoot before I got to the trees.

Splotches of blood on the ground—I followed them. In sand, Toby's tracks had the girth of telephone poles but were soon absorbed by the soggy forest floor. High above, broken limbs also marked the way. Every few steps, I peered ahead. I didn't want to surprise a wounded bull elephant. The silence troubled me—no bulldozer crack of shattering wood. Toby was close, though. His musk clung to the trees like mist.

Quirt felt the weight of that musk and tried to stop me again, saying, "Hoss . . . I'm not so sure this is a good idea."

Until then, I hadn't risked more than a glance over my shoulder. I stopped and turned, more interested in the distance that separated us. Quirt was closer than I'd hoped but walking with an obvious limp. The spill from his Harley had done something to his hip or back and the pain was getting worse.

"How many rounds do you have left?" I asked.

He leaned against a tree, saying, "Shit, it's hot. Out west, we got dry heat. Maybe we should go back and get some water." Using the glove on his good hand, he dabbed at his scars.

"If that magazine doesn't hold more than seven," I said, "the elephant's going to kill us both. You've already fired six."

"No I didn't. Fired five."

I said, "You're wrong," and left him there, walked slowly inland, while he raised his voice to say, "Besides, I got *this*."

Quirt's hand would be touching the pistol. No need for a look to clarify, and I wouldn't have bothered even if confused. It was because of what I saw not far away: a sizable bundle of clothing . . . no, a hunter's tarp suspended high in the limbs of a tree.

Or was it a . . . ?"

I moved closer, Quirt saying, "This is more of your bullshit psychology. A Winchester holds seven in the tube and one in the chamber. To prove it, I'll check. But stop right there. I can draw and shoot before you take two steps."

I said, "You do that," and kept walking, but not far, then stood there, looking, while my brain pieced the scene together . . . an eerie scene that clung to chaos and noise despite the silence. Small trees leaned as if a tornado had swept through. A few lay crushed on the ground, creating a ragged circle. In the middle of the circle was an oak, bark shaved on one side. White scars worked their way up the trunk to what I'd thought was a tarp, but it was too high off the ground for a hunter's blind.

It wasn't a tarp. It wasn't a bundle of clothing either, but there was *some* clothing.

Behind me, Quirt shucked the rifle, then spoke to himself, saying, "Oh . . . *shit*." Then worked the lever several times as if hoping for a miracle.

I put the chain saw down and started toward the oak. "I was right, wasn't I?"

"No! Goddamn thing's empty, which wouldn't of happened if you hadn't played your bullshit games. What you did was trick me into wasting lead. But it don't matter a bit because I still got—" He went silent, aware that I was moving quietly for a reason. Then, whispering, demanded, "Hey . . . what do you see?"

I heard the empty Winchester clatter to the ground—Quirt had tried to lean it against a tree.

"Don't bother with the pistol," I told him.

"Is it the elephant? Tell me, damn you. Is he dead?"

I said, "You'd better hope so," and pointed toward the tree canopy, which brought him creeping to investigate. It allowed me freedom to concentrate on the ground and circle the oak while the biker stood staring. I found a spent brass shell casing, three inches long . . . then another casing that pulled me outside the ring where chaos had occurred. I slipped one of the casings into my pocket and kept searching.

Quirt, oblivious, continued to stare, transfixed by what hung from the tree. Finally said, "Jesus mother Mary . . . *are you shittin' me?*"

I asked, "Do you think it's him?" Said it to focus the biker's attention because in bushes near the brass casings lay a rifle: a glistening walnut stock with a recoil pad protruding from the leaves.

Quirt said, "Poor bastard's gotta be fourteen, fifteen feet off the ground. You think an elephant could do that?"

I wandered toward the rifle. "Unless the guy fell out of an airplane. Can you make out his face?"

"Shit, man . . . *what face?*"

That was true. Harris Sanford, the good-looking gambler and fossil guide, had been tromped beyond recognition and then impaled on a limb that had sheared upon impact. Blood dripped as if from a high balcony after rain, the man limp as a deflated balloon.

Quirt, after changing angles, started to say, "We gotta get the hell out—" but then stopped when he turned and saw what I was holding: A rifle, barrel pointed—*Remington Safari 700* etched on the stock. And a monogram: *DSS.*

Dalton Sanford, middle name unknown. His nephew or grandson, Harris, had used it to terrorize Toby—but for the last time. Like Owen Hall, he had been stomped to death. The look on the crazy biker's face when he saw the rifle—shock on overload while he tried to recover, saying, "Good . . . *good,* you found it. That's what we need. Is it loaded?"

"Unbuckle your belt," I told him. "Don't touch the pistol, let it fall. When it hits the ground"—I paused, aware of a distant plodding vibration, limbs cracking somewhere to our right, so raised my voice to continue—"When the pistol falls, kick it toward me."

Quirt clicked the pincers on his bionic hand, beginning to panic. "Hear that? The big son of a bitch is coming back."

"Then you'd better hurry," I told him.

"Hoss, it'll take both of us to kill something that size."

"Not if I shoot you. He won't care if you're bleeding—as long as you're still alive."

"As long as I'm . . . shit, man"—Quirt shoveled his hair back—"I can't run, my back's hurt. You can't just go off and *leave me* . . . not after what happened to—" His eyes drifted to Harris Sanford, Harris's disjointed arm swinging while the ground vibrated, the rest of him pinned flat to the tree.

"It's the best I can do without a boat," I said.

Quirt's eyes glazed for an instant, remembering Deon's story. He had wanted to believe I'd done it, left Deon out there to drown among sharks, and now he had proof—he was living it—and the reality sucked the air out of him.

Dry-mouthed, he said, "I'll split the ivory with you fifty-fifty," but, as he spoke, I noticed his hand drift toward his belt.

I told him, "Drop your damn pants, kick the pistol toward me, then throw me my wallet. And Leland's." I managed not to raise my voice.

It froze his hand. "Okay," he said, "but you got to promise we'll come to an agreement."

"Maybe we will," I said, which gave him something to cling to. Instead of bothering with his belt, he reached and lobbed both wallets at me, then the pistol—almost got himself shot for that, but he was too spooked to care.

To our right, much closer, roots of a tree made a slow keening sound. The tree crashed to earth, and the musk of heavy breathing flowed toward us in a wave.

Hurrying, I tucked the wallets and pistol away, then let Quirt watch as I shucked a live round from the Remington and caught it—a stiletto-shaped cartridge as thick as my finger. I held it to the light, then checked the empty magazine, saying, "You've got one chance. The woman who died in the house fire—did you knock her out first?"

"What?"

I said, "I don't have to outrun the elephant. I just have to outrun you," and turned as if to leave.

"Wait! I'll tell you. She . . . Hell, she was a dried-up old prune who loved to talk. I got a few rums down her, but then she did something stupid. She tried to slap me—"

A shrill trumpeting drowned out the rest—an unexpected sound because it came from the pasture, not the woods. Immediately, the call was answered by an elephant duet to our right where the tree canopy pushed closer and showed a wedge of sky as more trees toppled.

Florida Elephant Rescue . . . it adjoined the old Mammoth Mines property—the only explanation. Toby, the solitary captive, had company.

It was not a gathering I wanted to stick around and witness.

To Quirt I said, "One bullet, one chance," and let him watch me slide a brass casing into the chamber and slam the bolt closed. Then skidded the rifle toward him and turned . . . and there was Toby, watching us, his black mass separating me from the pasture.

I spread my arms to show him two empty hands while the crazy biker, still oblivious, knelt and picked up the Remington, a Safari 700.

I said softly, "Quirt, I don't think you're going to make it to the beach."

Looking up, he asked me, *"Huh?"*

A second later, he stood and hollered, "Hey . . . hoss! Why are you running?"

I didn't look back—even when I heard Quirt bellow after cursing the empty rifle . . . then scream.

EPILOGUE

THE DAY AFTER OWEN'S FUNERAL, I FINALLY GOT MY CHANCE TO DIVE WHAT Leland, on the phone, referred to as "Toby's Pond." Just me. The man had no knowledge of diving's "buddy system" and even less interest.

The invitation wasn't negotiable. Leland, a loner all his life, tried hard to sound in control, which told me he was agitated. My guess was, he had no one to talk to—no one he trusted anyway.

"A news helicopter spotted vultures over a woods near the interstate," he said. "They're sending people to check. The cable networks are all over it, of course."

For nearly a week, "three killer rogue elephants" had been on the loose, and the national media couldn't get enough. Should the animals be euthanized or rehabilitated? And how could three adult pachyderms evade detection in a state that was as densely populated as Florida?

Every time I heard that—and I'd heard it a lot—I rolled my eyes.

Leland said, "Even if they're wrong about the vultures, there's something I want you to see. Bring your scuba stuff—that's up to you—otherwise, jeans and boots. I'm the only one here."

"Have you gotten any sleep?" It was a polite way of asking how he was holding up.

"No, but it doesn't matter," he replied. "Try to get here by noon. I won't put the backhoe away until you see what I'm talking about."

He had dug Toby's grave. Why else would the heir to the Albright fortune be alone on his ranch using a backhoe?

I had been sitting on the deck with coffee, waiting for Tomlinson to arrive. On a nearby table was an envelope that contained the retriever's DNA results and a newspaper.

Not my newspaper. I avoid the damn things, even when "killer elephants" aren't running wild. Palm trees and tropic June mornings are too fragile to compete with a litany of the world's woes. Choose one or the other. I made my choice long ago.

Today was different, so I'd walked to the mailbox, then the marina, and returned with the paper folded to a small headline:

FWC STING NETS "BONE HUNTER" RING, UNDERCOVER AGENTS POSE AS COLLECTORS

My name wasn't included in the story, which was the only reason I'd bothered checking. But my cop friend from Tallahassee was mentioned several times:

> In charge of the operation was Capt. Shelly Brown, a twelve-year FWC veteran who spent months working undercover before staging a "relics sale" on public land north of the Peace River.

Fallsdown had guessed correctly about the woman with the cute chin and marathoner's body. Shelly, a former jogging partner, had drafted me to help after we'd struck a deal about the contents of the duffel bag.

The sting had taken place three days ago—Saturday. I had accompanied Mick but slipped away before cops descended on dozens of bone hunters and dealers, who were convinced they were safely gathered on private property.

Among those arrested was a tall blonde. She had arrived in a VW van adorned with peace signs and belching smoke because the radiator was overheating. After money exchanged hands, the woman was charged with selling stolen property, and with more than a hundred felony counts of "violation of historical resources." The collection she had brought included mastodon ivory, a bezoar stone on a gold chain, and the hilt from a Conquistador's sword.

Ava Albright had been cuffed and taken to jail. Now she and her attorney Dalton Sanford were claiming entrapment.

It wasn't true.

Tomlinson had made good on his vow to produce the person responsible for Lillian's death and he had done it all on his own. Didn't say one word to me. The proof was that he, too, had spent the night in jail.

Before hanging up, Leland, the cuckolded husband, paid mild tribute to Tomlinson's cunning.

"I figured your friend for a harmless flake. Tell him thanks."

WHILE I LUGGED DIVE GEAR from the house to my truck, the harmless flake followed the dog walking at my side. Tomlinson saying, "The woman cop might be an old jogging buddy, but that doesn't mean she won't arrest you. She's doing her undercover cop routine again. I'm afraid Dunk's going to find out the hard way."

I said, "Shelly? Stop worrying. Has he called since he got back to Montana?"

"Let me finish. Remember asking where he disappeared to this weekend? Shelly drafted his tracking skills as an excuse to take him camping—you know, search for Toby and the other two elephants. Dunk took his drum, which tells me the trip turned into a sex fest, John and Yoko doing the Little Bighorn thing, while she infiltrated his redskin brain. Shelly drove him to the airport last night. And get this: She plans to fly out there next week."

I said, "Then you have spoken to him."

"*Yes*. Dunk's worried she's falling in love, but the whole time what she's really doing is gathering evidence. You know, pay a visit, meet Rachel. While they're not looking, she'll get video of the Little People you stole from Dalton Sanford's lockbox thing."

It was true that before police and EMTs had arrived, I had opened the box and removed two owl stones. One was the crested carving in the photo Harris Sanford had sent. All possessed a pearly white sheen around the eyes.

By now, the owls were with Rachel Fallsdown.

I smiled. "Your feelings are hurt because Shelly cuffed you instead of inviting you to go camping. Maybe if you owned a drum, things would've been different."

"Like that's going to help find a dying elephant," Tomlinson scoffed. "The moment Dunk told me, I knew."

"I think some of Ava's ego rubbed off on you," I said. "Too much time doing that yoga mind-link business. What color was her aura the day you led her into your little trap? Check the mirror, ol' buddy. Or do you use a prism?"

"Hers was greenish gray," Tomlinson said after thinking back. "But you're wrong. Vegas dancers are like honest men—they can't be tricked. Ava hung herself. All I did was zone in on her objectives and steer her back into the web. Doc, you should know by now my instincts are about ninety percent right on."

"Only because you don't remember the times you're wrong," I said. I swung a fresh tank into the truck, secured it, and walked toward the house while Tomlinson prattled on about fears that only illustrated his police paranoia . . . but stopped me cold when he said, "What's Hannah going to think if Shelly nails you for theft? I'm pretty sure she knows about the saber cat skull."

"How?" I asked him, which sounded like an admission, so I covered my tracks. "I took pictures of the thing and moved it. Big deal."

"All I know is, Shelly asked Dunk what you took from the river that day. He's the one who brought it up. Let's hope Shelly doesn't get him love-drunk and trick him into spilling the beans."

I continued walking, and told the dog, "Go swim."

The dog did. Tomlinson moved up beside me and watched him catapult off the walkway, where a cormorant dived for its life, then slapped the water until airborne.

"You've got to admit it's weird," Tomlinson said. "I've still never heard him bark."

I replied, "You never will," then changed the subject.

I WAS STILL ON THE PHONE with Hannah when I parked beside Leland's Escalade, so ended our conversation, asking, "Can I call you later?"

The way she fumbled around told me she had plans for the night, but the woman recovered nicely. "How about I call you in the morning? I still owe you a fishing trip."

Because of confidential paperwork on the sting operation, I'd had to cancel our date on Monday. My wobbly excuse hadn't meshed with the woman's iron morals, but on the phone she had been cheery and sweet and quick to laugh—Hannah's normal self.

Another reprieve . . . or maybe we actually were becoming friends again.

On the floor of my truck, passenger side, was a five-gallon bucket covered with a towel. It had slopped water because of the bumpy road—distilled water to which I had added a careful amount of a chemical, Acryloid, after using a meter to measure the amount of soluble salts.

I was sopping up the mess when Leland exited the office door, so I poked an arm out the window and held up a finger: *Give me a minute.*

He was dressed like a gentleman farmer, wearing baggy pants and Wellingtons, his khaki shirt dark with sweat. With a shrug, he walked toward the pond and waited.

I looked into the bucket and, once again, wrestled with my conscience. A saber-toothed tiger stared back through eons and the eye sockets of a skull. I couldn't let Leland see the thing—an obvious flaw in my hasty plan, a plan that was unraveling fast.

Before leaving, while in the systemized certainty of my lab, I had made two tough decisions: No, I would not tell Leland about the petroglyph. The mastodon tusk would soon be returned to him. That was enough. The man was in financial trouble and the temptation to auction a priceless artifact would only add to the trauma he had suffered—or so I rationalized.

I had also convinced myself that, yes, I would return the saber cat skull to the pond where snakes and gators and, possibly, an old elephant on the mend would return to guard it.

Now, however, in a place where chaos had reigned so recently, I was certain of nothing. Plus . . . by god, I wanted that skull with its lethal ivory fang. Forget the lies I had told Tomlinson, I felt *something* each and every time I touched the thing.

So I covered the bucket and reached for my dive bag but then left it all, thinking, *Do what you always do, Ford—make it up as you go.*

WHEN I JOINED LELAND, he referenced the flowers piled where Owen had died, saying, "I'm not a particularly spiritual person, but I had hopes for him. You know? I wish you could have seen the way he stood up to Harris that day. He was . . . He reminded me so much of . . ." Leland cleared his throat, his hands shaking.

I helped him out by mentioning his late wife, then let him talk for a while before asking, "Did you hear anything about what the helicopter spotted?"

"Oh . . . the vultures." He shook his head, then surprised me with an ironic smile. "Over the last few days, I've gotten to know the manager of the Elephant Rescue facility pretty well. Gwen. She's very sharp but as baffled as me about what happened. And she sees a kind of weird humor in it. Three very old, very large Asiatic elephants disappear without a trace. Well"—he glanced toward the flowers—"that's not entirely true."

He talked about the search still under way—that was the ironic aspect: helicopters and telemetry foiled by beasts from the Ice Age— then addressed a subject I couldn't bring up. "I don't have any hard feelings toward Toby. He was reacting to a situation—probably confused Owen with Harris. Or maybe Harris had already wounded him when Toby did what he did. I don't know, I was still unconscious. Gwen has been working with elephants for years and we talked about it. She agrees."

I didn't agree, so was relieved when he said, "There's something I want to show you." He looked at my feet. "Good. You're wearing boots. We don't have to take the road."

On the other side of the pond, the hill sloped downward into swamp, then flattened into a tractor path that cleaved through the trees. Harris and Owen, in the red Dodge, had disappeared into those trees before returning—and dying.

Leland led me around the pond toward a backhoe, a pyramid of black dirt piled high beside it. On the way, he caught me off guard, saying, "Your Indian friend is a pretty nice fellow. Duncan—I didn't feel comfortable calling him Dunk. He's a little strange, but so what? I was disappointed you weren't with him the other night."

I said, "He was here?" then amended, "Oh—that's right. He and a woman I know spent a couple of nights in the area. Shelly Brown. I haven't talked to him for a few days."

"I liked her, too. Monday late, he built a fire and did a little ceremony for the elephants. Gwen grew up in South Africa, so she's more tolerant of that sort of thing. The twins were there to encourage him, of course."

"I heard that Duncan brought his drum," I said.

"Brought his *what*?" Leland was confused for a moment. "*Oh.* No, that would have been too much for me. I wandered off anyway, figured he would take the hint and leave. Nothing against Duncan—Owen's funeral was yesterday, you know, and I wanted some time alone. But somehow he found me and we had a nice talk about . . . about various things."

Awkward, the silence that followed, me walking beside the man. Something was on his mind. He finally got to it by offering an apology that was a setup. "I have to admit I was wrong about him and your other friend Tomlinson. I made a snap judgment." He slowed but didn't turn. "Which makes me wonder if I was right about you, Ford."

"Oh?"

"I'm learning to be cautious. Thank Ava for that."

"If something's on your mind, Leland, out with it."

The man was sweating and used a handkerchief before he replied, "Okay. For one thing, Duncan knew I tend to drink more than I need at night. I'm not the sort who lets strangers get close enough to smell my breath, and I hold my liquor pretty damn well. So it was more than a guess."

The insinuation that I had blabbed was offensive but I let it go. "Why not ask him?"

"I did—but that part of our conversation is private. I'm more interested in the photos you took of the mastodon tusk. You *did* take them, didn't you? You had part of our collection the whole time."

"Duncan said that?"

"No, but it makes sense."

"I can't tell you how it happened, but, yes, I had some things I believed were yours."

"Had to be. That's why you thought I was being too hard on my father." He didn't wait for a response, kept talking. "Which might be true, but there's something unusual about that tusk my father never bothered to notice. I don't know how Tovar got it, but the fact my father parted with the thing sums up his whole . . . *Sloppy*, I guess is the word. His sloppy approach to life." Now Leland did stop, eyed me for a moment. "Do you know what I'm talking about?"

I said, "Your grandfather must have had a very good magnifying glass."

"Then you *do* know."

"That's why you're suspicious? Leland, ask yourself a simple question: Why did I give the damn thing back? I have photos of the petroglyph taken with an electronic microscope. I know what it's worth."

An earnest look; a man who wanted to understand. "Then why didn't you *keep* it? You could've made up a story or some damn thing."

I continued walking, let him follow me for a change. "Being arrested for grand theft ranks right up there. But the smart-ass answer is the most accurate: I didn't trust myself. How would my conscience handle stealing a piece of history from the big puzzle? What's my price? A million? Three million?" I glanced over. "I took the easy way out. Now it's your problem."

The man responded, "I'll be damned," then took longer strides to catch up. "I had to ask. Especially after what I found this morning."

"While you were digging?" We were close enough to the backhoe that I could smell fresh earth piled high, sulfur and humic musk.

"It was staring me in the face the whole time," he replied—an odd response. "I couldn't take photos because I don't have a new phone yet. Then I decided it was better to get someone else's opinion anyway."

Another pre-Columbian burial site—that was my guess, but let him explain why he'd chosen me. "Tricia is an emotional wreck, and I didn't want to risk getting Esther's hopes up. I could've brought my attorney out here, I suppose, but . . . Well, just in case I'm wrong, I want someone I trust on a personal level." Leland placed his hand on the backhoe's fender in a familiar way and faced me. "This is confidential, but you can tell Duncan. Also Tomlinson, I suppose.

Otherwise, I want your word not to say anything until I decide how to handle this."

A man's word means something. Leland had told me that.

"You have it," I replied, then reconsidered. "Wait—there's a woman I'm dating—or was dating . . . Anyway, it's a long story. I'm trying to be less secretive. Do you mind if I include her?"

After a year with Ava, the cynic in Leland was amused. "If I refuse, are you saying you're going to leave?"

"We're dating, not joined at the frontal lobe," I answered. "It was a request."

He shrugged and used the handkerchief again, then led me to the hole he'd dug. It was the size of a swimming pool, but deeper; deep enough to pierce the water table, which explained the need for boots. The walls were earthen black, the rim fringed with sludge and fossilized oysters, the spoil heaped twice as high as my head.

I said, "You dug this by yourself?"

"I started before sunrise yesterday—I couldn't sleep. Owen's funeral, everything that's happened, plus"—he balked for a moment—"And, to be honest, I stopped drinking two days ago, so sleeping's not easy."

That explained a lot: his sopping shirt and shaking hands, and also the private conversation he had alluded to—Duncan had taken Leland aside to confront a fellow alcoholic. Stopping cold turkey, however, might be dangerous if he was the drink-in-the-morning type—an unknown.

"You're holding up pretty well," I said. "A lot of people would need medical care. How are you feeling?"

Leland, a man who had seldom received compliments, didn't know how to handle that. "I just told myself, *Stay busy.* Why else would I be out here on a backhoe at three in the morning? And I worked until after midnight last night. But I had a good reason. All along, I've figured Toby is dead. Gwen thinks they all are. If not shot by Harris, dead from the trauma. The animals she lost were both damn-near sixty years old. So"—Leland gestured to the hole—"I decided to be ready when they found the bodies."

I said, "I didn't get a good look at Toby, but, from what I saw . . . well, I don't think he could have gotten very far. You chose a good spot—next to a graded road so a flatbed can get in."

"That's exactly what Duncan told me. A low place where the ground is softer."

"He suggested it?"

Leland, watching my reaction, nodded. "Being this close to the pond, Duncan said there was a spiritual aspect, which the twins appreciated. He used some odd wording—*Ivory Pot*. And there was another one: *time tunnel*. Then he mentioned your story about an elephant graveyard."

"That sounds like Dunk. But he was only repeating terms he'd heard from someone else," I said. "The rest is part of what he calls his medicine man act."

"That's what I figured. It all seemed rather strange at the time— until I found this."

"Found what?" I'd been peering down in the hole—nothing but water and muck—so I walked toward an incline created by the backhoe. "Am I missing something?"

Leland stuck out his arm when I tried to slog past. "Take a good look at what's sticking out of the water. But that's not why I want your professional opinion."

It was a bright June afternoon, no clouds or shadows to play visual tricks. I didn't have to clean my glasses but did before stepping back, shaking my head. "I'll be damned, you're right. When did you realize?"

What I had assumed was tree stubble was, in fact, a midden of Ice Age ivory—sodden tusks, many of them shattered. They created a ragged blue reef on the bottom where brown water flowed, the stream seeking the bed of an ancient creek.

"An elephant graveyard," he said. "Last night, after the funeral, I worked here until almost one. If the backhoe had better lights, I would've known I hadn't hit limestone. No telling how many tusks I ruined and how many are down there."

Smiling a strange smile, he turned, his face pale. "But this isn't why I brought you. *There*—take a look at those." He pointed a long finger at the incline where water slid over mud that was pocked with craters and ivory shards. "My grandfather could have explained them. But I can't. Those weren't here last night."

Responding to my blank expression, he edged closer so I could look down his arm, as if sighting over a rifle. I saw a mud plateau, water flowing a few inches deep over muddy craters, lots of them, the craters juxtaposed in a line, each hole the diameter of a telephone pole.

"Elephant tracks," Leland declared. "*Fresh*. Three sets. The largest has to be Toby's."

Nervous laughter—*my* nervous laughter—while I stood and moved a step away. Then pretended to give each random crater my attention, aware that water would soon erode the holes. It was better, I decided, to bring him back later so he could see for himself.

"Interesting," I said. "I should take pictures—but first, there's something in the truck I brought to show you."

The saber cat skull was my handy excuse. The man needed water and shade—and a doctor—but he pulled away when I tried to take his arm.

"There's nothing wrong with me. Ford . . . you still don't understand. A time tunnel, Duncan called this spot, and it's hard to argue with my own eyes."

Choosing my words carefully, I responded, "I understand most men would be in the hospital after what you've been through," and, once again, tried to steer him away.

"Those elephants were *here* last night," Leland Albright insisted. Then reached for his handkerchief. Stood staring for a moment before turning to me, his eyes glassy, while a single tear streaked his face. "What I don't understand is . . . all three sets of tracks lead into the hole—*but*, Doc—*there are no tracks leading out.*"